THE
SECRET
W♥UND

DEIRDRE QUIERY

THE

SECRET

W♥UND

urbanepublications.com

First published in Great Britain in 2017
by Urbane Publications Ltd
Suite 3, Brown Europe House, 33/34 Gleaming Wood Drive,
Chatham, Kent ME5 8RZ
Copyright © Deirdre Quiery, 2017

A CIP catalogue record for this book is available
from the British Library.

ISBN 978-1-911331-83-4
MOBI 978-1-911331-85-8
EPUB 978-1-911331-84-1

Design and Typeset by Michelle Morgan

Cover by The Invisible Man

Printed and bound by CPI Group (UK) Ltd, Croydon, CR0 4YY

urbanepublications.com

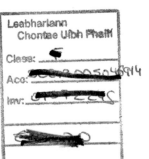

FSC
www.fsc.org
MIX
Paper from
responsible sources
FSC® C013604

"THE WOUND IS THE PLACE WHERE THE LIGHT ENTERS YOU."

J RUMI (1207 – 1273)

For Martin – for hanging in there and being the most fantastic support and muse.

For Matthew Smith, Founder and Director of Urbane Publications – for showing what it truly means to be collaborative.

THE SECRET WOUND

> "DON'T GRIEVE. ANYTHING YOU LOSE
> COMES ROUND IN ANOTHER FORM."
> **J RUMI**

AUGUST 2012 BELFAST

GURTHA OPENED the kitchen door calling out Nuala's name. He was about to call out for Paddy as well but the words stuck in his throat as he glimpsed Nuala lying at the bottom of the stairs, wearing her favourite navy blue pleated skirt, and a striped navy blue and white jumper. A sandal had broken loose from her left foot and lay turned over on the tiles like an abandoned child's sandal. Her head rested on her arms as if she were sleeping. Gurtha felt a coiling of energy as if someone had stabbed him with a dagger and his throat contracted, curling up like a snake. He held onto the stair bannister for a second, breathing deeply with perspiration breaking out on his temples and running down the sides of his cheeks before dropping to his knees to feel for a pulse. Her skin was taught like a drum – no pulse, although he thought that he detected a hint of warmth. He pressed two fingers a second time into her neck and then feverishly looked for a pulse at the wrist but her wrist was cold and motionless.

He rolled Nuala onto her back, attempting to bring her back to life with mouth-to-mouth resuscitation, pumping her chest with his fists joined together. Her eyes remained closed. There was no movement in her body. He fumbled once more to find a pulse in her neck but there was nothing. Maybe he imagined it, but it seemed in the short time he had been there that her body was already solidifying. He searched for his mobile, dialled 999 and asked for the emergency services. Maybe he should have done that first but he could hardly breathe, never mind think. He sat on the tiled floor beside Nuala, holding her hand, waiting for someone to arrive.

He thought that it had been a terrible accident – that she had fallen downstairs. However, the doctor who arrived to certify the death felt that there were sufficient grounds to justify an inquest. The coroner's verdict turned out to be one of unlawful killing. There had been evidence of a struggle – bruising to the arms before she had fallen or had been pushed. The body had been dragged after the fall and positioned in a way which was incompatible with an accidental fall downstairs.

There was no obvious motive for her murder and no suspect.

♥

Gurtha sat in the front row of the pews in Holy Cross Church, head in hands. On his left Paddy blew noisily into a cotton handkerchief. Kneeling to the left of Paddy, Tom and Lily stared straight ahead watching Father Jerome wipe the chalice clean. Cornelia, on Gurtha's right, patted her nose dry with a Lancome powder puff, flecks of powder flying into the air, sparkling into the sun shining through the stained glass windows. With the help of a Chanel mirror and her little finger she corrected a smudge of crimson lipstick at the corner of her mouth. Laura from the sweetie shop, on Cornelia's right, blessed herself on the forehead, lips and heart as Father Jerome gave the final blessing. He then walked swiftly towards the microphone where earlier in the Mass he had delivered his passionate eulogy for Nuala. He scanned the congregation with a slow, meaningful searching sweep of his eyes, left to right.

"We have been informed that it is more than likely that Nuala's murderer is now sitting in the Church beside one of you. There were a few gasps and a tut-tutting in the few seconds before he continued. "You have heard details of the profile of the person the police are looking for. Take courage and share whatever you know. We do not know why Nuala has been murdered but we have been cautioned by responsible professionals that the murderer is likely to strike again. May we raise our hearts in prayer once more for Nuala and pray also that the conscience of whoever committed this atrocity is awakened to allow them to admit the grievousness of their actions and, with remorse, receive pardon. Without remorse, a hardened heart lives in Hell – a Hell of their own creation, which they inflict on themselves and on loving families and friends." He gestured towards the front row.

"As you know, Nuala is …" He coughed, "*was* and I believe still *is* within the communion of saints, an active member of this community. Her faith was profound. She opened herself to the mystery of life and participated more than anyone I know in its dance. She enriched our community in many ways. In Nuala, I am reminded of the words of Pope John XXIII – "See everything, overlook a great deal, and correct a little." That was Nuala's way of being. She saw what was in your heart and what you could not see yourself. When she overlooked the flaws within your character, you knew them for what they were –minimising them had a way of magnifying them. When she corrected you a little, it was with the gentleness of love. You left her presence knowing what you had done wrong, yet rippling with love and sensing the unconditional love she transmitted. Love that came from a world Divine. How do I know this?" Father Jerome's voice trembled; he gripped the lectern with both hands and leaned even closer to the microphone.

"When Nuala came to Confession – it was I who confessed to her – not the other way around. When she began her Confession, I listened to her and to my surprise my response was one of hearing my own sins fall spontaneously from my tongue. I found myself waiting in the silence for Nuala's comments. Her words were wisdom thoughts imbued with directedness and love.

You understand how important it is for anyone who has information about who is responsible for this horrific murder to approach the police or call at the monastery and ask to speak to a priest. You can ring the confidential number. Nuala, we can all agree, deserves justice."

As if on cue, the altar boy snuffed out the two candles on either side of the altar. Smoke curled into the air in circles as a few muffled sobs were heard from the back of the Church. Everyone looked over their shoulder as if the murderer had revealed himself or herself and was about to confess but it was only Molly Devine from the choir who sang soprano with Nuala and who had momentarily lost her composure in response to Father Jerome's address. She shook her head rapidly from right to left as though denying the unspoken accusation then fell to her knees with a small gasp, clasping her hands in prayer.

Nuala's coffin rested on a wooden frame with a bouquet of red roses on top. Incense hung in the air from earlier devotions – its scent warm and comforting. Gurtha glanced sideways at the coffin. A coffin of oak wood with brass handles like a wardrobe toppled on its side, holding Nuala.

The previous day her coffin had lain open in the parlour, with cream coloured candles of varying shapes and sizes shimmering on the mantelpiece. The chair beside the coffin, which Gurtha had brought from his house on the Malone Road, was upholstered with fancy gold embroidery on red silk. Someone sat on it, leaning forward, resting their hands on top of Nuala's and whispering into her ear. Occasionally someone would jump from the chair, stand firmly on their feet and stare into the coffin to commune in silence with Nuala in what seemed a more intense way.

It was odd for Gurtha to witness this warmth of expression for Nuala as he crossed his arms and leant against the door frame of the parlour door. When alive, Nuala never seemed to demand intimacy in relationship which appeared paradoxical considering the impact she had on others. She was rather a detached figure which did not mean that she did not love – quite the opposite. She exuded joy, kindness, generosity, gentleness and self-control, although indulging in her favourite Neuhass chocolates which she hid in the bedroom. Her love was a mesmerising love, radiating in a non-possessive way. In its presence you felt compelled to gaze, to understand the mystery hidden within someone eternally being refreshed from a fountain . Like an unseen source of water for someone who never experienced thirst.

Although Gurtha, her only son, was closest to her, he didn't know what she really thought of him. She was not one of those mothers who talked about their children as if they were the centre of the Universe – or as if they were flawless and perfect. Gurtha knew that this was unusual. He thought it yet another sign of Nuala's sanity. In Nuala's company the deepest peace enveloped him. He couldn't decide if he was sending peace to Nuala or if he was receiving it from her. It was as if the billions of neurons and trillions of synapses in their brains were sending each other inhibitors calming the world into a still place.

The evening before, at the wake, Nuala's favourite music played loudly in the kitchen and visitors sang along to Frank Sinatra's "I did it my way" while nibbling bites of cheese and ham quiche and sipping wine and beer. Hardly anyone talked about the murder. There were one or two utterances of "Who could have done it?" or "Why did they do it?" These questions were snuffed out like the candles on the altar as conversation changed to an exploration of Nuala's sense of humour, her psychic tendencies, her knitting, baking, dancing skills, her love of singing in the choir and her fearless honesty.

Tom raised a glass of Harvey's Bristol Cream sherry into the air, "To Nuala. We're not here to investigate the murder. We'll leave that to the police. Let's celebrate her life. That's what she would want us to do – a good party. Let's enjoy ourselves."

The party which followed would have nearly wakened the dead if such a thing were possible. That didn't happen. Nuala lay waxen white, cold and still while the music got louder and people danced between the pickled onions which had rolled from the table onto the floor. Laughter crackled around the house that might have shocked someone not from Ireland. Mary Walsh broke a rib when her nephew Colin grabbed her around the waist and circled like a Dervish, Mary's legs flailing as she shrieked with laughter and begged to be set down before the rib snapped. An ambulance was called and Colin accompanied Mary to the hospital. Everyone seemed to think that it was a good sign and that Nuala would have been delighted that the wake was so wild.

Throughout the whole evening, Gurtha never strayed from his propped up position, leaning on the door frame of the parlour, watching everyone come and go to say their last goodbyes to Nuala. The questions of why had she been murdered and who had carried out the murder repeatedly and solemnly tolled in his head.

THE SECRET WOUND

The murder had taken place on his birthday – Wednesday 15th August 2012. It had taken the Coroner three months to deliver his solemn report and release the body for burial.

In his head Gurtha replayed over and over again what had happened on that day. Paddy, Nuala, Cornelia and Gurtha were due to go out to dinner to celebrate. Gurtha arrived at Paddy and Nuala's house at four thirty. He remembered the exact time because he checked to see if there was a text from Cornelia, before opening the back door with the spare key. There was no message but he noted that the time was four thirty and that Cornelia's plane should be landing at Belfast International airport at any time.

There was no sign of Paddy or Nuala in the kitchen. As he walked across the kitchen floor, he noticed that the table was set for tea for four. Four china tea cups on saucers, a small piece plate with a pastry fork set on top of each and the china teapot in the centre of the table with the lid off, waiting for the hot water to be boiled. At that precise moment his mobile buzzed - a text from Cornelia to say that her plane had landed. She would catch a taxi and be with them within the hour.

♥

The day after the wake, towards the end of the Requiem Mass, the choir in the Church sang "Oh Danny Boy" and everyone got to their feet. Gurtha tasted loneliness and despair within. A cold metallic film coating his tongue – an acidic burning at the back of his throat. He could not sing but instead allowed himself to be washed by the plaintive harmonies of the choir,

"But come ye back when summer's in the meadow
Or when the valley's hushed and white with snow
And I'll be here in sunshine or in shadow

Oh Danny Boy ... Oh Danny Boy ... I love you so."

He remembered Nuala tapping her feet as Gurtha played the guitar after dinner a few weeks before. Nuala sang 'Danny Boy', gently beating out the rhythm with her fingers on her knee as if playing a piano. There was a moment when she didn't quite hit the highest note. They held one another's gaze and he knew that it would be the last time she would ever sing 'Danny Boy'. He didn't know how he knew. He just did.

Once the choir had finished singing, Gurtha excused himself to file past Cornelia and Laura into the middle aisle where he stood beside the coffin. Although in his nineties, Tom insisted on being a pallbearer. He put his arm strongly around that of Gurtha and two members of the choir - one of them the choirmaster - stood behind Gurtha and Tom, grasping one another's arms as the coffin was gently placed on their shoulders. They began to walk slowly in unison towards the front Church door. The rest of the congregation followed like processionary caterpillars. Tom was slightly smaller than Gurtha and the coffin tilted slightly to one side. Gurtha imagined Nuala inside, rolling on the white silk cushioned sheets – as though slumbering in her sleep. She would typically give a snuffling sound and a small cough before she would waken. He would stand beside the bed with a mug of tea in one hand and toasted wheaten topped with honey on a plate in his other hand. That was in the days when he lived at home on the Crumlin Road before he moved into what Nuala called his millionaire Mansion on the Malone Road.

Gurtha couldn't bear to watch the coffin being lowered into the ground where her body would be eaten by worms or crawled over by beetles. Neither could he contemplate seeing the coffin slide into a furnace to weird tinkly music. He made the decision that he wouldn't watch either a burial or a cremation but would ask for the ashes to be delivered to him when the dreadful job had been completed. As the body burned, they would celebrate Nuala's life by having lunch in Pizza Express in the city centre. Today, they would remember the moments of deep friendship they had shared over the years with Paddy tucking into his lasagne and visualise Nuala eating her favourite American Hot pizza with extra jalapeno peppers, her false teeth wobbling in her mouth.

The funeral directors gently lowered the coffin into the back of the black hearse, as though placing a baby in her cot, before respectfully shaking Gurtha's hand.

Gurtha stepped into a large funeral car with Tom, Lily, Cornelia, Paddy and Laura. In silence, three sat facing three as the car pulled slowly away from the Church. Tom sat with a straight back, his silver hair brushed back from his forehead. His gnarled and wrinkled hand clasped Lily's. He closely watched Gurtha as though seeing him for the first time – his blue eyes squinting slightly and a deep wrinkle of concentration furrowing in the middle of his forehead. Lily closed her eyes, took a few deep breaths and sighed.

Sitting in the funeral car it was clear to Gurtha that his life had been divided into two parts. In the first he had gazed out at the world – separated from it, distant from it. How many hearses had he watched? How many lines of funeral cars following, as he removed his hat and stood passively, in silence? An invisible screen separated him from the feelings and experience of the passengers inside.

Then there was the second part of life which, with earthquake ferocity, had shaken him from being an observer into also being an experiencer of life. It felt like a 'oneing' taking place and the most significant 'oneing' was the sense that there was an umbilical cord attaching him to the marbleised body lying within the coffin.

He had gone back in time, become a baby again, and connected in a visceral way to his mother who was dead. His body did not pump blood but liquid pain from which he could not flee any more than he could stop his eyes from seeing. The two parts of life were one. Life trembled into being. It was organic and cellular – an osmosis – a membrane of being in which information and feelings were interchanged – from inner to outer and from outer to inner. He looked from the window of the car, watching an elderly man, curved over an ivory walking stick, remove his hat. Gurtha found himself lifting his hand and waving like a King at the man who bowed back and smiled in acknowledgement.

The car maintained a slow and respectful pace until it reached Carlisle Circus, an acceptable distance from the Church, at which point it picked up speed as if the funeral directors had another engagement for which they were late.

Cornelia, taking off her black gloves and popping them into a black paten handbag, broke the silence.

"I know it's a very difficult time for you with the horror of what has happened to Nuala – but it could be good for you to have a break from Belfast for a while – a transition in life to a new beginning. I know you love Mallorca. I can find you a house to rent for as long as you want and maybe you can even hold one of your art exhibitions there. I know of one or two galleries which would be ideal."

"I'll think about it." Gurtha replied listlessly, tightening his black tie and rubbing his sweating hands on his black linen suit. "It depends what happens with the police investigation." He raised his hands despairingly into the air. "And with Paddy."

Lily leaned forward, "We'll keep an eye on Paddy. You do what's right for yourself."

Laura rested her hand on top of Paddy's.

THE SECRET WOUND

"Anything at all Paddy that you need – you only have to say and we will take care of you."

Paddy rubbed his nose and stared out the window.

"It's odd that Nuala isn't here. Where is she? She wouldn't want to miss a party."

Laura brushed a tear away from her cheek and turned to Gurtha.

"It's only natural. He's in a state of shock."

Gurtha nodded as he looked out the window.

"Aren't we all?"

♥

A number of strands ran through Gurtha's professional life, including running art exhibitions for emerging new talent and part-time lecturing on Consciousness Studies at Queen's University, Belfast. He spent the greater portion of his time as an Executive Coach supporting senior leaders in creating a vision with their teams, identifying strategic priorities and executing strategy. The most lucrative part of his career was his work as a motivational speaker. He had a reputation for enlightening and amusing his audiences in equal measure.

♥

"The Troubles" in Northern Ireland had long since settled into a simmering unrest rather than a boiling cauldron of hatred. Belfast in 2012 was a place where hope flourished and few wanted to return to the old days of violence. That was what made Nuala's murder all the more shocking. It wasn't a sectarian murder as far as anyone could see – but it was murder nevertheless.

Cornelia, also in the car, was a long standing friend of Gurtha's who had recently been coming to terms with the death of her husband Henry. He had died three months earlier in June 2012 from a heart-related illness. Before retiring, he been a Bank Director. He was quite a bit older than Cornelia. His death at 69 was unexpected. Cornelia attributed it partly to the karma from many years of intense socialising in the 1970 and 1980s. She called those the years of plenty when, as a Bank Director, Henry was obliged to creatively use his vast monthly expense budget. His target was to host twenty lunches a month, a figure which he frequently exceeded. He also succeeded in overspending his clothes budget. Henry used clothes to reflect his character – bright orange jackets with silky navy blue trousers which, if inspected carefully, hid delicate orange flowers. His favourite was a cerise pink suit with a navy blue pin-stripe. To accompany these striking choices, he wore a different coloured cravat with a white shirt each day of the week – red on Sunday, purple on Monday, turquoise on Tuesday, green on Wednesday, orange on Thursday, indigo on Friday and amber on Saturday.

Once suitably attired, he revelled in inviting solicitors and accountants to spend hours consuming lobster thermidor, washed down with copious glasses of Moet, followed by beef bourguignon accompanied by Chateauneuf du Pape and a baked Alaska with more Moet or a glass of Sauternes. With all of this entertaining he was understandably a bit on the plump side with three chins which stylishly complemented a cravat rather than a tie.

Cornelia hinted that a secondary factor in Henry's heart problem was the fact that his love for the finer things in life meant he was more deeply affected by the stress triggered by the economic crisis of 2008 when his pension fund lost two thirds of its value over a few short weeks. He had planned to continue with a lavish lifestyle of entertaining in retirement and discovered that his pension barely covered his fixed costs. He found himself unwillingly pushed into an aesthetic lifestyle, which caused tension with Cornelia. She repeatedly ignored his pleas for austerity measures in her clothes budget, the visits to Vidal Sassoon and to lavishly redecorating their second home in the Port of Soller, Mallorca. After months of tortured aestheticism, Henry discovered that moderation could be avoided, at least in part, with drinkable wine retailing at under three pounds a bottle.

Gurtha saw Henry's life as an example of understanding life. Life was simultaneous expansion and contraction. A cloud appeared in the sky and blueness automatically contracted. A feeling of anxiety arose in the body and the experience of peace diminished. If he was to use a see-saw analogy, Gurtha experienced life as sitting on both ends of a wooden plank. As he shot into the sky, he simultaneously plummeted to the ground. Life contained a pivotal point which triggered all movement into being. Being open to this yin yang perspective on life, Gurtha was able to enjoy Henry's boisterous love of life before retirement, while at the same time being slightly repulsed by it. In a restaurant Henry would order wine insisting on knowing the location of the vineyard and requesting tasting notes.

A waiter held a bottle of AN/2 in his hand, showing it to Henry as though presenting him with an Oscar.

"It is a Falanis wine – thirty five per cent Callet, thirty five per cent Monto Negre and thirty per cent Cabernet Sauvignon. It has a typical Mediterranean, limpid colour with brilliant subtle aromas, spicy, elegant and balanced in the mouth with well integrated tannins. Would you like to taste?"

Henry nodded. The waiter poured a small amount of wine into the bulbous glass.

Henry tasted but not before sniffing. He pushed his thickened nose into the glass and everyone waited in silence for the response.

"Excellent."

The waiter smiled knowingly and topped up everyone's glass. Gurtha felt a hint of embarrassment tightening his stomach as Henry swilled the wine in the glass, sniffed it again, before taking the smallest of sips. Gurtha's discomfort converted into a sensation of disgust – a shrivelling around the heart and throat, as starters arrived. Gurtha observed as Henry and friends became gobbling geese lifting their heads into the air, opening their mouths wide. Henry, in particular, had developed the skill of allowing his uvula to shake in anticipation before his lips were drawn tightly closed and his jaw began to slide quickly from side to side. When he demolished his entrée, crumbs hung like spiders about to spin a web below his lower lip. There would be a smattering of tomato sauce forming a copy of a Miró painting on his orange cravat.

Over the years of friendship with Cornelia and Henry, Gurtha visited their Mallorcan home on a regular basis and sailed with them around the island in their small boat called "Pepino". Rather than see Henry as hedonistic and excessive, Gurtha chose to see him as a generous man with an abundant capacity to enjoy and be grateful for the unexpected financial bounties which dropped onto his lap with little or no effort.

Mallorca was an island where financial success and money in the bank were considered by many as indicators of greatness of character and of superior intelligence. Henry, therefore, found himself a popular person within the expatriate community. Friends liked to brush shoulders with his success – hoping that somehow or other it might be contagious.

Although Gurtha perfectly understood that everyone responds to grief in different ways, he had to admit to being slightly surprised at the rapidity with which Cornelia had found a new partner in Barry after Henry's death. Barry was a younger man from Cardiff who was lucky or unlucky enough to inherit a fortune from his father's construction business. This allowed him to retire at the age of thirty five when he joined Cornelia in her house rental business in Mallorca.

Laura, sitting with a straight back in the funeral car, worked in the corner shop close to where Paddy and Nuala lived. Whereas Holy Cross Church provided spiritual food for the local area, it was the corner shop which took care of the physical body. Its counters were piled high with Paris buns, Madeira cake, soda, wheaten, potato bread, slices of ham and a selection finest Irish and English cheeses. Laura swept the floor and mopped it every morning, cleaning the counter glasses while dreaming of one day going to University.

At seventy, Paddy had not aged well. Thick, dark, curly hairs grew out of the top of his nose, red blotches dappled his face, a thinning of hair in places where he would have preferred a quiff and flabbiness around the waistline, which from time to time he took solace in squeezing.

At school Paddy excelled in his Junior Certificate exams but life seemed to go downhill after that. Like Laura, he didn't go on to higher education as he felt obliged to earn money to pay the family bills.

There had been a couple of years when he first married Nuala during which Paddy experienced what might be called 'classical happiness' – an absence of emotional distress. He worked as a sheet metal worker as his father had done before him, earned enough money to have his suits made by a tailor and his shoes by a cobbler.

After two short years the relationship with Nuala deteriorated for reasons unknown to Paddy and he took refuge in drink. He hated being forced to retire at sixty five and managed to find a job taking money and handing out tickets to clients in a city centre car park. With every year that passed he felt more and more distant from Nuala – a distance which seemed to add pounds and then stones to his weight. He felt like a slug. Nuala called him 'the pig'.

♥

The funeral car slowed to a gentle speed approaching Pizza Express. The two funeral Directors jumped from their seats and slid the car doors open. Gurtha emerged first, almost stumbling onto the pavement and then turning around to help Paddy. Paddy took Gurtha's hand, lowering himself from the car as if into a swimming pool. Cornelia reached a hand towards Gurtha, waiting to be helped. For the first time that day Gurtha noticed she was dressed in a deep pink suit with a black trim around the cuffs, collar and skirt. A large beret circle of a hat perched in the middle of her head covered her hair, allowing a fine veil of black lace to cover her face. Before taking Gurtha's hand, as she descended from the funeral car, Cornelia pulled the veil back from her face and smiled. She waited for Gurtha to do something.

Gurtha reached for her hands.

Once inside Pizza Express, Paddy sat in silence, eating his lasagne with a spoon and drinking Peroni beer which he didn't much like but they didn't serve Guinness and Peroni was better than water. Tom and Lily attempted to lighten the mood by talking about Rose and Matthew and their family – four children – two boys and two girls and another baby expected any day. Laura tried to get a conversation going with Paddy as to whether or not he was enjoying his lasagne but he only nodded and kept eating.

Cornelia, did her best sales pitch.

"You've just suffered a major trauma in losing Nuala. You could benefit from having a break. Where better to go than to Mallorca? You know it well, you can walk in the mountains, swim in the sea – make a new life for yourself. You can even keep working – Palma is a great hub for Europe and long distant flights are a doddle from Barcelona or Madrid. You can run your art exhibitions. The island is a home to so many artists. I can find you a place to live and a gallery for your exhibitions. You know that it is the perfect place for you. Everyone is calling it the new Monaco of the Mediterranean. Promise me that you will at least consider it?"

DAY 1

SUNDAY 11TH AUGUST 2013, MALLORCA

"STOP ACTING SO SMALL.
YOU ARE THE UNIVERSE IN ECSTATIC MOTION."
J RUMI

ON THE 11th August 2013, Gurtha boarded Easyjet flight 5672 to Palma, Mallorca. He looked out of the window at 37,000 feet, seeing shadows fall on the deep valleys and craggy Pyrenees, flying over St Jean-Pied-de-Port.

It hadn't been an easy year since Nuala's murder. He had managed to continue lecturing but following Nuala's death he couldn't engage in the world of coaching or motivational speaking. Coaching involved him having to ask clients questions to help them explore new realities and to encourage them to see a world of infinite possibilities. Motivational speaking required him to energise people with a sense of humour, a lightness of touch, a penetrating depth of insight which, in his state of grief, was inaccessible.

Since Nuala's death, the world had contracted for Gurtha. He felt himself sucked into a black hole, where light, happiness and potentiality had ,with the snap of fingers, disappeared. Or perhaps it was more accurate to say that he felt that he existed within a vacuum. In a vacuum a ray of light is imperceptible unless there is dust to reflect the energy as light. Nuala's presence had been like stardust glittering light into darkness.

During his lectures on Consciousness studies, Gurtha spoke with authenticity following Nuala's death about the pain inherent within the human condition. With poetic intensity he drew upon the reality of grief. Students seemed to enjoy these lectures even more than they had done before. The descriptions of his descent into a private Hell stimulated interest. One of his students asked.

"Is Hell within the human condition finite or infinite?"

Gurtha answered.

"From the perspective of the great spiritual Masters we are told that Hell is a human construct, as is Heaven. Both are infinite in potential. Yet they can both be transcended. We are designed, as human beings, to have the potential to experience a consciousness beyond Heaven and Hell. To do so, there is work to be done. It has been described by great writers such as J Rumi that we have to find our secret wound which creates Heaven and Hell within us. Paradoxically, the wound, as thirteenth century Rumi has said, 'is the place where the Light enters you.'" It is seeing the wound that heals, allowing us to transcend Heaven and Hell.

Another student - Robby - tubby, pimply red-faced sitting at the back of the lecture hall, raised his hand, asking in a trembling voice.

"What does that mean?"

Gurtha hesitated.

"There is more than one answer to your question. I will give you a suggestion, which may help. Imagine that your body is giving you indications that all is not well. Perhaps you have a cough and there is blood in your phlegm. You ignore it. Six months later you still have blood when you cough and in addition you have a blinding headache. You ignore it. You see where I am going with this? Let's say that it is not your body that is sick but your soul –

your spirit – how will you know that you are sick in spirit and what will you do about it?"

Robby flushed, maroon patches around his neck resembling the appearance of Borneo, Indonesia and the upper part of Australia. He stuttered a question.

"How can you know that something which is not your body, is sick? You wouldn't feel anything unless that something was embodied – would you?"

Gurtha looked at the pleading eyes of his student. He felt overcome with a desire to loosen the tie around Robby's pink flowery Paul Smith shirt which he was sure was contributing to the puffiness of his face and the reddening of his neck. It also gave him a sense of existential isolation from his companions scattered on chairs flopped into sweaters from Fat Face, Gap and Nike.

"You are right – the sickness in the body and the sickness of spirit are not separate. They are not one and they are not two."

As Borneo faded from Robby's neck, Gurtha closed his notes registering the fleeting thought that he, not Robby, didn't have a clue what he was talking about. He coughed, clearing his throat.

"Enjoy your summer. I look forward to being with you again towards the end of September when no doubt our worlds will have tumbled in and out of being many times."

After that lecture, Gurtha proceeded with his plans to spend his summer on a forty days sabbatical in Mallorca, where he would find the equivalent of a log cabin by Walden Pond as did Henry David Thoreau in the nineteenth century. Like Thoreau, something called him to spend time observing nature, reflect on how to discover life's essential needs. He could, as Cornelia suggested, organise a small art exhibition. He would limit his stay to forty days.

He chose forty days as he knew that the number forty was symbolic of a period when something of great significance could be accomplished. The Great Flood caused by rain over forty days and nights forced Noah to build his Arc. After leaving Egypt the children of Israel wandered for forty years in the wilderness. Moses spent forty days and nights on Mount Sinai before receiving the Ten Commandments. Jesus was tempted for forty days in the desert. There were forty days between the resurrection of Jesus and the Ascension. There seemed to be enough evidence to suggest that something of substance could happen within forty days in Mallorca. Even though he was only planning to stay for forty days, he sold his house on the Malone Road. It was a statement that life was going to be different. He was determined not to return the same person, to the same house, living the same life.

♥

Gurtha drove out of Palma after collecting a hired car. Cars whipped past on the left and then in the lane to the right, heading in the direction of Palma and Andratx. He felt woozy, disorientated. He stayed in the middle lane, only swerving violently to the right, to avoid missing the exit for Soller.

He made his way towards the mountains which pushed into the sky like Gaudi sculptures – weird shapes which held their own beauty. They were not symmetrical but leaning, swerving, curling into the air. Emerging from the tunnel, he saw the olive terraced mountains, dotted with almond and carob trees and the town of Soller with its golden stone houses. He drove past field after field of orange and lemon trees before turning off the main road and winding his way towards La Torretta.

La Torretta overlooked Soller valley. Before opening the front door, Gurtha walked along the crazy paving to a stone hexagonal gazebo with its terracotta tiled roof and sat to drink in the view.

The sky was lightly covered in feathery clouds. The houses of Soller were small orange and grey rectangles with scattered mirrors twinkling in the sunshine. A plane growled overhead, like a thunderstorm in the distance. He listened to see if he could hear the moment that the sound disappeared. It became an attenuated rumble, a gentle purr, before it disappeared. Cicadas were singing loudly out of sight. He heard the click clacking of the wooden train before it emerged from the tunnel in the mountains. An almond tree to his left was covered in furry green shells. The carob tree beside it was full of black pods swinging gently in the breeze. A donkey sang its painful song nearby as a blackbird swooped to his right. The air was perfumed with pine. He took three deep breaths before getting to his feet and turning towards the front door. The earth outside the gazebo was tanned and loose. A single pink daisy nestled among bright green shoots near the door. The wind unexpectedly started to blow strongly, sounding like the sea in a storm. It had a hollow sound as if Gurtha had pressed an enormous conch shell to his ear. The olive tree beside the front door was waving its branches enthusiastically. Its bark light brown with black rough crevices – corrugated wrinkles hundreds of years old. The sun shone on the light green shoots, making the leaves glitter like small silver swords. A hawk settled on a rickety post to his right, it swayed from side to side before launching itself into the valley below with a wide opening of its wings. Gurtha turned the key in the lock.

Inside La Torretta, Gurtha creaked open the green shutters allowing sunlight to fall on the red tiled kitchen floor. He patted the two plump sofas in the sitting room covered in cushions and examined the wood burning stove before walking upstairs. He explored the two bedrooms and bathroom. He opened the windows and shutters in all of the rooms and threw a suitcase on

THE SECRET WOUND

the floor of the largest bedroom which had a view of Soller from one of the windows and the sea from the second. The bed smelt musty and was cold to the touch. A mosquito net dangled from the ceiling. Gurtha sat on the bed, listening to the silence which was interrupted by the tinkling of sheep bells as the sheep made their way up and down the mountain. Birds chirped overhead, making a nest in the roof. For the first time since Nuala's death, Gurtha felt a hint of peace moving within him. In the silence of the room his thoughts stopped churning. He lay back on the bed, stretched wide his arms to form a cross and breathed deeply.

That night Gurtha wakened to the sound of thunder. He pulled back the mosquito net and opened the bedroom window. Over the sea, in the distance, the black sky was ripped apart by streaks of silver. He looked up. Overhead it was a clear starry night. Huge black cumulus clouds moved from the horizon heading towards La Torretta. Thunder rumbled, muffled within the clouds which continued to swell and billow – their edges briefly etched in silver. Gurtha climbed onto the windowsill, dangling his legs into the blackness. He overflowed with excitement, like a child, as the thunder, now closer, shook the house; a strong wind banged the shutters on either side, forcing him to reluctantly climb back into the bedroom. He closed the shutters, leaving the windows open to listen to the storm. As he lay in bed, rain and hailstones like marbles, thrashed against the tiled roof. Thunder exploded directly overhead with lightning flickering through the shutters like strobe lighting. Tomorrow, he would go to Soller and make plans for the opening of the art exhibition. He had arranged to meet Cornelia and Barry at eleven for coffee. He realised, with a start, that he had forgotten to ring Paddy to tell him that he had arrived safely.

In Belfast, Paddy sat on a chair in the sitting room with a photograph of Nuala in his hands. It was taken somewhere by the sea, before they married on the 14th January 1967. He couldn't remember where. Was it Carnlough, Bangor, Portstewart or Newcastle, Co Down? He searched for any signs that would help identify the location but there was only a boat resting on the sandy beach, out of the water and twelve people smiling for the camera, including Nuala. She looked radiant, wearing a soft beige cashmere coat, her hair in curls down to her shoulders. She had reached a hand into the left pocket of the coat. Was she looking for a tissue or a sweet? Paddy was in the photo wearing an open-neck shirt and a V-neck jumper. He looked straight at the camera. The sun shone on the right side of his face leaving the left side in shadow. He had thick straight dark hair brushed off his forehead. Nuala looked absorbed in thought. She also looked invincible.

A tear rolled down his face.

"I've been a bad boy," he whispered to himself.

The fire had gone out. It was cold. He looked through the lace curtains and could see the cherry tree which Nuala had planted, cared for and loved. He hadn't eaten since breakfast. When Nuala was alive, he regularly cooked "an Ulster fry" for two - with bacon, egg, soda farl, tomato, potato bread and black pudding. Since Nuala's death, he merely fried an egg for breakfast. He cracked an egg into a bowl before placing it in the frying pan. Nuala had explained to him in the early days that putting the egg first into a bowl means that you can decide if it is "off". He smelt the egg. It was fine. He dropped it into the frying pan. It hissed, spat and sizzled. The edges burnt and curled. Little bubbles burst in whiteness. Popping sounds of brightness splashed onto his face.

THE SECRET WOUND

He stabbed a few of the bubbles with a fork. He found a spoon and caught the oil at the edge of the pan and poured it over the yolk. It glazed white like a dead fish eye. It was ready to eat. He ate it from the frying pan with his fork. It didn't taste of anything – there was only texture – crispness from the burnt white, softness from the yolk. No flavour. He threw the fork into the sink and sat at the table, looking at the chair where Nuala would have sat. He waited a few moments and then shuffled from his chair which faced the wall to sit in Nuala's chair with her view of the room, the window into the garden and the toilet. As he looked at the toilet door, he felt a little trickle run down his leg. He ignored it.

The house was strangely empty without Nuala. For Paddy, being in the house without Nuala felt like he didn't exist. It was a double emptiness. He looked at the telephone beside him. It didn't ring. He scratched his head and picked up the Irish News. Who else had died? Was there a wake he could go to? He turned the pages without recognising any names. He stared at the flameless coal, heaved himself to his feet and forgot what he was planning to do. He sat down again. There was always 'The Easter Rising Club'. He staggered again to his feet, pulled on a cap and a jacket and opened the front door.

♥

When Paddy turned the key in the lock five hours later it was four in the morning, about the time Gurtha dangled his legs over the windowsill of his bedroom in 'La Toretta'.

The sky was lightening; blackbirds were breaking their night's silence and called to each other. Paddy staggered up the first flight of stairs to his bedroom. He reached under the pillow for his pyjamas, peeled off his clothes, leaving them on the floor beside the bed and climbed in under the sheets. With the help of the moonlight he saw streaks of blood on the pillow. He was bleeding. He touched his head and looked at the bright red blood glistening on his fingers. What had happened to him? He couldn't remember. Where was his wallet?

He heaved one leg out of bed and then the second. He sat for a few minutes trying to remember the evening. He recalled entering 'The Easter Rising'. He remembered having a pint but couldn't remember with whom. He knew that he had laughed and so there had to be someone else there with him but couldn't remember who or what was said and or why he had laughed. Where was his wallet? The next memory that he had was of turning the key in the front door. He didn't remember looking into Nuala's bedroom before opening the door to his own bedroom.

He knew that he did not want Nuala to see the bloodied pillow cases and sheets. He dragged the sheets from the bed and hobbled downstairs, with the sheets and pillow cases under one arm and one hand gripping the bannister. He couldn't find the washing powder and used the Fairy Liquid to rinse away the blood. It wasn't so easy to do. His hands were wrinkling with the water before he stopped trying. He found bleach and poured it onto the pink sheets which turned yellow in patches. The water from the kitchen tap gushed fully open when he remembered the washing machine. He carried the soaking sheets and pillow cases and put them in the washing machine. He poured the washing powder which was sitting on top into the drawer, closed the door and left without turning it on.

The phone rang. It was Gurtha.

"How are you doing, Paddy?"

Silence.

"Are you there Paddy? It's Gurtha here. I'm in Mallorca."

THE SECRET WOUND

"Where's Mallorca?"

"It's in Spain, Paddy. Do you remember that film with Grace Kelley, driving around the coast of Mallorca? Nuala really liked it."

"When will I see you?"

"You'll see me Friday. You're coming out here for your holiday."

"Am I? How will I get out there?"

"I'll collect you. Don't worry about a thing. Remember Nuala always sang that Bobby Ferrin song?"

"Bobby who?" Paddy whispered.

Gurtha began to sing down the phone,

"Here's a little song I wrote
You might want to sing it note for note
Don't worry, be happy
In every life we have some trouble
But when you worry, you make it double
Don't worry, be happy."

"Do you not remember, Paddy – that was Nuala's favourite song?"

Paddy was silent again for a few seconds before asking.

"Are there any other songs that Nuala liked? Could you sing me another one? Could you sing 'Danny Boy' for me?"

DAY 2

GURTHA DROVE the winding track down to join the main road to Soller. Old men in slippers bent over wooden canes, shuffled through the Plaza. Alongside, the local Mallorquins drank coffee, read newspapers and chatted to one another under the leafy sycamore trees. Sunlight dappled the tables and chairs. A tram tooted its way across the square. Gurtha looked for Café Soller.

He spotted Cornelia. She was wearing a long tight-fitting jersey dress covered in pink and yellow flowers with an outline of black around the flowers like an artist's simple brush stroke to highlight features of an almost finished painting. Gurtha was surprised that his first feeling was not one of pleasure at seeing Cornelia again, but rather one of missing Henry at her side. Even when temperatures soared towards thirty degrees centigrade, Henry would have worn a navy pin-striped suit with a white shirt and, as it was Monday, a purple cravat. His shoes would be reflecting the world above him. His hair dyed a subtle dark brown, layered, glossy, falling in layers onto his shoulders. He would have reached a manicured hand towards Gurtha , before patting him on the back, the way you would a horse.

Cornelia kissed Gurtha before opening a white parasol – which – using only the slightest twist of her fingers on the mahogany handle, she circled above her head.

"Meet Barry."

Barry stood up and shook Gurtha's hand. It was a half-baked handshake – neither too firm nor too weak. He was half-baked all over – neither too tall nor too small – shorter than Gurtha – maybe five foot eight inches. He was neither too thin nor too fat – although he had the look of someone who would have a tendency to fatness rather than thinness – with rosy cheeks, a hedonistic smile, and sported a crisply ironed linen shirt over beige cotton shorts. Gurtha spotted his sandalled feet with two surprisingly gnarled big toe nails and wondered why anyone would not cover them up with a pair of leather boat shoes.

"How was your journey?" Cornelia lifted the white straw hat from the chair and placed it on her head, pulling the brim down to almost cover her eyes.

"Everything went to plan." Gurtha nodded as he requested sparkling water from the waitress.

"What do you think of La Torretta?" Cornelia leaned forward in her chair.

"I like it a lot."

"Oh good. That's a relief. I was hoping you would say that. Let's hope you like what I've chosen for you as the venue for your art exhibition. It's quaint." Cornelia sipped her Americano coffee.

"If you like it, I have the rental agreement. We can sign it today. You are sure that you only want to stay for forty days? We hardly need to bother signing a contract but we're in Mallorca and the world revolves around paperwork."

Gurtha sipped water and surveyed Barry who inspected his nails.

"Forty days will be sufficient."

Cornelia continued to twirl the parasol.

"So what else are you going to do during your forty days? After all, Angelina will be mostly taking care of the exhibition."

Gurtha looked into her eyes which were like button-green cat eyes, placed in her face but having a life of their own rather than being a part of her body.

"It will be good to have time to do nothing. I have no plans. No doubt a routine of sorts will emerge." The sunlight stung his eyes. He slid the chair into the shade.

"What about you, Barry – how are you enjoying retirement?"

Barry finished off Cornelia's croissant, before replying.

"There's always something to do to keep the women happy."

Gurtha was aware of a sense of irritation arising in his body. Trying not to let it affect his tone of voice, he attempted to sound jovial, aware that it sounded false, "How many women are you struggling with?"

Barry wiped his mouth with the napkin.

Three. Feels almost like full time – Cornelia, Angelina and Stephanie. I imagine that more will arrive – they always do when there's a handsome man like myself with money around."

Cornelia gave him a kick under the table.

"Behave yourself or you will be sent to the 'naughty room.'"

Barry laughed.

"I can't wait."

Cornelia ignored him.

"It needs a bit of work." Cornelia touched Gurtha's hand across the table.

"The gallery I mean. I could also have said that *he* needs a bit more work." She laughed, looked again in her purse for a mirror and applied fresh lipstick.

THE SECRET WOUND

"Are you ready to see the gallery?"

They walked from the Plaza towards the small alley of Son Joan. Cornelia handed Gurtha a long black iron key.

"You can open up. It's yours for the next forty days."

The door squeaked open and the first thing that Gurtha noticed was the aged, oak-panelled floor. Then his eyes moved towards the beams embedded in the ceiling, the white walls and a large door into the patio garden at the back. The front window was stained glass, which threw a kaleidoscope of blue, yellow and green onto the floor. Small flecks of gold and silver circled within golden sunbeams which pierced the clear air exploding onto the back wall.

"There's upstairs to see." Gurtha followed Cornelia up the first wobbly wooden staircase. He ducked his head to avoid swinging terracotta lamps. Even more sunshine flooded the first floor, lighting up the dark wood panelling and falling onto a range of agricultural tools pinned to the wall. There was an old mace with a cylinder studded with iron thorns on the end of a chain, which Gurtha imagined could have been used in Roman times by a gladiator, two sharp knives with wooden handles, strapped with cord, at least seven different ploughs, a long three pronged fork and a large wooden sieve almost a metre in diameter.

Gurtha felt himself falling back through the centuries to a time when these instruments would have been used. There was something about time being held unspoilt in this small terraced house that felt good - a sense of peace, stability, a palpable rootedness in the hands and hearts of those from the past. It was also smelt in old polish and varnish and heard in creaking floorboards.

"I wouldn't change it too much." Gurtha looked out from the first floor window onto the narrow street below with its flowerpots filled with aloe vera, cacti and ferns.

Cornelia stood beside him, wiping a glass with her finger,

"Well, it needs a bit of a clean, at least and everything taken off the walls to make room for the paintings."

Cornelia polished a small circle of window with a cotton handkerchief, turned to him and smiled, "How about dinner on Thursday? It's your birthday. Meet a few new friends." She opened her briefcase.

Gurtha opened the top button of his shirt,

"It's hard to believe that this day last year, Nuala was still alive."

Cornelia opened a plastic wallet containing the contract. She handed it to Gurtha with a fountain pen to sign.

"It must be hard for you – as it is for me with Henry. Is there any progress in the Police case about who murdered her?"

Gurtha placed the contract on top of a wooden bench and, as he prepared to sign the papers, he glanced at Cornelia.

"No. There have been no developments. It's frustrating. The longer there are no leads and the more time that passes, it is becomes more unlikely that the murderer will be found."

As he talked, he watched Cornelia lift Barry's hand and gently squeeze it. Then she touched his nose with the cotton handkerchief she had used earlier to clean a blemish on the window. They looked into one another's eyes with complicity – something which he had never seen her do before with Henry. The scene sent a slight shiver along his spine from top to bottom. He hesitated, without knowing why, in scratching the pen across the contract - but there was no going back. It was like the critical moment before take-off when the pilot commits and a ping tells the crew that there is no going back and that the plane is taking off, no matter what.

DAY 3

"IF YOU ARE IRRITATED BY EVERY RUB,
HOW WILL YOUR MIRROR BE POLISHED?"
J RUMI

BACK IN "La Torretta" Gurtha unpacked his cases. Nuala was on his mind. What was it that he missed so much about her? There was something intertwined with her flesh and blood that mysteriously glowed and burned in a way that he didn't understand. It pervaded her glance, her crooked smile, her gestures with the hand tapping on the sofa as she sang, her humour, the way she dressed, her gentleness. There was beauty in seeing her fringe plastered against a sweating forehead, beauty in the grey hair which needed another blonde rinse, in her swollen tummy, in her sitting on the bed at night in her pyjamas, taking out her dentures and placing them in a cup of Steradent. Watching her do all these simple things brought him peace.

One evening, more than a year before, Nuala, had stood beside the bed, looked at her swollen ankles and asked.

"I think it's spreading all over me. Am I going to get better?"

He knew that her heart problem wouldn't be cured, yet he couldn't bring himself to say, "No – you're not going to get any better. Yes, it is spreading all over you."

She gazed at him with that direct eye contact that he was used to receiving, insisting.

"My mother died like this. Her legs were swollen like mine. It was the end of it all for her."

Gurtha said nothing as he straightened the duvet. Nuala sighed.

"Thank you. You are very kind."

She smiled at him and sat on the bed. Gurtha kneeled on the carpet at her feet.

"Would you like me to help you put the elastic bandages on your legs?"

"Yes please." Nuala stretched a leg towards him and rolled up her trousers. "They feel good."

Nuala's death had surprised everyone by its unexpectedness. Nuala - a beautiful thrush sweeping over the ground at great speed knowing exactly where she was going and why. She was fearless – so different from Gurtha – who felt himself gripped by an anxiety about living which easily turned into a feeling of sheer panic. When Nuala was alive, her sense of direction, her confidence in the meaning of life, eased Gurtha's distress that ultimately life may hold no meaning other than what he chose to make of it.

Where was Nuala now? He had read somewhere that love could grow even in death. How could that happen? Hadn't Nuala said to him that she would always be with him – always around? Maybe she was wrong about that. He shuddered to think that Nuala lived a life believing in something which wasn't true. If what Nuala valued wasn't real, it negated her life. If everything she thought, felt and did was based on ignorance, then her life had no more reality than the short flickering dance of a Mayfly.

He suddenly remembered that he had forgotten Paddy again.

The phone rang for quite a while before Paddy picked it up.

"Hi Dad. How's it going?"

THE SECRET WOUND

"Who's that?"

"Gurtha."

"Where's your Mother?"

"What are you talking about Dad? You know that Mum's dead."
Gurtha took a deep breath.

"Are you OK?"

There was silence on the end of the phone. Gurtha's voice
increased in volume and intensity,

"Are you there Dad? Speak to me."

"Of course I'm here – sure where else would I be?"

"Dad, I'm coming over. You're coming on holiday here to
Mallorca. I'll see you on Friday. Don't forget. Get your swimming
trunks packed. You love swimming."

"I don't swim any more," Paddy rasped on the end of the phone.

"You'll love the sea here, it's warm. Didn't you swim in Bangor
on New Year's Day?"

"That was when Nuala was alive," Paddy whispered.

"Wasn't it?" Paddy searched to hear Gurtha's response.

"Yes Dad, it was. But you will have a great time here."

"I'm not so keen on flying," Paddy stuttered.

"I'll be with you. If we go down, we'll go down together." Gurtha
wished that he hadn't said that.

"That means that we will be with Nuala then does it?" Paddy
sounded anxious and pleased at the same time.

"Dad, Nuala is watching over us." The lie stuck in his throat.

"Do you not feel her around you?"

"I don't know where she has gone. She'll be back soon." Paddy
put the phone down.

Gurtha placed his mobile phone on the table in the gazebo. He
held his head in his hands. What was Paddy doing now?

He imagined him opening the front door, walking up the road to buy fish and chips for his tea. He might first call into Sean Graham's, the Bookies on the corner, to place a bet on a horse. What would he be wearing? Maybe he would have chosen his tweed jacket, a navy blue V-neck jumper, a blue shirt and tie, navy corduroys, brown loafers. On top of that he would be wearing loneliness. It was as though the air that touched Paddy was permeated with loneliness. He breathed it in and he breathed it out. Paddy was so soaked in loneliness that he became almost invisible like the air around him. Loneliness dissolved him. He would walk into Sean Graham's, place a bet and leave and no-one would even register that he had been and gone.

That was the story of Paddy's life. He moved almost unnoticed across the planet without any sense of motivation or intent. Those who looked at Paddy did so only with the curiosity with which you might watch at a beetle scurrying in a straight line and then taking a sharp turn to the right. You didn't know where it was going or why, or what feelings, if any, it had on its journey.

THE SECRET WOUND

DAY 4

THE NEXT day was Gurtha's birthday. He sat on a chair outside La Torretta. A gentle breeze blew through the olive trees waving the branches constantly from side to side. As they moved, the colour turned from olive green to silvery white. The trunks remained solid, rooted in the dry, red earth. The sky was blue – a light blue hiding the stars. Above, there existed a starry universe hidden by the light of the sun. Gurtha listened to the buzzing of the cicadas, feeling the scorching August sun tingle his body into awareness, smelling the pine needles roasting on the barbeque of the earth, seeing the movement within the olive and palm trees.

He could have brought Paddy with him when he left Belfast on Sunday 11th August but he wanted to make sure that La Torretta would be suitable, to purchase essential food supplies, minimising any agitation which could arise for Paddy being without Nuala. He placed a photo of Nuala and Paddy on their wedding day in Paddy's bedroom which was beside Gurtha's. He sat a packet of King Edward and Hamlet cigars beside Paddy's bed with a blue lighter with the words 'Mallorca' written on the side. He wondered what else he could do. He had bought bacon and there was wheaten bread in the freezer, Kerrygold butter and PG tips tea. He remembered that Paddy loved digestive biscuits. He could buy those later in the supermarket in Soller. He added biscuits to his list along with a reminder to buy Guinness and pushed the notebook into his pocket.

Protected from the late afternoon sun, he sat in the gazebo and tried to listen. He wasn't listening to the sounds of the birds outside, or the rustle of the breeze in the olive trees. He tried to listen to what was happening inside his head and what was whispering in his body. There were no words to be heard in his head – only a sensation of discomfort – almost nausea. As if he had eaten something which had disagreed with him. He found his breath shortening. Then he realised that the memory of finding Nuala dead flickered once again into his head, together with sensations of nausea, panic and difficulty breathing. Images on the wallpaper in the hallway where he had found Nuala were now magnified in his mind. Hummingbirds flew from the wallpaper and, rather than buzzing over purple flowers, they whirred around his head. He saw the skirting board with its flaking white paint, the hallway tiles with Molly's muddy cat footprints. These images were fading in and out of existence, speeding up and circling around the central image of Nuala's body.

The mobile rang. It was Cornelia.

"Don't forget it's your birthday tomorrow. The party is organised."

Gurtha replied. "It *is* Nuala's anniversary tomorrow."

Cornelia's voice mellowed.

"I'm sorry – of course you must be thinking of Nuala. I am as well."

THE SECRET WOUND

There was a moment of silence as Gurtha looked down into the valley of Soller where Saint Bartholomew's twin spires reached towards him. An intense nausea rolled through him making it difficult to speak. He heard words coming out of his mouth which he had previously no intention of saying.

"Barry seems to have helped you move on after Henry's death."

There was silence on the phone. He heard Cornelia take a few deep breaths before answering.

"Everyone has to find their own way to cope with what life throws at them. In the end everyone is on their own, no matter who is with them. You should have learnt how to be on your own with Nuala when she was alive and then you wouldn't find it so difficult now. Your relationship with her wasn't a healthy one as you can see by the state you are in a year after her death."

Gurtha coughed before spluttering down the phone.

"She didn't die. She was murdered. That's what makes it difficult."

DAY 5

"FORGET SAFETY. LIVE WHERE YOU FEAR TO LIVE.
DESTROY YOUR REPUTATION. BE NOTORIOUS."
J RUMI

GURTHA DECIDED to walk from La Torretta to Cornelia and Barry's house in the Port of Soller. Cornelia had apologised to him on the phone earlier, for her lack of sensitivity at how he was feeling with Nuala's anniversary approaching. Yet her comments about his relationship with Nuala had sown seeds of doubt in his mind. Was it love that he had felt for Nuala or had he twisted love into something which was about self-gratification – using Nuala to provide his life with meaning? Was he looking for approval from Nuala to confirm that his career, money, lifestyle meant something? She never gave him that approval. In fact she had told him that his life was built on shifting sand. He didn't know what she had meant by that. She had followed up by saying,

"Maybe you should give up your big job and find out what life is all about."

He never asked her why she thought that or how he was expected to find out what life was about.

He glanced at his watch to see if it was time to walk down to the Port. Temperatures had fallen and there was a slight breeze. It should be possible to walk down and arrive in a fairly respectable

THE SECRET WOUND

state without sweating too excessively. He could get a taxi back – although not all of the taxi drivers would be happy to twist the twenty seven bends on a stony track, leading from the main road to 'La Toretta'. Even if he got dropped off where the track began, he could walk home with the help of a torch. He had packed a small rucksack with a rope, a torch, a bottle of white wine and a bottle of red – both from the Bordoy vineyard in Mallorca. Henry would have approved.

He stood for a few minutes in the gazebo looking at Soller. There was a haze diluting the sunshine. He searched for something new to see. He spotted a house on the mountain across the valley. Who lived there? Wouldn't it be interesting if they were looking at him this very moment? That simple thought reminded him again of Nuala. He imagined that Nuala was watching him, that she filled the space around him. He wanted to hear her speak – to listen to her laugh. He looked at the olive trees swaying in the breeze, the cheese plant with its slit leaves and the blue delicate plant by the front door. He didn't know the names of many of these unfamiliar plants and flowers but the fact that he didn't only made him want to look at them more closely. He approached a small bush with tiny orange and yellow flowers. He picked one and looked more closely. The leaf was the shape of a mint leaf but bigger. The orange flowers were small – the size of your thumb in diameter, with the centre deep orange and the rim of each flower a lighter colour. Each flower in turn was made up of tiny miniature flowers so that each flower was like a bunch of flowers. All that intricacy and beauty and no-one to necessarily see it. As he examined the flower, it disintegrated in his hand – the miniature blossoms spiralling and tumbling onto the sandy earth.

It was five o'clock when he began to stumble along the uneven track towards a gate which hikers passed en route to Sa Costera. He turned right along the path to the Port. The path became narrow, with a steep drop to his left. He breathed shallowly, holding onto the branches of the olive trees to his right. The last time he had walked to the Port was when he was on holiday with Cornelia and Henry. There had been a thick wire on the right hand side which you could hold and steady yourself. It had gone. He knew that he shouldn't keep looking to the left but he couldn't stop himself. It was turning more into a cliff edge and the path itself almost too narrow for two feet to be placed side by side. Although it was obvious that he had to put one foot in front of the other to make progress, the fact that he couldn't stand still for a moment with his two feet together made him feel dizzy and anxious. He grasped at the olive tree branches to help steady himself but they felt too thin, too weak. He searched with his hand into the tree to see if there was a stronger branch and then froze. His breathing became even more shallow and rapid. What could he do? There was no-one around to help. He needed a hand to help him. He held the lower branches of the olive tree and got down onto his knees. That was worse. His left knee was barely on the path. He attempted to somehow sit down and push himself along a few feet on his bottom, ignoring the thorn bushes digging into his right thigh. Pulling himself again onto his knees, he tried holding onto the branches sticking out from the cliff face with both hands but that didn't feel right either. He was off balance. He grabbed at a rock jutting out from the terrace and managed to sit down. After five minutes of deep breathing, he resorted to inching along the path once more on his bottom. He made slow progress and eventually reached the half-way point which meant that he had to keep going. He couldn't turn back. A dog barked far below. He imagined it standing in a garden with a proper path. He so much wanted to be there with the dog. It wouldn't matter if it mauled him – anything

THE SECRET WOUND

would be better than struggling along this path in what was meant to be paradise. He looked at his watch. It was half past six. They would be wondering where he was. He had stupidly left his mobile phone behind. He realised that for the last hour he hadn't thought about Nuala.

♥

"What happened to you?" Cornelia in a floating red chiffon dress kissed him on the cheek.

"It took longer than I thought." Gurtha raised his hands into the air, "I apologise for being late."

"You're not late. We're still waiting for Angelina. Come in and let's get you introduced."

With arms outstretched Cornelia walked into the room as though walking on stage,

"Let me introduce you all to Gurtha Maloney – a lovely Irishman – my dearest, longest standing friend."

It sounded as though a round of applause would follow but instead a few heads turned around; there was a low level ripple of "hellos" after which everyone continued with their private conversations. Cornelia swung around to Gurtha, "Aren't they all sooo rude. I promise you we can educate them." She took his hand and brought him over to Todd and Stephanie.

"Don't be beastly to him. He's only here a few days. He's all alone and it is his birthday."

Todd stood up, grabbed Gurtha's hand, shook it firmly, slapped him on the shoulder with his right hand – it was almost a hug – and bellowed.

"Great to have a man on the scene. We're outnumbered here with the girlies. Barry, serve the man a drink."

Barry arrived with a tray of champagne cocktails. Gurtha helped himself. Barry sat the tray on the circular table covered with plates of olives, potato crisps, almonds and quails eggs. Todd lifted a glass and offered it to Barry.

"Don't forget yourself, Barry."

Barry shook his head.

"I'm not drinking until Angelina arrives."

Stephanie stepped forward, "Do you mind? You're ignoring our guest. That's frightfully bad mannered."

She pushed Todd to one side and pecked Gurtha forcefully on both cheeks.

"The first thing you have to tell us is what do you do. That's all that we're interested in around here. What do you do, how much are you worth and do you know anyone interesting?"

Stephanie laughed, throwing her head back, allowing her auburn hair to cover her bare shoulders. She crossed her legs and her blue silk halter neck dress fell in Grecian folds to the floor, hiding her diamantine slippers. Todd raised his eyes to the ceiling, drummed his fingers on the table, and shouted across to Stephanie.

"Do you have you any idea how boring you are?"

Stephanie pulled her fringe down over her forehead and slowly twiddled ringlets into her hair, lifting it into the air and then letting it fall down once more onto her shoulders.

"If there were a competition between Todd and I as to who is most boring who do you think would win, Gurtha?"

Gurtha lifted a quail's egg from a white ceramic frilled dish.

"I don't think boring would be an appropriate adjective for either of you."

He peeled the spotted shell into the adjoining dish, popping the egg into his mouth and managing to smile at the same time.

Stephanie shook her head from side to side,

THE SECRET WOUND

"Oh dear. We have a diplomat in our midst. How ghastly. What do you do when you're not being frustratingly polite?"

"I'm a University lecturer, from time to time I run art exhibitions but mostly I work within the business world."

Stephanie sat upright in her chair. Her eyes, although slanted temporarily, opened wider.

"Oh my God." She laughed. "We will expect to be educated and entertained then during your visit." She laughed, placing a hand over her mouth.

"No pressure then. How did you meet Cornelia?"

The question was swallowed into the silence which fell over the room as Angelina entered. Everyone stopped drinking, talking, smoking and stared at her. She was wearing the tiniest of blue jean shorts, a black and cream polka dot blouse and silver stiletto sandals.

"What would you like a drink Angelina?" Barry hurried to her side.

"What are you having?" Angelina smiled down on Barry below her, her blonde curls brushing against his face.

"I was waiting for you to arrive before deciding."

"That's very restrained of you." Angelina transferred her weight from one stiletto to the other.

"Can I show you something first?" Barry pointed to the spiral stairway.

"Of course." Angelina tottered across the floor and followed Barry upstairs.

♥

In Cornelia's bedroom, Barry whispered to Angelina,

"I haven't been able to stop thinking about you all day. I know what they mean about love driving you crazy. I'm madly, insanely, wildly, in love with you."

He lunged towards her, taking her in his arms, pulling her into an embrace. As he kissed her, he moved his head slightly to the right and left to deepen the contact with her lips. He closed his eyes, aware of the softness of their merging with one another. Then he felt Angelina resist and pull away from him. She moved her head backwards avoiding contact with his lips. He kissed her chin and neck as she pushed him towards the bed.

Barry sat shaking on the white linen duvet; eyes wide open, unable to speak. Angelina took a few steps backwards towards the bedroom door the way a cat moves when it is retreating from a potential fight. She hissed at him.

"I've told you – I don't want any more of this. It was a one-off mistake. I had too much to drink that night. It should never have happened. If you don't stop this – I am handing in my notice to Cornelia and you will never see me again. You can explain why that has happened to Cornelia or I will. Do you understand?"

Barry threw himself heavily back on the bed and covered his face with his hands. The words he uttered were hardly audible.

"But I love you. I don't love Cornelia. You're killing me."

Angelina clasped her hands together as though she was in prayer. Her voice softened a little.

"I'm not killing you. You are inventing something which is not real. You don't love me. You can't love someone you don't know. You don't know me. I came upstairs with you to beg you to stop sending me those texts, making innuendos and trying to catch my eye every time Cornelia is not looking at us. I find it harassing, embarrassing and frightening. I'll say it for the umpteenth time

THE SECRET WOUND

– it was a one-off mistake. Do you get it? You're right – you are crazy. So wise up or go and see a psychiatrist. If you can put this behind you, I can and we can be friends. If you can't ..." Angelina took a deep breath and steadied her voice, "So what we do now," Angelina paused, "is we go downstairs, act normal and stay that way. Am I making myself clear?"

Barry moved his hands away from his face, continued lying on the bed and staring at the ceiling, sobbed.

"I've never heard you sound like this before. Yes, you've made yourself clear. I'll do what you say. I don't want to lose you."

Barry struggled to sit up, resting his elbows on the bed, gazing at Angelina with soft teddy bear brown eyes. He listened as Angelina whispered before twisting around to face the door.

"Don't be a fool. You never found me. How can you lose me? You used me."

♥

Downstairs, Cornelia perched on the arm of the sofa, announcing.

"Dinner will be ready in five minutes. Gurtha as it is your birthday, I'm doing one of your favourites – green thai curry – with all the trimmings."

Stephanie schmoozed over to Gurtha, picking a glass from the silver tray on the table.

"You're staying in La Torretta – isn't it a bit isolated?"

"That's what I want – space, isolation, no fixed line telephone – only the mobile, no internet, no television, and no running water - stepping back to learn from Nature."

Stephanie sipped her wine and shook her head.

"I don't think I would like that. I'm too much of a Los Angeles girl."

"Santa Monica isn't Los Angeles" Todd interrupted. "It's a surreal world."

"Why do you say that?" Gurtha stabbed a toothpick into a crushed olive.

"It's a freak show. You see the weirdest people on Venice Beach creating a whole world of people endlessly distracting themselves."

"That's rich coming from you. All you have done in your life is to seek success by distracting people." Stephanie punched him playfully.

Cornelia walked into the centre of the lounge holding a flat bronze gong suspended from a thick cord. She thumped it with a wooden mallet. A discordant clash vibrated around the room.

"Dinner is served."

Barry and Angelina descended the stairs and, arriving first at the dining table, sat facing one another.

Gurtha surveyed the table. Todd had taken a seat beside Barry and was feeling the texture of his pink silk shirt and making a commentary on it which Gurtha couldn't hear. Stephanie was on Todd's left directly across the table from Gurtha. Cornelia swept into the room sitting herself down between Gurtha and Angelina and facing Todd. She took a deep breath, placing her hand on Angelina's shoulder.

"What was Barry showing you upstairs?"

Angelina laughed, passing the basket of bread, with alioli and olives.

"A very good product he discovered for removing the lime scale from beneath the rim of the toilet. The water is so hard here; it will make cleaning a lot quicker."

Barry nodded, "Firewater. Lethal if you mix it with bleach. If you breathe it in, you're dead."

THE SECRET WOUND

Cornelia interrupted - standing up and raising her glass, "Let's toast to Gurtha – to his birthday and to his forty days in Mallorca."

♥

For many years, Todd, originally from Los Angeles, had been a film Director primarily working on a well-known TV detective series called 'Cops Unleashed'. He kept a house in Palos Verdes to the south of Los Angeles, whereas Stephanie lived in Santa Monica in a small apartment on Venice Beach above a tattoo parlour. Stephanie was his girlfriend with Japanese eyes, the result of one too many skin pulls around her ears. If you had to guess at Todd's age, you would say that he was sixty-five. You would be wrong. Todd was eighty years old, thirty years older than Stephanie who was the same age as Cornelia.

Stephanie had met Todd on a film set when he was directing a TV comedy series in which Stephanie played a supporting role. She knew how to make a man laugh. She also knew how to make a man feel that he was being funny - a winning combination. They struck up a relationship within the first week on set.

Todd's large detached house on Seaside Boulevard had a manicured lawn and a track which led down to a path skirting the Pacific Ocean. Every morning before breakfast a newspaper would appear on the front lawn. Before the arrival of the flying paper, Todd could be found walking the path, watching the mist settle like cotton wool on the sea below and waiting for the orange sun to push its way through the clouds into a watery pale blue sky. It was the most peaceful part of the day for Todd, before the mid-day sun burnt the mist away and revealed the slow moving flow of the ocean below. He spent six months in Palos Verdes and six months in Mallorca each year. Stephanie, who continued her acting career, visited him for two months each year in Mallorca.

When they were in Los Angeles she lived in her apartment in Venice Beach and Todd in his mansion in Palos Verdes. In Mallorca, she stayed in Todd's house sharing the same bedroom.

Back in Cornelia's house Gurtha sipped the green thai curry sauce with a soup spoon as Cornelia served Thai sticky rice into a small bowl. The conversation hummed around the table, at times increasing in intensity, at times fading away to almost nothing. As Angelina passed spring rolls to Barry, Stephanie fed Todd with crispy seaweed skilfully delivered with clicking chop sticks and Todd rolled crispy duck with a hoisin sauce into a pancake for Cornelia. It seemed to Gurtha that they were communicating with one another like bees do with their pheromones. Gurtha reflected how each bee in a bee colony has a role – the worker bees, the queen and the drone - and wondered what might happen if conditions within the colony were disrupted. Dipping a prawn cracker into his green curry sauce, Gurtha continued to daydream. He glanced across at Barry and Todd - were there not now three drones around the table and only two queen bees? How would the imbalance created by his arrival affect the colony?

Angelina interrupted his reverie from the far end of the table,

"Gurtha – the paintings arrived safely yesterday. I will begin to organise the exhibition and we can finalise the opening when you are back. Are you OK with that? I have the notes you sent Cornelia about which paintings should go where and in which sequence. I can make a start on it if that works for you."

Gurtha held a glass of wine into the air.

"That would be marvellous. Thank you, Angelina for your offer of support and thank you, Cornelia for making such an effort in hosting a splendid evening."

THE SECRET WOUND

He nodded at Cornelia, clapped his hands and automatically everyone joined in.

DAY 6

THE DAY after Cornelia's party, Gurtha packed a small suitcase and boarded a plane for Belfast to collect Paddy.

He settled into the window seat in row three. He smiled at the woman who struggled to place a bag under the seat beside him.

"Did you have a good holiday?"

"In parts - it was a bit too hot for me." She sighed deeply. Her face was flushed red and beads of sweat drained around her eyebrows and formed two streamlets on either cheek.

"I'll be glad to get back to the rain."

She was a woman of about sixty five, most likely retired, with short spiky auburn hair, slightly grey at the temples. She wore a brightly coloured yellow and gold dress over black leggings.

She twiddled with a large jade-coloured ring on her right hand.

"I hope it's a smooth flight. You don't mind if it gets bumpy if I grab hold of you?" She touched him on the arm.

Gurtha laughed, "That's fine by me."

Gurtha closed his eyes. He thought about what had happened during his first six days. It was disappointing. Although 'La Torretta' provided him with a hermitage in nature, it hadn't yet brought him any new insights about his life, peace or a sense of progress. Meeting Cornelia's expatriate community gave him a sense of dissipating his time there rather than using it in a meaningful way. He began to think that maybe he had been hoping for something unrealistic. What did Gurtha think could happen in forty days? He had definitely hoped for something dramatic and transformative. He had imagined that forty days would offer an opportunity to stand on the edge of a metaphorical canyon, gazing down at the jagged edges of red outcrops razoring their way to a canyon floor. He could see the other side. That was where he needed to be. The only way to reach the other side was to fall into the canyon. Once there, he would be able to scramble up a small narrow path on the other side. It would be possible to fall into the canyon if he morphed into a white feather. Then he could drift, floating effortlessly wherever the thermals chose to take him and eventually settle on the pebbly, sandy floor, before morphing back into his body to commence his climb up the other side. Symbolically, that is what he had been hoping would happen. He would go to the depths of his being and soar to its heights – transformed – leaving his inner world of confusion behind and finding his feet treading on unfamiliar land with a certainty that he was on the right path, even if what would happen next was unknown.

Now six days into his journey what was he doing? Nothing other than embroiling himself with an expatriate community within whose company he felt more like an actor dragged onto a stage where they were enacting a Greek tragedy. He didn't know the part he had to play or which lines to say.

The plane shuddered; Gurtha opened his eyes, glancing at the woman beside him who had fallen asleep. She gently snored as the Airbus A320 climbed over the sea. Through the window small yachts buzzed like flies out to sea, leaving a trail of white foam in the water. He recognised the island of Sa Dragonera sleeping in the sea with its iguana-like jagged back. The plane banked steeply to the right and flew over the Port of Soller. He squinted to see if it was possible to identify La Torretta. No, it was hidden, tucked within folds of pine trees and terraced stone walls.

A refreshment trolley rolled by and the woman beside him sat up with a start, breathing heavily as she fumbled for her handbag under the seat in front,

"A gin and tonic please, with Sour Cream Pringles."

The air hostess rattled a drawer open, "Slimline or ordinary?"

"Slimline please." She fumbled in her purse for euros.

The airhostess tapped the order into a machine,

"Would you like a double and save two euros?"

"Yes please."

She turned to Gurtha, "I don't normally fall asleep on a flight. I'm normally too terrified. Were you on holiday?"

He looked into her eyes. They were blue, slightly bulbous. She wore heavy eye liner and sparkly green eye shadow. The eye liner was a little smudged as though her hand had shaken when putting it on. Or maybe she had been crying.

"No – I'm not on holiday. I'm on a sabbatical."

She sipped on her gin and tonic, "What's a sabbatical?"

Gurtha rubbed his hands over his face.

"It's a kind of break – a time to step back and try to get a new perspective on life."

She offered him the tube of Pringles.

"That sounds interesting. How will you know if the new perspective is better than the one you started with? Here, have some more."

She poured a third of the tube of Pringles into his hands.

"Stop ... thank you. That's a good question. Are you a psychologist?" Gurtha straightened his back in the seat as he munched on the Pringles.

"No. But I have been on the receiving end of help from a psychologist for three years. I've learnt how to be nosey."

Gurtha laughed.

"I haven't a clue how to answer your question. The best I can imagine is to say that some people think that life falls into two parts – the first part when you do things without really thinking – you're on automatic pilot – working, earning money, friends, and family – all the normal things are happening and you feel fine. Then there is a kind of mid-life crisis and you want to head in a different direction – to change your life. Maybe I want life to have more meaning. I would love to have something in my life that is important – a transcendent cause – you might call it – for which I would be prepared to sacrifice everything. I haven't got it. All I have got is a mid-life crisis."

Miriam looked away from Gurtha, her lips pulled into a solid line. She then looked at him directly and he noticed for the first time that her eyebrows were not real eyebrows but charcoal tattooed an inch above her eyes in a smooth arc. He smelt smoke from her clothes. Her hand shook only slightly but enough to draw his attention and to allow him to see the indentations in her stained orange first and second fingers.

"If you don't mind me asking, what caused this mid-life crisis?"

Gurtha hesitated for a few seconds, when he spoke his voice trembled a few notes higher, "My mother was murdered a year ago. We don't know why and the killer has never been found. Ever since then my brain feels scrambled. Everything that I used to like, I don't care for. I'm living in a flatland. If I was on a heart monitor

– it wouldn't register any peaks or troughs. I'm one of the living dead."

Miriam leaned towards Gurtha, taking his two hands and stared into his eyes, "How dreadful." She placed her hands on his cheeks. Gurtha felt his face stinging with the heat from her palms and fingers. A current of energy zapped through his body, tingling down both legs before reaching his feet. It felt like an electric shock. It wasn't unpleasant – only slightly unsettling. The warmth from Miriam's hands made his face feel as if it was dissolving into flowing warm water which provoked a wave of anxiety to ripple through his stomach. When it passed he felt extraordinarily calm as Miriam withdrew her hands from his cheeks and rested them on her lap.

"Some people call me a witch." She laughed.

"A white one of course."

She looked confidently into Gurtha's eyes,

"It will get better for you."

Gurtha smiled and nodded.

"I hope so." Enough about me – what about you - what do you like most about Mallorca?"

"I like the dancing. I'm not a day person. I don't like bright sunshine and heat. Isn't that strange?"

Gurtha lifted his hands in disbelief.

"It certainly is. Most people come to Mallorca for the sun and the warm weather. Can you not go dancing in the dark in Belfast? It would be cheaper."

She laughed, throwing back her head in a turkey fashion with folds of flesh around her neck wobbling like cylindrical tubing Gurtha had seen shudder in Mallorca when rubble emptied from a top floor apartment.

"But the darkness in Mallorca has a different quality to it."

She drained the last drop of gin from the plastic glass and closed her eyes.

"If you don't mind, I'll have a bit of shut eye. I didn't go to bed at all last night."

"Of course – sleep away."

Two hours later Gurtha looked again from the window as the plane began its descent into Aldergrove airport. The green fields of Ireland below speckled with munching black and white cows told him that he was home. It felt good to be back – a sense of ease and comfort flooded his body. The plane shook from side to side in the crosswinds. Miriam opened her eyes and sat upright with her eyes darting from right to left.

"What was that?"

Gurtha's hands sweated. He took a deep breath. The plane dipped into grey cumulus clouds. It shook violently, the wings quivering up and down, slicing at nothingness – a knife cutting air. He rested a hand on Miriam's arm.

"It's nothing - totally normal. It's like a boat bobbing on waves of the sea - mild turbulence. I remember flying out of Palma once when a tornado hit the airport. It should have been a short flight thirty minute flight to Barcelona but we flew into a tornado. The plane lost height, climbed, the pilot revved the engines, it shuddered, climbed again then almost dropped onto the runway. They closed the airport after our plane left. We should never have taken off."

Miriam put her hands over her eyes.

"Is this meant to make me feel better?"

Gurtha laughed.

"I'm only telling you because there's no need to worry – these planes are built to withstand stormy skies."

Gurtha looked into her eyes, "Would you like me to share with you what I did – it might help you when you're flying?"

Miriam nodded.

"Yes please."

"Close your eyes and take a few deep breaths. Breathe in, counting to seven and breathe out counting to eleven. Keep repeating it. It gives the body a physical message that you are relaxed. It fools the brain. Your body will begin to think that you are relaxed and not afraid."

Miriam obeyed. She closed her eyes and began to concentrate on her breathing.

After a few minutes with her eyes closed, her breathing slowed and she whispered, "Thank you. That really works."

As the plane dropped steeply through the clouds, Gurtha looked again at the green fields below, the white washed houses with grey tiled roofs, the silvery edge of Lough Neagh. He kept his hand resting firmly on Miriam's arm until the plane landed. She opened her eyes, smiling as she rubbed them – unaware of smudging her mascara.

"You've been an angel. I would need someone like you beside me every time I fly."

She looked at him with a quizzical sad expression nursing her handbag on her knees.

For a moment Gurtha thought that she was going to ask him to meet her for a coffee or say that she wanted to see him again. She didn't. Instead she dropped her head onto her chest and began to sob.

Gurtha leaned forward. He hesitated as to whether or not to say anything. He decided to ask,

"Are you OK?"

Miriam looked at him with one of those looks steady and

penetrating to your soul.

"Am I not a bit too old for dancing?"

Gurtha shook his head.

"No-one is ever too old for dancing."

Miriam smiled, "Thank you." She opened her handbag, found a mirror and a paper handkerchief which she used to remove the running mascara. "I don't normally cry. But you have a way of making me feel visible, as though I exist. I haven't felt that in a long time."

Gurtha patted her arm again and laughed,

"Are you telling me that I have the knack of making a stranger cry?"

Miriam blew her nose on the handkerchief and gave a hearty chuckle. "And laugh."

♥

After saying goodbye to Miriam, Gurtha drove into Ardoyne, parked at the back of Paddy's house and called into the shop to buy Paris buns. He opened the door of the shop, a bell tinkled and Laura grinned broadly at him.

"I know what you're after." She placed two Paris buns in a brown bag.

"How are you coping?"

"I'm not great." Gurtha sighed. "If anything maybe I am getting worse. When I am on my own in La Torretta I think I'm becoming an even more compulsive, obsessive thinker. I've always been a daydreamer but now I go round and around in circles with the same thoughts of Nuala."

"Sometimes you have to get worse before you get better." Laura handed over the Paris buns.

Gurtha laughed.

"It's worse I'm getting for sure. How's the old man faring?"

Laura bit her lip and frowned.

"Not so good. Be prepared for a shock. The wild man of Borneo comes to mind."

"I've only been away less than a week. Tell me the worst."

Laura shook her head.

"You'll see for yourself. You might have been away for less than a week, but I'm not sure that Paddy has any sense of time any more."

Gurtha opened the gate, walked up the pathway to the back door and saw that the rose bushes which Nuala had pruned and watered were withering, their yellow petals buried in a circle of overgrown grass. He picked a few petals and held them to his nose. The only smell was that of earthy moss. He dropped them again onto the grass and knocked on the door.

Paddy stood in front of him, unshaven, the locks on the side of each cheek bushy, his hair oiled with sweat and his shirt opened two buttons revealing his grey hairy chest. Paddy looked blankly at Gurtha. There was no smile, no taking a step towards him. Instead Paddy moved his head up and down, scanning Gurtha, his eyes looking puzzled and containing a hint of silent irritation.

"Hello Dad. How are you?"

Paddy's mouth opened and closed but no words came out. Gurtha took a step forward, reached his arms out to Paddy and hugged him. He smelt the greasiness of his hair and a stench of urine from his trousers. He pressed him tighter to his chest.

♥

The embrace reminded Gurtha of the one time when Nuala, Paddy and he had gone on holiday to Bangor. The first night, Paddy had told him a bed time story, hugged and kissed him. Gurtha

THE SECRET WOUND

remembered Paddy's lips soft and moist on his forehead. He had felt the warmth and pressure on his forehead long after Paddy left the bedroom. Paddy never kissed him again.

Without moving inside, Gurtha continued to hold Paddy in his arms, looking down on the circle of baldness on the top of Paddy's head with two or three hairs that had grown long in the middle. He took a deep breath. There on the back of Paddy's head was a six inch jagged scar, inflamed and red.

"What happened?" Gurtha dropped his arms and took a step back. His stomach heaved, and then tightened with anxiety.

"I was mugged." Paddy turned around and hobbled into the kitchen.

"There's no need to make a fuss. I think there was only a fiver in the wallet. There's many a man killed for less these days."

"Why didn't you tell me?"

"What could you have done? I caught a bus to the Mater Hospital. They patched me up."

There were two china cups and saucers on the wash board by the sink. The kitchen table was covered with Monday's Irish News.

"What are you doing Dad? You've got table cloths – you don't need to use newspapers." Gurtha pointed at the table.

"It keeps it clean. A table cloth gets dirty. I'll take it off if it annoys you." Paddy pulled the newspaper from the table and stuffed it in the bin.

Gurtha looked around the kitchen.

"Did you get my Marks and Spencer's parcel? It should have arrived on Monday."

"No." Paddy shook his head, sitting down at the table.

"Are you sure it didn't arrive?" Gurtha looked puzzled.

"No." Paddy repeated, swatting away a fly which had settled on his hand.

"They bite you."

"It had cheese, wine and your favourite raspberry jam."

"Never got it." Paddy sat unmoving on the chair, watching the fly circle in front of his eyes.

"Let me make you a pot of tea." Gurtha walked toward the kettle and filled it with water.

"Where's your friend Molly?"

Paddy shook his head from right to left.

"Lily found Molly dead on the floor beside the toilet. Nuala once said that when Molly died she didn't want another cat – that was the end of it. No more cats. She didn't want a cat to be left alone and the two of us dead."

"When did Molly die?"

"The day that Lily brought me chicken soup."

"That must have been Monday – she said that she would bring you something to eat on Monday and Wednesday. Would you not like to have another cat for company?" Gurtha poured tea into the china cups.

"No. Nuala said that we weren't going to have any more cats. Who would take care of it when I pop my clogs?"

"I will."

"You might but I will be in my wooden overcoat before Christmas. I don't want to trouble you with a cat. Sure you're never here."

Gurtha stood up to put wheaten bread in the toaster.

"Of course you won't be dead by Christmas. Don't be an old misery guts. You'll feel better after your holiday. Have you got your bag packed?"

Paddy sat staring ahead without moving.

"I don't need anything packed. I'm OK the way I am."

Gurtha filled a suitcase with shorts, tea-shirts and two pairs

THE SECRET WOUND

of Chino trousers, a pair of corduroys and two V-neck jumpers which Nuala had bought for Paddy the Christmas before. He folded two smart cotton shirts – one blue, one white – and rolled up two matching ties. Rummaging in the bottom drawer of the wardrobe, he discovered an old pair of black swimming trunks.

Images flashed into Gurtha's head of his father teaching him to swim many years before. He remembered black moles and pink warts on his shoulders, bandy legs doing the breast stroke, curly black hair over his back, his chest, shoulders and arms.

He poured Paddy a fresh cup of tea, placed a Paris bun and a cheese sandwich on a china plate before leaving him to search for his cap in the front parlour. He knew that he normally kept it sitting like a cat on the arm of the sofa. That's where he found it - on the arm of the sofa and on the floor beside it the box from Marks and Spencers. Inside the box were the wrappers of three packets of mature cheddar cheese, an empty champagne bottle and a half eaten jar of raspberry jam with a spoon sticking out of it. He looked around the room at the empty fireplace and the bare light bulb dangling above his head.

He returned to the kitchen where Paddy pushed the last crumbs from the Paris bun into his mouth.

Gurtha decided not to mention the hamper but inquire about the fire.

"Dad, why did you not light the fire? It's cold in the parlour. You've also removed the lampshade and the bulb's not working. What's going on?"

Paddy munched on his sandwich.

"I didn't pay the coal bill. They won't deliver any more coal until it's paid. I tried to fix the bulb but I couldn't unscrew it. It's stuck."

Gurtha took his father's hand. The fingers were swollen with arthritis. The skin was waxy to touch – like a plastic hand. He gripped it tightly. His voice quivered.

"You must tell me when you haven't any money. You know I can pay the bills. You'll catch your death of cold if you don't light the fire in the winter. A fire is like the heart of the house. It's company for you. Tell me where you have another bulb. I'll fix it for you now."

Paddy shook his head, looking slightly annoyed.

"There's nothing wrong with the light bulb. It will come on later."

Gurtha sat beside him, putting an arm around his shoulders.

"Let's get you to the Doctor."

Paddy touched the stitches in his head,

"There's nothing wrong with me. I'm all patched up. I told you that before."

In the surgery on the Springfield Road, Doctor Bramley wrote a note for Gurtha to take to the accident and emergency department.

"It's best you take him to the Royal Hospital. They'll run tests."

In the accident and emergency waiting room, Gurtha sat in silence with Paddy.

"It shouldn't be too long. Do you want a coffee?"

Paddy nodded. Gurtha walked to the vending machine, looking over at Paddy as he filled two frothing cappuccinos.

"Be careful. They're hot."

They watched as tall, skinny red haired man walked towards them with a coffee and a sandwich wrapped in cellophane. Gurtha and Paddy glanced at one another as the man approached. There was an empty seat on Paddy's left. The red headed man threw himself onto the chair. He leaned over slowly to place the plastic coffee cup on the ground. He then inspected the cling filmed sandwich in both hands, studying it closely, looking for a way to open it. He turned it over and over in his hands, muttering,

THE SECRET WOUND

"This fuckin' ... Fuck you ..."

A few minutes later he found the end of the cling film which he slowly removed, rolling it into a ball which he threw onto the ground at Paddy's feet.

Paddy looked at the ball of cling film on the marble floor. The sandy haired man and Paddy looked into one another's eyes. Paddy made the next move slipping his foot slowly towards the ball of cling film and gently pushing it in the direction of the sandy haired man.

"Paddy Maloney." A nurse interrupted. Gurtha and Paddy rose to their feet.

"We only need Paddy." Paddy followed her out of the waiting room with 'The Irish News' sticking out of his right pocket.

"Now tell me Mr Maloney, what day is it?" The Doctor looked into Paddy's eyes which had regained a certain spark.

Paddy pointed to the window, the Doctor eyes followed,

"It's a great day."

Paddy glanced at the front page of 'The Irish News'.

The Doctor turned a page in his notebook and with a fountain pen scratching the surface of a clean page, asked, "It sure is a great day. But could you tell me what day is it?"

Paddy sat upright in the chair, his eyes dark as sapphires,

"If you don't know what day it is Doctor – I would worry if I were you. It's Friday 16th August and you know the year don't you – 2013?"

The Doctor made a few notes on the page.

"Let's get your chest X-rayed Paddy. You've a little tendency to bronchitis, I see, which we wouldn't want to overlook, would we now?"

Gurtha watched Paddy being wheeled on an iron bed towards him. He was chatting to the Nurse and looked triumphantly at

Gurtha. Helping Paddy to dismount from the bed, the Nurse said in a cheerful voice.

"I'm happy to say that we have a clean bill of health for Mr Maloney. He's as fit as a fiddle."

♥

Back in Mallorca Todd looked at his watch for the third time. He pulled on a Panama hat, lifted a straw basket and swung it onto his shoulders. He surveyed Stephanie lying in bed on top of the sheets. He felt slightly unsettled watching her arms outstretched on his bed, her tangerine silk nightdress crumpled around her legs. She turned around slowly as though she knew that Todd was looking at her and opened her eyes,

"You're up early." She rubbed her eyes and sat up. "We weren't in bed until three. Aren't you tired?"

Todd shook his head.

"Not a bit. I'm off to buy those croissants for Barry and Cornelia. I'll save one for you."

Stephanie pulled the cotton sheet around her.

"It's too early to pester them. They'll still have the dishes to sort out from last night."

Todd blew her a kiss.

"You know that Barry's a morning person."

Stephanie fell back on the bed, mumbling.

"Come back before lunch-time. I'll be bored otherwise. Can't I tempt you to stay?" She crawled under the white sheet, peeping out with the sheet covering her mouth and nose.

Todd waved, "I promise I'll be back for lunch."

He walked along the seafront in the Port of Soller. Giant seagulls glided silently overhead, each reflected clearly in the mirror-like still water. Todd peered into the water, throwing bread for the fish that surfaced briefly. They gobbled it up, returning to deeper levels where they circled around one another.

He thought of Barry. How odd it was that he could find nothing wrong with him. In Barry's company, Todd felt paradoxically more alive and more at peace. Why would that be? As a Film Director he had grown used to being critical over the years. It was easier to find faults in objects, places and people than it was to find perfection. A scene could always be improved. He had never been happy with any of his finished films – not even the one which received an Oscar nomination. He agreed with those who criticised him. What was different about Barry?

Todd hated the way anger flooded his own body over the smallest inconvenience – the butter melting in the butter dish at breakfast, Stephanie's wrinkly neck, her insistence on playing Josephine Baker on her playlist, her irritating loudness, the way she put too much jam on his toast and the time she took to methodically cook the simplest of dinners.

Barry was never angry – at least not in front of Todd. He seemed almost too lazy to be angry. Maybe he had cultivated sloth rather than the virtue of patience. Todd liked the fact that it was difficult to move Barry to action. It made sense that the world could slow down after spending so much time in Los Angeles which felt to Todd to be a world driven by amphetamines. There was no time to think – only to react and people often reacted in anger – sitting on their horns in a traffic jam, trying to jump to the top of queues at the airport, flicking flies away with irritation and impatience. Todd felt in himself a sense of incessant drivenness – a need to do everything quickly and to keep doing something. Barry's laziness was a foil to Todd's need to be successful. He found Barry's slowness strangely attractive. He turned onto the Repic beach.

It was then that he spotted Cornelia standing alone scrunching her hair into a pony tail. She wore a tangerine bikini - the same colour as Stephanie's slip. She was standing sideways - flat stomach, small breasts hidden within a strip of bikini top and long delicate arms which she held out like a ballerina as he had seen her do many times before. She bent forward touching her toes, stretching then to the side in a yoga posture. She raised both arms into the sky and then clutched them together, twisting to the right when she saw Todd.

Cornelia ran towards him, stumbling slightly on the sand, reaching a small wall which she easily climbed over and stood with both arms stretched towards him.

"How lovely to see you. I thought that I would wash the cobwebs away with a swim before starting work. What brings you here?"

Todd kissed Cornelia on both cheeks. There was the taste of sweat and salt on her cheeks and the smell of last night's perfume – a flowery J'adore by Christian Dior. It reminded him of California and his garden full of jasmine and honeysuckle. He lingered a second or two longer than he should have. Cornelia smiled, moving her face slightly to the right as so as their lips nearly touched.

"Why don't you come for a swim? It's the best time of the day." She took his hand and urged him towards a gap in the wall which would allow him to walk easily on the sand. The waves were soaking into the sand as they broke making hardly a sound – only the gentlest hiss and fizz before the next one arrived and disappeared.

"I didn't bring any trunks."

"Don't be a fool. Who's looking?

Todd glanced at the café where he had planned to buy croissants. A voluptuous black waitress waved at him.

THE SECRET WOUND

"Who's looking? Cornelia repeated, pulling him onto the sand.

He felt slightly annoyed that his brown leather Barkers were covered in sand. Cornelia danced ahead of him. She looked younger from behind. He followed her to the water's edge, placed his bag inside her basket and removed the Barkers, striped blue and white socks, cream shorts, vest and Paul Smith flowery shirt.

Cornelia removed her bikini top, threw it onto the sand and dived into the smooth water – disappearing beneath the surface for a few seconds. When she bobbed up, she waved the bottom of her bikini into the air and shouted.

"I'm waiting for you."

Todd glanced at the café. The waitress was inside. There was no-one around – the only sign of life apart from Cornelia's head bobbing in the sea, was a scraggy terrier dog which ran quickly past him without so much as giving Todd a glance. He quickly removed his underpants and dived into the water. It was slightly cold, but exhilarating. He felt an incredible sense of freedom as his body slipped through the waves which caressed him with a soft and silky-finger touch. He instinctively spread his arms into a strong breast stroke, making a frog stroke with his legs and quickly closing the gap between himself and Cornelia. Cornelia flapped weakly in the water, one arm lifelessly being raised and then slapping the water as her head bobbed up and down. She rolled onto her back and cackled at him, gulping at the air as the seagulls swirled in circles above them.

♥

An hour later, Todd pressed his face against the sitting room window and watched Barry fill a kettle with water. He felt that warm glow flicker in his stomach and noticed that his heart was fluttering. He knocked gently on the window, holding the brown bag with the croissants high for Barry to see. Barry turned around as though in slow motion, waved at Todd, smiled, dried his hands on a towel and ambled towards the front door.

"You've been for a swim."

Todd threw himself onto the sofa, "No. I've had my weekly shower whether I needed it or not."

Barry rummaged in a drawer for two napkins.

Todd got to his feet, walked to the patio, sat at the table and, accepting a glass of freshly squeezed orange juice, asked.

"Where's Cornelia?"

"She's having a swim and then is going to help Angelina in the gallery."

♥

From the gallery Angelina looked onto the patio. There was an olive tree immediately in front of the window. The olives were plump and green. They would continue growing for another two months before being harvested. A small pink rose looked as if it needed watering. She stepped into the patio and picked up the garden hose as Cornelia arrived, drying her hair with a beach towel which she then threw on top of the kitchen table.

"Coffee?" Cornelia shouted from the back door.

Angelina switched the water off.

"An espresso would be perfect."

They sat sipping coffee. Cornelia deeply breathed in the jasmine scent hanging heavily in the air as her eyes followed Angelina's well defined collarbone, her long and slender neck leading to a heart shaped jaw-line, and then a broad smiling mouth, long narrow nose, hazel green eyes, covered in white glitter and framed with curling blue mascara.

THE SECRET WOUND

Angelina's face coloured slightly. She moved in the chair trying to find a more comfortable position.

"I could sit here all day, but I have to work. I need to have the exhibition ready for Gurtha's return."

Cornelia ignored her desire to start working, asking instead,

"Do you miss Argentina?"

"Some things, yes – conversations with friends, talking about poetry, philosophy and the meaning of life. I also miss the fact that there is no-one here who really knows me – friends from childhood or university – connections with people that go back years. When you leave your own country, you're uprooted. You are forced to live in a pot which you have chosen rather than in the earth you were born from. Human beings come out of the earth like an orange tree or a sheep – everything comes out of the land. I think you must lose something by leaving the land which gave birth to you."

She brushed a few olive leaves which had fallen onto the table to the ground.

"I know that I am not at home here, but on the other hand, I don't miss the chaos, the violence, the uncertainty of Argentina. I regret mistakes I have made being here. I don't think I would have made them in Argentina."

Cornelia tousled her drying hair.

"What mistakes?"

Angelina, closed her eyes, took a deep breath, rocked the chair onto its two back legs, lightening the tone of her response.

"Mistakes born of loneliness and opportunity. Maybe if I had stayed in Argentina there would have been different mistakes born of something else – maybe fear and frustration. Who knows? But then I haven't met anyone yet who hasn't made mistakes. Have you?"

Cornelia shook her head, remained silent, looking into the coffee cup resting in her hands.

Angelina jerked the chair back onto its four legs which had the effect of making the question which followed sound like an interrogation.

"You've never said why you left England – what made you come here?"

Cornelia's shoulders shuddered as if she had been touch by a cold breeze.

"The weather says it all doesn't it? It's dull, grey and boring. I was glad to get out of there after Henry's death."

Angelina looked up at the rectangle of blue sky above the patio.

"I don't know whether it is important or not where you live. Argentina is, after all, beautiful. Maybe I should have stayed there and appreciated what was good about it. There's beauty everywhere if you can only open your eyes. Look."

Angelina pointed to an aloe vera stridently growing to her left – dagger shaped leaves pushing energetically towards the blue sky. It sprouted two new leaves unfolding from a lighter green scroll. A hummingbird hawk-moth hovered over a lilac bush holding itself steady, with orange and grey wings whirring, and a small eye like a fish looking directly at Angelina.

"If there is beauty everywhere – maybe what makes a place special is more the quality of our relationships."

Cornelia gathered up the cups and saucers and nodded.

"That may be true. However, there is no guarantee that the people we chose to live with or who we find ourselves living with will bring out the best in us, or us in them – is there?"

Angelina followed Cornelia into the kitchen.

"There's no guarantee but there's always the possibility that they can. It depends upon how we circle around them."

Cornelia washed the cups and saucers and without looking at Angelina asked,

"What do you mean by 'circle around them'?"

"Well, everything is about relationship – how we move with others. If you think about an atom it has neutrons, protons and electrons circling around one another in space. It's mysterious how that movement holds together. Yet we can split the atom and release an immense destructive energy. Maybe relationships are like that – we can circle around one another in a magical dance of enjoying life or we can destroy one another."

Cornelia placed the cups on a drying rack.

"It's well seen that you studied Philosophy at University. Do you not think that there's a danger if you think about things too deeply that you can go crazy?"

Angelina laughed.

"What's the danger of not thinking deeply?"

Cornelia wiped her hands on the drying towel.

"I don't see danger. We need to be able to act quickly to protect ourselves – to survive. Thinking slows us down. Coming from Argentina – you know that the world is unpredictable – we need to move – do things to survive."

DAY 7

"DON'T BE SATISFIED WITH STORIES,
HOW THINGS HAVE GONE WITH OTHERS.
UNFOLD YOUR OWN MYTH."
J RUMI

PADDY'S MOOD improved on the flight to Palma. He passed Gurtha a rolled up bundle of notes - three hundred pounds in total which he had borrowed from the Credit Union. Gurtha placed the notes in Paddy's hand and gently pushed his hand away.

"Dad – what about the coal bill? You keep it." He lifted his wallet. "This is for you." Gurtha pressed a hundred euros into Paddy's hand.

"I wish that Nuala were here." He shook his head, placing the sterling notes into the left pocket of his jacket and the euros into the right pocket.

While Paddy slept his first night in La Torretta, Gurtha sat on the sofa alone. He listened to gentle snores from upstairs. It was too warm to light the wood burning stove. He stared at the olive and pine logs in the basket which he would burn if the temperatures dropped.

Lying stretched out on the sofa with Paddy safely in bed upstairs, Gurtha reached for a book by Bede Griffiths, a Benedictine monk who had lived in India. It was a book that he had read before but Gurtha liked to read and re-read books. He liked to feel the words sinking into him, taking root and sprouting new flowers of understanding. He opened the book and read a passage in which Bede talked about a ground of being, an ultimate reality experienced in all of the world's great religions, which revealed itself beyond thoughts and feelings. It was possible to enter the womb of creation and find that we are all attached to the same belly button. Everyone could experience this but it required the death of our identity as being separate from the world – death to all self-centredness.

Looking at the page he was reading, for a flicker of a moment Gurtha felt that there was no-*one* reading – only reading. In his body there was a stillness and peace. He closed his eyes. There were no thoughts, only a gentle warm glow of light behind his closed eyelids. His peaceful state was interrupted by a padding, scuffling sound of feet descending the stairs.

"Where am I?"

Paddy stood in front of him, wearing pyjama bottoms and no top. He had his arms crossed over his bare chest. His feet were also bare. His blue eyes were faded – like old postage stamps left too long in the sun.

Gurtha moved slowly to his feet, walking towards Paddy with his arms outstretched.

"It's OK Dad. You're here with me – on your holiday in Mallorca."

"Where's Nuala?"

"She's dead, Dad." Gurtha touched Paddy on the shoulder.

"Where has she gone to?"

"Home."

Paddy held his arms over his bare chest. His eyes brimmed with tears.

Gurtha gently repeated, "She's gone home – gone back to where she came from. She's at peace."

"Can I go home?" Paddy hugged himself tighter.

"You'll be home soon. Don't worry. Home isn't going to go away." Gurtha felt his eyes stinging. He blinked several times, turned his head away from Paddy and pointed at the fireplace, "Would you like me to light the fire?"

Paddy nodded, "That would be nice."

Gurtha searched for the kindling wood in the basket. He threw a newspaper towards Paddy,

"There are no fire lighters. Roll the pages up into balls. You make them tighter than I do."

On his knees beside Gurtha, Paddy pulled the middle pages of the paper out first and twisted them into dense little planets which he stacked in a careful pile on his right.

THE SECRET WOUND

DAY 8

SUNDAY 18TH AUGUST 2013

THE NEXT morning, Gurtha laid the table for breakfast in the gazebo. He made a fresh fruit salad with papaya, pineapple, raspberries, heated croissants in the oven and placed a jar of homemade apricot jam which Cornelia had given him on a white porcelain Beleek dish. He found a lighter and ash tray for Paddy. He set a packet of Hamlet cigars beside his coffee cup. Through the front door Gurtha could see Paddy sitting on a chair facing onto the terrace. He was wearing a green woollen V-neck jumper, an orange striped shirt and brown corduroy trousers.

"Dad, you won't need your jumper in this heat." Gurtha's voice was coaxing and gentle. Paddy didn't reply. Gurtha trod on the sun-warmed pine needles which crunched beneath his feet as he walked towards the house. A tram hooted in the valley below. Sheep ran along the terrace to the right, their bells vigorously clinking, and their feet throwing up a cloud of dust into the olive trees.

"Breakfast is served." Gurtha took Paddy by the hand. "It's beautiful outside. Come on, let's eat. I'm starving."

Paddy pulled his hand free, pointed at the olive tree, shook his head and asked, "Who's that man out there looking at me? I've seen him before."

Gurtha swallowed with difficulty. His heart thumped heavily in his chest. He sighed. He walked slowly towards the breakfast table, where a furry black bee hovered over the croissants and then settled on one of the pink roses Paddy had placed in a vase in memory of Nuala. He turned and beckoned to Paddy.

"Breakfast is ready. The croissants are getting cold."

Paddy, turned around, heading indoors.

Gurtha shouted after him.

"Where are you going?"

Paddy stopped , shuffled to face Gurtha.

"I'll be down in a minute. I've forgotten something."

In the gazebo, Gurtha lifted a rose from the vase. The water from the stem dripped onto the table cloth before he placed the rose on Paddy's plate. The drops reminded him of the nights when Nuala blessed the house with Holy Water.

There was one night in particular which came to his mind. Gurtha lay in bed struggling to get to sleep. Nuala with the Holy Water bottle in her hand opened the door of his room and whispered.

"Gurtha – you have to hear this."

Gurtha threw back the sheets and followed Nuala onto the landing. There was a flight of stairs which led down to a hallway. From the hallway you turned right to enter the sitting room, you walked a few steps further to open the door into the front room parlour or you walked to the front door. Nuala pointed downstairs.

"Listen."

There was a metallic scratching sound of a key turning in the

THE SECRET WOUND

front door lock, followed by a rasping of the door opening – the wooden frame trailing across the red tiles. Gurtha peered at the door. It was closed. He strained to hear what would happen next. There was the sound of heavy footsteps walking along the hallway, but with the light of the moon shining through the window of the door, it was easy to see that there was no-one there.

Nuala caught Gurtha by the arm and whispered in his ear.

"It's your father. He's on his way back home. The Devil is walking ahead of him. Let's get to bed before he sees us."

Gurtha climbed into bed. He listened in the darkness to a key turning in the front door, the door opening, then closing, footsteps thumping along the hallway. Paddy slowly climbed the stairs, walked past Nuala's bedroom, and opened the door into his bedroom.

The next morning not a word was said about what had happened the night before. Nuala poured Gurtha and Paddy a cup of tea. The three of them sat in silence until Paddy got up, put a cap on his head, threw on his raincoat and caught the bus to work.

Nuala patted Gurtha on the hand, "You don't need to worry about it. Neither the dead nor the Devil can harm you. It's the living you need to worry about."

♥

Gurtha looked at Paddy who stumbled towards him with slow, unsteady steps, arms hanging lifelessly by his side. He arrived at the table, squeezed himself onto the chair. He placed his hands like two door stops on the white table cloth – wrinkled, red with thick blue veins bulging from his wrist to his fingers. Clutched in his right hand was Nuala's purse.

"I found what I was looking for. There's nothing in it. Nuala must have taken the money to go shopping."

♥

After Nuala's death, Gurtha found her purse buried deep in her black leather handbag amongst a bag of fruit sherbets, rolled up paper handkerchiefs and reading glasses. When he opened the purse he pulled out a Saint Christopher medal, loose change, a twenty pound note and a small white piece of paper which had been folded carefully into four. He unfolded it and immediately recognised Nuala's handwriting. She had written "Violence against Women" and had noted below the number of a helpline – underscoring it twice in black.

Gurtha had kept the piece of paper and gave the purse to Paddy with its twenty pound note and spare coins. Paddy had then pressed it to his chest.

"I'll keep it for her. She wouldn't want to lose it. Nuala is careful with money."

♥

Now watching Paddy pull his croissant apart, an unbearable thought floated into Gurtha's head and lingered for a while – 'Was it possible that Paddy murdered Nuala?' A second thought immediately followed – 'Why had Gurtha not shown that piece of paper to the Police investigating Nuala's murder?'

He looked at Paddy who gave him a smile as he pushed the last morsel of croissant into his mouth. Disturbing thoughts continued to bubble up in Gurtha's head. If it wasn't Paddy, who was it that was Nuala frightened of? What had made her write that number down and underscore it twice?

He lifted the coffee cup to his lips and looked again at Paddy. Paddy winked at him. Gurtha winked back and a flash of inspiration occurred to him. He could ring the number which Nuala had underlined and ask if Nuala had been in contact. He hit himself on the head with the palm of his hand - why had he not thought of that before?

Gurtha sighed with relief when he opened his wallet and the piece of folded paper was still there. He checked his watch. It was ten o'clock. That would be nine o'clock in Belfast. Someone should be available to take his call.

His hand trembled almost imperceptibly as he dialled the number. A woman answered.

"Good morning, Violence against Women, how can I be of help?"

"Good morning. My name is Gurtha Maloney. My mother, Nuala Maloney, was murdered last year on the 15th August. I've recently been made aware that she was carrying this telephone number in her purse. The murderer has not been found. I wondered if perhaps you have any records of Nuala reporting concerns that someone may have been violent to her or if she was worried that it might happen in the future?" Gurtha listened carefully. The line crackled a little. He switched the phone to his other ear. The woman replied in a gentle voice.

"I'm so sorry to hear of your loss Mr Maloney. We normally would not give information of a confidential nature like this over the phone. However, I can look at our records. In view of the serious nature of this matter; I can give you a simple yes or no to whether your mother did contact us. If the answer is yes – all further information will be given to the Police and they will keep you informed of the situation. Is that OK for you?"

"Yes. Yes. I understand. Please can you look now for me? I will hold the line."

Gurtha sat down at the kitchen table. His legs were now also shaking.

He heard what must have been filing cabinets opening and closing, someone sneezing, a murmured conversation between two people, footsteps walking quickly across the floor.

"Mr Maloney?"

"Yes. I am here."

"We do have some information on file regarding a call by Nuala to our centre in July 2012. However, as I mentioned earlier – I cannot release any further details regarding this. I will immediately pass this information onto the Police and you can speak with them directly regarding the matter. Do you have the telephone number and name of the investigating Officer?"

"I do. It's in my mobile. Let me ring you back in one minute."

♥

Investigating Officer Andy Finn explained, "On the 25th July 2012 at 10.30 am, Nuala rang the offices of Violence against Women. We have it on record that she asked for advice about what she could do if she suspected that someone was planning to murder her. When the counsellor responding to her call asked Nuala the reason for this suspicion, Nuala said that she had a premonition and in the past other premonitions which she had turned into reality."

Officer Andy paused.

"I'm sorry. As you can imagine these situations are difficult to assess. I have closely questioned the counsellor who talked with Nuala in July 2012. She confirmed that Nuala did not provide any evidence of violence or abuse. There was no reason to believe that Nuala was at risk. I apologise if what I am going to say to you now causes offence – but Mr Maloney – twenty per cent of calls received by the helpline are bogus calls – from people suffering mental health issues. Would you say that there was a possibility that Nuala suffered from paranoia or had a delusional mind set?"

Gurtha took a quick intake of breath.

"Officer – you know that Nuala was murdered?"

"Yes. We are aware of that."

"Therefore Nuala's premonition which was logged became a reality. This is not someone suffering from paranoia having delusions but someone with a highly developed intuitive capacity. Nuala had an unusual capacity to know things which others did not know. This ability for human beings to do this is well documented. It is called intuitive wisdom – a knowing beyond the rational mind."

"I apologise Mr Maloney if I have caused offence by my question. I recognise that you are a professional in these matters of consciousness and higher states of mind. However, as the investigating Officer, I thought it important to check if there were any mental health issues. Nuala's murder may or may not have been connected to the premonition. We have to keep an open mind in this investigation to get to the truth and each small piece of what may seem insignificant data can, and often is, a vital piece of the jigsaw. I do have a further question for you Mr Maloney."

Gurtha listened anxiously, "Yes, what is that?"

"Why have we only been made aware of this new information today and not earlier in the investigation? I am obliged to ask you if there anything else which you are withholding from us and once again to ask you is there anyone you know may have had a reason or motivation to kill Nuala?"

Gurtha held his head in his hands, pressing the mobile to his ear, stuttered, "I really don't know why I didn't think of handing you the piece of paper which I found in Nuala's wallet with the telephone number and the name of the organisation which helps women who are subjected to violence. I can only suggest that I was in a state of shock and forgot about it until this morning when something triggered my memory."

"What was that something?" Officer Andy asked in a direct yet kind voice.

"I was having breakfast with my father here on holiday in Mallorca and … it was nothing … a memory of something Nuala had said to me years ago, came into my head."

"What was that memory Mr Maloney? It could be significant."

Gurtha hesitated. If he told Officer Andy that Nuala had called Paddy the Devil's companion that would make him a definite suspect. Yet if Paddy had murdered Nuala, he needed to be brought to justice. Nuala would be outraged that Gurtha did nothing about it. It would be a gross betrayal.

Officer Andy allowed the silence to unfold, "Take your time Mr Maloney. I understand that this is a stressful time and it can be difficult to immediately recall a painful memory."

Gurtha audibly swallowed,

"It was Nuala's purse. My father brought it to the breakfast table. I remembered that when I opened it after her death, there was the piece of paper with the number written on it."

"Mr Maloney, excuse me, but you said that the memory was of something that Nuala had said to you – not the memory of seeing the purse. What did Nuala say to you?"

"I'm sorry – it was the memory triggered by the purse this morning. I am confused. Sorry. This is all extremely upsetting."

"Mr Maloney, you know that we are doing everything we can to find Nuala's murderer. Can I emphasise that if any new information – including significant memories - comes to mind which provides a new perspective on why anyone would have had a reason to kill

Nuala, that you contact me immediately?"

"Of course Officer. I certainly will do that. Thank you for your help."

Gurtha looked at the screen of the mobile phone in his hand. 'Call ended.' He breathed deeply, noticing that his hand was still shaking. He would have to find out himself if Paddy had murdered Nuala, and if not Paddy, who had? With Paddy's state of mind, there was no way that the Police would make any headway interviewing him. Gurtha would have to find a way of discovering the truth. Gentleness with Paddy might allow the truth to spill out.

DAY 9

MONDAY 19TH AUGUST 2013

"SILENCE IS THE LANGUAGE OF GOD,
ALL ELSE IS POOR TRANSLATION."
J RUMI

A STRING quartet played Beethoven's string quartet No.19 in C Major at the entrance to the gallery. The golden light from the setting sun glowed on the terracotta roof tiles, the windows of the gallery sparkled from the flickering candles inside. Outside in the small alley, sitting on a wooden chair, Paddy puffed on a Hamlet.

Inside Cornelia, wearing a white turban and pink silk dress studded with pearls, gesticulated to the paintings hanging on the walls, "We are celebrating budding artists. The theme of the exhibition is 'The Secret Wound.'" She smiled at Gurtha who nodded in acknowledgement walking towards the centre of the room. "Thank you for taking the time to be here for the opening of the exhibition. I prefer to say little and let the works of art speak for themselves. Art has implicit rather than explicit meaning. The job of attempting to make its meaning explicit is left to the art critics rather than art lovers. I consider myself in the latter category. I would like to share only a sentence or two of orientation for the exhibition. 'The Secret Wound' is a symbol for what lies buried deep within. Each one of us is in need of healing. It is a wound of perception inflicted upon us by our ancestors in

THE SECRET WOUND

our genetic inheritance and by the circumstances and choices of our lives. When we find it, see it, feel it – we have the potential to be healed. In the ancient Shamanic tradition the healers were always the wounded who, in healing themselves, became the 'Wounded Healers' of others. Enough said. Enjoy."

There was a murmur around the room from those who didn't understand English asking friends to translate what Gurtha was saying and a whispering from the English speakers asking one another what Gurtha was talking about. Angelina passed around tapas of – 'boquerones', 'calamares', 'croquetas' and Spanish omelette and Barry served wine.

Cornelia filled a plate with tapas. She approached Gurtha.

"I'll bring this for Paddy. What do you think he would like to drink?"

"Guinness – but if there isn't any – red wine."

Cornelia placed the plate of tapas onto a wooden tray and poured a large glass of Ribero del Duero into a silver goblet. She looked around the gallery, lifted a small vase filled with white daisies, placed it on the tray, floated towards the front door and placed the tray on the small wooden table.

"Here you are Paddy. Are you OK sitting here or would you prefer to come inside?"

Paddy glanced up at Cornelia and unfolded the napkin,

"I'm fine here. I can have a smoke. Nuala knows where to find me."

"Are you sure you're OK? Gurtha is inside if you need him."

Paddy pushed an olive into his mouth.

"Could you tell Nuala that I am here? She doesn't always know what I'm up to."

Cornelia placed a glass of wine into his hand, pulling the small oak table a little closer.

"I'll tell her you're here. She will be out in a few minutes. I think she's in the loo."

Paddy nodded, "Yes she takes those tablets for her heart which means she has to go to the toilet nearly every hour."

Inside, Barry sat on a stool, smoothing his hair with a comb which he then popped into his shirt pocket. He then bit into a spinach croquette watching Angelina talking with Gurtha. He strained to catch the conversation.

"The still point?"

Angelina lifted a 'pimiento de padron' from her plate.

"T. S. Eliot." Angelina pointed at 'The New Eve' painting.

"Do you not think this artist has captured the 'Still point of the turning world' in this 'New Eve' painting?"

Gurtha helped himself to a cube of Spanish omelette.

"What do you know about T.S.Eliot?" Gurtha dragged a four legged stool from the corner to sit down.

"He was an interesting person." Angelina raised her chin, staring at the ceiling,

'At the still point of the turning world. Neither flesh nor fleshless;
Neither from nor towards; at the still point, there the dance is,
But neither arrest nor movement.
And do not call it fixity.
Where past and future are gathered. Neither movement from nor towards.
Neither ascent nor decline.
Except for the point, the still point.
There would be no dance, and there is only the dance.'

Gurtha nodded, "The Four Quartets."

Angelina offered Gurtha a glass of cava,

"I never quite understood T.S.Eliot."

"What didn't you understand?" Gurtha clinked his glass against hers. Barry watched and listened, hidden by a tall cheese plant.

"He seemed to be able to write poetry with great spiritual insight but I was confused by 'The Love Song of J Prufrock' which launched his career. I thought it bestial whereas 'The Four Quartets' sublime and esoteric. It is as though he could be animal, human or divine. He could alternate his identity at will. Do you not think so?"

Gurtha waved a hand, chasing away a mosquito buzzing around his eyes.

"Perhaps the more intellectual we are it becomes paradoxically more likely that we succumb to the temptations of the flesh – we indulge the animal side of our nature."

"Why would that be the case? It doesn't make sense. Is the rational mind not above animal instinct?"

Angelina found a stool to sit on. Gurtha apologised.

"Sorry, I should have offered you a seat first."

Angelina shook her head.

"Don't worry. I will be helping to serve the wine in a few minutes. What were you saying about the rational mind?"

Gurtha looked at the 'New Eve' painting.

"The rational mind is not necessarily a wise mind. After all we rationalise killing, racism, anger … The intellect fragments reality. Perhaps Eliot struggled with this as we all do. If you look at animals, the research shows that they are programmed to experience contentment and to nurture. It's we human beings who are capable of leaving contentment and nurturing behind."

Angelina listened carefully and asked. "Why do we do that?"

"I really don't know for sure. When I have reflected on this question – I see the possible answer visually or symbolically rather than intellectually."

Angelina placed her glass on the table, leant forward, with both hands clasped.

"And ....?"

Gurtha took a sip of Cava.

"It's like a ladder. But not a straight one – a spiral one. Each rung contains a certain level of consciousness. As human beings we step onto a rung which provides us with emotional consciousness. We feel happy or sad. We are interested or bored. There's an enormous spectrum of response attached to our emotional world. Then we step onto the thinking rung and we start to make judgements – liking, not liking, good and bad – dualistic thinking. We struggle to keep one foot on the rung of emotion with another on the rung of thinking and we never venture to the rungs above which would give us a new understanding of where we have come from." He paused. "Please stop me if I am boring you. I have that tendency to do that with others."

Angelina picked at the wax falling onto the table from a thick white candle.

"You're not boring me at all. What are on the rungs above thinking?"

Barry interrupted, slithering from behind the cheese plant, with a bottle of white wine. His shoulders curved, his eyes semi-closed, like a pig - his voice ingratiatingly, honey sweet.

"Angelina, would you like a top up?"

Angelina reached out her glass.

"Thank you." She smiled fleetingly at him and pointed to Gurtha's empty glass.

"What about Gurtha?"

She watched his shoulders become even more concave as he poured the Cava into Gurtha's glass. As the wine reached the top of the glass, he continued pouring. It cascaded with a bubbling

THE SECRET WOUND

exuberance onto Gurtha's white linen trousers.

"I do so apologise." Barry withdrew the bottle with feigned speed, ensuring that a final splutter of wine fell onto Gurtha's alligator skin Testoni shoes.

Gurtha pulled a cotton handkerchief from his jacket pocket, mopping first the shoes and then the trousers, dabbing at his thighs.

"I understand that you were trying to be generous."

Barry glanced at Angelina, "Would you like more?"

Angelina twisted her face into a look of disgust, "You've already topped my glass up."

As Barry repeatedly blinked at her, he seemed to her like a lecherous camera man – with each blink capturing a photo of her to be drooled over later. She pointed at the stairs,

"I don't think the people upstairs have any wine. Would you be good enough to take care of them?"

No sooner were those words uttered when Cornelia rushed towards them. She stood breathing rapidly and shallowly in front of them. Her pale face whiter than normal, lips trembling.

Gurtha jumped to his feet.

"What's happened?"

"It's Paddy. He's disappeared. He's gone."

Gurtha pushed his glass at Barry and shook his head.

"What do you mean 'gone'?" Without waiting for an answer he asked, "Who saw him last?"

Cornelia confessed, "I did. I brought him his tapas and a drink." She paused,

"He was asking about Nuala. I told him a lie. I said that she was in the loo to calm him down. He seemed to accept that. I thought that he was OK. He seemed tranquil. Maybe I shouldn't have told him a lie. I thought that he would come inside to look for her if he was confused. Not for a moment did I think that he would leave the gallery."

Gurtha took a deep breath.

"Let's stay calm."

Outside a circle formed around the wooden chair where Paddy had sat a few minutes earlier. Paddy's cap lay folded in the centre of the chair. The tapas uneaten, a blue paper napkin rolled in the breeze along the street, the glass of wine empty. Cornelia and Angelina glanced to the right and left. Gurtha asked, "Did anyone notice which way he went?"

Cornelia fanned herself,

"No. I've asked everyone."

Gurtha rubbed his eyes, "He can't have gone far if it was only ten minutes ago. I'll go this way. Get Barry, Todd and Stephanie. Ask everyone if they can help. We meet back here …." Gurtha glanced at his watch. "We meet back here at nine o'clock."

♥

Paddy listened to the violins playing inside. There was the gentlest of breezes moving the geraniums in the pots in front of him. A child in a turquoise cotton dress with a white bow in her hair sat on the pavement. He waved at her. She waved back.

He scratched the stubble on his chin. 'What time was it?' He looked at his watch. It was seven thirty. He thought, 'It must be time to shave.' He normally got up at six-thirty when he was working – seven thirty was a bit late. He carefully examined the tapas on the table and chose to ignore them, lighting, instead, a Hamlet and breathing in the aromatic smoke. Wonderful. He sniffed at the air. Timeless Hamlet taking him back to where he felt safe, to what he knew - the smell of home. It didn't matter that he didn't recognise the writing on the sign above the shop in front of him. He squinted – 'Sa Frontera' – what was that? It must be time to go home. He heaved himself onto his feet. What would be the best way home? He looked up the alley to his right. At the end of the alley, in the distance was a huge mountain – grey, towering over the orange terracotta roof tops. Home could not be to the right. He looked left. There was Molly. A black and white cat rolled onto its back, purring as it played with a green ball on piece of string.

"Molly come here." Paddy took a few steps towards the cat which bounced away from him, heading towards the end of the alley. "Don't be like that Molly. Nuala will be looking for you. Don't run away."

Paddy walked slowly down the alley towards the Calle de La Luna. He turned left. Molly was nowhere in sight. He reached the Plaza. On his left was the St Bartholomew's Church – grey stoned, sculptured greatness of Gaudi. Paddy looked at circular stained glass window, the spires above reaching into light blue sky. It didn't look like the twin spires of Holy Cross Church. It was a Church and maybe Nuala would be inside. He climbed the steps slowly. He counted the steps to take his attention away from his aching knees. There were twelve steps or was it thirteen? He disappeared into the darkness.

Paddy wandered up the middle aisle of the Church towards the main altar. One man sat leaning on his wooden stick. The inside was dark, with statues in gold to his left imprisoned behind black railings. Behind the statues were paintings in which obscure, cloaked, semi-naked bodies reached out their arms from dark corners.

There was no sign of Nuala. She must have gone home. It must be getting late. Nuala would have the kettle on for tea by now. He peered into the side altar and then walked slowly down the side aisle and out of the main door.

There were drummers playing in the Plaza and three men wearing swinging black coats, red tights and black hats brimmed with gold braid played guitars and sang a song he didn't recognise. He turned left. He always turned left after going to Mass in Holy Cross. He turned left again and walked uphill towards the railway station. On his right there was a row of white taxis with a blue diagonal band on the door. He approached the first one which had the number ten written on the door.

A tall blonde woman chatted with another taxi driver. When she saw Paddy, she opened the door of the taxi for him. At first she spoke to him in Spanish, but when she saw that he didn't understand, she asked in English,

"Where would you like to go?"

"Home." Paddy said confidently.

"Where's home?" The woman tentatively asked.

"Facing the Church." Paddy climbed into the back seat.

"The Church in the Port of Soller?" She started driving.

"That'll do nicely." Paddy nodded.

Ten minutes later they arrived in the Port of Soller, beside the Church of San Ramon, a few minutes' walk from Cornelia's house.

"That will be eight euros."

Paddy pulled out a handful of notes and passed them to the front.

"Do you have euros? These are sterling notes."

Paddy nodded. He handed over a second bundle of notes.

"One of these is enough." The taxi driver smiled returning Paddy's money, with his two euros of change.

"Are you sure that you know where you are going?" She looked over her shoulder.

THE SECRET WOUND

Paddy smiled as he stood on the pavement, he leaned into the front window of the taxi. "I do. Thank you. You are very kind."

The taxi pulled away. Paddy saw the sea sparkling at the end of the street in front of him. Maybe Nuala would be on the beach with Gurtha. Bangor. That's where he was – Ballyhome Beach in Bangor. He must have left them to buy cigars. He felt in his shirt pocket. He had his Hamlet and a lighter. It would be OK now. He only needed to find Gurtha and Nuala. He walked along the pavement and looked to the right towards the setting sun. The Faro lighthouse to the left of the bay on top of the hill was falling into shadow.

The sun dropped slowly towards the horizon. A large white yacht sailed quickly towards its mooring. A wooden boat groaning with drummers and pipers circled the harbour creating a medieval feel to the evening. Paddy looked at the people walking along the front –slim women in scanty bikinis, men with reddened faces and overstretched stomachs, children throwing lights into the air with elastic bands and seeing them fall like fireworks back onto the sand. There were couples eating hazelnut and vanilla ice cream in cones, hastily licking the edges as the ice cream melted. Paddy breathed in the warm air and the peace. He forgot for a moment that he was looking for Nuala. Then he spotted 'The Irish Bar'.

There were three wooden tables outside with couples drinking Duval and Guinness in chilled glasses. Paddy opened the door. Inside the walls were dotted with familiar photos of trams and buses in Dublin, O'Connell Street, and there were leather seats that reminded him of the Crown Bar in Belfast where he had sat alone celebrating his twenty fifth wedding anniversary. Paddy shuffled towards the bar, pulled crinkled notes from his pocket,

"A pint of Guinness."

The bartender waved a hand.

"Have a seat and I'll bring it over to you."

"Can you put a smiley face on it like Tommy does?"

Paddy sat with his back to the window and from his shirt pocket he removed a packet of five Hamlet and a plastic orange lighter which he placed side by side on the wooden table. As it was a beautiful evening most customers were sitting outside watching the sun set between the two lighthouses on either side of the bay. A tall man with a mottled overgrown freckled face sat on a stool at the bar studying his half-drunk pint of Guinness. He turned slowly to look at Paddy. His dyed orange hair curled over his shirt collar. Grey roots showed through, maybe an inch or more. He wore a white short sleeved cotton shirt with the collar crisply ironed and the rest of the shirt left wrinkled. There were three spots of blood, each the size of a one euro coin on the knees of his jeans. These might have come from an animal he had tried to help, a fish he had gutted, a wound to his own body – perhaps a self-inflicted injury or the splattering of someone else's blood onto his trousers during a brawl.

Paddy gave him one of those big smiles which showed neither teeth nor gums. When Paddy was thirty five he started to lose his teeth one by one from gum disease. One night, for reasons Paddy never shared with anyone, he pulled out all of the remaining wobbly teeth with a pair of pliers, popping them one by one into a blue ceramic cereal dish. He said to Nuala, "No hair, no teeth and the girls will still love me."

He never bothered to get a set of false teeth or go to the dentist. Later he joked, after chewing on an apple and pointing at the indentations made by his gums, that you could see teeth marks.

"I could be on TV like that Uri Geller chap you like."

The man at the bar slid off his stool and walked towards Paddy, with his pint of Guinness in hand. He walked in an unexpectedly steady way with his eyes trained firmly on the wood panelled floor.

"You look like a real Irishman. Can I join you?" Brian hoisted himself into the seat beside Paddy without waiting for an answer.

"Where are you from?"

"Belfast," Paddy said without hesitation and with a touch of pride.

Brian took a Hamlet from Paddy's packet. He cautioned.

"You're not meant to smoke inside but I act stupid and it works every time. Mind you – I don't have to try too hard."

After helping himself to a cigar Brian offered Paddy one. Paddy placed it in his mouth and waited for Brian to click the lighter. Paddy inhaled deeply.

"Do you fancy something to eat?" Brian waved at the barman for a menu.

"Now that you mention it, I am a bit peckish." Paddy puffed enthusiastically on his cigar.

"They do a mean prawn sandwich – on proper brown bread – you would nearly think that it was wheaten bread with the lovely mayonnaise and a slice of lemon. How does that sound?"

"Sounds perfect to me." Paddy reached into his pocket and pulled out his roll of sterling notes. Brian took them from him and shoved them into his own pocket.

"Have you any euros? That money is like monopoly here. It doesn't count." Brian stubbed out his cigar in the ashtray and waited in silence. Paddy set his pint of Guinness carefully on the beer mat, adjusted the beer mat so that it was straight, reached in to his second pocket and tossed the crumpled the bundle of euros onto the table.

"That's more like it. We'll have two of those open prawn sandwiches then and another pint. What do you think?"

"Why not? I'm on my holidays." Paddy offered Brian a second cigar. He took four attempts at lighting it before a red ember brightened like a hot poker. Brian rested his hand on Paddy's shoulder.

"After we have our tea, if you don't mind, I'll be getting home."

At ten o'clock Paddy sat alone, staring into space and chewing on a prawn, for his only company.

"Are you OK?" the bartender asked resting both hands on the table and staring into his eyes.

Paddy nodded. His lips were closed but his jaws were moving extensively up and down, his cheeks from time to time puffed up like balloons.

"Spit it out," The bartender anxiously urged, holding a paper napkin under Paddy's chin. Paddy kept staring ahead, past the bartender, towards the back of the bar. He continued chewing the prawn.

Paddy continued with his lips closed, jaws moving up and down in an attempt to configure the prawn into a condition where it might be swallowed. Not achieving this, at precisely ten twenty three, he got his feet, waved at the bartender and attempted to exit the pub.

Seeing his unsteady gait, the bartender rushed towards him. He grasped at the brass door handle, pulled it gently towards him, opening the door. He watched Paddy stumble from the Irish Pub –his feet pointing outwards, his bandy legs within floppy trousers shuddering like newly hoisted sails in a gentle August breeze.

It was dark now outside. There were three tables of people

chatting and drinking – two on Paddy's left and one to his right. He stopped for a moment to look at the table to his right where two women were in the process of downing a pint of Guinness.

Leaving them behind, Paddy released the prawn from captivity. It flew through the air towards the Mediterranean Sea. A small capsule of life after more than two hours in Paddy's mouth, heading senselessly home but falling short on the pavement, inches from the sand, only a short distance from the swishing waves from where once it had been free.

Paddy shuffled in the direction of the prawn. He silently passed it by, hobbling onto the sand towards the edge of the sea. The waves broke quietly with a swish rather than a roar. In the darkness he saw the whiteness of foam.

In Paddy's mind it was froth on the simple sands of Ballyhome Beach, County Down. It was dark. He had only swum once in the sea in the dark. It was in July of 1972. Gurtha was four years old. 'The Troubles' in Northern Ireland had been at an all-time high. He had decided to take Nuala and Gurtha for a weekend's holiday to Bangor. Nuala had enthusiastically packed two cases, singing 'All you need is love' as she ran between the ironing board and the upstairs bed where the clothes were neatly pressed and folded.

The train pulled out of Belfast and headed towards Bangor. Paddy remembered the comforting clickity clack .... sschuchhhzzz ... click ... click ... sschuchhhzzz ... clickity clack of wheels on the track.

Gurtha sat on Nuala's knee, Paddy sat opposite them in a wooden carriage watching Belfast disappear and the oak trees and green fields of County Down open up before them for the first time. Paddy's body buzzed with pleasure, with anticipation, with pride that he was taking his family on holiday. Fifteen minutes later, Belfast seemed a world away. There were new glimpses of the sea – steely grey smooth panels like those Paddy soldered for ships. They were followed by rolling hills with smooth curved backs of seated wild hares.

"Tickets please." A uniformed ticket collector slid open the wooden door and put his hand out. His presence didn't break this sense of sacred peace held within the carriage. As he returned the punched tickets to Gurtha, with outstretched hands, he was like a priest administering the Eucharist, looking into each other's eyes, slightly bowing to one another in respect. Paddy closed his eyes as though saying his prayers after Communion.

Gurtha didn't say a word, but only gave the occasional "Oooohhh" or "Aaaahhh" with a deep sigh of satisfaction, pointing his finger at the black bulls with their thick necks, long bodies, and thin dangling tails with a tassel on the end like Nuala's blinds. They stood unmoving in the long grass and didn't provoke fear in Gurtha, only awe and wonder. In another field there were Scottish Highland cattle with their long shaggy fringes and sticky out horns, curved at the end. Then there were the Jersey cows with their big soft eyes like teddy bears, fawn and beige coats which watched the passing train with curiosity before they broke into a gentle run towards the furthest end of the field. In another field there was a mix of black and white cattle which were Gurtha's favourites – the Belted Galways – huge, like the bulls he had seen earlier, with a broad saddle of white like a blanket around the middle of their torsos and Friesian cows with white skinny legs, a white star in the middle of a black forehead and patches of white and black over their bodies like maps of another world. Drinking in these animals, Gurtha felt that he was drinking in a magic substance, filling him with a special power that they possessed. It was seeding in him a sense of the peace and strength that they embodied, which he had never seen before.

The train juddered to a stop in Bangor and Paddy, Nuala and Gurtha walked the short distance to the Bed and Breakfast. The door was opened almost immediately by a bright eyed dark crimped haired woman with a slight lump on her left cheek. She wore a red and white striped apron. She smiled.

"I've been expecting you. I've made you a picnic. Leave your cases in your bedroom and make the most the day."

They dropped the cases in the bedroom with its four poster bed with draped yellowed chiffon curtains. Nuala spotted Gurtha's cot under the window. It was really a bit too small for him but would be fine for a couple of days if he curled up on his side to sleep.

While Nuala and Paddy talked to the landlady, organising the picnic, Gurtha listened to the sea calling with a gentle swish of waves on the pebbled beach. He heard the drag of the pebbles and sand like marbles rolling in a glass jar. He had never been so close to the sea before and tingled with its mystery. He knew from cartoons that it was a place which moved and was not solid, where strange animals survived without breathing in the way that humans breathe, where they could twist and turn and nibble food which humans would find repulsive. These strange beings lived in a hidden world not to be seen. When Nuala returned to the bedroom, Gurtha tugged at her hand.

"Let's go."

Paddy changed into swimming trunks and open toed sandals. Nuala wore a yellow halter neck swimming suit, crimped around her breast and tummy. She carefully pushed her toes into white sandals.

She clasped the picnic basket which Mrs Aspery had thoughtfully prepared. Before they headed for Ballyhome Beach Mrs Aspery caught her by hand arm and suggested.

"You might want to have a second look to make sure you have everything you need."

Nuala opened the basked and started to unpack it. There were an abundance of eggs. There were six hard boiled eggs, four rounds of egg, onion and tomato sandwiches.

"I've done an extra round for Mr Maloney. Maybe I should have done an extra one for you too?" Mrs Aspery smiled almost apologetically looking at Nuala and acknowledging her slightly rounded stomach. Nuala shook her head.

"You have been most generous."

There was a flask of tea and another flask of milk, chocolate digestive biscuits, three apples, one orange, three slices of fruit cake, two tomatoes and a bottle of ice cream soda.

"Is there anything else you would like? Perhaps I have forgotten something?"

Nuala smiled and shook her head.

"Of course not. You have thought of everything."

Curling his toes in his sandals, Paddy asked, "Would there be the chance of a bottle of Guinness?"

Mrs Aspery rubbed both hands down the side of her apron. Her cheeks blushed.

"How could I be so remiss, Mr Maloney. Of course there will be the chance of not one, but two bottles of Guinness. My deceased husband spoke highly of their medicinal qualities. Unfortunately they were unable to help him in the last stages of his life. You will need a glass I presume?"

Paddy nodded.

Nuala repacked the picnic and Paddy carried the basket down to the beach. He remembered every step of the way. The rose bushes blooming with yellow, pink and orange. Leaves falling on the pathway beneath their feet, like a blessing. There was an

THE SECRET WOUND

old man standing on the corner of the road pointing right to Ballyhome Beach. Paddy looked at him. He was like one of those men who wore sandwich boards stating 'The End is Nigh' on one side and 'Repent' on the other. He smiled like Father Christmas and gave a small bow to Gurtha and said, "Today will be one of the happiest days of your life."

They arrived, sweating but exhilarated, at the beach, which wasn't as full of people as you would expect in July. The sky was a turquoise blue with a dozen or so seagulls hovering overhead in place of clouds. Nuala stretched out three towels on the beach and a fourth for the picnic. Gurtha was stripped of his clothes and allowed to run around in white knickers. He headed straight for the waves and Paddy followed but not before pressing a kiss on Nuala's lips. Nuala sighed one of those sighs which come from a place of peace which may always be there but not always known and then rested back on her elbows and took a deep breath.

After Gurtha had splashed in the waves, covered himself in seaweed, dug a hole with a bucket and spade which the seawater magically filled within seconds, it was time to demolish the picnic.

Gurtha played on his own at the water's edge watched carefully by Nuala and Paddy. They stayed on the beach until seven o'clock. Nuala and Paddy each took Gurtha's hand and walked along the edge of the water. Gurtha walked on tip toes and squealed every so often with excitement. The sun was still a few hours from setting, balancing among drifting pink clouds which coloured the waves turquoise. The irony smell of seaweed felt healthy just to breathe in. It was time for Gurtha to be bundled into a soft while towel and gently dried.

They returned to Mrs Aspery's but not before buying Gurtha an ice-cream from Mr Whippy, a chocolate flake stuck into the swirls of soft cream. Mrs Aspery smiled, listening to the singing from the bathtub as Nuala scrubbed away the sand from Gurtha's tender body and found a third bottle of Guinness for Paddy who lit a cigar and sank into the leather sofa. His feet were on the ground but he didn't feel them there. He felt himself more in the smoke which swirled in front of his face and drifted towards the kitchen where Mrs Aspery basted the roasting chicken. The skin was crispy golden, with clear bubbles over the breast. The potatoes were fluffy and spiked at the edges with a crunchiness Nuala could never master. Mrs Aspery peeped through the door at Paddy and asked, "Would you like a bread sauce with your chicken and maybe a few sausages?"

Paddy sat up on the sofa, leaned forward and asked, "Do whatever you would do for Mr Aspery. It will be good enough for me."

She gave a short gasp – a breath like you might take in and never breathe out. It created a pause, a space in the room, only broken by Paddy holding his head in his hands and sobbing tears of joy.

After the roast chicken, with the tiny sausages, bread sauce, roasted potatoes and mashed carrots had been heartily finished; there was, of course, apple pie and cream. Paddy did something which he had never done before in his life. He asked Nuala if he could tell Gurtha a story, after she put Gurtha to bed. She looked at him with open eyes, her eyebrows raised, her jaw slightly dropped and without saying a word, nodded.

Paddy sat on the bed with Gurtha and Nuala retired to help Mrs Aspery with the washing up after a fierce fight to be allowed into the kitchen.

Paddy stroked Gurtha's head. Gurtha moved onto his side and pulled his legs up almost to his chin. He joined his hands together as though he was saying a prayer but then slipped his joined hands under his cheek, making his hands the pillow. He listened with eyes wide open to what Paddy had to say.

"There was a man called Athaneus who by the time he was quite old – forty to be exact – he had lost the ability to talk. It happened quite suddenly. One night he was able to talk normally to his wife – she was called Alaya – the next morning he had lost the power of speech. He couldn't tell her of course. He looked into her eyes that morning and he tried to tell her that he loved her. He made his mouth go all soft and curl up. When he did this dimples appeared on either cheek. Alaya knew that he was happy even though he couldn't talk. He wasn't sure what to do with his eyebrows and so he pulled them together – only a little and made them go a slightly higher on his forehead than he had ever been used to doing and with his nostrils he made them flare out ever so slightly.

Alaya looked at him, waiting for him to say a word. She tried to interpret what he was trying to tell her with his facial movements. He kept experimenting. When Alaya guessed accurately which animal he was imitating he smiled and put two thumbs in the air. At times he twitched his nose like a rabbit and found that made him want to bare his teeth. He raised his lips and stuck his teeth over his lower lip. At other times he smiled like a cat, keeping his nose perfectly still and staring straight ahead. After five years he had experimented with being almost every single animal that he could imagine – even a snake. When he tried to be a snake he stretched his neck high into the air and moved his head from side to side, keeping his eyes focused on Alaya's lips. He stuck his tongue out from time to time quickly as though he was catching an insect."

"What happened to him?" Gurtha didn't move on the pillow but rather stayed very still.

"It was on a Sunday, five years later when he wakened up in bed with Alaya – the sunlight was streaming through a chink in the floral curtains onto the bed. Athaneus knew before saying a word that he could talk again."

"What did he say?" Gurtha sat up in bed.

"Nothing. He went into the bathroom and tested out that words could come out of his mouth. Words came out. I can't tell you what those first words were you understand because he heard them and no-one else and then they floated into the air and disappeared. Even Athaneus could not remember what those words were. He became more fascinated by not the words themselves but how they appeared and disappeared. He found himself listening to the space that they appeared from and into which they disappeared. The words were not to be remembered. They were totally insignificant. He looked outside the bathroom door to make sure that Alaya hadn't heard them. He sprayed the bathroom with air freshener as though that would disguise the fact that words had one again filled the air. He had realised during his five years of silence that there were really no words worth saying. The world was more mysterious, more wonderful and awesome without words. He felt that words broke the world apart like an egg shell falling apart. "

Gurtha sat up in bed and whispered to Paddy.

"A chicken comes out of a broken shell."

Paddy looked at Gurtha in amazement. How could a child so young see this positive side of a disintegrating world? Before he could think of a response, Gurtha had another question.

"Did he not want to tell Alaya that he loved her?"

"No." Paddy shook his head. He regained a sense of where the story was going. "He found that there was love in the silence. It was as though the words were bubbles. They hold a small

THE SECRET WOUND

amount of love but when the bubble bursts you know that love is everywhere."

Paddy hugged and then kissed Gurtha on the forehead, pulling the sheets and blankets around him and silently left the room. He heard Mrs Aspery and Nuala in the kitchen still chatting and tidying the dishes. He went back to his bedroom, found his wet bathing trunks and a dry towel and slipped quietly out of the house, returning to the beach. It was ten thirty. The sun had set. Darkness had fallen over the sand and pebbles. There was luminous blue foam at the water's edge. The sea was still, a gentle black liquid coal, swirling in front of his eyes. He folded his clothes neatly at the water's edge, on top of the towel and pulled on his black swimming trunks and disappeared like a thick sea eel below the surface of the water. He remembered how in the darkness, he was only aware of water holding him, gently, rocking him. He turned on his back and floated, seeing the flickering stars fizz in the blackness above. The moon was a slither of a crescent. He could imagine sitting inside the curve of white and swinging from side to side.

♥

In the Port of Soller, outside the Irish Bar someone played a guitar and sang, 'Oh Danny Boy'. Paddy looked upwards and the moon was indeed once again a fine line of white, like a scythe lying on a plush velvet pillow. He looked into the sea, rolling towards him, each wave calling him in. He took off his shoes and started to undress at the water's edge.

♥

It was nine o'clock. Gurtha sat in a circle inside the Gallery with Cornelia, Barry, Stephanie, Todd and Angelina. Cornelia held Barry's hand. Barry lay back in the chair with his eyes closed. Stephanie stared at Gurtha. Todd picked at a tooth with toothpick. Angelina crossed her hands on top of her lap. Gurtha held Paddy's checked green cap in his hands and stared at the ceiling before taking a deep breath.

"We need to get the Police involved."

Todd dropped the toothpick into an ashtray on the table beside him.

"It's not necessary for us all to go to the Police station is it?"

Stephanie stood in front of Todd, placing her hands on her hips.

"Are you saying that you don't care what happens to Paddy?"

Todd glared back in disgust and annoyance before placing both hands on his knees and leaning forward, looking gently into Gurtha's eyes. "I'm only saying, Gurtha, that if we split up we will maximise our efficiency. You and Cornelia go to the Police. We keep in touch by phone. It's a small island. He's not going to escape. Has he got a passport and money?"

"I have his passport. He has some money." Gurtha held his hands over his eyes. His voice trembled, soaring in pitch.

"I gave him money."

Cornelia knelt down in front of Gurtha.

"It's good that he hasn't got his passport. I am so frightened about losing mine that I have it with me all the time."

She showed them a small white purse with a white cord which she criss-crossed over her shoulder.

"You always need to have identification on you here if the Police stop you or you buy anything with a credit card."

THE SECRET WOUND

Cornelia's eyes were unusually soft, eyebrows slightly raised in interest and her jaw dropped an inch or so as she whispered to Gurtha.

"Don't think the worst. He is not going off the island. Not unless he swims." Barry opened his eyes, abruptly sat up and glanced around the room.

"Does anyone want a drink or is it only me?"

Cornelia got to her feet in a graceful movement, resembling something between a yoga movement and an adage ballet twist. She took two steps towards Barry and placed her hands on his shoulders.

"There will be no drinks for you or for anyone until Paddy is found. What kind of people do we have here? For God's sake let's get out there and find him."

♥

Barry watched Gurtha and Cornelia scurry along the Calle Son Joan and turn left at the bottom. Cornelia's pink silk dress disappeared from sight like a Matador's cloak whisked from the eyes of the bull. When Barry was sure that they were definitely gone, he turned to Angelina who stood behind him, leaning against the closed gallery door, arms crossed, a small cream handbag with pink silk flowers slid along one arm like a bracelet. She closed her eyes slowly, let her head fall back took a deep breath and exhaled slowly. With her eyes closed she whispered,

"This is a nightmare. Poor Paddy. Where do we look first?"

Barry noticed a narrow line of silver eye shadow, long heavily mascara coated lashes which slowly opened to reveal hazel green eyes which were not unlike Cornelia's. Barry found that he had to look away from Cornelia's eyes as if they weren't human eyes. They were frightening at times – marbles of another world holding dark secrets. He asked Angelina, "Would you like to have something to eat first?"

He blushed. He looked at her to detect a response – a flicker of surprise, annoyance, or interest. Surprisingly a smile opened gently on Angelina's face.

"If you behave yourself. Don't spoil it." She reached out her arm to link it with his.

"These cobbled streets are hellish to walk on with high heels."

Barry felt her body press against his and then release, press and release with every step she tottered. Her linked arm pulled down on him and then relaxed, pulled down again and relaxed. All his attention was on the right side of his body where Angelina was tethered. The left side of his body scarcely seemed to exist at all. His face continued to blush and throb with heat.

An old woman sitting on a chair outside her house to the left watched him approach with Angelina. Her grey hair permed into tight curls. She wore a blue polyester dress with a wide yoked neck and no waist. Her hands rested on her thin thighs hidden in the swathes of blue. As they arrived beside the old woman, Angelina stopped.

"Do you think we should ask her if she's seen Paddy?"

Barry nodded, "You ask. You speak Spanish."

Angelina slipped her arm away from Barry, walked towards the old woman, crouched down beside her, taking her hand and caressing it as she asked.

"Have you seen an old man, bald, this height", she raised her arm above her head, "who was sitting over there", she pointed at the gallery. Paddy's chair was still outside.

The old woman shook her head, holding onto Angelina's hand. Angelina stood up, took a small step back releasing her grasp on

THE SECRET WOUND

the old woman's hand but the old woman continued to hold on. She stared into Angelina's eyes, "You're beautiful."

There was a silence. Angelina tugged a hand free. The old woman's hand fell back onto her lap. Keeping her eyes on Angelina, she repeated,

"You're beautiful. He knows that." She pointed at Barry. "He's the one for you."

Angelina touched the old woman's hand.

"Do you think so?"

The old woman held a finger to her lips.

"Sometimes you know, sometimes you don't."

Angelina turned towards Barry who was looking at her from a distance, and as she drew beside him, she linked her arm again with his.

"She didn't see anything."

The light was now falling and the tall narrow buildings were creating a black shadow against the blue sky which held the remnants of light from the day. Swifts flew energetically overhead, diving and soaring above the terracotta roof tops.

Barry's hands were sweating with the air humid and sticky without a breeze.

They arrived at an old house which had been converted into a restaurant at the end of a cul-de-sac. A thick candle burnt fiercely in the still air. Barry opened the door.

A waiter guided them through a corridor with blue and white tiles on the floor. A spiral staircase on their left wound its way up to the first floor - they continued walking into patio garden. The waiter found them a table for two at the far end of the patio terrace, beyond the illuminated swimming pool. There was a semi-circular stone seat with soft feather filled cushions in red, yellow and green and a table also made of stone with a lantern and a candle flickering inside.

Angelina rested her elbows on the table, moving her hands into a prayer symbol. Barry looked at her intently and commented, "You seemed to be getting along well with Gurtha."

Angelina lifted the menu and began reading it, "Yes – he's not like other people here."

"In what way?"

"He thinks differently."

"What do you mean?"

"He's not only thinking about making money, or buying a bigger house. He's thinking more deeply about life."

Barry set his menu to one side, "What do you think his relationship is like with Cornelia?"

Angelina also set her menu on the table. A waiter approached.

"Bacalao with tumbet. That's for me." Angelina smiled at him.

"Make that two." Barry took a sip of water.

"Can you bring us a bottle of your house white wine, please?"

Barry mopped the sweat away from his forehead and asked again.

"I'm curious what you make of the relationship between Gurtha and Cornelia."

Angelina removed the clips from her hair and allowed it to fall onto her shoulders. She shook her head from side to side, smoothing her hair with her hands, lowering her head over the table. She pulled her hair together again and wound it into a bun which sat on top of her head, securing it with three long hairpins.

"She seems very fond of him. They've know each other a long time. I would say that they're very good friends."

Barry sat upright, breathing heavily.

THE SECRET WOUND

"Do you think that they've ever been more than good friends?" Angelina shook her head.

"I don't think so. But why don't you ask Cornelia? After all, she is your partner. She would be the best person to tell you."

The waiter approached the table and filled their wine glasses.

Barry sipped on his wine.

"I don't think Cornelia would tell me. She isn't someone who tells the truth."

Angelina lifted her glass of wine and before taking a sip, looked at Barry in puzzlement, "That sounds odd coming from you. Is there not a bit of projection going on here? I'm assuming that you haven't told her about us?"

Barry shook his head.

"What is there to tell? You've said that it's over."

Angelina opened her napkin and folded it over her knees.

"Yes. It is over before it even started. However, you said that you didn't love Cornelia. What are you going to do about that? If you don't tell her – isn't that another lie?"

♥

"Are you getting into the boat or not?" Todd threw his jacket into Stephanie's basket.

"Shouldn't we keep looking for Paddy?" Stephanie reached for Todd's hand and shakily stepped into 'Pepino' – Cornelia's wooden boat. The brass fitting which Todd had been polishing earlier in the week, gleamed in the moonlight.

"Give me a break. You would have thought that Gurtha would have known that his father is crackers. It's his fault for leaving him on his own."

"I don't see it like that." Stephanie sat at the back of the boat near the motor. She instinctively dipped her left hand into the water. It was still warm, like tepid tea.

"Paddy may be a little forgetful but I don't think anyone would have anticipated that he would go 'walk about' without telling Gurtha where he was going."

Todd slipped the key into the 'dead man's switch' and ensured that it was safely attached to his wrist. He started the motor and 'Pepino' slowed edged away from the peer. Within minutes water began to slowly enter the boat, silently seeping around Stephanie's feet.

"Oh my God - is this boat seaworthy? Why is there so much water coming in?" She grimaced, swinging both legs onto the seat in front and clutching the straw basket to her chest.

"It's a wooden boat. It's perfectly natural for it to let in a little water." Todd pointed at a pump on board.

"I took it out last week with Barry. He needed to use the pump, but it was OK."

"Do we have to do this? What will the others think if they see us? It seems so self indulgent." She shivered. Todd ignored her, focusing his attention on steering 'Pepino' clear from a small outcrop of rocks. Stephanie insisted, "Isn't it dangerous? We haven't got lifejackets."

Todd increased the speed and the boat began to bounce over the waves.

"I need some space. We won't stay out too long."

Todd slowed 'Pepino' down a little and it moved smoothly into the bay. The lights from the restaurants in the Santa Catalina district fell onto the dark water in splashes of blue, orange and green. 'Pepino' cut through colours sending rainbow ripples to the right and left. Someone played a flamenco acoustic guitar outside the Marina hotel close by. The notes were carried like

THE SECRET WOUND

hidden night birds moving through the air softly before fading into infinity.

Todd licked the salty water from his lips, feeling the gentle rocking of the boat beneath his feet, as he negotiated around a yacht anchored in the middle of the bay. He nudged slowly forward, feeling the fingering of a warm breeze against his face – oblivious of Stephanie sitting silently behind him. With one hand on the rudder, he balanced his weight first on his right foot and then pressed down on his left. The waves were quietly swelling in rhythm to his touch. It was a dance between Todd, 'Pepino' and the waves. He felt the undulations of the waves below 'Pepino' move through his body in a gentle caress. He looked up into the sky. The stars flickering pin points of light and Mars holding still with its characteristic orange hue. The moon - a crescent slither of platinum –a scythe hanging in black velvet. The sparkling waves around 'Pepino' transformed into stars – the waves undulating black velvet. Everything flowing around him - sky, sea and space. A ripple of pure joy shuddered through him as Stephanie raised her voice anxiously.

"Todd, the water is really coming in. We need to turn back."

Stephanie placed her basket on the wooden seat, edged towards the front of the boat, to find the pump.

"Pass me the pump. This is turning into a nightmare. Can you not see that the water is now above our ankles?"

Todd turned around to see Stephanie hanging on with both hands to the side of the boat.

"I'm afraid to move. For God's sake, pass me the pump."

Todd extended a hand towards her.

"You're panicking. Take my hand. Come here, you steer. I'll do the pumping."

They changed seats – the boat wobbled at the transfer of

weight, the water inside rolling and swishing to the right and then left. Todd breathed deeply, pumped vigorously, and the water level inside 'Pepino' began to fall. Stephanie steered towards the beach. The waves lapped gently, licking the sides of the boat, a duck gave an occasional agitated squawk as they drew close to a family heading towards their nesting place in a Torrente near the Repic beach. Suddenly 'Pepino' slowed with a spluttering cough, coming to a halt – bobbing listlessly in the same place.

"Don't tell me we're out of petrol?" Stephanie leaned over grasping Todd's arm, her voice trembling.

"Where is the spare can of petrol?"

Todd looked around the boat and shouted at Stephanie,

"I told you to lift it. It was on the pier beside your basket."

Stephanie looked at the beach in the distance, back at Todd who continued to frenetically pump water back into the sea.

"The last time I saw it – it was in the boot of your car." Stephanie let go of the rudder and with her fingers raked her frizzled auburn hair.

"Calm down, Stephanie. For God's sake. We are not on 'The Titanic'. The beach is not far away. We have oars."

Todd clambered towards the front of the boat, loosening the oars tied inside on the left. He then splashed through the water, settled into middle seat, slotted the oars into their metal holders and began to row, shouting at Stephanie, "You keep pumping."

Holding the pump in one hand, Stephanie inched her way towards the back of the boat and began to pump furiously, breathing heavily, glancing every few seconds towards the beach. Then she caught sight of a head bobbing in the water. Someone swimming the breast stroke in a slow and determined way, headed in their direction.

Stephanie screamed, "Careful, Todd. A man in the water. Keep

THE SECRET WOUND

to the right. Try not to make waves."

Todd looked over his shoulder to his right. He saw a shape the size of a small dolphin raising itself out of the water and then disappearing under for a second or two before emerging again. Todd turned 'Pepino' to the right, slowing his pace. The waves almost made no movement now. Stephanie slowed her pumping, without taking her eyes off the man in the water. The water level inside 'Pepino' began to rise again. As they drifted closer to the swimmer, Stephanie and Todd saw that without a doubt - it was Paddy.

"Paddy," Stephanie, dropped the pump into the floor of the boat and waved her arms.

Todd rowed gently towards Paddy. Drawing alongside him, Stephanie lowered a metal ladder into the sea. Without saying a word, Paddy caught hold of the lower rung. He looked up at Stephanie, smiling his toothless smile. Todd rested the oars inside the boat and manoeuvred himself beside Stephanie. The boat dipped heavily to the right. Todd patted Stephanie on the back.

"I'll stand on the left hand side or the boat will capsize. Can you help him in."

Stephanie sobbed and whispered.

"OK."

Todd gently manoeuvred towards the left the boat. 'Pepino' steadied as Stephanie leaned over the side, her face covered in sea salt and tears.

"Paddy climb up. I'll help you."

Paddy put his hands on a higher rung and then a foot on the lower rung. Stephanie was able to slide her arms under Paddy's armpits, clasped her hands together behind his back and with a superhuman effort hauled him over the edge of the boat and then they both collapsed onto the watery floor.

Gurtha helped Paddy into the dry clothes retrieved by Todd and Stephanie, while Barry heaped logs onto the wood burning stove. The fire crackled and hissed as damp wood spluttered into life. Gurtha buttoned up a checked blue and white shirt and felt Paddy's hands again. They were cold. Paddy sat on a chair, Gurtha knelt in front of him pulling on two socks and then gently slipped on brown leather shoes. He looked into Paddy's eyes,

"What on earth were you doing Paddy? You gave us all a shock."

Paddy smiled, stretching his hands towards the wood burning stove, "That's a great fire you've got going. What are all these people doing looking at me?"

Gurtha poured a cup of tea and placed it in Paddy's hands.

"If it wasn't for Stephanie and Todd you would be still swimming to Barcelona."

Paddy sipped his tea.

"Barcelona? I'm not going near Barcelona. Do you have a custard cream biscuit?"

Gurtha shook his head.

"Not here but I have them at home."

Paddy took another sip of tea.

"When are we going home then? I'd like a custard cream or a jammy dodger."

Gurtha shook his head, "I don't know. I'll take you home. Don't worry. You don't like flying on your own."

Barry asked Todd,

"What made you think of searching at sea? That was a bit of luck wasn't it?"

Stephanie shivered and stared at the floor. Todd rubbed his hands on his trousers and leaned over to Barry.

THE SECRET WOUND

"Divine inspiration. Where did you and Angelina go to look for Paddy?"

"We stayed in Soller. We didn't think he would far away but that was a misjudgement." Angelina flushed red, holding her hands over her face for a moment and pretended to sneeze.

♥

They say that your body holds your life. That there is no thought or feeling that isn't registered and stored. That is why some people experience the past unfolding rapidly within minutes before they die.

Gurtha looked at Cornelia holding Paddy's hand, both gazing into the fire, and had a flashback.

♥

He was eighteen years old. It was his first day arriving at Nottingham University. The taxi swept up a curving driveway to Woodward Hall. A gentle mist settled over the grass beside a small pond. A peacock strutted along the gravel outside the front door – opening its tail with a swish and turning round and round. Large wooden doors led into reception. Before going inside, Gurtha looked at his new home for the next year – a nineteenth century building made of granite stone with large wooden windows made up of tiny square lead frames. There was a hanging basket to the left of the front door, filled with small blue and yellow flowers and in the centre three robust autumnal orange tubular plants which were topped by a cascade of white pearl flowers flowing down into the flurry of blue and yellow. It smelt different here from Belfast – there was sweetness in the air – maybe from the hyacinths in the lawn or from the roses to the right of the front door, grown into a tree shape in a wooden barrel pot, with more than thirty blossoms bursting into a symphony of bouquet.

Gurtha carried his suitcase inside and rang a brass bell sitting on the desk. There was a picture frame on the table detailing the history of Woodward Hall since its construction in the sixteenth century by Sir Thomas Fintonbury who made his money from the Nottinghamshire coal pits. The reception desk was made of solid oak as were the panelled walls behind it. There was a formidable portrait of Sir Thomas and Lady Sarah on the wall behind. Sir Thomas was standing, Lady Sarah sitting on a chair beside him and lower down a black pointer dog lay at their feet. Sir Thomas wore a black striped tunic which was tight at the waist before it opened up into a ballerina style skirt which had a puffed cream underskirt. He had a black hat tilted to one side with a feather in it, black trousers and the most delicate of silk flat pointed shoes. Lady Sarah wore a hat like a twisted curled snake on her head. You could see a strong widow's peak beneath the hat. She had a ruffled collar like something you would put on a dog to stop it scratching its ears, a long black velvet dress draped in pearls and a pink ornately-decorated left sleeve. Her hand rested on the dog's head. The dog's eyes looked directly into Gurtha's in an unsettling way. He was trying to work out why it felt uncomfortable when a door opened on his left and a sprightly elderly man dressed in a black suit with a white shirt and black tie, approached the desk.

"Welcome to Woodward Hall. Let's get you registered."

He searched through a list of white envelopes which were neatly laid out in rows on top of the desk, checked Gurtha's passport for identification and handed him the envelope and a key from a pigeon hole in the wall behind.

"Follow me. I'll show you your room and explain how it all

works here. Your neighbours have already checked in. You're a lucky man. This place will be sold next year by the University. You'll be the last year of students to enjoy it."

Mr Starkley opened the door into his bedroom.

"We serve breakfast at 7.00 am in the dining room which we will see in a moment and dinner at 6.00 pm. If you wish to have your dinner elsewhere, please let us know."

Gurtha saw a single bed to his left, neatly made with an orange quilted bedspread and white pillow on top. Two blue towels sat folded on top of the pillow. On his right was a small writing table and chair. Towards the window there was a large white washbasin with a glass tumbler.

"The TV can be watched in the sitting room and we have a shower and toilet along the hallway."

Gurtha walked towards the window with its small square leaden panels. He had a view over the front lawn with the drive snaking its way out of sight towards the main gates. He could see the pond with four ducks, the peacock and a newly appeared peahen stood, still unmoving, looking towards him.

Later that afternoon he met his two room neighbours - Bosie from Rotheram with red fuzzy candyfloss hair, a slightly bloated face and redeemingly clean fingernails. Bosie studied Physics. Andrew was a thin matchstick man with black hair and blue eyes studying Chemistry who even on that first afternoon couldn't be stopped sharing with Gurtha his insights into visual spatial thinking as it related to Chemistry. They were both in their second year.

Within a month, the three of them met Cornelia. Bosie literally stumbled over her on the way to order a drink at the bar. Cornelia was a mature student – studying English and a regular visitor to 'Ye Olde Trip to Jerusalem' near Nottingham Castle.

Cornelia was then twenty three, with a classic black bob, pale translucent white skin and that evening she wore a Moschino black quilted denim mini-skirt with a bodice make out of safety pins. A long thick blonde plait was woven into her raven hair. She had the habit of holding it and twiddling with it on her right shoulder. Her tights were black lacy roses and her boots were knee length patent leather with an unusual flap at the top like a butterfly wing. She smoked long thin menthol cigarettes, blowing the smoke into Gurtha's eyes, laughing.

"So you have talked a lot about Nuala. You are a real Mummy's boy aren't you? Don't they say that a man looks for his mother in the women he marries? Do I look like her? Does my mind tick like Nuala's? Of course I am already married to darling Henry but it's still an interesting question don't you think?"

She threw her head back and blew smoke towards the ceiling. Bosie poured Cornelia a glass of Pinot Grigio, before helping himself to a Rioja. A waiter lit a red candle in a Mateus Rose bottle, covered with the molten remains of previous intimate candlelit conversations.

Gurtha looked into Cornelia's green eyes, "I don't think any two people are the same or even similar. There is only one Nuala."

On the walls were photographs of Hollywood actors from the 1950s – Humphrey Bogart in a suit with a black tie looking as though he was going to a funeral, Clark Gable with a bow tie, Marlon Brando looking mean and moody in a stretch tight t-shirt. There were women - Hedy Lamarr with a perfectly symmetrical oval face, arched eyebrows leading in a fine line to a long straight nose and perfectly plumped cupid lips. Kathryn Hepburn, arms crossed, wearing a dark suit and white shirt, looking frostily away from the camera. Brigitte Bardot with a cascade of strawberry blonde curls over bare shoulders, her mouth hanging slightly open

THE SECRET WOUND

as though gasping for air. The walls were papered a warm rose colour with a gold vertical line which every so often converted into a gold heart. The lighting was soft and golden emanating from cream scallop shell lampshades perched on the walls.

From the table, Cornelia watched the kitchen where a red brick pizza oven vibrantly blazed with flames jumping into the air and the pizza makers slid long thin metal plates holding pizza into the oven. She turned to Gurtha, "Well if there is no-one else like Nuala in the world – do tell us what you like best about her. I'm sure we're all dying to know." She took another deep inhalation of smoke and released it making small circles of smoke which drifted towards Gurtha.

Gurtha waved the smoke away from his face, "That's easy. She is the most honest person I've ever met. She doesn't try to impress anyone. She's mysterious."

Cornelia stubbed the cigarette into the ashtray.

"Mysterious. What does that mean?"

Gurtha pushed the smouldering cigarette and ashtray to one side.

"It means that you feel that you can never know her. You can't pin her down and say that she is this or that. You can't control her. She won't try to please you. She is a mystery and although you attempt to plumb her depths you will never fully know her. You circle around – watching to know the unknown."

Cornelia pulled another cigarette from the packet; Bosie leant forward with a lighter, "Aren't we all a mystery? I find your attitude towards Nuala rather odd. She can't be more special than anyone else here."

She stubbed a second cigarette, almost unsmoken, into the ash tray.

"I'm paying remember." Cornelia smiled into Bosie's eyes. "I have a wealthy man at home to take care of me."

♥

The second time they were together, Cornelia wore a gold coloured satin dress with a plunging neckline and fake gold ear-rings in the shape of a cross. Over the dress she wore a blue satin jacket with three quarter length sleeves. On her hands were gold lacy gloves which finished at the end of the sleeve. She had matching gold high heels.

"Why don't we do something different?" Cornelia placed a menthol cigarette into a holder which she placed in her mouth and leaned across the table this time for Andrew to light.

Andrew flicked on his lighter several times before the flame smouldered orange. She closed her eyes in appreciation, giving a slight shiver of her shoulders.

"We're always eating and drinking. It's so boring. Can't we have a proper adventure? Don't you first year students do things like "Expeditions"? Why can't we have one of our own?"

Andrew spread his linen napkin over his knees and grabbed a black olive from the dish in front of him, scooping it with his fingers and then pushing it into his mouth, pressing his hand heavily against his lips.

"What are you thinking of – Kilimanjaro, a trip through the Congo following in the footsteps of Che Guevara or maybe to the Bolivian jungle tracing his last few weeks to investigate if he was betrayed by Fidel Castro?"

Cornelia leaned across the table and caught Andrew's hand before it reached for more olives as the waiter arrived with two sizzling pizzas – one for Andrew – with roasted artichokes, red caramelised onions, red pepper and goat's cheese and one for Gurtha – with spinach and egg. Andrew slipped his hand away from Cornelia's and sat back as the waiter grated fresh parmesan cheese on top.

Cornelia stabbed out her cigarette in the ashtray, "Well, I have in mind something simpler - a walk along Offa's Dyke towards Hay on Wye. Andrew, you can take Bosie in the mini. Gurtha will come with Henry and me. We will follow you to Hay and then you can all pile into the back and we'll go to the starting point in Henry's car."

"Don't look like that Bosie. You are eventually going to meet Henry. I am married to him. It's still quite in the Honeymoon period, you know, five years later. I can't leave him all alone for a whole weekend." She chuckled glancing at Gurtha, peeling off her gloves as her salad nicoise arrived.

"I think we should go next weekend – before snow falls. I'll book a hotel in Hay."

♥

Gurtha saw Cornelia first, leaning against the yellow Mercedes, looking up into a heavy grey sky threatening rain. Henry stood at her side holding a matching yellow umbrella with pink hearts above Cornelia's head. A few drops of rain fell on top of his abundantly curling hair. From a distance he looked majestic – tall, well built, broad shoulders, radiating a sense of energy and presence. They were appropriately dressed for a mountain hike – both wearing black waterproof trousers and red Gore-Tex jackets.

Cornelia walked towards Gurtha. Henry followed, stretching his arm with the umbrella above her to keep her dry.

"Gurtha, meet Henry."

They shook hands. At first sight, Gurtha liked Henry. What impressed him were his huge brown eyes - they had a steadiness about them which made Gurtha feel at ease. They bundled into the car with Gurtha in the back seat.

Henry looked into the mirror at Gurtha and asked.

"What are you reading?"

Gurtha answered. "Psychology, Spanish and History."

"Which do you like best?"

"Psychology and History are quite similar. We explore the motivation of key characters in history and what made them do what they did. Psychology helps a lot with that – using different vocabulary but looking at similar patterns of behaviour. I like them equally and Spanish is wonderful as Spain has an intriguing history and culture. Did you know that at one point in time Spain was the wealthiest nation in the world?"

Henry continued to keep his eyes on Gurtha using the mirror.

"Nope. I didn't know that. That must have been before my holidays to Magaluf."

Cornelia slapped him on the arm.

"You've never been on holiday in Magaluf."

Gurtha interrupted. "How long have you been working at the Bank?"

"Twenty years. I was working there before you were born. That's why I look the way I do."

"I was a baby of three when he started." Cornelia pulled the mirror down and tucked a few loose hairs behind her ears.

"Do you like it?"

"Not until I met Cornelia. I have to thank the bank for that. If it hadn't been for the bank, we would never have met."

Cornelia looked over her shoulder at Gurtha and smiled, "Yes.

I was his Personal Assistant until he gave me the opportunity to become a student, for which I am eternally grateful."

She patted Henry's leather glove on the steering wheel.

"Our life is meticulously planned and controlled. Henry will receive a handsome pension when he retires."

Henry rubbed his nose with the back of his leather glove, "I must confess to enjoying the finer things in life. A hefty pension will allow us to ensure we are tucked into a comfortable elegant duvet. However, please Cornelia – let us remember that is some years away. Between now and then, is the hard graft of working to ensure I can keep you in the style you have rather unfortunately become accustomed to."

Cornelia gave a little laugh, glancing over her shoulder at Gurtha.

"I so love a man who removes the burden from living. I can concentrate on my English literature, gaze at my navel, enquiring into the nature of life."

Henry beeped the horn as a lamb wandered onto the road. It scurried onto the verge to the right.

"That would make a wonderful supper – slow cooked in red wine with thyme, rosemary and garlic for at least four hours."

♥

At nine forty five Henry pulled into the car park of 'The Green Man'. The rain fell heavily onto the front windscreen. Henry turned the wipers to sweep frantically backwards and forwards, Cornelia leaned forward, wiped the mist on the inside of the window with a tissue and broke the silence, "There we go. Andrew and Bosie are predictably on time.

Cornelia and Henry climbed out of the car to shake hands

with Andrew and Bosie. Gurtha waited inside listening to the drops of rain splashing into the car park puddles, sending ripples shimmering across the small pools of water.

"We will be back here by four o'clock latest."

The first two hours of the hike went more or less to plan. Cornelia packed two flasks of tea, with Kendal mint cake and egg mayonnaise sandwiches which were shared around one o'clock. Gurtha, Andrew and Bosie had brought a small bottle of water each. They drank all three bottles one hour into the walk. The sweet tea was welcome as the temperatures dropped as they reached the top of the Dyke.

"Where do you think we are?" Cornelia passed the map to Bosie who shared it with Andrew.

"There's the trig point." Bosie pointed to the stone marker a few feet away.

"That must mean that we are here." He pointed to a dot on the map.

"Are you sure?" Cornelia stood beside him and peered at the map.

"That means we're making slower progress than I calculated. Are we not here?" Cornelia pointed to a second trig point further along the path.

"Definitely not. We're here. Look – there's the path signposted down to Llanthony Abbey. You can see the cliffs marked here." Bosie took out a piece of string from his pocket and traced out the path towards Hay.

"We need to walk faster if we are to arrive in Hay before dark. It's twice as far as we've come so far. Do we have a torch?"

Cornelia nodded, searching her rucksack and pulled out a small hand torch. She turned it on and it shone a yellow feeble light on her hand.

"I think the battery is low. Did you bring batteries, Henry?"

Henry shook his head tightening the scarf around his neck.

"I think you left them in the old rucksack. Do you remember?"

Cornelia shook her head.

"We better get moving then."

Gurtha got to his feet and led the way along the path. Andrew had lent him a lightweight waterproof but the rain still soaked through to his fleece. There was only a light breeze but it was cold – the temperature was not much above freezing. His jeans were heavy with rain and his trainers covered in mud. The breeze touching his face had a hint of sleet in it. He shivered. The path deteriorated as it widened out on top. It was difficult to see exactly where to walk. The narrow path with muddy footsteps from other walkers had degenerated into soft mud with the occasional tuft of heather flourishing within puddle of cold murky water. Leading the way, Gurtha shouted to those following,

"It's turning into a bog. Walk on the clumps of heather. The puddles are pot holes."

As if to prove the point, with his next step, he missed the heather clump he was aiming for and his foot sank into the muddy water all the way up to his thigh. Bosie behind, attempted to avoid doing the same but nearly all the pools of water were at least a foot deep. Everyone walked slowly. At the back, Cornelia slid her arm around Henry's, stumbling twice within a few seconds. They were making slow progress towards Hay. Andrew counselled from the back, "We need to get off the mountain or we are going to be stranded."

Gurtha stopped, waiting for everyone to huddle in a circle.

Bosie's face and hands were mottled blue and red. He had forgotten to bring gloves. He rubbed his hands together to get the circulation moving.

Gurtha pulled his gloves off,

"Wear these, Bosie."

Blowing on his fingertips held close to his mouth, Bosie reached for the gloves.

"For a few minutes and you can have them back."

"There are cliffs here," Cornelia commented, referring to the map she shared with Henry.

"I can't see a way down."

"What's that?" Andrew pointed to a small path no wider than a single boot width, snaking through the rocks.

"It's a sheep track. If we try to go down and it runs out, we will be lost." Henry squinted at the map, holding it close to his face.

"There's no marked path. I say we go back to the trig point and take the marked path down to Llanthony Abbey."

"How do we then get to Hay?" Cornelia snatched the map from Henry.

"If there are no taxis, we stay the night in Llanthony Abbey and walk along the valley floor to Hay tomorrow morning."

"Our suitcases are in Andrew's car." Cornelia wiped mascara running down her face with her leather glove.

Henry stated calmly, "Let's take a reality check. We have no food, no water, the light is already dropping, a torch with batteries running out and we are experiencing extreme cold."

Cornelia took several deep breaths, removed her rucksack, opened it, pulling out two aluminium sheets.

"We've two survival blankets."

"We are five people," Henry said, taking the survival blanket from Cornelia and wrapping it into a smaller square, he replaced it in the rucksack.

"It will be dark before we find Llanthony Abbey." Cornelia's voice quivered.

THE SECRET WOUND

"Let's not waste time. Let's try the sheep track." Henry took the lead pointing to a small path winding into the valley.

With the help of the fading light from the torch, they descended one behind another towards Llanthony. An hour later, Llanthony Abbey lay a hundred feet below.

With the light of the moon, they could see four arches – holding a silvery light within the darkness. There was a warmer orange light to the left in a small building from which flowed the sound of voices.

"We're nearly there." Henry increased his pace. Within fifteen minutes they arrived at the doorway of the pub at Llanthony Abbey.

"We've made it." Cornelia turned and embraced Henry. "Look at the state of us. You would think that we had made that expedition to the Bolivian jungle."

The scent of chargrilled chicken and lasagne filled the air. Tables made from oak were scattered with white candles held in wrought iron spiral holders. Henry followed after Cornelia and then Gurtha, Andrew and Bosie. The restaurant noise levels fell as diners observed them and whispered to one another, as Cornelia asked the waiter,

"What time do you stop serving food?"

He looked at his watch, "In five minutes."

Cornelia pointed to an empty table at the bottom of the dining room, "Could you bring the menus. Henry, I'll order for you. You sort out accommodation."

They sat around an oak table – all four covered in mud up to the waist – all four soaking wet. Cornelia removed her Gore-Tex coat.

"Remove whatever you can, retaining as much decency as possible. At least it is beautifully, wonderfully warm in here."

With food orders placed, Henry pushed open the door leading from Reception, stripping off his coat before reaching their table.

"We're sorted. I'm ravishing."

Cornelia opened a compact from a pocket in her rucksack and inspected her face. She patted Henry on the shoulder.

"Do you not think I'm the one who's ravishing? Although I'm sure we're all 'famished'."

Afterwards, having coffee by an open log fire, Gurtha opened the Visitors' Book and read the last entry.

"This sounds curious. Someone has written that this place is … 'A mystical, magical place which will transform you overnight in the most mysterious of ways'. What do you think?"

Bosie sniggered.

"Not that I'm an expert in hotels, but I would say this place is basic and bloody freezing. I'm not complaining. It's better than being stranded on the mountain."

Gurtha gazed into the fire as the burning logs spat sizzling sparks onto the tiled floor.

"Let's see."

♥

Gurtha lay in bed listening. There was nothing to hear only thick silence like a blanket around him. Then, the silence was broken by the sound of wind rattling the metal window frames and heavy rain with hailstones furiously pounding at the window.

He listened. He imagined that he heard a gentle, yet insistent tap, tap, tap, inside. It persisted. Tap, tap, tap. Gentle knuckles tapping on a hard oak door. Tap, tap, tap on his bedroom door.

He pulled on the t-shirt he had worn during the day and scrambled into damp jeans before opening the door.

THE SECRET WOUND

Cornelia stood outside. Gurtha scanned her face. She had no make-up. He wasn't used to seeing her face bare, lips empty of gloss and hair slightly tousled.

Cornelia's hands were dropped by her side. She stood in bare feet, wearing Henry's shirt. Gurtha's heart thumped against his rib cage. He breathed deeply before asking,

"What's happened?"

Cornelia touched the door as she stepped into the room as if to steady herself.

"Nothing and everything."

Gurtha followed her, stubbing his toe against the iron bed. He bent to rub his big toe.

"Is Henry OK?"

Cornelia walked as if in her sleep towards the bed.

"Henry is exhausted."

At first she sat on top of the bed, sinking into the fluffed up Nordic quilt. She then swung her legs onto the bed and lay with her head on the pillow. She rolled onto her side and leaning with one hand on her cheek, as Gurtha rushed back to close the door, she asked,

"Would you mind if I took my clothes off?"

Gurtha's heart thumped wildly, yet he managed a gentle tone to his question.

"Why?"

Cornelia slid off the bed, unbuttoning Henry's shirt.

"Purity of intent. If you know what I mean? Clothes can be a disguise."

Gurtha nodded.

She slithered naked under the quilt.

"Please. Keep your clothes on."

Gurtha pulled off his t-shirt off, discarding his jeans on the floor. He climbed into the bed beneath the quilt.

"Purity of intent is mutual."

Staring at the ceiling, Cornelia inched closer. Gurtha asked, "You are not to be touched, I take it."

Cornelia laughed,

"I knew you would understand. However, I can touch you."

Gurtha nodded with his eyes closed as Cornelia ran her fingers gently across his forehead, then she drew a line above his eyebrows before lightly caressing his nose, and tracing her fingers along his cheek bones.

"Don't think. Allow yourself to feel the touch, smell and taste it. You have ways of doing that. Find them. No-one experiences anything in the same way."

Gurtha breathed deeply. There was a smooth white light behind his closed eyes which shimmered into waves at Cornelia's touch. He listened to her words which floated into the light breaking it up into scintillations of white and black.

"You adore me don't you?"

Without waiting for a response, she continued stroking his forehead.

"Do you accept that we all hold holiness and horror within us at the same time?"

Gurtha smelt perfume like honeysuckle on a hot summer's evening. The pillow was soft; the sheets silk-like and cool against his skin.

"Holiness and horror?"

"Yes, exactly that. Can you adore that combination? If you can't you don't really adore me."

Gurtha felt the touch of her fingers tracing his lips.

"You're married to Henry."

"I am, but it changes nothing..."

THE SECRET WOUND

Gurtha rolled onto his side opening his eyes. Cornelia covered her face with the cotton sheet. Gurtha asked, "What do you want from me?"

Cornelia whispered, "I'll think about it."

"What about Henry?"

Cornelia rolled away from him. With her back to Gurtha she whispered, "There will be nothing to tell. It will be a cleansing, purifying relationship for us both. It will be 'Nothing and Everything'. Do you not feel it? Do you not feel the 'Nothing' which I have with Henry and the 'Everything' which I have with you?"

Gurtha shook his head.

"I don't."

Cornelia took his hand.

"It's simple. With Henry there is security. With you there is innocence and adventure."

Gurtha opened his eyes, without looking at Cornelia, "What am I expected to do?"

"Nothing more than to stay innocent and childlike."

She lifted the golden plait embedded within her shiny black bob. Then began to caress it. She let it fall onto her shoulder.

Gurtha touched it.

"I noticed this the first time we met. It's striking. I've never seen anything quite like it. It suits you."

Cornelia rolled onto her side with her back to Gurtha.

"It's a lock of my sister's hair. She died when I was ten and she was seven. She was my best friend. This is to remind me always of her. She's with me."

Gurtha stroked the plait.

"How did she die?"

Cornelia turned over, pressing her face into the pillow.

"It was an accident. I don't like to talk about it."

He felt her slip from beneath the sheets. She dressed before placing a finger over his lips.

"Have courage to stay fearless like a child."

He watched her turn the knob on the door and glance at him once more before gently closing the door behind her. The wind increased in intensity, howling a slow, low moan.

♥

Gurtha entered the breakfast room first at around eight thirty. The other guests had not emerged from sleep. A woman swept the floor with a long bristle brush. It made a scratching sound as it moved over the red tiles. Sunlight beamed through the window to his right. Dust rose up into the beam of light and was held there, curling and moving in circles. The woman, dressed in white with a long cotton skirt which reached to the floor, kept her head bent, intently sweeping. It was a scene of ageless peace. Gurtha imagined the monks sitting at the wooden bench, their heads bent in prayer, while the sweeping would have taken place in the same way, with the same golden light beam holding the clouds of dust in a mesmerising display of minute movement.

The woman raised her gaze, "Would you like to wait for your friends or would you like to eat now?"

Gurtha slid along the wooden bench, folded his arms on the oak table, "I'll wait, thank you."

Ten minutes later, all four of them arrived, talking and laughing as they entered the dining room.

Bosie and Andrew joined Gurtha on his side of the table. Cornelia and Henry sat opposite. Helping himself to wheaten bread which sat in baskets along the table, Bosie was the first to speak, "Did you hear the storm last night? How lucky were we to find this place? I've never had a better night's sleep in my life. Maybe it was made better by thinking about what it could have been like on that mountain."

Andrew clicked a ballpoint pen on the table, "Pass me the Visitors' Book. I'm going to have to write something."

Henry nodded,

"Yes. It's the utter simplicity of it that is special. "Sanctus Simplicitus" – Holy Simplicity. How did you sleep?"

Andrew helped himself to a piece of chunky toast which he buttered, cutting it in two.

"Superbly. I'm writing, 'It almost felt as though an angel visited my room.' He glanced at Cornelia, penned his remarks, looked quickly away before stealing half of Bosie's toast.

"What about you Bosie?"

"Add my name beside yours."

Andrew passed the Visitor's Book to Gurtha,

"Your turn."

Gurtha took the pen from Andrew and wrote, "A mysterious – possibly dangerous place."

The book was passed to Henry who laughed at Gurtha's entry and added his name beside it.

"I know what you mean. Did you see how steep those stairs are going up to the bedrooms."

Cornelia, paused for a moment as she received the Book, she sipped her coffee and wrote, "A life filled with danger – needs a haven of rest. Thank you Llanthony Abbey."

♥

Gurtha looked at Cornelia sitting beside Paddy in the art gallery, holding his hand and staring into the wood burning stove. She turned towards Barry, "Barry, we promised you a drink when we had a happy ending by finding Paddy. Stephanie would you be a darling and find the champagne and nibbles?"

Paddy pulled his hand free from Cornelia's grasp.

"Who is this woman? I don't know her. Can you tell her to get her hands off me?"

The room swallowed a collective gasp.

THE SECRET WOUND

DAY 10

TUESDAY 20TH AUGUST 2013

NEXT MORNING in La Torretta whilst Paddy slept, Gurtha wondered about how he could find out if Paddy had murdered Nuala. He scanned through his memory, trying to remember what Nuala had said to him in the weeks before she was murdered. Why, he thought, did she not share her premonitions with him – rather than phone a help line? He tried to remember her exact words. He remembered a day in July. She had poured a cup of tea into a china cup dotted with pink flowers. It sat in a saucer with a fine line of gold leaf around the rim. She had placed a small piece of Madeira cake onto a matching plate beside the cup. Her translucent skin shining with light like the china cup. She hadn't looked at Gurtha, but tapped her fingers on the white table cloth especially produced for his visit.

"Your father told me, the night before last, that he had never felt himself loved. He's never talked to me like that before. I told him that God loved him. He shook his head at me. I knew he didn't believe in God or God's love."

Nuala had looked at him, her eyes a little watery. Yet she smiled, "Then that night, I had a dream. I dreamt that he was a baby of six months old. He had to be taken care of like a baby."

In La Torreta Gurtha heated milk and pressed a Nespresso pod into the machine. It gurgled happily into a white mug.

Maybe Nuala was right. Maybe that was what was happening to Paddy. He was turning into a baby again - no teeth, no hair. Yet there was no sign from Nuala that she was concerned that he might be violent. The opposite – she seemed to be softening her attitude towards him – becoming more loving.

He waited while the Nespresso machine finished filtering a second coffee. Then he opened the wooden lid of the well in the kitchen and peered into the darkness. There was an echo below – as though the well held hostage a mysterious beast. He heard its growl reverberate off the circular walls. He smelt the damp graveyard mustiness. He imagined a beast standing– with only a head above the water line – emerald green eyes glimmering with light, flickering like fireflies, waiting for him to throw food. On the marble shelf beside him was a dish made from olive wood, holding a few coins. He took a five cents coin and threw it into the well. He counted the seconds before he heard it splash. Only one second. He listened to the hollowness arising from within the well. The dampness now reminded him of catacombs. He imagined the water hiding layer after layer of hollowed skulls. His mind felt hollow. He poured the steaming milk into the coffee, took a sip and walked to the front door, opening it to look into the valley of Soller. Far away a dog barked agitatedly. There was an intense loneliness in the harsh rhythmic hacking at the air. There was an anguish which no-one could take away because no-one knew where it came from and what it meant.

For Gurtha, it was as though the dog had been sent to earth to voice despair, howling from the ends of the Universe. Maybe that's

THE SECRET WOUND

where despair and Hell were – not in some mythological fire in the depths of the earth, but in the intense loneliness and isolation where every soul found themselves alone in an infinite blackness with not even the earth to touch for comfort, or for relationship.

The dog in the valley below seemed to sense that Gurtha listened. It changed his husky bark into a long, quivering howl which rose from the depths of its innards, pushing its way past its heart to escape through the doorway of a mouth held wide open, past sharp teeth into which the next gulp of air would be snapped shut against.

Even though it was early morning, the pine needles lying on the path in front were already sending a cleansing perfume into the air. Gurtha looked to his right where a flock of white and black vultures circled – their necks long but not so long as the neck of a swan or a goose – with the edges of their wings feathered. They drifted towards him. He walked towards the gazebo, watching their hypnotic circling overhead. Three swooped lower, almost tangling their long wings with one another. They made no noise. He couldn't even hear the flapping of wings or the squawks he was used to from the seagulls in Belfast. They were eyes watching him. What did they see? He sipped on his coffee which had gone cold. He threw it on the ground with a gesture of a sower of wheat, or was it with disgust? By the time he looked up, the vultures had gone. They now seemed more like an omen than something real. He hurried into the house to see if Paddy was OK.

Paddy managed to dress himself in khaki shorts, a white vest, blue checked shirt and sturdy brown loafers. He opened a cupboard door looking for a mug. He looked serene and smiled at Gurtha as he turned the kettle on to boil.

"Do you want a cup of tea?

"I'll stick with coffee. Let me get you some toast."

He poached him an egg, placing it on top of the brown toast and topped up Paddy's mug of tea a second time. They sat at the table inside rather than go to the gazebo. Paddy sat in silence.

"What did you think of your adventure last night?" Gurtha asked gently.

Paddy searched in his shirt pocket for his Hamlet cigars.

"They were nice people. Good people. Although I don't like that woman with the dark hair and that funny blonde plait. I would cut that off if I had a chance. It looks like nothing."

Gurtha got up from the table and searched in Paddy's tweed jacket for a lighter. There were two in the pocket. He lifted a brown ashtray from the shelf and sat it on the table. Paddy held the cigar to his lips, Gurtha pulled at the metal clasp, allowing a long flame to turn the end of the cigar smouldering red.

"What do you not like about her?"

Paddy shook his head.

"I don't know. I don't think Nuala liked her – do you?"

Paddy opened his book, flicking ash into the ashtray.

"Nuala can tell you for herself what she thinks about that woman."

Gurtha stood up and placed a hand on Paddy's shoulder.

"Well, you read and I'll drive down into the Port to buy us some fish for supper."

Paddy nodded.

"I'll be fine here. Maybe you could get me some Hamlet – the small ones?"

"I'll only be an hour or so."

He looked at Paddy. He had moved to the sofa and looked relaxed; glasses perched on his nose, hands gripping his book from the Belfast library, head down, immersed. He couldn't escape from the olive grove. With the gate locked, the olive grove was well fenced in. Not a single sheep or goat had managed to find a way in. Paddy certainly wouldn't find a way out.

Paddy asked, "Can I come with you?"

Gurtha gently insisted, "You'll be exhausted after yesterday. You stay here and read. When I get back, we'll have a beer together and I'll make dinner. The front door is open in case you want to sit in the gazebo but I'm going to lock the front gate after me. No-one will bother you."

Paddy held the book in his hands and looked into Gurtha's eyes. Paddy's face relaxed again.

"You go on then. I'll be alright."

As the grey Clio bumped its way down and around the bends towards the Port of Soller, clouds of dust puffed into the air behind him.

♥

That first holiday after Llanthony Abbey dictated the way their relationship developed. Henry and Cornelia typically found a holiday home somewhere. Andrew and Bosie were no longer invited – only Gurtha. The year after Llantony they rented a house in a small hamlet outside of Saint-Beat in the foothills of the Pyrenees.

The three of them drove the final stretch of the journey climbing into the mountains. Gurtha sat in the back of the car watching Cornelia. Her skin paper thin and white. Her hair cut into a thick black bob sleek like seal. She wore a pink ribbon tied around her neck fastened with a gold heart. He felt waves of peace flood through him as though he was at home. Outside, poplar trees whizzed by like thick feathers tickling the sky. Cornelia talked but he couldn't make out what she was saying. It didn't matter.

He listened to her words the way you listen to a babbling stream. He didn't feel a need to say anything. He wished that the journey would never end.

It was dark by the time they arrived at the hamlet. There were two or three houses apart from their chateau which stood on a small mound, silhouetted against the starry sky like a small castle in a fairy tale. A wrought iron gate opened onto a jasmine covered terrace. In the darkness the sweet, musky smell of honeysuckle and jasmine hung in the air. As Henry searched his pockets for the keys, Gurtha looked over the wall amazed to see a two hundred and fifty foot drop. He sat on the cold stone watching Henry. After looking over the wall, Cornelia put her hands over her eyes, shouting,

"Don't sit there – it's dangerous."

Gurtha leant back, swung his legs up and lay on the top of the wall, looking at the stars.

"I don't think we're going to have another incident like Llanthony do you? What amazes me is that when I look at the stars instead of looking down, I don't feel afraid. If I were to look down, I would be terrified."

Cornelia took hold of his jacket, gripping it tightly.

"Don't be silly. Get off the wall."

As Henry turned the key in the lock of an arched wooden door, they heard the noise for the first time. It sounded as though someone was breathing heavily nearby.

"What's that?" Cornelia stepped back from the wall and looked up at the shuttered windows.

"It sounds as though it's coming from inside the house." Gurtha was now on his feet, standing beside Henry who was wearing a white Panama hat with a black ribbon, white shorts, a Polo t-shirt rather than his white shirt and cravat, knee length white socks and open-toed sandals. He placed a finger on his lips, tilted his head to the left and listened.

There was not a sound at first and then all three heard it again. It was distinctly the sound of deep breathing – a relaxed breathing – as though someone was soundly asleep. But there was no-one to be seen. The noise seemed to be coming from just above the first floor window. It was outside, not inside.

Henry whispered, "How curious." Gurtha moved towards the opened front door.

"Let's investigate. It could be coming from the bedroom. There could be someone inside."

Once inside, Gurtha marched towards the downstairs window of the sitting room. He pointed at a door covered in black velvet, "It's the room above this one. The entrance has to be through this door, but how strange." He tried to turn the brass door knob but the door was locked.

"Oh please don't," Cornelia whispered in a high pitched voice, as if afraid that someone might hear.

"Why have they covered the door in black velvet? It's sinister … creepy … Satanic."

Henry calmly placed his Panama hat on the kitchen table.

"I don't think so my dear. That is an over reaction. I think bed is called for and we will investigate in the morning. There is always a rational explanation. Don't you agree, Gurtha?"

"Nuala would be open to other possibilities."

"Like what?" Cornelia dropped her handbag on the sofa beside the window.

"Exactly like what? Now I'll never sleep."

Gurtha laughed.

"Where's your sense of adventure?"

Gurtha's room was at the end of a long corridor. He opened the door and moonlight fell onto a panelled wooden floor. The moon was full, rising from behind a craggy black mountain which lay still, like a spiky iguana, on the flat valley floor. He threw open the window and drank in the warm scented air. Frogs croaked to his left, beside a lily pool. A breeze unexpectedly swept through the garden below and then disappeared. All was still again. He left the windows open and sat on a patchwork quilted bed, wondering what the night would bring. There was no sign of Cornelia until early morning. There was no knock at the door but he heard the handle turn. He glanced at his watch; it was five in the morning.

He closed his eyes and pretended to be asleep. He heard his own breath turning shallow and more rapid. He felt Cornelia's lips against his. She gently rested her lips then against his cheek – as light a touch as a butterfly settling on a rose petal. He couldn't pretend anymore. He opened his eyes and she slid under the sheets and slipped her arms around his shoulders, laying her head on his chest, listening to the beat of his heart. He reached his hand to touch her and felt the smooth silkiness of her nightdress. He took his hand away quickly and placed it on the cotton sheets. Cornelia rolled onto her back and placed her hands beside her. They stared together at the ceiling, listening to the birds breaking the silence of the night with intermittent cheeps. Cornelia whispered, "Do you believe in such a thing as perfection?"

Gurtha felt this mouth dry up and his words came out in a crackled way, "I do."

He heard Cornelia sigh deeply before asking, "What is it?"

"It's a moment of freedom." Gurtha closed his eyes. He was not thinking about what he was saying.

"Freedom from what?" There was stillness in Cornelia's body beside him, which made Gurtha feel as though time was collapsing into itself, disappearing into a vortex.

THE SECRET WOUND

"Freedom from wanting anything to be different. Letting the moment be."

"Like now?"

Gurtha smiled, "Yes, like now."

Cornelia twisted the blonde plait on her shoulder.

"My sister, Amelia, was perfect. Not like me."

Gurtha's voice was soft and gentle.

"Why don't you tell me what happened to her? I would like to know."

Cornelia shook her head on the pillow.

"Nobody knows, you see. How can you talk about something that you don't know?"

They lay together in silence for almost thirty minutes, before Cornelia left the bed, without saying another word. He heard her feet pad across the floor and the door clicked closed as Gurtha breathed deeply. There was a hint of her scent in air – herbiness, like rosemary and thyme roasting in a summer sun, with a slight whiff of mint. She was a sacrament for him.

Over breakfast they ate fresh baguettes which Henry had discovered in a patisserie in a village a few kilometres from their hamlet. Cornelia sat very straight in a Van Gogh-like wooden chair. She had placed a pink bow in her hair, which made her look even more child-like. She was dressed completely in white – with a long flowing skirt and a sleeveless white blouse with rippled layers of fine silk. She ate her bread with her lips closed. She stared straight at him as Henry served coffee. Gurtha couldn't make out what her eyes were telling him.

Cornelia jumped to her feet as though she had suddenly remembered something.

"Let's find out what made the noise last night."

She took Gurtha by the hand and then caught Henry's hand and pulled them both behind her, laughing as they burst through the front door, turned left past the lily pond, onto the terrace studded with crimson geraniums.

"Sschuuhhh. Listen." Cornelia continued to hold onto Henry and Gurtha. She looked up towards the rooftop .

There was silence. From the silence emerged the sound of breathing – a deep husky breathing.

"It's still here." Cornelia dropped the hands of Henry and Gurtha and covered her face.

"What is it?"

As she asked the question there was another sound of stirring in the air – a movement of form – quickening into life. All three now looked upwards and witnessed the slow flapping feathered wings of a snowy owl circle three times around them before taking a course of flight towards the iguana mountain in the distance.

"The wise old owl – it's a good sign," Cornelia whispered, staring at the owl until it disappeared from sight.

There was a day towards the end of the week, when Henry had a cold and chose to sit in a café and read while the others went canyoning. Cornelia momentarily returned to her energetic old self. She and Gurtha scrambled into wet suits at the bottom of the iguana mountain and then, with the help of a guide, they climbed the mountain. The path became increasingly narrow. At times there was only enough space for one foot to be placed in front of the other. To stay on the path, they had to hold onto plants growing out from cliff edges. Cornelia moved quickly, without hesitation, whereas Gurtha could feel his stomach tightening and his breathing rasping at the back of his throat. Cornelia looked around at him and laughed, "Don't worry; we definitely won't be coming back down on this path. It will be easier in the water."

They reached the canyon after two hours. The guide instructed

THE SECRET WOUND

them, "Follow me. Don't wade to the left. There are several underground caves and strong currents. Six people died here last year after being swept underground and not being able to find a way out."

Cornelia didn't wait. She jumped into the water first, rolled onto her back and waved at them, "Come on – don't be cowards. It's easy."

Gurtha was the last to jump. If he could have walked back down the mountain along an easier path, he would have, but he knew that the path down would be worse than facing the waters in the canyon. He jumped. It took an hour to descend – scrambling over rocks, walking through emerald pools surrounded by trees, jumping from small waterfalls. Cornelia walked and swam side by side with the guide while Gurtha struggled to keep up. After half an hour, when the waterfalls were behind them, Gurtha was able to swim more freely and for the rest of the journey he felt like a salmon, his body flooding with excitement, in anticipation of what was coming next.

The letters started arriving one week after leaving Saint-Beat.

Dear Gurtha,

You said that "perfection" is freedom from wanting anything to be different. Letting the moment be. How does that relate to Good and Evil? I can decide to commit an act which others may consider "Evil". Is that perfection – if it is letting the moment be?

Cornelia

Gurtha found himself waiting for the post to arrive with a sense of excitement. What question would Cornelia ask him? What answer would he give? It was like a game of chess without rules. He didn't know into which square he would move – it depended upon the question posed by Cornelia.

Whether it was the hot Mallorcan August breeze or the smell of rosemary, thyme and mint blowing through the window of Clio which made him remember Saint-Beat after such a long time, he wasn't sure. The memories of that week surfaced with the force of a tsunami, crushing over the top of him. Laying stark his primal desire to know what had happened to Henry and what had changed Cornelia. How could she have begun a relationship with Barry?

♥

He parked the car some distance from the house. He didn't want Barry to see it. He opened the wooden gate leading into a small rose garden. As he walked along the path, he felt strangely disorientated, nauseous and dizzy. As he knocked on the front door, he caught sight of his reflection in the glass and it frightened him. He didn't recognise himself. His hair was dishevelled; his eyes looked a little wild – opened too wide – staring, as though he had seen a ghost. He heard the familiar click of heels along the marble hallway. Cornelia looked at him through the glass panel. Her appearance wiped out his reflection. He thought he saw a faint smile on her lips, as though she had guessed that he would visit. The door swung open.

"Where's Paddy?" She leaned forward to kiss him on both cheeks. He looked into her eyes. He could see now that she had aged. He noticed that her eyes were slightly puffy and lined at the corners. Had she been crying? She was wearing eye liner and it made her eyes look more sunken in her face. He noticed a small blemish on her nose with concealer to hide it. Her hair looked

THE SECRET WOUND

slightly brittle and broken compared to what he remembered – her neck wrinkled when she bent her head forward.

"Come in. Where's Paddy?" She repeated.

Gurtha stepped into the hallway and trailed his fingers through his hair, "He's reading."

"Coffee?" Cornelia turned into the kitchen.

Gurtha hesitated in the hallway, almost tempted to retrace his steps and leave. He was filled with a strong sense of foreboding. He listened as a chainsaw cranked into life in the back garden. Its drone insistent and deliberate – then a splutter – silence. It started again with increased intensity.

"Barry's cutting wood for the winter."

Unaware that Gurtha was there, Barry stood beside a pile of pine, almond and olive trunks, wearing a white shirt and jeans. He took an axe from the ground, placed a log on a plinth of wood and began to axe it into kindling. His face glowed in the early morning sunshine. He raised the axe above his head and swung down swiftly on the pine log. It splintered in two. He straightened the two halves and swung again at one of them. His eyes focused on the wood. Beside him a small fire was smouldering.

"We're not meant to burn anything until October. It's illegal. Don't you love it when you get away with it?"

Gurtha caught Cornelia by the wrist.

"You have to tell me what happened to Henry."

Cornelia pulled her wrist free, "What do you mean? What happened to Henry? He died."

Gurtha looked through the window again. Barry lifted the chainsaw and plunged it into an olive tree trunk.

"At Easter when we were together in La Quinta, he seemed well."

Cornelia spooned coffee into a filter jug. She glanced at him with what he recognised as total disdain.

"Henry was not a young man. He had a heart condition. He died from heart failure. Admittedly, it was shocking that he had only just been discharged from hospital and I thought that he was recovering. I do not know where you are going with this line of questioning. What do you think happened to him? No-one lives forever."

Gurtha took two steps back and looked again through the window. Barry rubbed his hands on a cloth before he placed on top of the axe. He walked towards the house. Gurtha whispered,

"He's coming."

Pouring the boiling water through the coffee filter, Cornelia whispered,

"Please go. We need to talk, but not now. It's not the right time."

She gently pushed Gurtha towards the door. She hesitated, her voice trembling.

"Did Nuala say something to you about Henry? Is that what this is about?"

Gurtha found himself intuitively lying.

"Yes she did. That's what I wanted to talk to you about."

Cornelia opened the door and kissed him briefly on the cheek.

"It's complicated, but I do want to tell you. We owe it to one another, don't we? Honesty – no matter how painful it is. That was our motto, was it not? You said our relationship was about 'The Good, the True and the Beautiful.' You said that to live up to that was terrifying to others. When you don't live up to it yourself – life isn't worth living is it?"

The kitchen door creaked open as Barry came in from the garden. Cornelia gently pushed Gurtha out of the front door and closed it, leaning back, sighing deeply before gathering herself into a state of composure and walking lightly towards Barry.

"I knew that you would be needing a coffee."

She threw her arms around him, hugging him, unable to stop crying.

Barry stepped back and held her at a distance, looking into her eyes which no longer seemed so threatening but more like dulled emeralds.

"What's going on?"

Cornelia lifted a tissue and wiped her eyes.

"You don't love me do you? I know it – even if you won't admit it."

♥

Driving back to Paddy in La Torretta, Gurtha remembered the bedroom in Saint-Beat, the moonlight streaming through the window, the owl sleeping above in the rafters, the sense of Cornelia's presence by his side, requiring nothing more than stillness and silence in response. It was then he knew that, with her, he was capable of touching something beyond, something mysterious and deeply joyful. It needed nothing else than listening to her breathing, feeling her closeness, smelling the aura around her as though Cornelia was a burning stick of incense. Why did he now feel impelled to control her beauty, her spirit, her will? It was like wishing to pin a butterfly to a board and give it a label. He had no idea why he had tried to influence her by lying that Nuala had said something about Henry. Maybe it was a bait to continue an intimate conversation with her – an attempt to return to the feelings they both shared at Saint-Beat.

As he rounded the last bend and the car bumped roughly over the rocky path, he knew that it was the absence of her questions which he missed most, more than the absence of her physical presence. In her presence there was an awakening of some kind of intuition of a beauty beyond form – a knowing. Her questions were the bridge to a connection to a spirit greater than either of them. As he stopped at the gate leading to La Torretta, he knew that in one way they were soul mates but in another way there was a dark energy which swirled around their being. A dark cloud enveloped them; a cloud veiling what was hidden, veiling the unspoken lies which nourished them.

♥

That night Gurtha had a dream in which he walked along a narrow path. On his left was a wire fence beyond which lay a long flat field leading to West where the sun was setting. To his right was a steep drop into a canyon with sheer sides. The narrow path was covered with glossy magazine pages which had been scattered as far the eye could see ahead of him. It was slippery to walk on these, so he walked slowly, becoming more aware with every step, of the danger of falling. It became increasingly harder to know where the path lay below the shiny pages. He felt a familiar sense of panic arise in his stomach and chest. The fence to his left was too high to climb, yet the flat ground leading to the sunset so attractive and easy to walk. The sun was touching the horizon. There was nothing familiar around – only wide open spaces which seemed more appealing than continuing alone on this narrow slippery path. He felt trapped – no way forward, no way back no way to the right, no way to the left. He stopped, frozen with fear. Then on his left, on the other side of the fence stood the shadowy figure of a man. The sun had set now and it was not possible to make out his features – only that he was smaller than Gurtha and that his head was shaved. It was also difficult to say what he was wearing. He was more like a walking shadow, an embodied presence. The

　　　　　　　　　THE SECRET WOUND

man reached his hand towards Gurtha. Gurtha grasped it tightly and then, with his help, heaved himself over the fence and fell on the grass on the other side. The man disappeared. Gurtha walked towards the horizon where the sun had also vanished. He felt relief. He knew who the man was. It was Paddy. He looked back at the fence and the ravine. He knew he would have to return, but not now – for the time being, he was safe and so was Paddy.

DAY 11

WEDNESDAY 21ST AUGUST 2013

"I WANT TO SING LIKE THE BIRDS SING,
NOT WORRYING ABOUT WHO HEARS OR
WHAT THEY THINK."
J RUMI

GURTHA WAKENED early and turned on his side to see the alarm clock – 3.00 am. His heart sank – he could not get back to sleep. He remembered another dream from the previous night. Nuala and he were flying through the air together as though they had sky dived from a plane without parachutes. Gurtha felt strong and peaceful and caught hold of Nuala's hand saying, "Look we can do this … We can float down like a leaf." They held both hands together, circling around and around, laughing, enjoying the descent. They were not afraid. Gurtha let go of Nuala's hand and spun away from her on his own. He landed – bouncing on springy green grass. There was a house to his right, which he entered. It was an old tumble down house with wooden window frames and crumbly stone walls. There was glass in the windows. He stood behind the window on the bottom floor, watching Nuala descend, falling through the sky, effortlessly dropping. She landed, tumbling ever so gently like a child rolling down a hill on Easter Monday side by side with her Easter Egg. He rushed out to meet her. They embraced one another. He sat on the grass beside her, waiting for her to speak. She whispered to him, "You're on the

THE SECRET WOUND

right path. It's going to be OK. You'll find out."

Inside La Torretta, he closed his eyes. There was silence within the room and outside. It was not a calming silence because he became increasingly aware of the churning thoughts in his head. Not that he knew what he was thinking about – only that his mind was not still. Neither was his body. His legs were restless. They wanted to move but he forced them to stay still. He pressed his head into the pillow which was so soft that he could feel through to the hardness of the mattress below. The pillow was soaking with sweat. He turned it over and for a moment it was cool and soft – almost delicious – until he became aware of thoughts again – whirring endlessly within the space of his head. His heart began to thump and quiver in his chest in a frightening way. It boomed so loud, he heard it in his ears, a wild thumping, a drumming, a warning of his own fragility, mortality – that one day it would stop. One moment would be its last palpitation. Fibrillatio and exhalation of the breath would follow. The awareness of that seem to make it beat even faster, louder, heavier within an arising cloud of seething anxiety and panic. How would he find out who had murdered Nuala? If it was Paddy – what would Nuala want him to do about that?

He sat upright. The night before he hadn't closed the shutters. It was a full moon. The steely light bathed the room. He placed his feet on the tiled floor and allowed the coolness to seep through him like spring water in a stream. He listened for noises from Paddy in the bedroom next door. There was a low level snore, barely audible. He got to his feet and walked to the window. Nothing moved. Everything held in stillness – the silver fleck of the sea in the distance, the pine trees to his right puffy black clouds pushing into the sky, the twisted olive trees to his left, ancient arms posing relentlessly in an unknown dance of minute movement only detected in time with eyes like Gurtha's which occasionally could see through time, present past and future. He glanced at the clock again – 3.30 am. Only half an hour since he had awakened and the stretch of time that remained for the sun at dawn felt unbearable.

He fumbled for his slippers – shaking each one before placing it on his feet in case there were scorpions inside. He had seen one, on the second day – only a few centimetres long, transparent with small pincers like a crab. He pulled the sheet over the pillows, as though he covering a corpse, before making his way into the box room where in his suitcase he had stored letters which Cornelia had sent him since Llanthony Abbey. He opened one from those early days. Cornelia had written,

"When Socrates was in prison awaiting his execution, he heard a fellow prisoner singing a complex lyric by the poet Stesichorus. He begged the man to teach him the poem. He was asked why. He replied, "So I can die knowing one thing more."

Cornelia asked, *"What would you want to learn if you only had one week to live?"*

Gurtha couldn't remember how he had replied. He hadn't the energy to look through the remaining letters for the answer. He only had Cornelia's letters – not his replies. What would he want to learn with only one week to live? He didn't know. He only knew that by the end of his forty days in Mallorca he wanted to find out what had happened to Nuala and what had happened to Henry. There was something which Cornelia was holding back. With Barry around it was going to be difficult to find out what she was concealing. At least yesterday he had made a small step forward in opening up a conversation.

He returned to his bedroom and looked at the clock – 4.00 am. He craved sleep – to be able to lie down, close his eyes and drift into that place which was always unknown and yet always like home

– dreamless sleep – leaving thoughts completely behind - finding peace in the small death – the disappearance of the world with all its pushes and pulls. He crawled under the sheets, stretched his hands down by his side, stared at the ceiling and felt a gentleness welling within him, stirring calmness from the deep. He allowed himself to sink into it. It felt that he was being taken somewhere, softly, leaving thoughts behind on the surface. He was sinking at last into sleep. Sleep. Sleep. Beautiful sleep.

DAY 12

THURSDAY 22ND AUGUST 2013

THE NEXT day Gurtha wakened with the smell of tobacco in the bedroom. Paddy was making noises downstairs. A frying pan, which Paddy had made for Nuala, was being put to work as Paddy cooked a traditional Ulster 'fry'. Bacon sizzled, mingling with the tobacco and, before opening his eyes, Gurtha took a few minutes to enjoy imagining the scene below – Paddy in his element, slicing tomatoes in half, crisping the bacon, no doubt searching for his potato bread and soda bread and in their absence settling to fry any bread he could find. He wouldn't be able to find the wheaten bread which Gurtha had put in the freezer. That would be a surprise for him.

He threw the sheets back and stretched, picked up the journal beside the clock and lifted his mobile phone. There was a message. It was from Cornelia. He eagerly tapped it open:

"Sorry for yesterday. Didn't mean to be so horrible. You know that everything has changed with Henry's death. Bring Paddy to the Feast of St Bartholomew on Saturday. We can have dinner with everyone. Afterwards, we need to talk. Cx"

Gurtha immediately texted back:

THE SECRET WOUND

"See you in the Plaza, Saturday at 8.00 pm. Gx"

He jumped downstairs two stairs at a time and slapped Paddy on the back.

"Thanks for breakfast. I'm starving. How did you sleep?"

Paddy scooped a fried egg onto a plate.

"Not bad. Not the same as home, but not bad. That's a great frying pan Michael made for me. Nothing sticks to it. Your mother would griddle potato bread the best on it."

He juggled two fried tomatoes onto the spoon. Gurtha carried the plates to the table, "I thought you had made the frying pan. Did you not?" Gurtha questioned in a low pitched, matter of fact way.

"No. It was Michael who was a dab hand with metal. We called him the cast master." Paddy chuckled. "He made them for anyone who asked. I helped him to sneak them out of the factory under my jacket. We were never found out. One of those frying pans flew out every week to a new home."

Gurtha looked at Paddy. He had a sense that this was the truth. Michael had made the frying pan. It was not so significant, yet it seemed important. Paddy had always said that he had made the pan. The fact that Paddy had made it was the only reason Gurtha had brought it all the way to Mallorca. He had imagined Paddy bringing all of his skills into the making of the pan which symbolised the pride of his trade. If it wasn't Paddy's at all and he admitted this, maybe there would be no more lies from Paddy. Gurtha looked at him across the table - he had shaved quite well, with only a small nick of blood on his chin. He seemed to know what Gurtha was thinking.

"I got too close to the razor."

Gurtha patted his hand, "You're all spruced up. We'll have to find somewhere to go. How about a little tour of the island? Then tomorrow it's back to work. You can help me in the gallery."

Paddy dipped his wheaten bread into his runny fried egg.

"When's your mother coming?"

"Paddy, where do you think Nuala is?"

Paddy shook his head, "I don't think she died."

"What do you suppose happened to her, then?"

"It was a funny business. I didn't like what I saw."

Gurtha watched the egg run down the side of Paddy's chin. Paddy fumbled in his pocket for a rolled up white tissue.

"I don't know why I was sent out. If I had stayed with her, she might still have been alive." There was wateriness in his eyes. His nose began to run. He wiped his mouth several times with the tissue which was now shrinking into a small circular ball which he rolled across his upper lip.

Gurtha searched for a new tissue in the kitchen drawer. He sat down beside him, lifted his box of Hamlet, pulled one out, lit it for him and passed it to Paddy who whispered.

"It wasn't an accident."

Gurtha listened carefully. He asked, "What happened, Paddy? Do you remember?"

Paddy shook his head.

"She had no reason to go up those stairs. She was dressed to go out. There was the downstairs toilet. With her bad heart, why would she have gone upstairs? She only went up to bed at night. Once she was dressed for the day that was it – downstairs."

Gurtha wiped his eyes with the tissue, got to his feet, lifted the two empty plates and took them to the sink.

"What made her go upstairs Paddy?"

Paddy carried the cups to the sink, "She would want the truth to be known. She was an awful one for the truth. She never listened to a word I'd say, you know. She thought I was a liar."

THE SECRET WOUND

Gurtha rinsed the plates and placed them in the wooded slotted shelf above the sink for drying.

"Were you?"

Paddy took the drying cloth and started to dry the plates.

"Was I what?"

"A liar."

"Show me someone who says they aren't and I'll show you a liar."

Gurtha laughed.

"There's no arguing with that now, is there? But tell me what made her go up the stairs and why did you go out?"

"She told me to go out. She wanted me to buy bread and milk."

"Why would she have gone upstairs?"

"There was something funny about that. But then, she liked her secrets."

Paddy lit another cigar.

"You know, I loved Nuala but I never told her. When she comes home, I'll tell her. I don't know what she will say, mind you. It will be a shock for her. But I have to tell her anyway, even if she doesn't like it."

DAY 13

FRIDAY 23RD AUGUST 2013

"LET YOURSELF BE DRAWN BY THE STRONGER
PULL OF THAT WHICH YOU TRULY LOVE."
J RUMI

GURTHA DECIDED to take Paddy back to Belfast earlier than planned. It was clear that he was suffering from dementia. He needed to be properly assessed and Gurtha had to decide what was the best care that could be provided for him in Belfast.

He texted Cornelia to explain that he wouldn't be able to attend dinner on the Feast of St Bartholomew, asked her to confirm that Angelina was happy to manage the exhibition and that he would let them both know when he planned to return.

Outside, Paddy agitatedly waved a rolled up newspaper to scare a hawk moth which was hovering beside a bush of delicate blue flowers. Its wings whirred and hummed. Paddy was wearing only a white vest on top of his khaki shorts. He threw the newspaper on the ground as Gurtha approached with a cup of coffee.

The hawk moth lay dead on the gravel.

"I didn't touch it." He shook his head. "Never touched it."

Gurtha sat the mug of coffee on the table set for breakfast and picked up the dead hawk moth.

"It had to be an accident then, didn't it? Shame. It's beautiful and it wouldn't hurt you."

THE SECRET WOUND

Paddy slid onto the wooden chair beside the table.

"These tiny black flies bite you."

Gurtha shook his head,

"I don't think they do. They're like the flies in Belfast. They don't bite you, do they?"

Paddy shook his head.

"We're flying back to Belfast this evening. You'll be glad to get home – won't you?

Gurtha buttered some toast for Paddy and placed a large teaspoonful of orange marmalade on top.

Paddy lifted the toast slowly to his mouth, mumbling as he chewed on it, "Can I not stay with you?"

"Well I am going back with you. We will be together."

Paddy smiled and nodded, "That's good. We will be on holiday together, like the old times with Nuala." He rested his swollen arthritic hand on the table cloth. He stared straight ahead of him, peering into the distance, down the track which led to the front gate. The donkey in the field to the left brayed loudly three times. Paddy turned to look at Gurtha,

"That donkey has got some lungs on it. Who's that man at the gate? Does he own the donkey?"

Gurtha jumped to his feet. There was a man at the front gate, opening it. It was Barry. He threw the gates wide open jumped into his Range Rover, and skidded along the path to the front door. He jumped out, his leather sandals crunching on the gravel and sending small clouds of dust into the air.

Although it was early morning, Barry was sweating, his face blotchy red, his eyes staring wide open and the skin above his upper lip solid and white.

"What's the matter, Barry? Has something happened? Where's Cornelia?"

Barry wiped his forehead with a white handkerchief which he then stuffed in his trouser pocket.

"She's gone for a walk with Angelina to Ramon Llull's cave."

Gurtha pulled out a chair for Barry to sit down. He asked, "Off the road to Valledemosa?"

"No on the Puig de Randa, near the Sanctuary of Cura. Cornelia's obsessed by sacred sites."

Paddy watched with his mouth open. He crossed his two arms over his chest.

Gurtha got to his feet, "Let me get you a coffee."

He left Barry sitting beside Paddy and walked slowly towards the kitchen. Paddy picked up the rolled up newspaper which Gurtha had left on an empty chair. He held onto it tightly looking at Barry in silent curiosity.

Over coffee, Barry explained, "She is very jealous, you see. Jealous and angry. Her anger is frightening. But you must know that. Vitriolic. You know her longer than I do. You'll have seen that side to her?"

Gurtha listened intently with his head to one side. He nodded at Barry although it was a lie. He had never seen Cornelia seethe with caustic anger the like of which Barry described.

Barry continued, sipping his coffee quickly so that it dripped down his chin.

"She frightens me. She accused me of not loving her. But she's the one who has never loved me."

Gurtha folded his hands on his lap, asking in a soft voice, "Why does she frighten you?"

"I know what she did to Henry. If she could do that to someone she was married to for such a long time, what could she do to me?"

"What did she do to Henry?"

THE SECRET WOUND

"She was heartless in the way she treated him." He hesitated as though about to say more, but coughed, pulling a cotton handkerchief out from his trouser pocket.

"In what way?"

"He found us in his bed two weeks before he died. It might have been the shock of that that killed him. Why did she make it so easy for him to see us?"

He blew his nose again and asked Gurtha.

"Did you have sex with her?"

Gurtha looked at Paddy who was dozing and then back at Barry, "Of course not." He whispered, "Who do you take me for? I was a friend to both of them – Cornelia and Henry."

Barry's face flushed even redder. He rubbed it with the palms of both hands; he sniffed at the air like a rabbit, his nostrils quivering quickly in and out. His ears twitched as he whispered, "Have you ever regretted getting yourself into a bad place?"

He shook his head, catching sight of Gurtha's eyes, "No. I didn't think you would have. Once you go there – it's downhill all the way – you can't escape. You're either the lucky one or you're telling lies. I find it hard to tell the difference these days with people."

Gurtha glanced again at Paddy, now snoring, his mouth open, in the chair beside him. Without taking his eyes away from Paddy's stubbly chin, he asked Barry, "I don't understand why you are telling me this. What do you want from me?"

Barry laughed harshly.

"I want you to work it out. You know her better than I do. When you work it out, for God's sake help me know what to do."

Gurtha straightened up in the chair and sipped on his coffee.

"You said that she accused you of not loving her – is that true?"

Barry held his head in his hands.

"Maybe is. She entrapped me. She fell in love with my money not with me. I was a fool not to see it."

"But Henry had money. He was one of most generous people I have ever met."

Barry shook his head.

"No, he didn't. His pension fund was badly hit by the economic crisis. He only received a quarter of what he anticipated. Cornelia was angry with him for that. You would have thought to hear her talk that he was personally responsible for the global economic recession. She called him incompetent and selfish for expecting her to live on a pittance of a pension."

Gurtha poured Barry another coffee.

"She never spoke badly of him to me or complained about money."

Barry spooned three teaspoons of sugar into his coffee and stirred it thoughtfully.

"She didn't want you to know who she really is. Apart from wanting my money, I think she enjoyed not hiding her dark side from me. She had kept it hidden for years – since childhood – from what I've heard. She is a complex woman. Dangerous I would say. You have experienced one side of her. I another. I don't think that either of us really knows her or what she is capable of doing. "

♥

Cornelia parked the car at the bottom of the hill in Randa. It was eleven in the morning. The houses were shuttered with green persianas firmly closed to exclude the fierce summer sun. A small bar spilt over onto the street where two cyclists sat in slinky cycling gear having a glass of orange juice, recovering from

THE SECRET WOUND

their heat acclimatisation training. The rays from the sun seared Cornelia's shoulders as she stepped from the car. She brushed at her shoulders with her hand as though she was flicking away a fly, as thyme and rosemary scents filled the air.

Inside the car, Angelina pulled down the mirror in the passenger seat and adjusted her lipstick before pulling a wide brimmed straw hat into place. She stepped delicately out, looking around her as though waiting for cameras to flash before walking to the back to help Cornelia with the rucksack.

Cornelia replaced her high heels with sturdy walking sandals. She pulled a loose long sleeved linen shirt over her brightly coloured t-shirt and linen skirt.

"Isn't it amazing to think that *he* would have walked up this road" She glanced at Angelina from under her hat. "I like to imagine that I *am* him. Once we leave the town behind, the views, sights and sounds will be almost exactly the same as he would have experienced over 700 years ago. I could be him. I'm smelling what he smelt, seeing what he saw, hearing bird noises like he heard, feeling the heat against my face as he could have felt it. I love this kind of pilgrimage. We can become one with Ramon Llull. He's alive again. He's walking the earth. The only thing to bear in mind is not to let your own thoughts intrude. Then you've given birth to him again."

Angelina laughed as she lifted a pineapple from the boot of the car and placed it in Cornelia's rucksack, "He did have a wonderful mind."

"The spaces between his thoughts allowed wisdom to emerge. We can see, touch, smell, taste and hear in the way that he did. So let's do it."

With the pineapple safely inside the bag, Cornelia added four oranges, a coconut and a tall red candle. She swung the rucksack onto her back, and began the slow walk uphill. Angelina followed a few steps behind. Cornelia stopped, looked around, "You go first. You set the pace. I'll follow."

Wearing denim shorts, a white t-shirt and trainers, Angelina ran a few steps ahead. Cornelia shouted after her, "Take the rucksack then if you have so much energy."

Angelina stood with her hands on her hips breathing in the perfumed air, one hand stretched out for the rucksack.

"It's OK. I'm training for the Iron Man. This is easy peasy."

They walked at first in silence, one behind the other, on the left hand side of the road, crossing over to the right each time the bend swung sharply to the left. The valley floor quickly lay below. They passed the Sanctuary of la Gracia without stopping and ten minutes later arrived at a sign for La Ermita de Sant Honorat.

"Turn right. I've been here before. I'd like you to see it. Angelina turned right up a small path which led into the courtyard of the Hermitage. Angelina was about to walk into the doorway of the small Church when Cornelia caught her by the arm.

"First, over here. You have to read this." She pointed to a noticeboard, very similar to a noticeboard you would see in an old English Church. It had a poem written in several languages. "This changed my life. I came here on a school trip when I was eighteen."

Angelina wiped the sweat from her forehead with the back of her hand, removed the rucksack and sat it on the ground. Her t-shirt was sticking to her back.

"I can't read it without my glasses."

Cornelia placed a hand on her shoulder, "I've never seen you wear glasses."

Angelina rubbed her eyes, "No, I don't, except when driving. I quite like the outside world being a blur. It can be an advantage,

THE SECRET WOUND

you know. Nothing looks really ugly as it's never properly seen." She laughed, "I will grow old without worrying."

Keeping her hand on Angelina's shoulder, Cornelia began to read in loud measured tones:

To the Pilgrim

Set Out!
You were born for the road.

Set Out!
You have a meeting to keep.
Where? With whom?
You don't yet know
Perhaps with yourself?

Set Out!
Your steps will be your words
the road your song.
The weariness your prayer
And at the end
your silence will speak to you

Set Out!
Alone, or with others,
but get out of yourself.
You have created rivals –
you will find companions
You envisaged enemies –
you will find brothers and sisters.

Set Out!
You were born for the road,
the pilgrim's road
Someone is coming to meet you
is seeking you,
so that you can find Him.
In the shrine at the end of the road,
in the shrine at the depths of your heart.
He is your peace,
He is your joy.

Go!
God already walks with you.

"Is that why you came to Mallorca?" said Angelina, wriggling her shoulder free from Cornelia's hand.

"Yes. I suppose so. Henry and I bought the house in the Port over twenty years ago. We would come out three or four times a year. When he died it seemed the logical choice to move here permanently."

Angelina hoisted the rucksack onto her back.

"Did you know Barry before Henry died?"

"No. I met him shortly after Henry died." Cornelia swatted at a fly which settled on her lower lip.

"How did you meet him?" Angelina pulled her hat over her eyes.

"In a restaurant with friends. It was a coincidence that his father was a client of Henry's before Henry retired."

Cornelia took Angelina by the hand.

"Don't leave the path. There are crevasses in the ground into which people have been known to fall and disappear forever. Two

THE SECRET WOUND

years ago there was a woman walking near Valledemosa. They think that is what happened to her. She was never found. People say that the ground opens up, swallows you up and closes over again. They don't know where all the crevasses are. I think what really happens is that the crevasses are covered with ferns and other plants. It is easy to step on what seems to be safe ground."

Angelina quickened her pace behind Cornelia, "So nobody knows what happened to that poor women?"

Cornelia shook her head, "Nobody knows. What is horrific is that she must have been lying at the bottom of the crevasse and not have been able to find a way out. How long do you think it would have taken her to die?"

Angelina walked side by side with Cornelia, "Please don't talk about it. It's upsetting."

"Don't be so squeamish." Cornelia put her arm around Angelina' shoulder as they entered the courtyard. On their right was a wrought iron gate covered on the inside with fine bamboo cane.

"Through there." Cornelia pointed right.

Angelina rattled the handle, "It's locked."

Cornelia whispered, "I know the secret."

She reached her hand through a space in the cane fencing which looked as though it had been cut only to allow the handle to be grasped. She twiddled with something below the handle.

"It will open now."

She swung the gate open into the cloistered quadrangle.

Angelina took a deep breath.

"How beautiful."

The valley lay directly below them, falling from a steep cliff edge. To the right, the glass windows of houses in the town of Llucmajor twinkled. To the left, the steely stillness of the

Mediterranean sea lay, its grey sheen broken only by the island of Cabrera stretching out like a slumbering, elongated seal. Further left again could be seen the outline of a sweeping sketch of a majestic wave of mountains made by a flamboyant impressionist artist.

"In the fourteenth century the Hermitage was commissioned by two Knights who had lived previously as hermits for thirty years on the mountain. I've tried to discover where they lived but no-one seems to know. They only know of Ramon Llull's cave.

Cornelia passed three tall sentinel cypress trees daggering the turquoise blue sky, then increased her pace along a pathway with cabbages, lettuces and onions growing in the vegetable garden on her left. She spun around,

"We don't want to be seen. Quick - you're walking behind me again. You go first. Do you like it?"

Angelina tightened the straps on the rucksack so that it would sit higher on her back and walked ahead of Cornelia glancing to her right.

"Apart from the fact that you've put me in front, I don't know where I am going and I'm as blind as a bat - yes, I'm enjoying it. That's quite a drop isn't it?"

There was a low wall on her right with a sheer drop down into a valley cultivated with light green olive trees and a deeper emerald green oak. There were a few fields tilled already – the grass cut and resplendent with circular tubes of gold. Three gentle rolling hills signposted the way to the town of Manacor in the distance. Two small yellow finches threw themselves into the valley below.

Cornelia followed Angelina's gaze.

"In the morning, before the sun comes up and before a slither of moon disappears, Llucmajor is at its most magical. All of the lights on the roads are turned off and there is an orange glow from a scattering of houses where people have wakened. The buildings still haven't caught the golden light of the rising sun and lie charcoal grey against the green of the valley floor. It looks like a giant has let a fire go out and the last embers are fading. That's my favourite time of the day here."

Angelina stopped for a moment.

"It's magical."

"Yes. Keep walking. The monks live in these rooms. She pointed to the left where there was a row of closed windows but one open French door leading into the vegetable patch.

"I have something else to show you."

There was a small path which left the Hermitage behind and climbed further up the mountain, past a building which looked like a small Church. It was, in fact, the sepulchre for the monks who had died. Cornelia led the way to a hidden viewing point where there was no wall but only a sheer cliff face drop from an overhanging rock. She walked to the edge and stood looking into the distance.

Angelina shouted after her, "Be careful. It could crumble. It doesn't look safe."

Cornelia inched closer to the edge and turned to Angelina, "Come and see the view."

Angelina's heart fluttered, her breathing quickened.

"You're making me nervous."

Cornelia dropped to her knees and then sat on the outcrop and dangled her legs over the edge. A breeze had picked up from the valley floor blowing in from the West. Her linen skirt opened like a parachute. She laughed as she threw herself back on the smooth grey slab of stone that was the outcrop.

"What a coward you are."

Lying on her back she pointed at the clouds which were forming not so far above them, "Look, a seahorse. What do you see?"

Angelina's eyes were closed. She felt her lower lip tremble, her eyes watered uncontrollably. She turned away from the outcrop of rock and began to stumble back along the path they had come. The rucksack caught in the branches of an oak tree. She pulled forward and it released. She shot forward a few steps like an arrow from a bow. Tears ran down her face, mingling with rivulets of sweat. She panted and gulped at the air, stopping only to catch her breath when she reached the vegetable patch. She thought that she heard Cornelia scrambling down the path behind her. There were certainly stones rolling and twigs snapping behind her. She ran along the path ignoring the lettuces and onions pushing their way through dampened red soil on her right. A small black and tan dog ran out from the opened French windows, wagged its tail and followed her. A hawk flew in front of her, so close she heard its wings whistle before it dived into the valley. She fumbled with the secret lock on the gate. Out of the corner of her eye, she saw Cornelia walking along the path, stopping to pet the dog. The dog gave a small bark and then fell silent. Once in the courtyard, she turned right into the Church. She threw herself heavily onto the wooden pew. Her breathing quickly returned to normal. She felt her heart slowing down.

Cornelia slid into the seat beside her and rested her hands on her knees.

"I didn't mean to frighten you. It's so beautiful at the edge. You feel that you could fly with the hawks and falcons – dive at a delicious speed, dropping into the valley, fearlessly. You should be here when the sun sets. The clouds are layered – fine parchment white on top, then a layer of patched grey, with fluffy Scotties, Golden Retrievers and Poodles edged in tangerine. The sun sinks onto the horizon as though covered with a fine gauze. A halo of golden light sits above it, surrounded in turquoise like the sea at mid-day. It gently drops towards the horizon which is like purple wine. It dips in slowly, until the valley floor darkens, the edge of the mountain cuts a silhouette against the sky. Then it's gone. Gone. There's a hint of orange of where it has been above the dark charcoal horizon – like the glow around a candle. The turquoise turns even more green, the Poodle, Retriever and Scottie dogs head for home, moving south towards the island of Cabrera. As if by magic, you turn left and a path of pink and tangerine opens in the sky towards Manacor as though the sun has sent a last wave, a gesture of goodbye – a kiss to the East to remind it that it will be back tomorrow. You see it's beautiful – not scary."

Angelina pulled her hat off and tied her hair into a ponytail.

"It's the heights and edges. They remind me of Argentina."

Cornelia stared straight ahead. She twisted a handkerchief in her hands.

"Well - let's find Ramon Llull's cave before it gets too hot."

They climbed towards the top of Puig de Randa. Before they got to the Sanctuary of Cura, Cornelia pointed left where a small track wound its way along the top of the mountain.

"It's not so far."

There were no signposts to indicate the way.

"How did you originally find it? Angelina walked quickly behind Cornelia.

"I knew that it had to be somewhere near. I kept looking until I found it."

The path swung to the right and the cave was in sight. It was south facing and caught the sun rising and setting. Outside there was a stone statute of Ramon Llull with the head and arms missing.

Angelina placed the rucksack on the stony path.

"Maybe someone stole the head and arms for their olive grove. I can imagine the two arms sticking out the dry earth somewhere. They would look quite good. The head could sit in a dish on a garden table, like the head of John the Baptist."

Cornelia climbed into the cave with the pineapple in her hand.

"I think you've been working too hard in the art gallery. Pass me the rest of the fruit and we will leave Ramon Llull lunch."

After assembling the pineapple, kiwis, coconut and oranges in a circle on the sandy floor of the cave, Cornelia crossed her legs and sat at the entrance to the cave looking over Angelina's head into the valley below.

Angelina placed her hands on her hips and took a deep breath.

"It's not so steep at this point. Maybe he would have scrambled down the hillside here to find wild strawberries and oranges in the valley below."

Cornelia stood beside Angelina, "There is another cave – near to Valldemosa. We can see the sun setting over the sea. Would you like to see it? Few people know that it is there."

Angelina nodded.

"If you wear hiking boots you will feel safer." She paused and placed a hand once again on Angelina's shoulder, "What happened to you in Argentina to give you such a panic attack today?"

Angelina placed her hands over her face and gave a muffled response.

"It was my father. He was a journalist. He wrote articles exposing what the military junta were doing. When they captured my father we think that they drugged him, put him on a plane and dropped him alive into the Atlantic Ocean. They didn't want his body to be found. But we don't know for sure. We only know that he was taken at gunpoint from my aunt's house and

THE SECRET WOUND

never came back. I've tried to imagine what happened to him. It's terrible when you don't know for sure. Your imagination can take you into such frightening places. You fall deeper and deeper into your own worst nightmare. Every day I think of him and what might have happened to him. With each second of his descent must have felt as if he was crossing a terrifying Universe of space and time."

Cornelia shuddered, "Well, you're safe here. No-one is going to kidnap you in Mallorca."

"Maybe not, but Mallorca isn't exactly an island of saints is it? There are people with lots of money here and where there is money there are people who are predators on people with money. Even when you don't have money – there are still people who are predators. Their motivation is not about money but power and control. I realised that when I was taken hostage in Argentina."

Cornelia moved to sit on a smooth rock with a clearer view of the valley below.

"You never mentioned before that you were taken hostage. What happened?"

Cornelia handed Angelina a segment of orange.

Angelina nibbled at it.

"I was asleep. The 'militares' climbed over the roof and entered my bedroom. I shouldn't have left the window open but it was a sultry night and I needed a breeze in the room."

"What did they want from you?"

"They wanted someone to control – someone to terrify – nothing more. I wondered if they knew about my father but I don't think so. They never mentioned him. I think that if they had known – they would have liked to use that information to torture me. They would have enjoyed telling me what they did to him."

"How did you survive? You could have been another 'disaparecido'.

Angelina's shoulders shook.

"I did whatever they asked me to do, until they got bored and left me. We all do that don't we? We do whatever we have to do to survive."

DAY 14

SATURDAY 24TH AUGUST 2013,

GURTHA AND Paddy flew back to Belfast on Saturday 24th August. Once they landed, Gurtha hired a car and drove to the Accident and Emergency Department at the Royal Hospital. They sat together in the Waiting Room. Paddy smiled at Gurtha,

"What's wrong with you, son?"

Gurtha answered, "It's you Dad - your chest. We need to get it checked out. It shouldn't take long."

He had dressed Paddy in his best grey trousers, a white shirt and a royal blue cashmere jumper. His hair badly needed cutting as it curled greasily over the neck of his shirt. He had packed a small overnight case with Paddy's pyjamas, dressing gown and slippers in case they were needed. After a Nurse completed her admission forms, he was admitted to a private room and Gurtha helped him into his pyjamas. He slid down in the bed, with his head only just on the pillow, pulling the crisp white sheets up over his mouth.

"Where am I?" Paddy appealed to Gurtha.

"You're getting tests done. Remember I said that you needed to have your chest checked out?"

"I want to go home."

Gurtha nodded, "I'll get you home."

Paddy pushed the sheets away. His grey hairy chest visible under his white vest. The striped blue and red pyjama top was opened a button or two too many. Gurtha leaned forward and closed the two buttons. Paddy smiled at him, not moving away, not resisting, his head sinking once again deeply into the freshly starched pillow case.

When Paddy fell asleep, Gurtha continued to sit by his bedside. He felt waves of emotions lapping inside him without being able to label them. Then his body flooded with the dull ache of an ancient familiar sadness. He felt confused about the nature of this man in the bed who was breathing deeply. Who was Paddy? What was his relationship with Nuala? He realised that although he had lived with them for more than forty years, he really did not know.

He felt a surge of despair rise through his stomach and lodge itself, thumping like a heartbeat, in this throat. His hand moved towards Paddy's hand which lay like a claw knocker on top of the blue cotton cover. He hesitated to touch it. He didn't want to waken him. He swallowed deeply and placed his head on top of his arms resting on the sheets. He cried – not knowing why.

Images of Paddy's mother – Kathleen – 'Granny Maloney' came to Gurtha's mind. He had visited her with Paddy every Sunday until the age of eleven. Paddy deliberately took him the long way along a country lane over Black Mountain on the outskirts of Belfast. He didn't hold Gurtha's hand. He told him that he used to run along that road as a teenager and that he loved cross country running. He would train alone. A solitary thin runner in the mountains, running along the lane and then through fields, not stopping, running from home and running back, smelling the freshly cut grass, hearing the deep breathing of black bulls lying on a carpet of daisies, looking up and seeing white clouds tinged with orange change shapes from scotty terriers into dolphins. Paddy didn't say much on these walks to Granny Maloney, yet the silence wasn't an awkward one between them. It felt that there was something being communicated in the silence which didn't need words.

In those days, before Gurtha was twelve, they would knock on the door of a small terrace house at the bottom of the Glen Road. Granny Maloney would open the door, unsmiling, and turn her back on Paddy as she jerked the door open, allowing it to crash against the plaster wall. Sometimes the handle would dig into the plaster and a few flakes would fall onto the floor like snow drops. She was a hefty woman with bandaged, ulcerated legs. A skilfully located safety pin ensured the bandages didn't unravel. She sat on a large armchair and every evening Paddy's sister, Eilish, would bring a tray holding a large plate of dinner and a bottle of HP brown sauce.

Gurtha watched her tip the acrid sticky brown liquid onto the potatoes where it formed a small brown lake and then flowed over onto the steak and onions. When she had finished, she would lift a long metal box with seven slots onto her knees. Paddy would put coins and notes into each slot. That was his debt paid for the week.

These images flickered through Gurtha's mind as he rested his hand on top of Paddy's. He felt the gold ring on Paddy's pinky left finger. It was Kathleen's wedding ring. He had returned from his mother's funeral wearing it. That was a quarter of a century before. Gurtha couldn't remember why he didn't go to his grandmother's funeral or why he didn't say anything to Paddy about the fact that he was sorry that Paddy had lost his mother. Now the hardness of the ring touching his hand was like a judgement.

Since Nuala had died, this was the way his memory operated. It was as though he was going back in time – the way they say you do when you are about to die and you see your life flash in front of your eyes. For Gurtha it wasn't so much a single rapid picture show but more isolated images here and there of his sins of omission – of all of the missed opportunities for kindness with Paddy and Nuala. Now he knew the feelings of remorse, guilt and shame. It was not Paddy reminding him – only himself awakening the past. Gurtha recalled how Kierkegaard had said 'Life can only be understood backwards; but it must be lived forwards.' Waiting for Paddy to waken from his sleep, he began to understand what Kierkegaard might have meant. There is too much information to be taken in now – in the present moment. It's registered but not understood and then, when sufficient time has passed, it can be replayed on a screen – the film of our own life. You can laugh or cry for the first time as you begin to understand it.

He remembered walking with Nuala along the same road as a child. She dragged him by the hand into Kathleen's house. Inside the sitting room Granny Maloney sat on her favourite chair by the coal fire as Nuala screamed hysterically at her,

"You've taken the money from him. It's our money. We have nothing to eat and we can't pay the mortgage. What he hasn't given you, he has spent on horses and drink and you've encouraged him. You've had the nerve to take the very wages he earned to feed the family. What kind of mother are you?"

Nuala sweated and shook as she shouted across the room, standing over Kathleen. Kathleen looked white – all white. White curly hair with a small white clip holding her fringe to one side, a white woollen jumper and white bubbly knitted skirt which covered her knees and the white swollen bandaged legs. There was also a white ball of saliva appearing and disappearing in the corner of her mouth. It appeared when she opened her mouth, said nothing and disappeared when she closed it.

Kathleen lifted the tin box awkwardly onto her knees from under the armchair. She opened it, handing a roll of notes to

Nuala who fell silent for a few seconds, took the money and said in a calmer tone of voice, "If you take any more money from him, I'll divorce him. I'm going to see a solicitor this afternoon. You've been warned."

She turned on her high heels, caught Gurtha's hand, and pulled him through the open front door. Once in the street, she dropped Gurtha's hand, reached for the door knocker and slammed it shut. That was the last visit Gurtha ever made to Granny Maloney. There were no more walks over Black Mountain and no more stories from Paddy about his childhood.

DAY 15

SUNDAY 25TH AUGUST 2013

"SET YOUR LIFE ON FIRE.
SEEK THOSE WHO FAN YOUR FLAMES."
J RUMI

GURTHA PHONED the hospital early on Sunday morning to see if Paddy's test results were through. They were. He made an appointment to meet with the Senior Care Team Leader who would share the updated situation with him at 3.00 pm. The night before, he stayed in the Holiday Inn in the city centre. He had got up early and had gone for a swim before breakfast. He hadn't stayed in Paddy's house since Nuala died. The thought of sleeping there made his stomach flutter and flood with anxiety. The memory of Nuala's murder seemed more real at night. He decided to go there and find extra clothes for Paddy in case he had to stay longer in the hospital. He called into the corner shop to update Laura.

"Awful isn't it. He's worked all his life. You would think he would be able to enjoy a happy retirement. You must be worried about him."

He looked at Laura. She was biting her lower lip and looking tearful.

"You need to be careful that you don't end up like that – on your own. You should meet someone. It's lonely to live a life with no partner, no children to care about you."

Gurtha placed the coins for the wheaten bread into her hand.

"In reality we're all alone. We come into the world alone and we die alone – no matter how many people are with us. Maybe there are more lonely people in loveless relationships than there are those who live alone. If you are attached and dependent on anyone at some point you have to suffer – even if it is only when they die."

"Are you talking about Nuala?" Laura rang the money into the till.

"Yes. But I'm not getting something. I have something to learn from Nuala's death. I haven't learnt it yet. But it feels so close – that I am looking at it and not seeing it. I know that death is natural – that it goes with life. You see it everywhere – in the leaves falling from the trees, the oranges growing from flowers – the flower has to die to allow the orange to come into being. I get that intellectually but I'm not really getting it deeply. I can't think my way into understanding this. That's my problem. I'm thinking about it too much and it's driving me crazy. Yet that's what my job is. I'm a professional thinker." Gurtha laughed.

Laura laughed with him.

"I've no doubt that you will work it out. Don't forget to come and tell me what it is. Although from what you're saying – I will still have to work it out for myself.

Gurtha climbed the stairs to the front bedroom where Nuala stored her clothes. He had only looked briefly into it since Nuala had died – although the police had made a thorough forensic investigation. He opened the door slowly.

The room was like a burial tomb within a Pyramid. Here were all the relics Nuala would have wanted to take with her to the next land if she had been the wife of a Pharaoh. Nuala was a hoarder – storing everything in plastic bags. On the floor to his left there must have been a dozen different Pringle jumpers – unworn – in different colours – beige, fuchsia, marigold and emerald green. Another bundle of blouses, then skirts and trousers, all unworn, all of the highest quality. He felt his eyes stinging. He imagined her buying them – the pleasure – the dreams about when she would wear them. She never did. She kept buying more and more. Each jumper, blouse, pair of trousers, pleated skirt – small consolations stacked away in plastic bags to compensate for the lack of love from Paddy.

Cardboard boxes neatly stacked one on top of the other lined the far bedroom wall. He lifted one and opened it. His school jotters with his arithmetic notes, his essays and books from Primary School, enshrined. Nothing thrown away. His own life strangely dead in those boxes. There were even two small baby shoes from when he was less than a year old. What hopes and dreams did Nuala have for him?

He spotted a white box sitting on top of the dresser. He knew it contained the wedding album. He opened the box. The album was wrapped in white tissue paper, as if new. He lifted it out and removed the paper. It felt sacrilegious to open. It was something that Nuala had wanted to keep unspoilt. It had a padded white leather cover. In silver it said, "Our Wedding by Vogue". There was a page to write the details ... The Marriage of ... and ... Son of ... Daughter of ... on ... at ... Bridesmaids ... Best Man ... Groomsmen ... Reception at ... Honeymoon at ...Officiating Clergy ...

Nothing had been filled in. He turned a hard thick page and then slid back a page of fine transparent tissue paper which covered the first photo of Paddy's Mother, Kathleen and his sister Eilish. There were three other women whom Gurtha didn't recognise but he did recognise his cousins – Eilish's children Maeve and Thomas - who looked about seven and five. He carried the album over to the window to see it more clearly. Paddy's Mother was a big woman with a face like putty. She had a double chin. Her lips pulled into a straight line. Her eyebrows, two slanted lines on her forehead like the pitch of a steep roof. She wore a dark coat buttoned up to her neck. You couldn't see any blouse or hint of colour below the coat, only a small triangle of flesh. In her lapel she wore a carnation wrapped in silver foil. Eilish looked happier. Blonde hair curled onto her jacket. Her suit was lighter in colour. She had a white shirt below the jacket and pearls. She had two carnations in her lapel and smiled. Beside Eilish stood a long narrow-faced women with sad eyes, her lips pulled into the same expression as Kathleen's. Her coat buttoned up with enormous buttons all the way to her throat. She held a dark handbag with black leather gloves.

He turned the page. There was Paddy with his brother Dennis, who had died ten years before, standing outside the Church. His shoes were so shiny that you could see the clouds in the sky sitting on top of them. He had a double breasted jacket with a silky tie and white carnation. His arms were hanging by his side with his hands slightly closed. It was his hands; the way he was holding them hadn't changed. They were the same hands which Gurtha had patted the day before.

All of Paddy's soul – the part that never changes - seemed to be in his hands, not in his face. They even looked slightly swollen and arthritic but they couldn't have been. You would never have recognised Paddy by his face. He had a high forehead – unwrinkled, a full head of hair with a clear parting to the left, two sticky out ears and a forced smile.

Gurtha felt his eyes water again as he looked at Paddy staring at him. The space between Paddy in the photo and Gurtha seemed to get mixed up. It was as though Gurtha's non-existence at that point in time was held in the space between them and around them. As though Gurtha was aching to be born in that space, waiting for his being to happen, watching his father get ready to be married. There was something solemn about the occasion – something almost frightening about the commitment that was being made.

He turned another page. There was Nuala, her best friend and Matron of Honour, Veronica and Nuala's father John. Nuala wore a long white silk dress with tiny mother of pearl buttons on the upper part. A long veil covered her face. This must have been before she walked into the Church when the veil would lifted back from her face and Paddy would see her clearly for the first time that day. She was holding a bouquet of roses which were probably red – the photo was in black and white and the roses looked black. She looked at the camera out of the side of her eyes. She wasn't smiling; instead there was a look of great determination, as if she knew what she was stepping into. Yes that was it. She had the look of a martyr going to her death. Her father, John, looked as if he was attending her funeral, with the saddest eyes and the same putty face as his wife.

He flicked through the remaining photographs quickly to see if he could find one photograph where they were smiling. He found one, taken in the grounds of the Church. Nuala was holding Paddy's arm and they were looking into one another's eyes and smiling. The deed had been done.

The very last photograph was at the reception. A room filled with faces straining to turn to the camera. They were looking over their shoulders peeping into spaces to be seen. Nuala and

THE SECRET WOUND

Paddy were at the top table towards the back of the room. Gurtha shuddered as he realised that everyone in that photo was dead – everyone apart from Paddy. All of their lives up to that point had been lived with their hopes and fears, their joys and anxieties, their frustrations and fulfilments. Gone. Now they seemed to be held in the space between their faces in the photo and Gurtha. They were all around him in that empty space looking at themselves incarnate for an instant on Earth.

He wrapped the album once again in its tissue paper, which now felt like a shroud and placed it in the box, which seemed like a coffin and back onto the table, which felt like a sepulchre. He walked out of the room into the bathroom, turned on the cold tap and splashed his face with water. As he towelled himself dry, he noticed that a long legged spider had been in the basin all the time he was washing. Its legs were flailing in circles and then crossing over one another as it frantically tried to stop itself going down the plughole. Gurtha quickly pulled a piece of toilet paper and placed it in the basin beside the spider. It took a few wobbly steps onto the paper. He gently placed the paper and the spider on the floor, the spider's legs now all contracted towards its small body. Then it lay completely still. Gurtha didn't know whether to flush it down the toilet or to see whether it would survive. He thought that its legs might be broken; maybe it would be kinder to kill it than to leave it to live as a spider without legs. He left it to see what would happen.

He opened the door into Paddy's bedroom. The light fell onto the floor from a large window beside the bed. Gurtha surveyed the bed with shock. The bed didn't have a mattress. How had he not noticed that when searching for Paddy's clothes for his holiday in Mallorca? Instead of a mattress there were blankets crumpled into small hills underneath a sheet. When, how and why had Paddy got disposed of his mattress?

The small hills of Paddy's bed sparked the memory of the house on the Malone Road which Gurtha had sold. There was a four poster bed, smothered in a powdery blue silk surround, mock gold taps in the bathroom where an ivory bath with gold lion feet crouched on the Fired Earth tiled floor. How could Gurtha have lived there while Paddy slept in this room? He sat on Paddy's bed, holding his head in his hands for quite some time before slowly getting to his feet and returning to the bathroom where the two squares of white toilet paper lay moist on the bathroom floor. The spider was gone.

♥

In the hospital at 3.30 pm Gurtha waited in a consulting room filled with the smells of anaesthetic, disinfectant and something unusual. He looked around and a candle burned in the corner sending out a hint of vanilla. On the wall, a pine trimmed board held letters from patients expressing their thanks for the care they had received from the doctors and nurses. Gurtha walked towards the board just as the door swung open. He turned around with a start, as though he had been caught doing something he shouldn't have been doing, to see Cornelia standing in front of him.

"What on Earth are you doing here? How did you know where to find me?"

Cornelia laughed.

"The shop – Laura told me where you were. I thought you might want company."

Cornelia moved towards him and kissed him on both cheeks.

"How's Paddy?"

"They've done all of the tests. I've a meeting with the Care Team

Leader in a few minutes to hear what they think needs to happen next."

Cornelia sighed.

"That's good. So you will know this afternoon. Where are you staying?"

Gurtha hesitated, and then said,

"The Holiday Inn by the BBC."

"I'll check in to the Holiday Inn and maybe see you for dinner at 7.00 pm?"

Gurtha nodded.

"I'll text you later."

♥

In the Holiday Inn, Cornelia unpacked her case, and reapplied her lipstick. Sipping on her tea and leaving the usual red stains on the rim of the teacup, Cornelia recalled how her mother, Anne, had once asked, "Imagine if you were born to sing. You would go to school to learn how to sing – nothing else. The world would be filled with human beings singing like larks at daybreak. Would you like that?"

Anne looked into Cornelia's green eyes waiting for a response. Cornelia placed both hands on the kitchen table as though to steady herself. Taking a deep breath and without answering Anne's question, asked her own, "Why do birds sing at dawn and human beings don't?"

Anne twiddled her long black hair into a ringlets, "To attract a mate, defend where they are living. Maybe they're glad to be alive."

Cornelia shook her head, in disbelief, removing her hands from the table and placing them on her red and white gingham dress.

"I can't imagine Daddy singing."

Anne laughed, got to her feet and went around to where Cornelia was sitting, standing behind her she crossed her arms over Cornelia's chest and in a gentle yet firm voice said, "Of course he can sing. Simon sings every morning. He's got a voice like a blackbird or maybe at times a corncrake." She smiled to herself.

Cornelia squeezed her Mother's hands.

"Do I have to go to school today? Can't I stay here with you? Amelia doesn't have to go to school."

"Amelia is only two. She will go to school when she is five. She's only a baby."

Cornelia dreaded leaving the house. The world outside was so strange, so confusing. She imagined that she would get lost and that her Mother would not be able to find her. She would be stranded in a city which she didn't know. The city of Cardiff was a whole planet circling round and around in space, with people walking along the streets knowing what to do and where to go, but not Cornelia. How did they know where to go? How did other people find their way home? Standing at the school gate, waiting for her Mother to arrive gave her a sense of being invisible – no-one could see her. If she started walking down any street, even her Mother would not be able to see her. But here, holding onto Anne's hands, she was safe. She looked at the picture of "the Sacred Heart of Jesus" hanging on the wall in front of her.

That night she had a dream.

The picture of 'the Sacred Heart' appeared in the dream. It was enormous. If filled the entire wall. Cornelia was shrunken small like an Alice in Wonderland looking up at the painting and wanting to see Christ's eyes. She couldn't see them from the floor where she was standing but she could see that the painting was alive – Christ was breathing – his chest moving. Then she was lifted gently up into the air. She didn't feel afraid but excited, as though she was in a fair ground with her Mother and about to get onto a roller coaster ride. As she floated towards the ceiling, she was able to look into Christ's eyes. He was smiling at her and his hand came out from the painting – large, white and warm. She shook it and her body trembled with happiness. She then drifted effortlessly back to the floor. She knew that she would always be safe in this room with 'the Sacred Heart' and her Mother. She didn't ever need to leave this room. The world could spin on and on without her needing to know it.

Anne helped Cornelia into her school blazer.

"Why don't you like school?"

Cornelia threw her arms around her Mother's waist.

"Miss Matthews slapped me with a ruler. I didn't do anything."

Anne stroked Cornelia on the head, firmly yet gently.

"You know that I have spoken with Miss Matthews and she said that never happened."

"But it did Mummy, it did. She's telling you lies." She cried pressing her face into her Mother's polka dot dress.

"Miss Matthews doesn't believe in Jesus. I told her that he is alive. I told her that I saw him in the garden. He was buried up to his neck near the rose bushes – only his head was showing. It had a crown of thorns on it. He told me that he was alive. He wasn't dead. Miss Matthews told me to stop telling untruths. Then she hit me with the ruler."

The door of the kitchen swung open with such force that the door handle scratched a line of white paint from the wall. Simon strode towards the pine table,

"Cornelia, shut up. I've told you to stop talking about Jesus. I don't want to hear another word about Jesus Christ."

He poured himself a cup of filtered coffee which Anne had earlier percolated and threw himself onto the Van Gogh chair, gulping at black coffee, coughing and then wiping his chin with the edge of the white table cloth, he glared at Anne.

"Stop encouraging her with these delusional thoughts and take that bloody picture off the wall before I get home this evening."

Anne took Cornelia's hand. It was cold. She rubbed it, turning her back on Simon and wiping tears away with the back of her hand. She said in a low, controlled voice, "Do you remember it is Cornelia's birthday today."

Cornelia felt a scream sounding within her. A frustration ballooning within her which needed to burst. She hadn't asked to be born into this frightening world with Simon as her father.

♥

In the Holiday Inn Cornelia pulled on a turquoise swimsuit and walked towards the obligatory shower before going to the pool. She was alone. The shower water was cold. It was late August and she was pleased to see that she had managed not to get tanned. There were many examples in Mallorca of sun drenched, wrinkled, carved faces like the bark of the olive tree.

She lowered herself into the water, staring straight ahead, as if in a daze. She began to swim, a gentle unhurried breast stroke, moving her arms through the water, pushing the water aside, spreading open her fingers to feel the water massaging her arms and hands. She brought her awareness into her body. She knew what would happen next. It always did when she had her body in such a state of suspended relaxation. Images would begin to play incessantly in her head. The internal chatter which accompanied them producing a familiar anxiety in her stomach. The images were of her sister, Amelia, aged seven – the year she died. It was as if Amelia was floating inside Cornelia's head. It started with a

THE SECRET WOUND

simple image of her face smiling at her. She had fine blonde hair with natural ringlets, a stark contrast to Cornelia's straight dark bob. Her face was more rounded than that of Cornelia – cherubic and angelic. She looked peaceful, tranquil, serene. Their mother Anne used to sit with Amelia on her lap brushing her hair. On Easter Sunday Anne would dress Amelia in a pink suit and Cornelia would be given blue. The rosy pinkness of Amelia's suit contrasted with the creamy whiteness of her hair. Her cheeks had a natural smudge of cerise. Her eyes were a watery deep blue. Cornelia pinched her cheeks in the bathroom in an attempt to imitate Amelia's beauty. Yet her cheeks only looked swollen and painful as if she had been crying. As they walked hand in hand with Anne along Tyn y Cae Road in Cardiff, strangers would stop Anne, bend down, touch Amelia on the chin and say, "What a beautiful child. One day she will break someone's heart."

They ignored Cornelia. It was as if she didn't exist. She learnt how to stamp her feet and cry to get attention. What worked even more effectively was when she panted and couldn't breathe. Anne would then give her anything she asked for, explaining to everyone that Cornelia had asthma and needed to be treated gently. Amelia was told not to annoy her, to let her play with her dolls and that she had to be kind to Cornelia. It never stopped Cornelia thinking that her parents loved Amelia more than her. Everyone loved Amelia more than Cornelia.

♥

Cornelia was ten when it happened. They were in the park playing. There was a roundabout which could go really fast if Cornelia held onto the bar and pushed with all her might. Amelia sat gripping onto the bar - that angelic look of patience quickly replaced by

tears as she cried, "Stop it Cornelia, you're going too fast. It's scary."
When there was no-one around, Cornelia pushed the roundabout
faster, jumping onto the wooden platform at the bottom of the
roundabout, feeling the wind in her hair, ignoring Amelia gasping
for air. Her cries could not be heard. Instead, they were whisked
away on the breeze, then scattered like rain over Cardiff. When the
roundabout eventually slowed down, Amelia looked at Cornelia
with fear in her eyes. She reached into her pocket and handed
Cornelia a strawberry lollipop.

"You can have this."

Cornelia looked at the flat circular lolly covered in transparent
plastic. She reached a hand towards it. She held it in her hand,
staring at it before throwing it across the playground.

"I don't want it."

Amelia scrambled off the roundabout. One of her sandals
was loose and she bent over to tighten it. She kept her eyes on
Cornelia. Cornelia walked towards the swings. The two swings
hung low, the wooden seats close to the ground. She sat on one
and waited for Amelia to join her. Amelia didn't move quickly
from where she had fixed her sandal. She hesitated. She then
took a few steps towards Cornelia and gently sat in the swing at
her side. She pushed back with her right foot against the sandy
ground. The swing moved slowly in a small arc. Amelia's two feet
dragged through the sand. She didn't want to go too high. Cornelia
hadn't started to swing at all. Instead she watched Amelia out of
the corner of her eye. Then she jumped off the swing, spun around
to see if there was anyone in the playground. It was empty. Like a
pendulum, Amelia's swing swung higher and higher, rushing into
the blue sky filling with thick black clouds which would later bring
rain. Her tiny feet no longer searched for contact with the brown
sand but her toes stretched and pointed out straight in front of

THE SECRET WOUND

her. There was a sense of abandonment to the sky and earth. She allowed herself to be thrown between the two. She made another effort to bend forward and make the swing go higher and then to bend backwards with the legs still straight out and toes pointing like a ballet dancer's into the sky. She laughed out loud.

"Higher. Higher," she shouted as if to God and then to Cornelia. "Push me higher."

Cornelia grasped the wooden seat as it swung towards her and swung it forward with all her might. There were two sweeping arcs, then three. Amelia screamed with excitement. She tried to slow the swing down but her feet only scratched at the earth before swinging high into the sky. Cornelia pushed again with all her strength as the swing flew horizontal. Amelia now shrieked,

"Stop it. You're frightening me. Stop."

Cornelia laughed and shouted into the air, "Enjoy it. It's fun."

Amelia screamed with fear as the swing shuddered, now pushing higher than horizontal. It trembled in the air before rattling to earth. Cornelia had to jump into the air to catch the seat of the swing at its highest point. She pulled it down to earth with all her strength, focusing on Amelia's red school jumper pulled down over her navy skirt. The swing almost seemed to have reached a point where it could complete a circle over the top of the bar holding the thick metal chains. She jumped a second time into the air catching the seat of the swing as it fell towards earth. She laughed, "I'll stop it now for you."

As Cornelia's hands gripped the seat of the swing for the last time, Amelia's hands let go of the cold chains on either side. Cornelia watched as the red woollen jumper, navy skirt, white socks and sandals hurtled through the air. Amelia's legs circled for a while in the air in slow motion as though she was doing a long jump before she began to fall backwards and landed on the ground with a sickening thump – like a hammer in a judge's hand as he drops it onto a rubber mat on top of a teak table and pronounces his sentence.

Cornelia was transfixed. Amelia lay motionless, her head to one side. A trail of deep red blood flowed from her nose, seeping into the sand. Cornelia raced towards her, kneeling beside her on the ground. A wind twisted fallen autumn leaves from an oak tree into the air. She stared at Amelia's chest. It didn't move. Cornelia leaned over Amelia and moved her head from the sand, positioning it as if onto a pillow, preparing her for a night's sleep. Amelia's eyes were open – staring at Cornelia like one of Amelia's dolls. Margaret Mary had white nylon hair and eyes which closed when you put her in her pram and which opened again when you lifted her out to have her bottle.

Cornelia tried to remember what you were meant to do if you wanted to save someone's life. She had been shown in school at a First Aid class. She couldn't quite remember but she leaned over Amelia's still body and breathed into her open lips three times. There was no movement in Amelia's body – only a slight smile which seemed to settle after the third breath. It was the smile she seemed to have been born with. Even death couldn't take it away.

Cornelia gathered Amelia into her arms and held her against her chest and cried. It was the first time that she had ever hugged her. She buried her head into the scarlet jumper and smelt the baby cleanness of Amelia's body through her clothes. She didn't dare to look into her eyes again. Instead she squeezed her own eyes tightly closed, pressing her head deeper into Amelia's shoulder. A sense of loss flooded her body. What had she done? Tears flowed. She stayed like that with Amelia, unmoving, until Anne found them. In the stillness of holding Amelia during what seemed to be an infinite period of waiting, something died within Cornelia. Or was

THE SECRET WOUND

something born? Cornelia continued swimming, knowing that the film within her head was nearing its end. There was another scene to watch.

She climbed slowly from the tepid water and walked towards the sauna, opening the wooden door, removing her gold earrings and placing them on the wooden bench beside her. She twisted the egg timer hanging on the wall for fifteen minutes and closed her eyes. The film rolled. She knew that it would. There was no stopping it.

Cornelia heard her mother Anne scream as she ran towards them, as she held Amelia, her head bowed. Anne had to prise her away. Cornelia and Amelia had merged into a closed oyster shell which Anne desperately struggled to separate. There was one soul – a pearl inside – not two. Anne eventually dragged Cornelia away from Amelia and called for an ambulance. Cornelia watched as Anne placed herself over Amelia's body and she did what Cornelia had forgotten to do – she put her hands on Amelia's chest and rhythmically pressed as she breathed air into her body. For a few moments it seemed as though Amelia had come back to life –she quivered and spluttered – only briefly. It was not be. It was only Anne's breath moving in Amelia's body.

At the funeral, Cornelia listened to the mourners whisper.

"She was so brave. She tried to save her. She loved her sister so much. It will be difficult for her now."

At the funeral Cornelia learnt how to bow her head down over her chest to avoid the gazes of everyone looking at her. She cried. Anne knelt on one knee beside her, wiped her face with a cotton handkerchief soaked in lavender oil, kissed her on the cheek. Cornelia felt a warm flame fanning in her heart which spluttered into a roaring furnace as the white coffin was lowered into the ground.

For the first time at the funeral, Cornelia wore the blonde plait from Amelia's hair which Anne had woven into her black bob. Amelia's DNA was one with her's. Nobody, or nothing, could separate them.

It was almost over as the coffin was laid in the grave. Although not entirely. Cornelia asked herself if she had killed Amelia or had it been an accident? She wasn't sure. Had she held onto the swing for a few seconds deliberately forcing Amelia to fly through the air? Had it been her intention to kill Amelia?

♥

One year later, on her eleventh birthday, the film played again. Cornelia showered after school, getting ready for her birthday party. As she ran the sponge over her body, she was disappointed at how it was developing. Breasts were pushing into existence. There was nothing she could do to stop it happening. She was not in control of her own body. The year before her legs were smooth and fine – like the legs on the new cherry wood kitchen table. This year, hairs had insisted on emerging like a plague of spider legs from toe to knee. She inspected them with a sense of curiosity. She was fat. Francis Turner couldn't like her.

Downstairs Anne was singing John Denver's 'Sunshine On My Shoulders Makes Me Happy'. The rain was pelting against the bedroom window. She hoped that the sun would be shining and Francis and she could be alone in the garden. They could find an excuse. She could show him the new wooden bird house or hideaway cave which she had woven into the hedge at the bottom of the garden. That wasn't likely to happen if the rain continued to batter the windows. She listened to the heavy tread of feet on the stairs. That had to be her father, Simon. She slipped on her platform shoes, sat up on the bed and waited.

The door swung quickly open as she knew it would. Simon entered, holding onto the door handle. Cornelia gasped and then closed her mouth again breathing in and out quickly and noisily – her breath like a saw chewing its way through hard wood. She watched Simon, recognising the red circles on his cheeks which meant that he had been drinking – although her Mother told her that it was high blood pressure. His dark hair greyed at the temples, eyes dark brown with thick black lashes and his mouth drawn into a straight line – pinched and straight. He sat on the bed beside her and reached for her hand, "I'm sorry about last night." He didn't look at her but stared at the floor. His hand resting lightly on top of hers.

"I should never have hit you. But I care for you, Cornelia. You need to learn to live in the real world. The Christ you want to hang on a Cross around your neck doesn't exist. We're here because of random chance – atoms bumping off one another - not because of some Great Plan of salvation. It was inexcusable of me to hit you. I get frustrated when I can't make people understand. It's for you own good. As a parent it is my duty to prepare you to survive in a real world."

Cornelia briefly noticed his broken uneven teeth before quickly moving her head to the left and stared at the pillow where her white teddy bear lay, arms stretched out.

"It won't happen again. I promise you. I won't hit your Mother again either. I'm sorry. Will you forgive me?"

Cornelia kept her eyes on teddy's still brown stare and nodded. She felt this whirling sensation in her stomach which made her feel dizzy. She didn't want to cry but could feel the familiar prickling sensations beneath her eyelids and one tear escaped. She breathed quickly and deeply to stop any more falling. She didn't know what to do to change the feelings inside. With her Father so close to her, the room felt small. There wasn't enough space for both of them. Without moving her hand from his, she slowly turned to face him. He stopped looking at the floor and raised his head to look at her. She saw a face twisted like an animal caught in a snare. Her hand was the trap. His upper lip once again sewn in a tight line. He had a white moustache – not a hairy one – only the area above his upper lip was creamy white. His cheeks still red, but now like splashes of raspberry on each cheek. He didn't look so scary now. Not like last night. She made herself look into his eyes. They looked surprisingly like teddy's eyes but warmer, softer. She felt a smile opening around her mouth but she didn't know why. Inside the swirling of the vortex in her stomach had turned into a gentle swish of waves on a beach. Words formed in her mouth as she heard herself say,

"I should help Mummy prepare for the party."

Simon looked again at the floor, pressed her hand into the patchwork quilt, released his hand and slowly got to his feet.

"That's a good girl. So I'm forgiven then?"

"Yes." Cornelia's legs shook at little as she walked towards the door behind her Father. He opened it for her, stood back and made a bow with the sweep of an arm to let her leave first.

In the kitchen Anne looked up with a smile as Cornelia rushed towards her and gave her a hug. Anne whispered into Cornelia's ear,

"Where's your Daddy?"

Cornelia looked into her Mother's eyes.

"He's watching TV in the sitting room."

"You've forgiven him haven't you? You know that he can't help himself."

She stroked Cornelia's hair.

"You mustn't tell anyone."

THE SECRET WOUND

Cornelia nodded, "I know." Together they prepared plates with white doilies, placed angel buns, apple creams, custard slices to the left of the kitchen table and sausage rolls, hamburgers, crisps and cheese sticks to the right. On a small table beside a pine dresser, Anne had taken the vinyl record player from the sitting room and placed a bundle of singles and long players. There was Diana Ross, the Hollies, Elton John, the Carpenters and Paper Lace playing "Billy Don't be a Hero". Cornelia took a handful of crisps as she inspected the back garden through the glass kitchen door and sighed with relief as the rain had stopped and there was still enough light for the party to take place outside for a few hours. Anne took Cornelia's hands, waved them in the air with her own, belting out loud the chorus of 'Billy, Don't Be A Hero'. Cornelia felt a wave of a smile move into place on her lips.

Anne walked to the pine dresser and lifted a small red velvet box and handed it to Cornelia.

"It's for you."

Cornelia wrinkled her face, "What will he say?"

Anne shook her head, "Nothing if you make sure that he doesn't see it."

Cornelia opened the box, inside lay a small golden crucifix studded with three tiny rubies.

"It is our secret."

There was a timid knock at the front door. Anne patted Cornelia on the back, "One of your friends has arrived. Let them in."

It wasn't Francis Turner – it was Sandy Strathroy who bounced along the hall with her box of chocolate Maltesers as her present, and the news,

"Francis rang me to say he can't come. He's sorry. He fell off his bike and broke his leg this afternoon. He's still in the hospital."

Cornelia fell onto the chair closest to the angel buns.

"Why didn't he ring me?"

Sandy raised her shoulders and threw her hands into the air, "He didn't remember your number."

"But you could have given it to him."

Sandy grabbed at a sausage roll and dipped it into the dish of Heinz Ketchup.

"What would have been the point of that when I can tell you?"

Cornelia turned to Anne.

"That's it Mother – no more birthday parties. This is the last one ever."

♥

For the year following her eleventh birthday Cornelia fell out with Sandy because she had stolen Francis Turner from right under her nose. He had never fallen off his bike and broken his leg. It was all a lie. What annoyed Cornelia more than anything was that it was such a stupid lie. Of course, she found out when she went to school on Monday and there he was playing football in the school grounds at lunchtime. It puzzled Cornelia why Sandy would tell such a bad lie. It was only at the end of Monday's classes when Cornelia saw Francis carrying Sandy's satchel that the penny dropped. Sandy wanted it to be a bad lie. The two of them smirked at her as they squeezed past her in the corridor.

She wondered how had she not known that there was something going on between Sandy and Francis. Cornelia and Sandy walked to and from school together. There was never any sign of Francis until break time. They went their separate ways after school and did their homework in the evenings. Sometimes Sandy would copy Cornelia's homework before classes started saying that she had had a headache the night before.

How could Sandy have come to her birthday party and dance with Cornelia to Diana Ross singing 'You Are Everything', when she knew that Cornelia would find out about her lies afterwards? For a year she harboured resentment against Sandy more than she did against Francis. She thought that Francis had been manipulated or brainwashed by Sandy. How? Cornelia decided to become friends again with Sandy to discover how Sandy had such power over boys. Sandy knew how to be mysterious and have secrets so that no-one – especially adults – had any idea about her life and how she was living it.

Sandy had dropped Francis as her 'steady' boyfriend, so the conversation was easier than Cornelia anticipated.

"Corneeeelia," Sandy purred down the telephone. Cornelia imagined her standing by the phone wrapped in a huge white bath towel, her hair still wet and falling in thick curls onto her bony shoulders. She was more than likely wearing oversized fluffy pig slippers.

"I am soooo glad that you rang. I have missed you."

Cornelia cleared her throat before speaking, "Me too. I thought we could still be friends. It's silly to let someone like Francis come between us." She paused. It sounded as if she meant it.

Sandy replied, "I'm sorry for what he did to you."

It was a conversation as comfortable as toasting marshmallows on a fork in a cosy sitting room close to Christmas.

Cornelia kept a close eye on Sandy once the friendship had been re-established. She noticed that in Sandy's world, there was a lot of smiling going on. Sandy beamed at everyone when they were within range, but as soon as they drifted into the distance, the smile melted from her face, her tone of voice turned sarcastic as she leant over to whisper an insult into Cornelia's ear about who had walked by.

Within a month Cornelia confirmed the Sandy knew the importance of secrecy. New boyfriends appeared on the scene. Sandy and the new boyfriends didn't hold one another by the hand or catch one another by the arm. Cornelia watched them disappear out of sight and wondered what happened then. The next day Sandy would sit cross legged on Cornelia's bed after school with a different smile on her face. It was as though she was remembering the night before and whatever took place, but she wouldn't say.

One Friday after school, Cornelia asked, "Do you want to come in and we can do our homework together and then we are free to do whatever we want for the weekend?"

Sandy turned the belt on her pleated tartan school skirt up twice so that her skirt would be four inches shorter. She had that familiar dreamy look in her eyes, looking away from Cornelia. She pulled her hair into a pony tail and whispered, "No. I couldn't face homework now. What a week. I'm exhausted. I'll give you a call tomorrow."

Cornelia opened the gate at the bottom of the path to her door and watched Sandy walk down the street and turn left at the bottom. Cornelia ran after her. She hid behind a thick oak tree on the corner and watched Sandy walk past her own house on the left. There was no cover along the road until the next tree.

A playful breeze blew Cornelia's hair over her face. Two sparrows chittered away above her head, swooping around and around one another. Cornelia took a deep breath and walked at the same pace as Sandy, a hundred yards or so behind her. She felt her stomach tense with excitement. She took a couple of deep breaths and ensured that her pace was measured and equal. There was a primary school playing field on Sandy's left. Sandy turned left through a wooden gate. Cornelia ran to the gate. She

THE SECRET WOUND

didn't need to worry. Sandy was not out of sight. She was standing outside the sports pavilion to the edge of the playing fields. It was a wooden pavilion with a steep pointed roof. It had steps leading to a terrace, also made of wood. There were four windows on the front. Three of them were shuttered and closed. One was open. Cornelia recognised the person standing inside waving at Sandy. It was Eoin Mahoney – the Head Boy. He moved away from the window and a few seconds later the front door opened. Sandy looked over her shoulder to her left but not to her right, and so didn't see Cornelia. She took Eoin's hand and kissed him on the lips. They disappeared inside.

Cornelia walked towards the pavilion. She was breathless and filled with a buzzing energy. She decided not to walk up the steps in case they creaked, but walked on the grass around the pavilion towards the back. There was a second set of stairs. She took off her shoes, set them out of sight with her school satchel, behind a barrel shaped flower tub and tip toed onto the terrace, making her way around to the open window at the front. Once on the front terrace she got onto her hands and knees and crawled until she was level with the window. She winced a little as two large splinters of wood pushed into the flesh of the palm of her hand. The breeze was still being playful, lifting up her hair and making a pendulum of her striped green and yellow tie. She listened beneath the window. At first she could hear nothing from inside – only the breeze rustling within the evergreen hedgerow edging the playing fields. Then she heard Eoin's voice sounding slightly scared and surprisingly high pitched. He sang baritone in the school choir.

"We haven't long."

There was a pause, then Sandy's voice, softer and gentler than normal, whispering, "Don't panic. Let me help you."

Cornelia slowly got to her knees, placed two hands on the windowsill and looked inside. Her breathing stopped for a couple of seconds. She smelt teak oil as someone had prepared the wood for Summer. There was a scuffling sounds like rats playing in straw to her right. She turned her head slightly. Although it was semi-dark, she could see the outline of Sandy's naked body on top of Eoin. He was still wearing his school trousers, socks and shoes, not his school shirt and tie which had been abandoned on the floor. Sandy was smothering him. He was gulping for air and staring at the ceiling. He didn't much look as though he was enjoying himself.

Cornelia dropped back onto her hands and knees. She had a terrible urge to throw something through the window. Instead, she stood up once she reached the side terrace and walked gently towards the stairs, salvaged her shoes and satchel from behind the flower tub and ran home.

♥

"Sorry I'm late," Cornelia called to Anne, "I called into the library." She threw her satchel on the sofa. "Let me get changed."

As she pulled on her jeans, she thought that for the first time in her life that her Father was right. There was no Jesus alive, no Christ to find. If she was to be happy, she needed to take responsibility for her life. She could fight Sandy for Eoin's love and win. She removed the cross and chain with its rubies from around her neck and buried it in a pink purse with rosary beads.

♥

THE SECRET WOUND

"Why did you do it?" Sandy screamed at Cornelia. She turned around to face her and glared into Cornelia's eyes. Cornelia stared back without moving.

"Because I could and he was willing."

Sandy was now crying, her mascara running down her face. Her shoulders were moving up and down as she gasped at the air. It was late June; swallows were flying overhead, curving out wide arcs in the blue. They were both standing on the daisy covered grass. Someone was having a barbeque close by – the smells of sizzling steaks giving the sense that summer was beginning and that they should be partying rather than having this row.

"But I loved him. You know that." Her sobs were now hysterical. She clenched her fists and for a moment Cornelia thought that she would punch her, but instead she continued to open and close them.

Sandy stopped crying, took two steps back from Cornelia and sobbed. "You've destroyed him for life. I know that you have. He's different. I'm going to tell everyone. They'll hate you."

Cornelia tightened a bow which had loosened around her head.

"I don't think that they'll hate me as much as they'll think that you are a Loser. They'll admire me. After all he's Head Boy and that makes me the real Head Girl – not you. Loser."

♥

At school Miss Toner, the Form Teacher, announced that the school trip for Upper Sixth would give everyone the opportunity to do a silent retreat in the monastery of San Honorat in Mallorca. When she made the announcement a ripple of laughter spread around the room.

"Are you really saying we won't talk for five days?" Kathleen shouted from the back of the classroom. Cornelia and Miriam sat in the front row.

"Could she not make it Santa Ponsa or Magaluff?" Miriam whispered to Cornelia. "We're going to have to do a creeping Jesus holiday."

Miss Toner continued, "This year you will make a significant transition in your lives. You will be faced with many decisions over the next three to four years. Sister Maureen and I thought that a wonderful way to mark this rite of transition would be to offer you an opportunity to connect with what is deepest in your being – to harmonise mind, body and soul – in preparation for your encounter with a world beyond the protected environment of this school and your home. It will be challenging – simple, but not easy. We hope it will provide you with a base and a discipline for your life going forward enabling you to expand into the infinite love and potential which are your heritage."

Miriam gave Cornelia a dig in ribs, "We could sit in our bedrooms for five days and sneak in vodka." She sniggered,

"I wonder if they're going to ask us to fast and put on a hair shirt."

Cornelia looked intently at Miss Toner. She was wearing the same mouse coloured straight haired wig that she always wore but today it looked slightly out of place as if she had forgotten to straighten it. Her make-up was a couple of shades too light, which gave her a slightly clown-like appearance. In addition, she hadn't rubbed it in well around her nose and the pores were open, as though someone had scattered poppy seeds on top of a beige matt finish. In the last year her face had turned jowly. Before, you could see fine definition in her chin – now, it was as though she had acquired the neck of a pelican.

She looked at Cornelia.

"Cornelia, you have been usually quiet. Will you be joining us in San Honorat?"

Cornelia jumped in her chair.

"Off course, Miss Toner."

Miss Toner smiled.

"I´m glad. At the end of the retreat there will be a weekend to explore the island. We are thinking of a day in Palma and a day in Soller."

There was a sigh of relief in the classroom. Miriam nudged Cornelia again, "Now we're talking. That's when we will let our hair down and go wild."

♥

Cornelia remembered looking out of the window of the plane as it descended towards Palma. There were pillars of cumulus clouds all around – simmering golden in the setting sun. The plane plunged into the middle of one shaped like an elephant. The plane shuddered from side to side, dropped height so quickly that children towards the back of the plane screamed. It then banked left, slicing through the meringue, levelled out and, leaving the clouds behind, glided over rugged grey mountains towards Palma.

Miss Toner rang the bell at the front door of San Honorat. It was the end of June and the sweet smell of jasmine hung heavily in the air. Crimson hibiscus flowers were dropping their silky petals onto the sandy ground. At five o'clock in the afternoon it was still intensely hot. The twelve girls who had volunteered for the school trip buzzed around her, peering through the wrought iron gate. She wiped beads of sweat which were falling from her chin onto her woollen skirt and removed her jacket.

Father Miguel walked briskly towards them. He opened the gate with a flourish and held out a hand to Miss Toner who seemed to courtesy as she placed her hand in his. He led them towards the monastery along a crazy paving path with tiny blue flowers growing between the stones. To the right, Miss Toner peered into the valley below. The monastery had been built at a cliff edge with a sheer drop to the valley floor, shimmering in a mirage-like mirror. In the distance she could detect a streak of blue like a stained glass window – the Mediterranean.

Father Miguel gestured left and they followed him through the monastery door. There was a list of names and rooms. Miss Toner took charge.

"Girls and boys. Follow Father Miguel and he will show you to your rooms. It's five o'clock. Father Miguel will carry out his orientation for the retreat at seven o'clock in the chapel. Please take the opportunity to settle into your rooms, explore the gardens and we will meet at seven."

Cornelia walked into her room and gently sighed with relief. The exams were over. The world outside was opening. She would be leaving home and start working as a Personal Assistant in a Bank in Nottingham – a job organised by her father. She was so looking forward to life changing. It had been a suffocating year. Simon, her father had been unable to keep his promise of not hitting her. He had an incredible rage bottled up inside him – like a pressure cooker – which had to be released on a regular basis.

Then Sandy had been horrible to her. She told everyone what had happened with Eion. No-one, apart from Miriam, would talk to her. She was suspicious about why Miriam was friendly. What did she want?

Five days of silence. At least it wouldn't be so obvious that no-one wanted to know her. The bedroom was lovely. A single bed with crisp white sheets and a primrose blanket. A small basin. A writing desk and chair and a wardrobe. She felt that she could live in this one room for ever. She didn't need more. She breathed deeply. The air seemed filled with peace. Each breath brought her a sense of groundedness. She was weighted to the earth. She walked to the window. There was a view of the valley below and the sea to the left. A hawk soared to her right and then dived, pulled onto the yellowing grass on the valley floor.

In the meditation room Cornelia breathed in frankincense - food for her soul. She settled onto the cushion – legs half crossed over one another. She fixed her eyes on the crucifix on the wall in front of her. The rest of the group had not arrived. She was alone. There was a silence in the room deeper than anything she had experienced before - a stillness which she found herself sinking into.

Where was Father Miguel? She suddenly felt anxious about the loneliness of being in the room without others. She took a deep breath and looked at the crucifix. That helped. Christ wasn't only pinned to a Cross - he was here, around her. She wasn't alone. She breathed deeply. Breathing in Christ. Was she mad? Was she going totally insane? Or for the first time in her life was she totally sane?

She closed her eyes. Could it be this easy? To sit and do nothing? Again she breathed deeply. There seemed to be a lead weight dragging her down into her centre – was it her centre – or the centre of everything? Whatever it was – it was dropping into something in which she knew a sweetness of being, an escape from thinking, a liberation from feeling – a touching of the silkiness of life and its bubbliness of being.

Father Miguel opened the door of the Church and stepped gently towards the front of the room.

He whispered with the voice of a lark – sweet, clear and penetrating, "Are you wishing to confess?"

"Yes Father I would like to confess but what happens if I do it again? You see it's like a sleeping wild animal within me. When it awakens, I can't stop it."

♥

At 3.30 pm Cecilia, the Care Team manager, swept into the room and reached a hand to Gurtha, "Paddy - what a lovely man."

Cecilia gestured to a comfortable chair beside a wooden table with a Nespresso machine.

"Would you like a coffee?"

Gurtha shook his head and sat down, feeling his body sink into the softness of brown leather.

Cecilia helped herself to an espresso, opened her handbag and pulled out a small plastic bag of walnuts,

"They're good for the brain. I need all the help I can get." She looked a little awkward, "I didn't mean that in a disrespectful way."

Gurtha raised his two hands in the air as if in surrender and smiled, "No offence taken. What about Paddy?"

Cecilia munched on her walnuts and looked at him with what could only be called a direct stare,

"It's clear cut. He has dementia. Drugs won't alleviate his symptoms and he can't live alone – no matter what the Psychiatrist says." She paused to shake the salt from her hands. "Mr Collins – the Psychiatrist - insists on recommending that people with dementia stay at home due to the importance of familiarity with the surroundings. However, that is a nonsense in Paddy's case – although it may work for others. If Paddy is left alone, he will leave the house and is unlikely ever to be around for the planned

THE SECRET WOUND

visits to administer his drugs and provide him with food. There is no way he can cook for himself. The Occupational Therapist confirmed that he will leave the gas rings burning, forget about the toast he has just put on and will be a risk to himself and to others."

Gurtha moved to the edge of the chair.

"What do you mean to others? Is he violent?"

Cornelia slammed her cup and saucer on the table.

"Absolutely not. He is a gentleman in the true meaning of the word. I only mean that he could burn the house down and in doing that put at risk those houses on either side of him. I'm afraid it's residential care which is now necessary as I understand that you are not in a position to be a full-time Carer?"

Gurtha nodded and bowed his head.

"I need to work. My work involves travel."

Cecilia stared at the crown of his head, noticing the smallest of patches of thinning hair, about the size of a two pence coin.

"We see that it is an emergency situation and so he has shot to the top of the table of people waiting for …" She hesitated, then coughed and continued, "a vacancy to occur. You are very lucky …" She paused. "There is an unexpected vacancy at Milthorn Residential Care Home. We have very good reports about that particular home. There is also a vacancy at Shenalon. We have had mixed reports but perhaps you should review them both."

Gurtha looked up.

"Paddy will not want to go into residential care. He'll fight against it."

Cornelia increased the volume of her voice and deepened it in reply, "There will always be a period of adjustment. He will get used to it."

Gurtha opened the top button on his shirt and loosened the flowery tie.

"When does he need to move from here?"

"Tomorrow if you are ready. There is some paperwork to be completed – but basically when you tell me whether it is the Milthorn or the Shenalon, I will ring them and they will be able to accommodate you within hours. I know this is a stressful situation, but you should be looking at the bright side. There is normally a minimum two year waiting list. I have known people to be on a waiting list for ten years. That's when the relatives are holding out for a special place." She shook Gurtha's hand again, "I'm thinking of putting my name down for the Milthorn myself." She laughed. "Don't leave it too late for yourself."

♥

Gurtha decided not to say anything to Paddy about the move until it was all decided – the Milthorn or the Shenalon. He drove to the Shenalon first. The Manager – Paul Donohue, welcomed him with a strong handshake,

"We would be delighted to have Paddy stay with us. Follow me. I'll show you around."

He followed Paul. He was a small, stocky man with dark hair and tight trousers over an inflated bottom. He walked quickly along a narrow corridor and, as though reading Gurtha's mind, said, "No problem here for a wheelchair and there's a lift to Paddy's room."

The very fact that he said, "Paddy's room" created a sense of unexpected tension in Gurtha's stomach. It was too familiar for someone he had never met. He felt like sticking his finger into Paul's chest and asking, "Paddy who?"

Instead, he had to quicken his pace to follow Paul as he ran along the corridor. In the lift Paul didn't stop talking about the kindness and care which Paddy would receive. Gurtha ⟨…⟩ that ripping sense of betrayal for what he was about to do to Paddy. Why couldn't Paddy have bloomin' well held onto his senses for a bit longer?

The lift doors opened, Gurtha stepped out and there were three rooms along a corridor, all vacant.

"Another two unexpected deaths yesterday which Cecilia won't have known about means you have a choice of rooms – most unusual." As he threw his arms open to indicate the vastness of choice, Gurtha gazed into the closest room. It had a metal hospital bed with a long red cord hanging beside it, a button to press for an emergency and a strong smell of Dettol. Everything was white and steel.

Gurtha asked, "Is there an en suite room?"

Paul turned to look at him with a certain curiosity,

"Pardon?"

Gurtha repeated, "En suite?"

Paul breathed in deeply, so deeply that one of the buttons popped open above the waistband. The button above that one looked under pressure too.

"I realise that this is very recent news for you. However, it is unlikely your father will even remember that he needs to go to the toilet. We have Care Assistants who will help him to these facilities." He indicated to an open door where a man slumped over in his wheelchair was being pushed by a young girl with pink hair and a ring in her nose to a room a little further along the corridor.

Gurtha shook Paul's hand warmly and said that he would be in touch.

His next stop was the Milthorn. As Gurtha walked through the front door, he knew immediately that this was the place for Paddy. It was true that there was a smell of pee more than Dettol, but that didn't seem to matter. There was something in the air that felt different. Maggie, the Manager brought him into her Office and talked about the practicalities of moving Paddy in.

"It will take time for him to settle. If you can bring photos, anything at all that reminds him of home – that will help. Let me show you his room."

They walked upstairs along a corridor where there was a dining room on the right.

"We like them to eat together and have grouped them in small tables. Sometimes they like to eat alone in their rooms and we respect that also."

The dining room had a sense of being a small restaurant with five circular tables, a coffee area and a large window looking out onto a car park and beyond to the mountains which Paddy would recognise.

Along the corridor there were photos and names attached to each of the rooms. They reached a room with an empty space which invited a new photo. As they entered, the room was flooded with sunlight. The walls were painted primrose gold. The whole room was warm and inviting. From the window a football pitch, on which young boys were practising for a match, was visible. The hills surrounding Belfast lay beyond the football pitch. There was a normal bed in the room – not a steel hospital bed – a wardrobe, a kettle, a few cups and saucers and a cupboard for biscuits. Paddy loved his biscuits – custard creams, jammy dodgers and McVities digestives with a mug of tea.

There was an en suite – with a step in shower with toilet and an emergency cord with a red button to be pulled should help be needed. Gurtha heard the tremor in his voice as he asked, "Can I bring Paddy's clothes?"

"Of course."

The door opened and Elizabeth walked in. She smiled at them both.

"I want to get out of here. Can you help me? Let me out."

She was a thin, frail, white haired woman with an anxiety about what would happen next.

"You're going out – aren't you?" She pointed at Gurtha. "I have to get out of here." She sat on the bed. "I never smoked. They said I smoked but I never did." She clicked the heels of her shoes together. "Do you have a cigarette?"

Maggie took her by the arm, "Let me take you back to your room. This is Paddy's room."

Maggie left and Gurtha sat on the bed, imagining Paddy's photos on the wall, his clothes in the wardrobe and how he would hobble every night to the en suite toilet where he would leave a little puddle on the tiles and no-one would think it strange.

He looked at his watch. It was seven o'clock. Cornelia would be in the Holiday Inn waiting for him. It would take him another two hours to move Paddy's clothes, pictures and photos to the new room in his new home. He would spend the night in Paddy's house – as a last farewell to it. Cornelia would have to have dinner alone.

♥

Gurtha drove back to Paddy's house thinking that it would probably be the last time he would stay there. He climbed the stairs to his old bedroom. He pulled back the candlewick bedspread and undressed, finding himself a pair of Paddy's pyjamas, as his clothes were in the Holiday Inn. At this very minute Cornelia would most likely be knocking on his door. He checked his mobile phone.

There were no messages. He knew that he should have rung her, especially as she had gone to all the trouble of coming over, but he didn't want to have a conversation and instead he sent a short text:

"Sorry not to be able to meet tonight. I'm sleeping in Paddy's house. I need to organise his clothes as he is going into residential care. See you tomorrow at 2.00 pm. Enjoy your evening. Gurtha."

DAY 16

MONDAY 26TH AUGUST 2013

GURTHA DROVE Paddy from the Royal Hospital to the Milthorn Residential Care Centre. It was a sunny day; clouds were puffing up over Black Mountain. Paddy sat very still in the front passenger seat. He looked straight ahead and asked, "Where are we going?"

Gurtha answered, "We're going home."

"You've taken the wrong road. That's Casement Park. That's not the way home." He was wearing a green Magee tweed jacket and olive green corduroys, a cream shirt and a dotted dark blue tie. He pulled his cap a little further down over his face.

Gurtha felt a solid ache in his stomach. He breathed deeply.

"It's a new home for you. It will be easier to manage. That house was too big for you after Nuala died."

"Nuala's not dead." Paddy shook his head. "She's shopping or she's gone over to the Church to sing in the choir." His voice was soft and gentle. Gurtha patted him on the knee.

"We're nearly there."

He spun the hired car into the car park of the Milthorn and helped Paddy to swing his arthritic legs around and then pulled him onto his feet. Maggie met them at reception beside the hairdressers where three women were waiting in a row to have their weekly hair wash, curlers rolled into place and a hair brush to follow up. Maggie walked quickly to room 11 and opened the door. Paddy shuffled inside and sat on the bed.

"What all this then?" He looked up into Gurtha's eyes.

Gurtha put the kettle on to make a pot of tea and opened the jammy dodgers and placed them on the china plate. Maggie hesitated at the door.

"Paddy, I'm Maggie. Anything you need just walk down the hallway and you'll find me by reception. I'll see you later and introduce you to your new friends at lunchtime. Paddy munched on his jammy dodgers. Crumbs fell onto the ground. They sat in silence beside one another. Gurtha looked at his watch.

"I'll leave you to settle in. Do you want to know where the bathroom is?"

Paddy shook his head, "No. I don't want anyone washing me."

"That's fine. The toilet is in that room beside the door if you need it. Let's put the TV on." He switched the channels until he found an old Western movie.

"You'll enjoy that until I get back."

Paddy reached for another jammy dodger and sipped his tea, "I'll see you later then."

Gurtha left the room, gently closing the door behind him. He felt as if he was crumbling inside. It was much harder to leave Paddy here than he had ever imagined. It really felt as though he was abandoning a child to strangers. He felt his eyes prick with tears.

He looked into the dining room. Six or seven residents sat at a table, waiting for lunch to arrive. They didn't talk to one another, but sat in silence, hands folded on the table. Each of their lives seemed to Gurtha to be a bundle of secrets contained within a disintegrating body. Eventually no-one would know or care what their lives had meant to them. Now, to ask them a question – to extract a moment from the past to know it deeply, seemed important. What was the present for them now? Nothing. The future? Nothing. But to experience again a moment in which they had felt their lives filled with love – even one moment when they knew with total certainty that they were loved – wouldn't that be wonderful? Could it not be possible to replay and replay again and again that moment of knowing, a moment which was, after all, only the unfolding of love within and beyond time?

The movement of their lives now coloured in leaves of gold, orange, then black before dropping onto the soil and being reabsorbed into the tree from which they fell. Where was the love in that? Gurtha knew that there was love in the total movement of life, but he couldn't feel it. He knew that there was something which held the tragic, the irrational and absurd with meaning in meaninglessness. He knew that there was something holding order within disorder, life within tragedy, the Divine within what was human. He didn't know exactly what it was. William Blake knew.

'He who binds to himself a joy
Does the winged life destroy;
But he who kisses the joy as it flies
Lives in eternity's sun rise'.

♥

Elizabeth stood by the door still hoping to escape, wearing white slippers. Her grey hair looked as if it hadn't been brushed for a few days. Her legs were little sticks of legs – boney and brittle, which you could see beneath the transparency of a white and blue cotton skirt. She folded her arms as he approached, hugging herself, "You'll take me home. Won't you?" She smiled at him, "Have you got a cigarette?"

Gurtha took her by the hand, "Elizabeth, you don't smoke."

Elizabeth looked directly into his eyes and pulled herself up straight, "You're right. I don't."

She turned to face the corridor leading back to her room. She walked quickly with her head jutting out slightly and turned around only once before she reached the bottom and had to turn left. He couldn't see her eyes but she gave him a look of reproach – like that of a deer heading into a forest, alone, without a mate.

♥

Gurtha suggested that Cornelia and he had lunch in Pizza Express across the road from the Holiday Inn. He opened the door for her. Cornelia wore white lace gloves, a cream hat with a pink band of silk around it and a long vanilla dress which moved like melting ice-cream. Her shoes had a little strap across them. She would have been perfectly at home in a 1920s black and white movie or having afternoon tea at the Ritz.

"What would you like to drink?" The waitress, with a ring in her nose and a heart shaped tattoo on her neck, asked.

"A Margarita, thank you." Cornelia removed the lace gloves and sat them on top of the side dish. She turned her head slightly to the right and looked at Gurtha. The waitress waited for Gurtha to order.

"Sparkling water."

She handed Gurtha the menus. Cornelia smiled one of those vacant smiles Gurtha had seen several times before. It was as if she was thinking of something private which made her chuckle or that she was in a black and white film, sitting across the table from John Gilbert. Perhaps she was Greta Garbo appearing with him in 'Flesh and the Devil'. Although she looked at Gurtha, she didn't see him, but saw a man with a centre parting in his dark slicked hair, a smile which indicated total adoration of her and a moustache which looked inked into his upper lip rather than real.

She tapped her lips again with her fingers.

"I loved Nuala."

Gurtha felt the blood drain to his feet which felt like blocks of cement against the tiled floor.

"What do you mean that you loved her?"

Cornelia touched her lips with her fingers as though playing a piano and picking out the white keys.

"We had our differences, but I loved her."

Gurtha repeated her words slowly.

"You loved Nuala? You can't love someone you don't know."

"I knew her well enough. You would like to think that you were the only person to love her, but that wasn't true. You heard what the priest said at the Requiem Mass. There were many people who loved Nuala – including me."

She pushed a strand of her bobbed hair behind her ear.

"When you first told me about her all those years ago – I have to confess to being a little jealous. You seemed so in awe of her. You know I didn't think it was - well - a normal relationship that you had with her."

Gurtha felt a choking sensation in his throat. He looked at the menu and then at Cornelia. He asked her in a direct tone of voice.

"Do you think our relationship is, or ever was, normal?"

Cornelia opened a mirror and inspected her face as the waitress approached.

"No. I don't. I never did. Whose fault was that? I'm having the aubergine paramagiana with a mixed side salad. What about you?"

Gurtha felt his heart furiously beating and heard his breathing gurgling around his throat as he responded to the waitress.

"Pizza Fiorentina."

Cornelia touched the plate and took hold of the knife and fork, polishing them with her napkin.

Gurtha felt his cheeks burn.

Laura sat alone at a table by the window. She looked out, watching the world go by. Then she opened her book and started reading, before glancing left as Cornelia in a loud voice challenged Gurtha.

"You said that Nuala told you something about Henry and I."

Cornelia signalled to the waitress,

"Another Margarita please." She looked at her watch.

"I'm catching a flight back tomorrow. If there is something that you want to tell me, now would be a good time."

Cornelia placed a finger behind her ear.

"I'm listening."

Gurtha said nothing.

Cornelia continued, "You were going to tell me the other day when you came to see me. So tell me now."

Gurtha hesitated.

"Is that why you've come here? To find out what Nuala thought about you and Henry?"

THE SECRET WOUND

"Gurtha, I have come here as a long standing friend, to accompany you on your journey with Paddy. I know that the situation with Paddy is stressful. However, you did say that you wanted to talk and that it had something to do with Nuala and Henry. It's easier to talk when we are alone and Barry isn't here. Is it not? I also have something which I need to share with you."

Gurtha nodded.

"OK. There is nothing to say, really. I have been confused that you began a relationship with Barry so soon after Henry's death. I wanted to tell you that. I felt that there was something untrue in your reasons for being with him. If you remember all those years ago you said that our relationship was about 'The Good, the True and the Beautiful'. I feel that there are lies in your relationship with Barry. Yet I have no right or reason to do anything other than to accept them. As for Nuala she merely expressed concerns that perhaps Henry didn't receive the appropriate care for his heart condition. She knew the symptoms well as she suffered from heart failure."

Cornelia breathed in deeply and rested her hand on top of Gurtha's.

"You know that Henry's medication was difficult to control. It was a delicate balance which got out of control in spite of the best efforts of the medical staff. In the last few weeks his Warfarin was impossible to stabilise. He suffered from internal bleeding, which damaged his vital organs. It was sad, but you know that he was admitted to the hospital for tests and he died in spite of all efforts of save him. I was lucky enough to have him at home two days before he died. They were sweet days which I will never forget and which bring me much comfort. I have no idea why Nuala thought he was neglected. Nothing could have been further from the truth. As for Barry – it is true that maybe I looked for someone too quickly. Someone I felt would fill the gap caused by Henry's death. It may have been a mistake. However, you also had a part to play in this."

Gurtha pulled his hand away and sat upright.

"What do you mean? I don't understand."

"Can you not see? Did you not know? I have always loved you. If you had given me any indication that this love was reciprocated – then I wouldn't have sought solace in Barry. I was prepared to wait for you. But that last holiday in La Quinta de Los Cedros – you were so disinterested – cold – heartless. You were changing. I am not someone who can live alone, like you. I need companionship. When Henry died, I needed friendship desperately and Barry offered me that. He seemed interested in me, listened to me in the way that you used to and he desired me physically. I felt that I was in a relationship with him which allowed me to feel loved. With you it was a mental game which we played together. With Barry it was quite the opposite. It had pleasure and comfort which came from our physicality together. Maybe that was a mistake."

Cornelia finished her Margarita, slowly sipping the last drops.

"So – I've confessed. What else can I do? What more do you expect from me?"

Gurtha held his glass of water with both hands, "You told me all those years ago at Llanthony Abbey to 'stay innocent and childlike'. Was that only for me? Were you excluded?"

Cornelia pulled on her lace gloves.

"I lost my innocence and my childlike nature when I was ten or even before that. That advice was to protect you. I didn't want what had happened to me, to twist you."

She touched his face with her gloved hand.

"I don't want to lose your friendship. There is no reason why it can't be even stronger than before. In difficult times if you

THE SECRET WOUND

persevere, a relationship can deepen. Do you not think so?"

Gurtha searched in his wallet to pay for lunch.

"It can go either way – deepen or fall apart."

♥

As Cornelia and Gurtha opened the door to leave Pizza Express, they failed to see Laura with her head bowed, pretending to read her book. She watched from the window and saw Cornelia hold Gurtha's hand as they crossed the road. She watched as she threw her arms around him, kissing him on the cheek, the blonde plait falling onto her shoulder. As she left him, she scurried towards The Holiday Inn, twisting the plait with her fingers, glancing over her shoulder to the left as Gurtha opened the door of his BMW. She waved at him, but he didn't see her.

DAY 17

TUESDAY 27TH AUGUST 2013

"WE COME SPINNING OUT OF NOTHINGNESS,
SCATTERING STARS LIKE DUST."
J RUMI

GURTHA LAY in bed in the Holiday Inn. It was his favourite moment of the day, when he opened his eyes and the world flowered into being. He pulled the crisp linen sheets up to his lips and turned his head to the right. It was a large room with white wallpapered walls. There was a painting on the wall –a beige, grey background with a swirl of granite red into a broken circle. It had the sense of a Zen painting – simple, emphasising emptiness – the brush strokes thick and strong – one stroke or maybe two at the most – nothing to be changed or improved – everything perfect as it is.

He turned onto his stomach, pulled the pillow down and lay on the mattress with his hands on the pillow like two sleeping tarantulas. He breathed deeply. His legs were tingling with vibratory energy. His stomach lay heavy against the mattress. His face burning as though with fever. He looked at the alarm clock. Seven o'clock. Cornelia would be down at breakfast. He pushed his head into the pillow. He couldn't face her this morning. She would have reserved a breakfast table for two, looking at the entrance to the dining area to see him approach.

THE SECRET WOUND

He rolled onto his back and stared at the white ceiling. He looked left towards the windows – white curtains. It felt as if he was in an institution designed to deprive him of sensory stimuli. Maybe it was meant to be restful – in keeping with the Zen painting. A blank screen. A state of not thinking, not imaging, not … desiring. Dropping into that big void – the circle in the middle of that blood red painting.

♥

What had happened on that last holiday when the three of them were together? Henry had gone to bed as he typically did around eleven. It was Easter 2012. They were staying in a small boutique hotel called La Quinta de Los Cedros in a suburb of Madrid. They sat at their table in the garden, surrounded by white rose beds and pink bougainvillea. A waiter came to crumb the table with a silver dustpan and brush. He bowed over the white cotton table cloth, his tight glossy black curls catching the light from the moon. They waited in silence for him to finish. He raised his head and smiled at them. His crisp white shirt impeccable after an evening's work. It still had creases along each arm, not a smudge of anything spilt on the black waistcoat or tie. Gurtha placed his napkin over three drops of lobster soup beside his hand. The waiter asked, "Would you like a 'chupita' on the house?"

Cornelia answered for both of them, as she had the habit of doing, "Two gin and tonics please." She smiled at him. The waiter responded with another curtsy. Gurtha looked deeply at Cornelia. She seemed to know he was looking and didn't return his gaze. Instead she let it linger. She wore a long blue, sleeveless silk dress. Her arms were so thin that she was able to wear a golden bracelet above her elbow. She had tied a ribbon with artificial daisies around her forehead. She crossed her legs and slowly moved her hand across the table, stopping short of touching his. She allowed the silence to grow between them like a harmonic into which they both vibrated. It was only when the waiter returned with drinks, settled them onto the table and left, that she spoke.

Gurtha's formal black suit, white shirt and bow tie felt exaggerated to him. He loosened the bow tie and let it fall onto the shirt like misplaced priest's Stole. He closed his eyes briefly as Cornelia began to whisper, as though she was afraid that what she was about to say would be heard by the people still dining at the tables to their right and left.

"You know that love is not an emotion – don't you?"

Gurtha opened his eyes. He responded.

"You've talked about this many times before. Why are you saying it again? It's becoming quite boring to hear it repeated."

The crickets sang wildly around them with a steady loud hum, like a generator. The pine needles which lay scattered on the ground, smouldered their fragrance-like incense. He breathed in deeply. He knew that Cornelia would continue with her obsession.

"It's an election. Love is a choice. Emotions are irrelevant."

She sipped on her gin and tonic and gazed at the stars.

"What tiny brains and arrogance we have to think that we know."

Gurtha watched her move her hand in a sweeping gesture around the garden. He coughed gently.

"If you forgive me - it sounds as if you think that you do know."

She leaned her chin on her hand, propping it up a few degrees, and moistened her lips.

"Do I indeed? You're calling me a hypocrite?"

Gurtha sipped on his gin and tonic, listening to the woman sitting at the table to his right break into a loud cackle of laughter before she leant forward and kissed her partner on the lips.

"I'm not calling you anything. I feel sorry for Henry. Whether love is or isn't an emotion can be debated. I think that wisdom without compassion is an act of cruelty. You seem to be dispassionate with Henry. I wouldn't like to be in his shoes."

Cornelia searched in her handbag for a cigarette.

"There is no emotional quality to my relationship with Henry. I do not need to explain or apologise to you for the fact that I feel neither pleasure nor pain with him. Henry doesn't complain."

Gurtha dabbed at beads of sweat on his forehead with the napkin.

"And you call that love?"

Cornelia's face reddened. Her face flushed into purplish blotches. She pushed her gin and tonic to one side, slid the chair back on the patio floor, stood up and said in a low voice, "How dare you. Who do you think you are?"

She lifted her hand as though slap Gurtha but instead dropped it to her side, pulled a rose from the vase on the table, stomped across the garden patio, swung through the French doors, waving to a waiter who ran after her and, dismissing him, she turned right to climb the oak stairway to Henry's room.

When she was gone from sight, Gurtha whispered to himself in a soft voice, heard by those who had fallen silent at the surrounding tables.

"Love isn't a choice. It just is."

♥

In the Holiday Inn, Gurtha decided that he was definitely not going to meet Cornelia for breakfast even if that meant completely missing breakfast. He pulled himself into a sitting position, swinging his legs onto the wooden floor. He spied the kettle on the formica table. A Nescafe would be fine. He boiled water in the kettle and was pouring it into the black ceramic mug when his mobile rang.

"Gurtha?" A woman's voice shook slightly at the other end. It was Maggie from the Milthorn.

"Yes, Maggie. What's wrong?"

Maggie, coughed before she replied, "It's your father – Paddy. There is no other way than to say this but, he's gone - escaped. We don't know where he is."

"How, Maggie?" Gurtha's stomach shrivelled.

"I'm so sorry, Gurtha. We don't know how. We have called the Police. We will find him. It would be helpful if you could bring some photos of him to help the police with their search."

Maggie continued, "We are having our audit today." He could hear her breathing deeply.

"I know that's not important." There was a clinking sound. He realised that she was drinking.

He breathed deeply. He closed his eyes. For a second or two he said nothing.

"Maggie, I will be with you within the hour."

Maggie kept talking, as if to herself, "Last night at 9.00 pm he had his cup of tea and a digestive biscuit. He asked for a second biscuit. He smiled when Anne, his care taker, gave him two more. She said that she would return to help him get into his pyjamas at 9.30 pm. When she returned, he was gone." She hesitated. "Elizabeth is also gone. We believe that they have flown the nest together."

♥

Paddy had finished his third digestive biscuit when Elizabeth opened the door of his bedroom and plonked herself down on the visitor's chair. Her hair had been set in neat curls and brushed into Judge-wig perfection. She wore a navy pleated skirt, shiny tan tights and patent black brogues. She had buttoned up her tweed blue and white jacket and placed a navy silk scarf on her head, tying it in a knot under her chin. She lifted a black paten handbag onto her lap, opened it and removed a packet of cigarettes which she offered to Paddy.

"Time to go home. Do you want a ciggie first?"

Paddy reached his hand to take a Lucky Strike. They sat for a few moments looking at one another before each putting an unlit cigarette between their lips. Paddy got to his feet. He looked for his shoes. They were under Elizabeth's chair. He pointed at them. Elizabeth removed the cigarette from her mouth, placed Paddy's shoes at his feet and, clutching her handbag in her left hand, whispered.

"Put a jacket on. It's cold out there."

Paddy slipped his feet into the shoes, shuffled towards the wardrobe, found the North Face walking jacket which Gurtha had bought him, pulled his cap from the shelf and headed for the door. Elizabeth followed. They walked along the corridor, Elizabeth linking his arm with hers. As they approached the exit door, it swung open and a burly man with dark black hair and a grey moustache, grunted heavily as he held the door open for them to leave.

"Do you know which room Tommy McNeil is in? He's dying. I can't find anyone in reception. That man gave me the code but I don't know the room."

He pointed at the revolving front door where a man was spiralling around into the car park.

Paddy smiled at him, nodded and pointed down the corridor.

"He's in room 11. He will be alright. He's not too bad. I've seen him worse." Elizabeth patted the visitor on the shoulder. "He will be so glad to see you."

The visitor sighed with relief.

"Thank you. That's a relief I can tell you."

Paddy shook his hand and together they continued through the revolving door into the car park.

"Where are we going?" Paddy asked, as Elizabeth picked up a bit of pace in her walking.

"We're going home. Where do you think we would be going after all this time? Don't you want your dinner on the table?"

"What are you making for dinner?"

Elizabeth smiled and squeezed his arm.

"Your favourite. Irish stew."

Paddy shook his head.

"I like steak and onions."

Elizabeth winked at him.

"You'll eat what's put in front of you. None of your cheek now."

It was dark outside; the road was busy with taxis hurtling in and out of the City. Paddy sniffed at the evening air. He smelt grass which had been cut hours earlier. There was a hint of drizzle against his face. He felt the pressure of Elizabeth balancing herself on his arm. He held his arm straight, like a bannister for her to hold onto. With the other arm he hailed a taxi which screeched to a halt beside them.

♥

Cornelia lay in bed in the Holiday Inn. She wakened with her heart racing and watched the second hand on the alarm clock click forward, rhythmically, with purpose; she attempted to settle her breathing into a steady pace. She felt that Gurtha was drifting away from her. She was standing on the shore watching him untie his boat from a mooring and navigate out to sea without saying goodbye. It was as if he knew the truth about her. But he couldn't know. That would be impossible. Unless Nuala had revealed more than Gurtha had admitted. But Nuala didn't know the truth before that day – Gurtha's birthday. If Gurtha was to love her, she would have to tell him the truth. Yet if she did that – how would he ever love her? It was an impossible situation. The only way to be with him seemed to be to continue to lie. But she didn't want to lie any more. The lies in her life were razors edges – peeling her into nothingness. A life of lies was a life not worth living.

She took special care with her hair, brushing it slowly into the bob style of her youth. When she placed the rouge lipstick on her lips, it felt as though her face was gently coming alive again. She pulled on a cerise pink long jersey dress, cream leather shoes with a strap and buckles and opened the door to search for Gurtha.

She knocked at first gently on the door of room 412. There was no reply. She pressed her ear against the door. No sound. It was 7.30 am. He had to be inside. She had checked the breakfast restaurant and he wasn't there. After the first soft knocking, she hammered the door with her fist, shouting,

"Gurtha. I know that you are in there. Please open the door."

A waiter approached carrying a tray for someone requesting room service. For a moment her heart lightened. Maybe it was for Gurtha. However, he walked past Gurtha's door giving her a curious look out of the corner of his eye and murmuring, "Good morning."

She pressed her forehead against the door and tapped it once more, lightly. Silence. She turned around, retraced her steps back to the lift and back to the breakfast room. She would wait for him.

♥

Gurtha ordered a taxi at reception in the Holiday Inn and asked to be taken to the Milthorn Residential home. It was 7.30 am. It was a gloomy day with rain falling and a chilly breeze encouraging those walking to work to bury their heads into their chins and hide beneath black umbrellas. He wondered where Paddy was now. It would soon be twelve hours since he and Elizabeth had gone missing. Where would they have slept? He looked into each doorway on either side of the street as the taxi moved slowly through the morning traffic.

Arriving at the Milthorn, he quickly paid the taxi driver as Maggie waited for him at the front door. She had dark rings under her eyes and her cream linen suit was wrinkled. She shook Gurtha's hand and weakly smiled at him.

"I received a call from the Police five minutes ago. They've found them. They're on their way here."

Gurtha breathed deeply as he followed Maggie towards the Reception room.

"Where were they?"

"They were standing at the entrance of the Titanic Visitor Centre. A member of staff had arrived early, realised that there was a problem and called the Police.

♥

THE SECRET WOUND

The night before, as Paddy hailed a taxi, Elizabeth held his hand. The palm felt solid and smooth and the top, hairy and coarse. It reminded her of her cat, Snoopy. His coat was like that - smooth and coarse at the same time. She watched Paddy intently. He was staring straight ahead, saying nothing. There was no response to her touch. She squeezed his hand a little and continued to watch him.

"Where are you going?" The taxi driver asked looking over his shoulder.

Elizabeth answered,

"22 Limestone Road. The house on the corner."

Paddy turned to look at her.

"Are we not going to the Crumlin Road?"

Elizabeth shook her head.

"Not tonight. We'll go there tomorrow. I have steak and onions in the house for you already cooked."

Paddy looked ahead again.

"I thought you said Irish stew."

"Why would I have said that when I know you like steak and onions? It's good to be going home isn't it?" Elizabeth squeezed his hand again. "I'm glad we're going home. I didn't like that place. I think they're all crackers in there. What did you think?"

Paddy touched the peak of his cap with his free hand.

"I think there are some good people in there. Wee Tommy's nice."

Elizabeth shook her head,

"He's an exception. He gave me the cigarettes. His son gave him a packet. Tommy told me that he's given up smoking. It's not good for your health. He showed me the photos on the packet. You know, the ones of the cancerous lumps growing on someone's lip. Sure you don't die a minute before you're meant to. Those photos don't frighten me. Anyway, Tommy died last night. It didn't do him much good stopping smoking."

"Tommy's dead?" Paddy looked at Elizabeth.

Elizabeth nodded.

"Yes. I was getting my hair done for coming home and they told me. He mightn't have died if he had smoked these."

Elizabeth pulled a cigarette from the packet and started to light up.

The taxi driver, in a soft voice, said, "This is a non-smoking taxi. If you don't mind."

Elizabeth snapped the lighter shut. She leant forward.

"If you're not careful you'll end up dead, like Tommy. He didn't smoke." She sat back, resting her head on Paddy's shoulder. "What do you think Paddy?"

Paddy nodded.

The taxi stopped outside 22 Limestone Road. It was a small end of terrace house. Paddy reached into his pocket to pay. Elizabeth smiled at him.

"You're a hardworking man who isn't afraid to bring the money in, thanks be to God."

"Good night." The taxi driver handed Paddy his change and watched them slowly ease their way out of the car.

Elizabeth walked quickly ahead, opening her handbag and peering inside as they neared the front door.

"I don't think that I have my key. Do you have it?" She looked at Paddy, now beside her. He began to search his pockets. Apart from the roll of ten pound notes and a few coins, there were only the sodden remains of a paper handkerchief.

"I must have left them on the mantelpiece. Will there be anyone at home?"

Elizabeth snapped closed her handbag and pressed the doorbell. "Jimmy might be in."

Paddy rubbed his nose with the disintegrating handkerchief. "Who's Jimmy?"

Elizabeth gave him a caustic look.

"Who do you think? My husband, of course."

There was no reply to the door bell ringing. The house remained in darkness with the curtains drawn.

Elizabeth took Paddy's hand.

"He must be out. We'll wait for him around the back."

She opened a small gate leading along a path of crazy paving with begonias growing to their left. As they got to the back garden, Elizabeth pointed to the right.

"That's where we can sit." There was a wooden swing bench with a green and white striped tarpaulin over the top edged with a white fringe. "He would normally have put the cushions out but it will be OK. Tomorrow, after we have a good night's sleep, we can go to the Titanic Visitor Centre. That's my favourite place in Belfast. My father used to work in the shipyard. You can buy cigarettes there."

Elizabeth pulled Paddy over to the bench and continued to hold his hand as they sat under the tarpaulin. The occasional car rumbled by on the Limestone Road. Paddy sang in a low voice:

"*Who knows if we shall meet again?*
But when the morning chimes ring sweet again...
I'll be seeing you in all the old familiar places

...and when the night is new,
I'll be looking at the moon,
But I'll be seeing you."

Elizabeth leaned over and kissed him on the cheek.

"You've a lovely voice. You could be on the stage. Aren't you glad we're home? You never know, we might even have a wee dance under the moon the way you're going. I don't mind if you don't. Sure you're only young once."

DAY 18

WEDNESDAY 28TH AUGUST 2013

BARRY SAT on a wooden chair in the Art Gallery and watched Angelina stick another red dot on a painting – another sale. The exhibition was going extraordinarily well. He couldn't help thinking that the majority of the success was due to Angelina rather than the quality of the paintings. He watched her place a pencil between her teeth as she straightened the painting she had sold - her hair curling onto her shoulders like glossy syrup spreading onto porcelain. She was wearing a long white lacy blouse over spotted pink and white leggings.

"When is Cornelia back?" Angelina sat on a wooden stool, leaning forward, resting her arms on her thighs.

Barry coughed, ran his fingers through his hair and looked to his left towards the door.

"She's already back. She got back yesterday evening. She sends her love." Angelina twisted her hair above her head, catching it into a pony tail.

"Do you not think that it's strange that she took off like that and went to Belfast to be with Gurtha?"

Barry held his face in his hands before talking through his fingers.

"I know why she went."

Cornelia walked over to the Nespresso machine and pressed the button.

"Why?" She lifted a glass of sugar from the oak cabinet.

"She is in love with Gurtha or at least she thinks she is. He's not in love with her."

Angelina reached him a 'cortado' and asked, "How do you know that?"

Barry placed his 'cortado' on the table.

"I've seen the way he looks at her. I would say that in the past she might have meant something to him, but not now."

Angelina poured a glass of water and handed it to Barry.

"What has changed? I don't understand why he would come out here, if he wasn't fond of her."

Barry wiped his sweaty hands on his beige chinos.

"Maybe Henry meant more to Gurtha than he did to Cornelia? What if Henry was the real friend?"

He rubbed his eyes.

"Relationships are complicated are they not?"

He brought Angelina's hand to his lips. He gently bit her knuckles.

"Thank you for friendship. I promise not to overstep the mark."

"You've bitten me – you've already done it." She laughed. "I forgive you."

She moved towards the painting of Samson and Delilah.

It's a good story isn't it – Samson and Delilah? I sometimes feel that Cornelia is like a Delilah."

Barry asked, "Who is Samson?"

Angelina thoughtfully place a finger on her chin.

"Hmmm. Could be you."

Angelina touched the painting and looked at it closely. There was an intensity of movement within the thick oil swirls which filled the sky with muddied orange, yellow, blue and green. Delilah merged into the background, sitting under a twisted olive tree holding Samson's head on her lap. It was hard to tell if she had cut his hair or was about to do so.

Angelina sat on the floor beside him.

"Maybe it's not you as you haven't got much hair, have you? Anyway - the point of the story is that Samson's hair grew back. He accomplished what he was meant to do. He had the strength to push the pillars of the temple apart. OK, he died in the process, but at least he fulfilled his destiny."

Barry took her hand.

"If only it was easy to know your destiny, it would be easier to live it. What do you think is yours?"

Angelina looked thoughtful.

"Maybe to marry Gurtha."

Barry shook his head and tutted.

"Cornelia would not like that."

Angelina clambered to her feet.

"Maybe that's her destiny. To discover that she can't control people or life itself. Both need the freedom to be what they need to be."

DAY 19

THURSDAY 29TH AUGUST 2013

"WHEREVER YOU ARE, AND WHATEVER YOU DO,
BE IN LOVE."
J RUMI

PADDY WAKENED and stared at the ceiling. Where was he? He looked at the lampshade with its yellow tassels and then at the wall where a Papal Blessing for his marriage to Nuala hung beside a picture of the Secret Heart of Jesus. The eyes of Jesus stared at Paddy, a gentle stare. In the picture, his heart was covered with a ring of thorns. There was a gold heart on top, with a small crucifix. There was a halo around the heart and also around his head. That painting had been in the sitting room ever since he had been married to Nuala.

He remembered her putting rosary beads over it. It had hung above the fireplace. He looked around the room. There was no fireplace.

Where was he? Was he on holiday with Nuala? Why was he on his own? He felt a nauseous feeling in his stomach. It was like a heavy sludge, a pool of mud sliding towards his heart. It stopped there, crushing him. This wasn't his bed. He rolled his legs onto the floor and looked at his blue and white striped pyjamas. The pyjamas were his pyjamas. He pulled the white cord tight into a small bow. He was getting thinner. He undid the bow and peeped

THE SECRET WOUND

down his pyjama bottoms. Yes, his stomach was flatter. For years he had a thick band of fat which made it difficult for him to close the button on his trousers. He pulled up his pyjama top. His chest was familiarly hairy. That was reassuring. He tied the bow once again on his pyjama bottoms and walked towards the window. Just outside there was a car park with a few parked cars and beyond that a road with black taxis driving up and down. It wasn't the Crumlin Road. There was no Holy Cross Church opposite.

He turned to look into the mirror above a small basin. They were his eyes, blue like Gurtha's. His face was unsmiling. There were hairs growing out of the bridge of his nose. He pulled at one of them with his thick fingers. He lifted a toothbrush from a mug, turned on the cold tap and rinsed the brush before opening his mouth. He looked again into the mirror and into his toothless mouth. That was his mouth but whose toothbrush was that? He replaced it in the mug. He could catch something from someone else's toothbrush. He walked back to the bed and sat on the quilt. Maybe someone would come to see him. He couldn't remember. Had Gurtha died? He hadn't seen him for a long time. Maybe he had died in a plane crash. He travelled a lot. Those planes were falling out of the sky all over the place these days. Who would visit him if Gurtha was dead?

He remembered. His mother would come and see him or maybe he would go and see her and give her his wages. Where had he put the money? Paddy searched in the pockets of his pyjamas. There was only a damp tissue and a menthol sweet. He threw them both on the floor.

He was sitting on the sofa at home. His mother sat on a chair with her legs wrapped in white bandages. The Headmaster from the school was sitting facing his mother. He was fourteen years old. The Headmaster was telling his mother that he had highest marks in Northern Ireland for his Junior Certificate. The Headmaster wanted Paddy to stay at school and go on to further education. He said that he had the brains to study whatever he wanted.

He looked at Paddy.

"Would you like to be a Doctor, Paddy?" Paddy nodded yes.

His mother shook her head. Her double chin wobbled. She patted the arm of the chair for emphasis.

"He'll have to go out to work with his father. There are five kids younger than him. We need the money. I don't need you to be putting highfalutin' ideas in his head, Mr McCaffrey."

That day Paddy had a feeling in his stomach and around his heart that he was turning into stone. He was becoming solid, petrified. There was nothing that he could do to stop it happening. If his mother had let him become a Doctor, did she not know that he could have taken care of her legs?

THE SECRET WOUND

DAY 20

FRIDAY 30TH AUGUST 2013

GURTHA CHECKED out of the Holiday Inn. He walked towards the City Centre for breakfast before visiting Paddy.

Nuala was dead. How quickly had the image of her face and the sound of her voice vanished. When she was alive, he had dreaded her impending death. Now that she was dead – she was somehow like a wisp of the edge of a cloud that had no meaning, no heaviness, no weight. What was that wisp - delicate, changing, transparent – holding enormous wisdom. How could someone so fragile be so strong?

Even though it was August, there was a chill in the air. He pulled a woollen scarf around his neck and straightened Paddy's cap on his head. He glanced to his left where someone was lying in a sleeping bag in a doorway. The bag covered with a cardboard box. The head of a man with greasy dark hair stuck out from the bag, like a snail's head. The man was pressing both hands against his eyes. He couldn't be asleep. You couldn't do that if you were asleep, could you – hold your hands over your eyes and sleep?

A woman wearing wedge sandals, a pink dress, a turquoise leather jacket and matching handbag overtook Gurtha, walking quickly on his right. Gurtha stopped. He wasn't sure about what to do next. He waited beside the snail in his cardboard shell. A man approached with shoes which clicked like a grandfather clock. He walked quickly past. From behind, Gurtha watched him disappear in what he knew to be a Paul Smith suit and Barker shoes. Gurtha placed a few coins on the ground.

The corridor in the Milthorn was circular so that the residents could keep walking and not feel confused by choices of going right and left. There was only one path and you kept circling it. Gurtha circled until he spotted Paddy.

Paddy was dressed as though going to a wedding – in a striped blue and white shirt, a dark blue silk tie and a petrel blue V-neck woollen jumper over navy blue trousers. He was leaning against the doorway leading into the TV room. His arms were crossed. He gazed into the room, carefully inspecting the inhabitants. Gurtha joined him and gave him a hug. Paddy smiled back without saying a word. They stood together silently, looking into the sitting room. There were four men, sitting in separate chairs. The TV was on. A reporter talked about the global economic crisis and evidence of a financial recovery.

The men watched the screen intently, seemingly interested. Their mouths hanging open, hands lightly gripping the sides of the chairs, eyes staring straight ahead, lost in a world which no longer had meaning for them but within which they still had to exist. Paddy seemed to be curious about them – as though he was different – as if he knew that, although he was there with them, he was not really like them. He had been imprisoned under false pretences.

"Can I go with you?"

Gurtha felt his innards quiver – a trembling inside – knowing that the answer was no. Yet did it have to be no? Could he not take Paddy with him and take care of him? Paddy's loneliness soaked into Gurtha. The enormity of the terrible paradox and tragedy of life itself. The mystery of an abundant creative, intelligence holding everything in existence – making sense and being meaningless at the same time.

DAY 21

SATURDAY 31SH AUGUST 2013

"YOU ARE NOT A DROP IN THE OCEAN.
YOU ARE THE ENTIRE OCEAN IN A DROP."
J RUMI

GURTHA FOUND himself back in Paddy's house on the Crumlin Road. The keys were to be returned to the Housing Executive later that afternoon. Even though he had cleaned the downstairs toilet half a dozen times, it still smelt strongly of urine. He pulled the bleach out from under the sink, filled a bucket with hot water and opened the door of the toilet to give it a final clean.

After bleaching the toilet floor and throwing rubbish for the last time into the skip, he visited Laura in the shop. The door resisted his push, as it always did. Laura polished the windows on the shelves displaying soda and potato bread. She jumped, her eyes opening wide with surprise.

"Hi. What the news?"

She smiled at him, hugging him, pressing her face against his. He felt her skin slightly cold and damp against his cheek.

"Probably what you already know, Laura. Paddy has been diagnosed with dementia. He's in the Milthorn."

Laura searched for a tissue and wiped her eyes.

"But he's so independent. How will he live in a place like that?"

THE SECRET WOUND

Laura pulled a scrunchie from her hair and allowed her hair fall onto her shoulders.

She looked into Gurtha's eyes.

"What's the news from that Geisha girl who was at Nuala's funeral?"

Gurtha audibly gasped.

"Geisha girl - you mean Cornelia?"

"Yes. Cornelia."

Gurtha shook his head.

"She's back in Mallorca."

Laura dropped her arms to her side and stared at the ceiling. She bit on her lower lip before speaking.

"Are you … in a relationship with her?"

She waited for an answer.

"We are friends. Why do you ask that?"

"I saw you with her in Pizza Express on Monday. You didn't see me. I was sitting by the window. Watching you together, I wondered what, with her husband being dead, if maybe your relationship had changed?"

"Well, it hasn't changed for the better if that's what you mean. I'm upset that you didn't come over and join us for a meal. I would have liked that."

"You seemed to be having a deep conversation. I didn't want to interrupt."

"It's impossible not to have a deep conversation with Cornelia. That's the way she is."

Laura looked around as if afraid that someone would hear what she was going to say next.

"At the funeral, she wore a hat with a veil."

"Yes – that's right."

"I didn't see her hair. She didn't take her hat off at all."

"That's true. But I don't understand why that is important."

"In Pizza Express I saw her hair for the first time. It's distinctive – that blonde plait falling onto her shoulder, with her hair so black. It's also because the plait is so much longer than her black hair – it looks odd."

"Yes. I suppose it does if you're seeing it for the first time. She has had that hairstyle ever since I've known her. It looks normal to me. Why are you commenting on it – now?"

Laura's voice trembled.

"This is maybe crazy – but you know Michael Donovan – the taxi driver?"

"Yes. He used to drive Nuala to the hospital for her check ups."

"Yes, that's him. The day Nuala died, he came here to buy some bread. He told me that he'd had a strange woman in his taxi. He said that she seemed agitated. Even though he asked her not to, she insisted on smoking in the taxi. He decided to ignore it as he thought she seemed a little crazy. She asked to be dropped off at the bottom of Brompton Park. Michael had the feeling that she didn't want him to know where she was going."

Laura fiddled with the cloth in her hand. She polished the counter.

"Michael said that happens a lot when people have something to hide – normally they're having an affair. He asked me if I had seen her. He described that she was wearing black – a long black dress with a black leather jacket. He mentioned her hair – with a blonde plait buried in what he called raven black hair. I remembered that I had seen someone like that walk on the other side of the road, past the shop on the day that Nuala died. But I never thought anything about it until I saw you both arguing together in Pizza Express."

Gurtha interrupted.

THE SECRET WOUND

"We weren't arguing. Cornelia had a little too much to drink and was being a bit loud. But on the day that Nuala was murdered, Cornelia caught a taxi from the airport. It would be quite normal that you might have seen her walk past the shop if she decided that she wanted a little exercise."

Laura shook her head.

"No. You see, I saw her at mid-day. That was before Nuala died. Didn't you say that the coroner said that the time of death was around one o'clock? You discovered Nuala at four thirty."

"Yes, but Cornelia texted me from the airport at four thirty saying she had just landed at Belfast International. She landed after Nuala had been murdered. It couldn't have been Cornelia that you saw."

"She walked past the shop without looking in. It was mid-day. I remember that the bells of the Church were chiming for the Angelus. There isn't another person with a hairstyle like that around here. I imagine that she deliberately wore a hat at the funeral in case anyone, like Michael Donovan for example, recognised her."

Gurtha took a few seconds to reply.

"But even if Michael Donovan recognised her at the funeral, there would be no reason for him to be suspicious of her."

Laura stared straight into Gurtha's eyes.

"You've forgotten that people are intelligent. They make connections. She's a stranger, in a district where most people know one another. She is acting rather oddly. If the Police were asking questions about whether anyone had seen anything or anyone strange - which they were, of course – Michael Donovan would have come forward to share what he knew about Cornelia. He would have done that if he had recognised her at Mass - if she hadn't put on that hat for disguise."

Gurtha's hands began to tremble. He felt a dull ache at the base of his spine. His head felt thick with a shooting pain moving across his forehead.

"He could have come forward and told the Police what he saw and what he thought. He didn't need to see her in the Church to tell the Police that there was a stranger acting oddly in the area."

Laura placed the polishing cloth gently on the glass counter and looked directly at Gurtha.

"Say that Michael saw her in the Church, sitting in the row of mourners beside you, powdering her nose, her hair covered by a beret and her face by a veil, he wouldn't make a connection would he? Do you not see that? It happened to me. I saw Cornelia walk past the shop but it was only when I saw her with you in Pizza Express that the penny dropped."

Gurtha clenched his fists and looked at the floor.

"God. What do I do now?"

Laura took his hands in hers.

"Do you not need to tell the Police?"

"But I need to talk to her first. There might be an explanation."

"But why would she not have told you that on the day Nuala was murdered she was in the house? You're not going to cover up for her are you?"

Laura placed her hands over her mouth.

"When you talked about her, in the past I used to think that maybe you were having an affair. Even if that were true, it wouldn't mean that you would let Nuala's murderer go free, would you?"

Gurtha held onto the counter and steadied himself. His legs felt wobbly and he struggled to breathe.

"Laura, I can imagine that it might have looked as if Cornelia and I were having an affair but it was never like that. We had an unusual friendship. We shared our deepest secrets with another.

THE SECRET WOUND

When you do that – something is released. You are liberated. Something opens up between you which is more than an affair could ever be. You glimpse into someone's soul and they see yours. Everything in the relationship is transparent and shining. You've fallen into something Divine in them and they have fallen into the Divine in you. It used to be like that with Cornelia, but that isn't how it is now."

"What has changed?"

Gurtha pressed the bag of buns to his chest.

"She changed in the months before Henry died."

Laura rubbed her eyes.

"How?"

"It's hard to explain. You know that film about the 'Stepford Wives' where the women were robots. It began to feel like that with Cornelia – that someone had programmed her – or maybe she had programmed herself. She was distant from herself, from Henry and from me. She was playing an act – pretending to be someone who wasn't real. Or that she had decided to be someone else."

Laura sighed.

"That is what I am saying to you. She has lied to you. She is still lying."

Gurtha shook his head vigorously.

"I can't believe that she would murder Nuala. On Monday she told me that she loved Nuala."

Laura listened carefully before responding.

"What did Nuala think of Cornelia? That would be revealing."

"She had concerns about her. I know that she didn't like the way she treated Henry."

Gurtha held his head in his hands.

"OK. Let's take it one step at a time. I'll see Paddy tomorrow and the day after I'll fly to Mallorca and have a conversation with Cornelia as soon as I possibly can. If there is not a satisfactory explanation from her, I'll let the Police know and they can investigate."

Laura looked at Gurtha in a way that reminded him of Nuala – fearless, honest and compassionate.

"You need to do that. It's important for Nuala and for me. I feel uncomfortable about not going immediately to the Police."

DAY 22

SUNDAY 1ST SEPTEMBER 2013

GURTHA FOLLOWED Maggie's wobbling hips along the corridor until they reached Room 11. Paddy's photograph had been placed on the door. He stared at Gurtha, as if from his passport. Maggie opened the door slowly.

"Morning Paddy. Gurtha to see you. Remember, lunch will be ready for you shortly."

Gurtha filled the kettle in the room to make tea. Paddy sat in the chair beside the window – overlooking the car park. Gurtha sat on the bed and they smiled at one another. Now, more than ever, Gurtha wanted to look into Paddy's face – to see who he was changing into. At times if felt as if he was there but wasn't there – a shadow of himself – a ghost of himself. Gurtha gently asked,

"Paddy do you remember the day that Nuala died. We now think that there was a visitor to the house. Do you remember what she looked like?"

Paddy's eyes faded a little as he attempted to retrieve something from a space far inside or outside. He remained silent, staring ahead for at least a minute. Gurtha didn't interrupt. Eventually he spoke.

"I don't think Nuala died."

Gurtha leaned forward to offer a custard cream biscuit.

"I know it is a little while ago, Paddy. It's not so easy to remember. I find it hard to remember some things myself. I have to write them down.

Paddy nodded.

"Nuala wrote it down."

"What did she write down Paddy?"

Paddy shook the crumbs from the biscuit off his corduroy trousers onto the floor.

"Pass me my wallet and I'll show you."

Gurtha got quickly to his feet.

"Where's your wallet Paddy? In your jacket?"

Gurtha walked to the wardrobe and searched Paddy's green tweed jacket pockets, pulling out a black wallet. He handed it over.

Paddy looked at it with a bulb of brightness returning to his eyes.

"It's not that one."

Gurtha took it from him, opened it and looked through it. There was a photo of Nuala, forty pounds which Gurtha had placed there a few days ago, still untouched and a few pound coins in the purse section. Nothing else.

"Which one Paddy, if it's not this one?"

Paddy shook his head.

"The one where Nuala used to put a list of messages. She wrote down the times that I had to take my tablets."

Gurtha remembered a pink wallet with owls on it that Nuala used to give Paddy. She would joke, saying that he was turning into 'a wise old owl'. Maybe Gurtha had thrown it, by mistake, into the skip. He started by checking the pockets of the three jackets hanging in the wardrobe. Nothing. Then he noticed the plastic bag containing items he had collected from Crumlin Road. He opened

THE SECRET WOUND

it. Inside were three of Paddy's caps – each folded in three. Gurtha remembered finding them in a drawer in Paddy's bedroom. He unfolded the first cap, a green tweed with a blue check, to find a roll of money bound with a plastic band. He counted it – three hundred pounds. He unfolded the second cap, grey and covered in cat hairs, to reveal a photo of Paddy and Nuala smiling into one another's eyes many years before at a Christmas Party. They were wearing Christmas Cracker hats and blowing squeaky whistles like snakes into each other's faces. He dropped the photo on the bed and breathlessly unfolded the third cap . Inside lay the pink wallet with the owl cover. His heart thumped as he walked back to Paddy.

"Is this it?"

Paddy looked at him, catching the excitement in Gurtha's voice, shouting in a loud voice.

"Yes. I told you it would be there."

Gurtha opened the wallet. There were two pieces of paper. One with list of Paddy's medications and the timings for him to take them. It was dated Wednesday 15th August 2012. There was a second piece of paper with Nuala's writing.

"Ask Laura to get help."

The paper had been crumpled several times and then opened, closed, folded into four and placed into the wallet.

Gurtha fell back on the bed, the letter dropping onto the floor. His head spun. He felt as though he was on a twister ride in an amusement park. He closed his eyes. Stabbing pain, followed by deep rolling nausea, started in his back and rolled like a tsunami towards his throat and down into his legs. His heart trembled – sending shockwaves into other organs – pains around his liver, a tightness of air in his lungs. He coughed – a dry movement in his throat, as he struggled to breathe.

Paddy struggled to his feet and stood over Gurtha – looking down at him.

Gurtha opened his eyes as Paddy placed a hand on Gurtha's shoulder.

"It's OK son. You found the wallet. I knew you would. It's going to be OK now isn't it?"

Gurtha lifted the two pieces of paper from the floor and placed them in his wallet.

"Yes. Everything is going to be fine. Laura said that she will visit you every day until I get back."

Paddy sat on the bed beside Gurtha.

"Why do you have to go son? Can you not stay here?"

DAY 23

MONDAY 2ND SEPTEMBER 2013

"DANCE, WHEN YOU'RE BROKEN OPEN. DANCE, IF YOU'VE TORN THE BANDAGE OFF. DANCE IN THE MIDDLE OF THE FIGHTING. DANCE IN YOUR BLOOD. DANCE WHEN YOU'RE PERFECTLY FREE."

J RUMI

AS SOON as Gurtha landed at Palma airport there was a message on his mobile from Cornelia:

"We need to talk. Get in touch as soon as you're back."

Gurtha texted back:

"Just landed. Yes urgent that we talk."

♥

Cornelia sighed as she read Gurtha's reply. He hadn't said when he would be calling around. She really needed to talk with him. It felt as if her life was spiralling once again out of control. She needed to stop it and Gurtha was her best chance to get it back on track before it was too late.

Barry opened the door of the sitting room searching for his Nike trainers. He found them beside the TV. As he tied the laces, he looked up at Cornelia.

"Are you sure that you don't want to come too."

She shook her head.

"It will be too hot. Anyway, you know that I have to open the

Gallery as Angelina has the day off. When will you be back?"

Barry ran his fingers through his hair. He had gelled his fringe to sit up on his forehead. Cornelia could smell his aftershave. It had a sweet flowery scent which she hadn't noticed before.

Barry hesitated before replying.

"It will be around mid-day. I've got a key. I'll come back to the house for a shower and then I'll join you in the Gallery and we can have lunch in Soller – if you like?"

"That sounds good." Cornelia looked at his hairy neck above his t-shirt and flabby arms lying almost lifeless by his side. He seemed disgusting to her now. It was hard to believe that she had ever enjoyed kissing him. Yet when Henry was alive, she had. Henry would go out for one of his afternoon walks, Barry would knock on the front door and they would immediately deeply kiss one another in the hallway. He continued to kiss her as he carried her upstairs. They collapsed on top of the bed which Cornelia had previously sprayed with Coco Chanel. Barry undressed her. His hands moved roughly over her naked body before they had sex, as Cornelia kept an eye on the alarm clock on the bedside table, anticipating Henry's return.

In those months before Henry died, it had felt briefly as if Barry had opened up a world in which every love song had been written for them. When Cornelia closed her eyes, she didn't feel Barry's body beside her, but the music quivering within her body as Barry's lips continued to press incessantly against hers. It was no longer as if he was kissing her but rather that she had dropped into the wave of the song. Norah Jones honeyed voice singing.

"Sleepless nights aren't so bad ... I don't want anything to change."

♥

THE SECRET WOUND

She heard the door close as Barry left for his walk. She waited for a minute before opening it.

It might be difficult not to be seen. She was lucky. A group of walkers were being guided up the road towards the Torre Picada, a small fort overlooking the sea. She tucked in behind them, wishing that she had remembered her hat. The September sun was still intense even though there was a gentle breeze from the sea. Carob pods hung like black witches fingers from the carob trees. Roses were wizened on the wire trellises as orange and red hibiscus flowers opened in the morning sun. Barry walked quickly ahead. She pushed her way toward the front of the walking group in order not to lose sight of him.

When she saw him turn left onto Calle Belgica, she smiled to herself. She knew it. He shouldn't be turning onto Calle Belgica if he was doing the walk that he said he had planned. He should instead be walking straight ahead. She felt a warm rush of energy and excitement flood her body. It would be easy now. She knew where he was going. He would walk along the Calle Belgica, drop down past the Jumeirah Hotel, down into the Santa Catalina district by the fishing Port. She could let him walk quite far ahead now. She only needed to make sure that when he got to the Santa Catalina district, she witnessed him turning right to climb the narrow street leading to Angelina's apartment.

He did. She continued to follow him. She now had to make sure that he entered the apartment. Barry stopped to talk to three black cats near the apartment. Seagulls hovered overhead, swirling in an enormous cloud of several hundred, strangely quiet. Barry pushed open the door of Angelina's apartment without ringing the bell. Cornelia did not need to go any further. She looked at her watch. It was nine-thirty. There was time to get the tram to Soller and open the Gallery.

She sat on the tram, as it clicked its steady way along the sea front in the Port and looked out to sea. She felt a sense of relief knowing that Barry would predictably call into the Gallery and tell lies about what he had done. She felt vindicated for her own sins. She tasted the sweetness of righteousness which comes with anticipating revenge.

She descended from the tram near the Plaza in Soller. Old men sat on benches leaning on walking sticks – the friendship of a lifetime soothing the passage of time – faces carved into grooves, imitating the olive trees. It was tempting to have a coffee but she was afraid that Gurtha might arrive and find the Gallery closed. She quickened her pace. It was already after ten.

She opened the Gallery to find the light falling onto the floor as it always did. Today it looked even more wonderful. She searched for her playlist and connected her phone to her Bose speaker. The song reminded her of being a child in Cardiff, listening to the rain beating against the window, holding Amelia's hand:

> *The rain tapped on the window*
> *Calling from above*
> *A quiet insistent yearning*
> *That seemed to talk of love*
>
> *Then there was a moment*
> *When no one was alone*
> *A fleeting, empty presence*
> *Filled with all and none*
>
> *What can you say*
> *When words have gone?*
> *What can you say when all alone?*

What can you say
When all you hear
For sure
Is a whisper within the silence of love?

She made a cup of coffee and checked the fridge to make sure that there was a bottle of chilled champagne - in case Gurtha arrived. A bottle of Moet, which a client had bought after purchasing one of the paintings, would do the job perfectly.

She checked her mobile – no messages from Gurtha. She pulled a wooden stool into a broad ray of sunlight and wondered how she could explain to Gurtha what had happened to Nuala. Would he believe her? There was one more problem which had to be resolved. She was happy to allow Angelina and Barry to squirm in one another's arms. They deserved one another. However, she had heard Angelina flirt with Gurtha, quoting T S Eliot. What was worse was that Gurtha responded to her with apparent interest. How could he do that? It was Cornelia's role in life to ask Gurtha questions that made him think. It was not Angelina's. Then there was the change in Gurtha's attitude towards her – his coldness. Was this intensified by his attraction for Angelina?

She began to breathe quickly and shallowly. She felt beads of sweat running down her temples which she didn't bother to wipe away. A scene played in her head of Angelina sitting cross legged on a tartan picnic rug. Beside her on the rug, a picnic basket had been opened. The white delph china plates inside removed and placed on the rug with an artisan whole grain loaf, a bottle of red wine, a circle of Cambazola cheese and a jar of olives. She opened the wine with four twists of her hand, removed two crystal glasses, filled them only half way up and passed a glass to Gurtha who held a six month old baby in his arms. They looked into one another's eyes and he smiled. It was the smile that he should have kept for her.

Cornelia brought her hands to her temples and squeezed them, shaking her head from side to side.

♥

Gurtha drove through the tunnel into Soller. The valley opened up before him dropping into Soller with the Church of Saint Bartholomew spiking the sky and the mountains around protecting the valley and isolating it from the rest of the world. He twisted and turned the twenty seven bends to La Torretta. The dust rose in a cloud behind him as the car struggled over the pot holes and gullies carved out by the winter rains. He opened the windows to hear the cicadas sing their incessant song of life. The hot air from outside swarmed through the car stinging his face and arms.

Once at 'La Torretta', he made a coffee and carried it out to the gazebo. The ghost of Paddy seemed to be sitting at the small table in the shade, overlooking Soller. He almost felt like making a second cup of coffee and leaving it there for him. He checked his mobile. There were no messages.

He sipped on his coffee. He thought about what he would say to Cornelia. How would he start the conversation? What kind of person was Cornelia, really? He had known her for twenty seven years. Did he know her at all? Did he know himself at all?

He thought about the number of people he had coached – the executives who had struggled with relationships in their high powered jobs. How he had asked them provocative, powerful questions to help them reflect and break through into insights into what they needed to do to improve these relationships. How he encouraged them to create clear objectives which they would

THE SECRET WOUND

review together. They would explore what made work challenging, the impact of global dynamics, the pace of change, the need for innovation and agility. How he talked about the role of emotions, the importance of developing self-awareness, self-control, executive disposition and stress tolerance.

Now he was unable to decide how to approach Cornelia. He felt nervous about asking her if she had been with Nuala earlier the day that she died and frightened of how Cornelia would react.

He tried to do what he encouraged others to do – to get in touch with his feelings. What was he feeling now? He was confused, afraid, anxious and also feeling like a fool – a hypocrite, a Pharisee. Someone who could talk about relationships, someone who knew all the theory about emotional intelligence but couldn't live it out in practice. If Cornelia had murdered Nuala, he felt a sense of self-loathing for having allowed this to happen by maintaining his friendship with Cornelia. Maybe in some way, he was to blame for Nuala's death.

What about Henry? Had Gurtha not betrayed Henry? Not by having sex with Cornelia, but with something much deeper. He had tried to possess Cornelia's soul. Was that not a more significant treachery than possessing her body?

As these thoughts and these feelings of remorse, confusion and despair surged within him like lava from a volcano, he reached down to his side, where there was a deep twisting pain, as if someone had stabbed him. It was a physical pain – buried deeper than his seeking for approval from the academic world, his coachees, the rounds of applause and laughter at his after dinner speeches. He felt a sense of humiliation, a disintegration of who he had known himself to be. He felt himself melting into nothingness – or the somethingness of a burning stream of lava, moving downhill. Previously he had searched for ascent in life, acquiring what he had thought brought greatness. He now knew it was a tale of empty promises and false hopes.

♥

At twelve thirty in the Gallery, Barry kissed Cornelia on the cheek. His fringe back in its normal position. His lips felt soft and soggy on her skin. She felt her cheek contract and shrivel. As he moved towards the Nespresso machine, she wiped her cheek with a handkerchief.

"Did you enjoy your walk?"

Barry pressed the espresso button and opened the cake tin.

"It was too hot – like you said. But I need to lose weight." He patted his stomach.

She noticed that his face was red and blotchy, as was his neck. He swivelled right and left surveying the room, cramming a piece of fruit cake into his mouth.

Cornelia turned up her nose,

"You'll find that if you don't eat so much, it's an easier way to lose weight than walking in thirty five degrees centigrade. Not pleasant I'm sure. You look as if you've caught the sun."

THE SECRET WOUND

DAY 24

TUESDAY 3RD SEPTEMBER 2013

GURTHA TRIED to pluck up courage to speak to Cornelia. Laura had texted him to insist that he call her immediately, reminding him that investigating Police officer Andy Finn would not be impressed if Gurtha again delayed in providing new information relevant to the case.

♥

He reassembled once again the jigsaw pieces from which he had created a picture of Cornelia in the past – a picture in which he no longer believed. In those first University days he remembered the pleasure he took from their conversations. It was like a sparring match. They exchanged words without ever hurting one another, preparing themselves for the jousts of life. These conversations were intense, delving deeper and deeper – words mingling onto a page and reassembling sense and meaning. They would try to catch one another out, to respond with new insights and dealing blows to old ways of being. It was intoxicatingly exciting. They were creating their own wisdom together. Henry wouldn't contribute to the discussions but instead searched for exotic recipes which they prepared together. As Cornelia sliced a lettuce leaf into small pieces, Henry broke open a crab's leg and removed the flesh. Cornelia pontificated.

"Religion is dead. It is as Marx said, 'The opium of the people'. It is designed to instil fear, to control people, to make them believe that there is a God who is watching them and who will punish them. It doesn't exist. We have to think for ourselves."

Gurtha lay back on the sofa, looking into the flames of logs burning on an open fire.

"Henry – what do you think?"

As it was a Friday, Henry was wearing his indigo blue cravat with a white shirt and navy blue silk trousers. He sucked on a crab leg.

"I think we complicate life. It's simple. Enjoy it. This crab has done a wonderful job sacrificing itself for my pleasure. I am grateful to it."

Gurtha laughed, walked over to Henry, lifted a second crab leg and sucked it.

"Let me also be grateful. Thank you Mr Crabby."

Then he turned to Cornelia who was removing charcoaled skin from a roasted pepper. Gurtha patted Cornelia on the head as he said, "I think that you're wrong. Rules are made to protect us because we have not developed a level of consciousness which sees a reality beyond the superficial thinking mind and emotional body. That consciousness moving towards the depths of our being is a different awareness. If we could access that awareness, we would see differently and would not need the rules made for children who need protection until they know."

Cornelia inspected an anchovy which she removed from a gourmet jar.

"How elitist of you, as always. I suppose you see yourself as one of the highly vibrating energy forces pulsating love into the world, whilst the rest of us are fools and inferior human beings?"

Gurtha was unmoved by her petulance.

"Do the science. Observe the consequences in your own life. Of your actions and the impact which they have on you and others. I don't need to read any books to work that one out."

Cornelia pushed the anchovy to one side and dissected the last remaining lettuce leaf.

"If I happen to have a lower level consciousness than you do – whatever created me – if anything did – must have wanted me to enjoy this – to experience my limitations and humiliations."

Gurtha picked up a poker and stirred the burning embers.

"Yes, but the purpose could be to guide you to an experience of love."

Cornelia looked at him out of the corner of her eye.

"What's holding this intelligence back then from doing it?"

Gurtha threw another long log on the fire.

"You know. I don't."

Cornelia laughed, throwing her head back in a way which was so familiar.

"I think I know what it means in one word."

Cornelia snorted,

"Of course you would Mr Bright Guy. One word. Spit it out then."

Gurtha gently said, "Sacrifice."

He remembered how she seemed to tremble at that word, falling unusually silent.

Gurtha decided to ring Cornelia and stop procrastinating over the conversation about Nuala's death.

"Cornelia can I meet you for a coffee in the Plaza?"

"Of course. When?"

"Now, if it is OK for you."

"It sounds urgent. Is it something to worry about?"

"I'd rather tell you when we're face to face."

"Oh dear. That does sound like something to worry about. Let's meet in Café Es Planet in half an hour."

Gurtha looked at his watch.

"Can we make it in one hour? I'd like to walk down."

"That's perfect."

He lifted his rucksack, checked that he had a torch and rope as always and looked for a bottle of chilled water in the fridge. He began his descent, walking along a track which would join the main hiking path into the town. Wasps buzzed low over lavender. Their long bodies held together as though by a black thread – not like the sturdy wasps from Belfast. He crossed the main road leading to Lluc and continued down a pathway covered in small yellow flowers, past a convent and a small chapel. He passed a man and a woman who were building a stone wall. The woman had no hands, only stumps which ended below her elbows. They allowed her to lift the stones and set them into place whilst the man , who Gurtha imagined to be her husband, looked for new stones a little further along the path.

Everything which appeared before Gurtha was a story being told. A story with hidden, deep messages. From now on, everyone and everything would tell him a story and what part it had to play in his life.

Descending, he passed a house where, through the gate, a giant black dog the size of a small horse, was chained to a pole. The dog snarled ferociously. Gurtha shuddered, imagining that it might break loose, leap over the gate and sink its fangs into his neck.

Cornelia now seemed like that Mallorcan Shepherd dog – dark haired, potentially aggressive and guarding secrets.

In the Plaza, Cornelia was already sitting at a table on the terrace outside Es Planet. Beside her were stalls filled with cheeses, olives, honey, local Mallorcan salt, bread, curled up sausages and sobrasada. A musky smell hung over everything, lightened by flower stalls crammed with pots of gerberas, herbs and delicate begonias and petunias.

Cornelia removed her sunglasses as Gurtha approached. She was wearing a straw hat with a black ribbon tied in a bow, the ends of which fell onto her shoulders. Her dress was emerald green, a mixture of silk on top and a chiffon skirt with matching emerald sandals. She held both arms out, warmly embracing him as he reached the table.

"How is Paddy?"

Gurtha heard himself say words which he hadn't plan to say. The tone was gruff.

"Missing Nuala, as you can imagine."

Cornelia didn't react to his aggression but smiled at him.

"That's normal. With his dementia, it's probably even more difficult for him. I'm sure he finds it hard to believe that she is dead." She sat down.

"Would you like a coffee, or maybe a beer in this heat?"

Gurtha took off his hat and sat down beside her, lowering his rucksack onto the ground.

"I'll have a beer, thank you."

The waiter approached, a smiling broad faced, slightly unshaven man who spoke excellent English.

"What would the gentleman like? I was afraid that this beautiful woman was going to be left alone." He smiled at Cornelia and then looked at Gurtha.

"She is so dainty – a chocolate in a fine chocolate box. I can see you are a man of taste."

Cornelia dropped her eyes demurely to the table. When the waiter disappeared, she said.

"I've been thinking a lot about Nuala. Do you remember the last time we were all together – you, me, Nuala and Paddy? Henry wasn't able to join us. He was quite ill – all puffed up and inflated like a hot air balloon." She gave a short laugh, caught Gurtha's expression and adopted a more sober tone.

"That's what he called himself. A hot air merchant. He said that was what being in the world of banking turned him into." Her smile changed to sadness and regret.

"I so miss him, too. I know what Paddy must feel like."

Gurtha watched her intently, attempting to read between the lines. Was she telling the truth or telling lies? He decided to ask her a question.

"So, you're saying that the last time you saw Nuala alive was that evening on Paddy and Nuala's 40th wedding anniversary in Belfast at my house. Is that the case?"

He was rather proud of the way he was interrogating her, like a prosecuting Barrister. He was also feeling a little uncomfortable, remembering that the reason he had chosen his house to celebrate their wedding anniversary rather than Nuala and Paddy's was that he was ashamed of their home. Gurtha had arranged for a catering company to cook and serve for them. They had lychees for starter. Paddy couldn't eat them because he had no teeth and no way to remove the flesh of the lychees from the stones. This was followed by crab bisque which Nuala thought was going to be a crab dressed up in a risqué costume and they all laughed. Then there was a stuffed pork fillet with roast potatoes and apple sauce. They finished with a chocolate bombe with a hot toffee sauce. Nuala joked that there had been enough bombs going off in Belfast during the Troubles without needing to eat another one.

The first question that Nuala directed to Cornelia that evening was, "What are the symptoms of Henry's ill health? It's always interesting to know, as I have a bad heart myself."

Cornelia raised her eyes towards the ceiling and answered,

"He's very tired, lethargic, has put on a lot of weight, arthritis, diabetes, depression, gasping for air in the middle of the night, at times not breathing in his sleep and I have to give him a push to waken him up … Not good."

Nuala took a sip of her coffee,

"You must be really upset not to be with him this evening if he is in such a poor condition."

Cornelia gave Nuala a withering look.

"Life has to go on – do you not think?"

She then grabbed her glass of white wine and finished it in one large gulp as a silence fell over the room.

Gurtha broke the silence asking, "Anyone for a digestif?"

Paddy brightened up.

"I'll have three digestive biscuits and a cup of tea, if you don't mind."

In the Plaza, Gurtha took a sip of chilled San Miguel.

Cornelia straightened her hat to cover her face from the sun. She hadn't answered Gurtha's question. He decided on a more direct approach.

"Did you see Nuala on the day that she died?"

There was silence. Gurtha sat with his hands on his knees waiting.

Eventually Cornelia spoke, with a certain hesitation.

"Well, yes, I was with her."

Gurtha sat upright.

"At what time were you with her?"

"It must have been close to mid-day."

"But you have never mentioned this before. Knowing that Nuala was murdered, you never said a thing to me, or for that matter, to the Police. What were you doing with Nuala?"

"I had arrived early as I had bought you a present for your birthday. I wanted it to be a surprise."

Gurtha asked,

"What was it?"

"A box of Roses. You said that they grow on you. I thought that you would get the joke and know they were from me."

"What happened?"

"I arrived at the house and Nuala opened the door. I explained why I was there. She took the chocolates from me and said that she would give them to you." Cornelia began to sniffle and look for a handkerchief.

"I asked if I could see your bedroom. We had a bit of an argument. Argument is too strong a word. It was a slight disagreement over nothing really. She said that she didn't like to show me your room without you being there. Paddy looked a bit upset and she sent him out to buy some milk - I think – she wrote something down on a piece of paper.

After Paddy left, I explained how upset I had been since Henry's death and that this small act of generosity as a surprise for you made me feel better. I know that you sleep in your big house on the Malone Road but I wanted to see where you used to sleep and to leave the chocolates on top of your pillow. It would be as if an angel had dropped by."

"What happened next?"

She hesitated, looking as if she was about to leave the table and then, gripping her handbag close to her chest, she took a deep breath.

"She tripped on the carpet on the landing after showing me the room. She tumbled downstairs. There was nothing I could do about it. Why didn't you make sure the carpet was tacked down safely?"

"Why did you leave her and not stay with her and call an ambulance?"

"She was dead. There was no pulse. I checked."

"Anyone normal would still have called for an ambulance. It's called abandoning the scene of a crime. It's an offence."

"Nobody would have believed that it was an accident if I had stayed."

"Why not?"

"Because nobody ever believes a word that I say. They never have done."

"Maybe there is a good reason for that."

"What?"

"That you are a confounded liar. How do you explain the Coroner's report said that Nuala had been murdered?"

The waiter rushed towards the table as Cornelia pulled at the glass of beer in Gurtha's hand. He let go of it. She threw the contents into his face.

"Don't call me a liar. It wouldn't be the first time that a coroner has made a mistake."

The beer trickled down his face. Gurtha stared after Cornelia as she ran towards the tram. The waiter used a napkin to dab the beer from Gurtha's t-shirt. Then Gurtha got slowly to his feet, gathered the rucksack from the ground, paid the waiter and walked slowly away from the Plaza in the opposite direction. The tram tooted as it passed by with Cornelia inside.

♥

Gurtha walked along the sea front and turned right to follow the road which would take him past Cornelia and Barry's house. From the Port, he would have to climb the steep path home. The heat sizzled below a cloudless sky and not a bird was to be seen. Suddenly, an eagle swooped in a quick curve from a tall pine in the hill in front. It disappeared into the long dry grass.

What was the truth about what had happened to Nuala? He was ashamed at his own behaviour during the conversation with Cornelia. He had wanted to find out the truth but to do so gently. Yet it had descended into an unsightly brawl rather their usual sparring match. Barry had commented on Cornelia's vitriolic anger. Gurtha had witnessed her mood swings in La Quinta and now in the Plaza. What might she have been capable of doing to Nuala? The coroner's report contradicted Cornelia's story. Yet there was no obvious motivation for why Cornelia would want to kill Nuala. It didn't make sense.

The story of the box of chocolates did not seem credible. A box of chocolates is hardly an extravagant present which would make an impression on anyone – least of all Gurtha. What did she do later with the chocolates? The box of chocolates would have been covered with the fingerprints of Cornelia and Nuala. If Cornelia had stayed with Nuala, called an ambulance, the box of 'Roses' chocolates lying upstairs on the pillow might have given weight to Cornelia's story that it had been an unfortunate accident. But what about the fact that the coroner had said that there had been evidence of a struggle? In fact, Gurtha hadn't told anyone as it was too upsetting to imagine. The coroner thought that it likely that Nuala had not fallen down the stairs but had been violently pushed over the bannister after a desperate struggle with her killer. It was only then that she had been dragged into a position to make it look as if she had fallen downstairs.

He breathed deeply as the road became steeper. He passed a house with a basket of oranges outside and was tempted to buy a few as he was already thirsty but there was no-one around to pay. He swallowed deeply. He had found a small consolation in what Cornelia had said. Paddy could no longer be a suspect.

He turned left onto the stony path which narrowed and began to drop away sharply to the right. His heart pounded. This walk terrified him. He knew to look straight ahead. He grasped at the bushes to his left, but the leaves and thin branches came away in his hand. In another hundred metres or so it would get worse. He tried to stop himself thinking, but his body trembled. He thought about finding a way to use the rope in his rucksack. Maybe he could lasso it to the branches of a tree further along the path.

He was annoyed at the recurrence of these panic attacks. He had to learn how to go beyond these animal instincts for self preservation. He had to go beyond fear. He opened the rucksack and took out his bottle of water. He perched on the edge of a craggy rock and drank deeply. When he had drained the bottle, he continued slowly along the sandy path. It became narrower, as he knew it would. The pebbles were smaller and skidded off the edge. He heard them bounce down into the heathers in the valley below. He looked ahead. There, sitting on the path cross legged, was Cornelia.

She was wearing the same green dress she had worn earlier in the Plaza but had replaced her sandals with a pair of white trainers. She also had a white scarf tied around her head instead of a hat. She smiled at him.

"What are you doing here?" Gurtha struggled to find words.

"I knew that you would be walking this way and that this part of the walk frightens you. I can help."

She reached a hand towards him. Gurtha stretched and grasped her fingers. She intertwined her fingers with his and gave him a gentle pull.

"Take it easy. Don't rush," she whispered, drawing him towards her. She took a few small steps back and whispered again, "There's nothing to be afraid of."

Gurtha took a few shaky steps forward. Cornelia walked backwards holding his hand. When they arrived at the top where the path levelled out and broadened, close to La Torretta, they walked side by side, smelling the pine needles roasting on the ground. At first they said nothing and then Cornelia spoke.

"I was horrible to you this afternoon. I'm sorry. It must have been a shock for you to know that I was with Nuala when she died. I should have told you earlier."

Cornelia caught his hand and squeezed it.

"We've been through a lot together. Haven't we? What are you going to do about it?"

Gurtha shook his head and they continued in silence.

Then he spoke.

"I don't know. If you were in my shoes what would you suggest?"

Cornelia tightened the scarf on her head.

"I didn't know either. I think you can understand why I ran away from the scene. I imagine that you think I am not telling the truth. Do whatever you have to do."

They continued walking in silence.

Half an hour later, they approached La Torretta. Gurtha opened the gate for Cornelia to enter. He calmly stated.

"I'll drive you back home. It will be getting dark soon."

Cornelia shrugged her shoulders.

"You don't need to. I can walk."

Gurtha let her step ahead of him.

"I insist."

DAY 25

WEDNESDAY 4TH SEPTEMBER 2013

"THERE IS A CANDLE IN YOUR HEART, READY TO BE KINDLED. THERE IS A VOID IN YOUR SOUL, READY TO BE FILLED. YOU FEEL IT, DON'T YOU?"
J RUMI

NEXT MORNING Gurtha rang Laura to explain how the conversation with Cornelia had gone. He correctly imagined her response.

"Her story is not believable. You need to speak with Police Officer Andy Finn today."

Gurtha replied, "I'll ring him immediately we finish this call. It's not impossible that she is telling the truth. I can imagine that the shock of Nuala falling to her death could provoke a panic reaction."

Laura sounded cross as she said,

"Gurtha – let the Police judge the evidence. I know that there has to be justice for Nuala and for Cornelia. You've known Cornelia for over twenty five years and in many ways it is admirable that you don't want to jump to assumptions about her being guilty. Let the Police continue their investigations and if she's innocent, she will be proven innocent. It is as simple as that. I personally think that she is as guilty as sin."

Gurtha asked, "What makes you so sure?"

Laura paused before answering.

"The fact that she has lied to you and pretended that she landed at the airport at 4.30 pm and the way she behaved at the funeral. She didn't seem like someone who was grieving for anyone."

"What way did she behave? Maybe I missed something."

Laura sounded slightly agitated.

"How many times did she open up that mirror and apply that gaudy red lipstick? It's not something you do at a funeral. You would think she was about to walk up a red carpet to receive an Oscar. Maybe she deserves an Oscar for managing to keep a lie like that going for over a year."

Gurtha listened carefully. He said slowly, "I'm struggling with what her motivation would have been. I don't get that at all. If there's no motivation it has to be more likely that it was an accident and that the coroner has misinterpreted the evidence."

"I suppose that is what Cornelia would say – that there is no motivation for her to kill Nuala."

Gurtha replied, "Well – yes – it is what she suggested after she threw the beer around me."

Laura laughed.

"I know this is really upsetting. But the beer incident was slightly funny. Maybe we need to imagine that if she were guilty what could be her possible motivations in wanting to murder Nuala. Have you no idea after all the conversations you must have had with Henry and her over the years?"

"Not really. If I think back over the years, I would say right from the start that she was 'interested' in Nuala. She wanted to know what Nuala thought and how she would respond to situations. They only met face to face for the first time at the 40th wedding anniversary. One small fact which may be relevant is that, at times she seemed a little jealous of my relationship with Nuala, but nothing that then or now seems significant. I was more concerned about the change in her behaviour with Henry. I definitely saw behaviours which I would have described as cruel. I told her as much when we were on holiday at La Quinta de los Cedros and she was very angry with me. There is also the fact that Barry confirmed that she was furious with Henry after he retired because Henry didn't receive the pension that Cornelia was looking forward to."

He could hear Laura trying to synthesise what he was saying.

"So money, lifestyle and intellectual jousting with you are important to her – but I can't see why that would encourage her to murder Nuala. In their investigations, the Police will have more experience of what might be going on and also greater skill in questioning her. Let's move it over to them. You will go crazy trying to work this out."

♥

Gurtha immediately phoned Police Inspector Andy Finn to bring him up to date with the new information about Cornelia. The Inspector remained silent – waiting for Gurtha to finish, before saying, "Mr Maloney. I don't think you realise the seriousness of this situation. You received a report on Saturday 31st August from your friend Laura whilst you were in Belfast to indicate that Cornelia had been seen close to Nuala's house at mid-day on the day Nuala was murdered. Cornelia had not revealed this information either to you or to the Police. It is now Wednesday the 4th September and you have only just informed us of new information about what happened that day. Why did you not contact us while you were in Belfast?"

Gurtha took a deep breath. He hadn't expected such a strong response from Andy Finn.

THE SECRET WOUND

"This was a serious allegation made about Cornelia. I have known her for twenty seven years. I thought I owed it to her to ask for an explanation face to face before reporting something which may not have any relevance to the case."

Andy Finn continued in an even more stern voice, "Mr Maloney, I repeat that you do not seem to understand that, not only is Cornelia guilty of withholding information and obstructing a Police investigation, but these charges could also be made against you. It is not up to you to decide whether new evidence is relevant or not to the case. That is for the Police to decide. I hope I am making myself clear. We need your full co-operation now. In our initial warning to the public we stated that we believe that the person who murdered Nuala has a profile which would indicate that he or she would be capable of murdering again. You are not only jeapordising the chance to find Nuala's murderer, but may also be putting other lives in danger. We cannot rule out that Cornelia is not the murderer at this stage and so here is what I need you do.

Firstly, do not tell her that you have contacted me. Attempt to keep her in a stable and unemotional state of mind. Continue with normal activities in order not to arouse suspicion. We will continue further investigations here. I will speak to Laura, the taxi driver and others who now may be able to confirm what they saw at around mid-day on 15th August 2012. We will also speak with Paddy. I will contact the local police to advise them that we may need their help. In the meantime, I need you to scan me the documents you found in Paddy's wallet. We may need a week to complete our checks here, which will including requesting the coroner to review the report in the light of the new evidence and a further forensic investigation of the house to see if we can find any new evidence which relates to Cornelia being present. As soon as we have data collated from all sources, I will personally fly to the island to interview Cornelia. What questions do you have?"

Gurtha stuttered slightly as he asked, "What should I say if she directly asks me if I have contacted the Police?"

"Mr Maloney, you have known Cornelia for twenty seven years. I urge you to make the appropriate response which will keep the situation stable until I arrive."

When Gurtha finished his call with Andy Finn, he found himself shivering. He walked onto the patio and stood with his back against the grey and orange stone walls which were warm from the morning sun. He closed his eyes. There was a ping on the mobile he was still holding – a message from Cornelia.

"How are you feeling today?"

"A little bit shivery and cold – even though it 35 degrees. I might be catching something. I'll see you tomorrow. Hope you are well."

Andy Finn would be proud of him.

DAY 26

THURSDAY 5TH SEPTEMBER 2013

AS GURTHA mulled over what had happened and was happening in his relationship with Cornelia, what surprised him most was how little he knew about her – how little he knew about everything and everyone – including Paddy and Nuala.

He accessed his voicemail messages. He had forgotten to listen to them the day before. There were over twenty messages from Paddy. He seemed relaxed and not agitated. Each message identical:

"Hello Gurtha. It's your father – Paddy. Give me a ring."

Gurtha phoned the Milthorn. Maggie had said that everything was fine and that the only the minor problem was that Paddy refused to get washed.

"I don't think he likes to be showered by a woman. It's normal for a man of his age. I think he might be afraid of falling in the shower as well. You told me that he didn't have a shower at home – only a bath."

Gurtha explained to Maggie that Paddy and Nuala hadn't slept in the same bed for years – so it was unlikely that he would want a strange woman undressing him and showering him.

Paddy opened his eyes. Where was he? The walls were yellow. He closed his eyes. Yellow was nice. He opened them again. He looked around the room. A kettle sat on a shelf to his right. Mugs hung from a wooden tree. Who put them there?

He looked down. The duvet was covered in flowers – roses, Nuala's favourites. He lifted the duvet and looked at his body. Striped blue and white pyjamas with a white cord tied in a bow. How do you tie a bow like that? Did he do that?

He sniffed the air, disinfectant. Had Nuala been cleaning? There was another smell. He lifted the duvet again. There was a wet stain on his trousers. The bed felt wet.

What had happened? He folded back the duvet and manoeuvred his legs out of bed. He laughed out loud as he looked at his feet on the floor. Whose feet were they? Whoever they belonged to, they couldn't be happy with them – they were ugly feet. He moved his toes. They weren't useless feet. They were capable of doing something. He put both hands on the duvet and pushed himself into a standing position. What now?

He felt something moving along his leg, heading south – like a line of caterpillars. They were inside his pyjamas bottoms. He looked down at his legs and started to slap them. That would frighten them off. He stared at the strange shape of his feet, resting on the ground holding him up. What were they? One, two, three, four, five. Another to the left. One, two, three, four, five. He leaned forward to look more closely at his toes. What were they doing there? He raised his right big toe from the ground and released it back again to the floor. Curious. He bent forward and touched it. What would it do next?

He was still aware of the caterpillars in his pyjamas. He slapped his legs again to chase them away. A pool of liquid appeared on the

THE SECRET WOUND

floor. He took two steps to the right. It reminded him of dancing with Nuala. Two steps to the left. Two back and two forward.

♥

Maggie opened the door with a phone in her hand,

"Paddy – it's Gurtha for you. He got your messages. Do you want to have a word?"

Paddy took the phone.

"Gurtha. When am I going to see you?"

Gurtha replied, "Very soon. You're in your yellow room, aren't you?"

Paddy looked around.

"If you walk over to the window you can see the car park, can't you?"

Paddy walked over to the window.

"Yes."

"So you're fine. You keep behaving yourself. Don't forget to get washed now. You know it's good for you."

Paddy laughed down the phone.

"Sure we never had a bath – only a tin out in the yard and you only got in there once every couple of months. It was freezing. Everyone had to use the same water."

He handed the phone back to Maggie before Gurtha could say goodbye.

♥

Back in La Torretta Gurtha looked at his watch. It was nearly two o'clock. He recalled how Andy Finn had emphasised the importance of keeping Cornelia calm and unsuspecting of any investigation. He had told her yesterday that he would see her today. She would be wondering what his reaction was and she might be annoyed with him for not getting in touch. Yet he didn't feel he had the strength to see her today.

Without thinking more about it, he lifted the phone and dialled her number. It would be better to speak than leave a text for a second day in a row.

She answered immediately.

"How are you? Are you coming down to the Gallery? Angelina wants to show you how well the exhibition is going."

Gurtha coughed twice.

"Thank you both for all the hard work. I feel a bit mean, but if you don't mind, I'll have another quiet day and see you tomorrow. The cold is getting better. I don't feel so shivery but I don't want to spread any bugs. How does that sound?"

Cornelia was silent for a second or two before replying.

"Of course. If you want, you can leave it to Saturday – didn't you say we were all invited to your neighbour Toni's fiesta?"

Gurtha attempted to sound enthusiastic.

"I'd forgotten about that. There will be quite a few people here. It should be fun. So, I may see you tomorrow in the Gallery and if not, it's definitely everyone at Toni's on Saturday evening around eight o'clock."

He set the phone on the table with a sigh of relief. The more people that were around, the easier it would be to keep Cornelia off the scent of what was really happening.

♥

Gurtha felt that he needed a break after the intensity of the previous twenty six days. He decided to have lunch in a restaurant a little further up the mountain - the Mirador de ses Barques. He walked along a broad stony path, before veering steeply to the right and climbing towards the Mirador. The wind moved through the valley with the sound of waves crashing onto sand. Olive trees seemed appearances of twisted shapes of previous thoughts, planted into soil feeding them in mysterious ways. Olive trees bending, bulging, unknown, unseen works of art. The artist's hand painting in the dark, form emerging from no known cause. Leaves now waving silvery green - movement embedded within stillness of crooked trunks. No straight lines anywhere.

The final climb towards the Mirador took him through a shadowy ancient passageway. He trod it as he imagined a climber would pick his way carefully towards the summit of Everest. Dead bodies on either side of the path, acorns sinking into sandy earth rather than snow.

He lifted a warm acorn from the ground – inspecting the hard brown egg shell with the green protection of a Buddha stupa. It was alive. A genetic imprint of greatness.

As he climbed, he felt himself surrounded by a life of possibilities. The acorn had to die to become the oak tree. The bodies scattered on the slopes of Everest? What did they become? Memories in a loved one's mind, laughter, tears incarnate, frozen until the end of time.

When he reached the Mirador he walked onto the balcony with its tables set for lunch. He sat alone, looking down on the Port of Soller. There was a sheer drop from the balcony to the valley below which stretched towards the sea. He felt familiar waves of vertigo move through his body – dizziness with a hint of nausea. He gazed into the vast sky.

What kind of relationship did he have with Cornelia? In Pizza Express, she had said that it wasn't a normal relationship. That was true. Yet, even though the relationship had changed before Henry's death, he knew that whatever happened, he still loved Cornelia. He had whispered in La Quinta after their row that "Love Just Is". Looking down at the Port of Soller – he knew that even if Cornelia had murdered Nuala, it was impossible for him not to love her. If 'Love Just Is' – he couldn't stop it – no matter how terrible her actions. What would be his loving response to her? He didn't know. But Love would know how to respond.

One night, before the big row, while staying at La Quinta, they had gone to a Thai restaurant where Henry, wearing his amber cravat, extolled the beauty of Thai food. He ordered a salad filled with beansprouts, tofu, peppers and a picante dressing. Cornelia and Gurtha began to talk about different kinds of relationships. Gurtha started by talking about marriages in which there was a 'symbiosis' – a long term co-existence of two different biological species which is beneficial to one or to both parties.

Cornelia asked Henry, "What do you think about that Henry, do we have a symbiotic marriage?"

Henry smiled at the Thai waitress who served them Tom Yum soup. "Of course darling. We are like two turtle doves."

Cornelia snorted rather than laughed,

"We meet the criteria for a long term living together and being two different biological species – but as for beneficial to one or two parties – I think the jury is out on that one."

Henry responded, sipping his soup, "This is superb. You can taste the lemongrass, galangal and kaffir lime leaves – a soup to die for."

Cornelia ignored him and continued the conversation by talking about relationships which where 'parasitic', those in which one member benefits while the other is harmed. She then asked, "Henry, darling – I think that is more like us – do you not?"

THE SECRET WOUND

Henry shook his head and said, "Well it would have to be me who has benefitted. I recommend the Thai larb. Rarely have I tasted such quality - perfect sticky rice."

It all felt rather embarrassing to Gurtha. He wondered if this was the kind of conversation which Henry now had to constantly endure. Gurtha felt obliged to finish the topic by explaining that there were also relationships which existed in a state of 'synnecrosis' - where any interaction was detrimental to both organisms. He waited for Cornelia to make another sarcastic comment but thankfully she only topped up each of their glasses and said, "So we have a trio of possibilities and none of them sounds particularly marvellous."

♥

As Gurtha tucked into Spanish Tortilla and salad, it occurred to him that there was a fourth level of relationship which hadn't occurred to him that evening in the Thai restaurant. Maybe it was just as well, as Cornelia would undoubtedly have made fun of Henry again. Could this fourth level of relationship be a rare event which happened without you doing anything? It was born when you died. It was love, but not as most people would know it. It was the 'Love that Just Is'. All that you needed to do was to get out of the way and it was there. It was like a Russian doll. As you remove one layer after another, you eventually get to the last doll. When you open it and there is nothing - only emptiness - love waiting in the emptiness. Love covered up, disguised and no longer recognised.

DAY 27

FRIDAY 6TH SEPTEMBER 2013

> "TWO THERE ARE WHO ARE NEVER SATISFIED —
> THE LOVER OF THE WORLD AND THE LOVER
> OF KNOWLEDGE."
> ### J RUMI

GURTHA WAKENED to birdsong and to feeling a glimmer of peace in his heart. He hadn't heard anything from Andy Finn, which he took as good news. Andy seemed to have a sharp intellect. If something had been discovered regarding Cornelia which needed to be acted upon by Gurtha in Mallorca, he had no doubt that Andy would have been in touch.

Gurtha didn't need to contact Andy as there was nothing new to add to the investigation, made easier by not having had contact with Cornelia. As he lay in bed, he wondered what Cornelia was thinking. If she had murdered Nuala, she might be thinking that she had got away with it – with no negative response from Gurtha.

There was a lie and a truth in what was known about what had happened to Nuala. Gurtha held onto that faint sense of peace within his body, wondering if it was the peace of a coward. He didn't want to rock the boat. He preferred what might be the lie of Cornelia's innocence to the truth of her possible guilt. He said to himself.

"That's who I am. I am a liar and a coward. I don't want to face the truth."

THE SECRET WOUND

He knew that Nuala was different. She looked for truth, found it, drank from it like a Holy Grail and lived it by what she said and did.

♥

He didn't want to spend all day alone thinking such thoughts. So he decided to visit the Gallery and not to ring Cornelia.

♥

Gurtha opened the creaking wooden door into the Gallery where Angelina, a feather duster in hand, was flicking away cobwebs from the painting of 'Eve'.

She jumped as the door swung closed.

"You gave me a scare."

Gurtha laughed.

"Sorry about that." He kissed her on the cheek, noticing her blushing.

"Where is the great general public? Have they disappeared from planet Earth?"

It was Angelina's turn to laugh.

"It's too early. It will be at least another hour before anyone turns up, but the exhibition is going well. We're nearly sold out. Let me show you what we've sold. Everything downstairs." She waved an arm around the paintings.

Angelina was wearing a pair of flowery pink and green leggings and a long white smocked cotton shirt. With her golden ballerina shoes she skipped along the wooden floors, as if on a stage.

"Follow me. You will love seeing this. They're nearly all sold. Only five left."

Gurtha followed her upstairs, smelling a warm herbal wave of mint, rosemary, lemon balm flowing over him.

He walked towards the painting which Angelina was standing beside.

"You smell like Mallorca."

Angelina turned to him,

"I hope Mallorca smells good."

"Of course it does. How are you getting on?"

Angelina looked at him quizzically.

"You mean with the exhibition?"

"Not necessarily. With your dreams."

Angelina laughed.

"Dreams? What restrictions do dreams have?"

Gurtha shook his head.

"None - the bigger the dream, the better. The only advice is that if you want to dream big, let go of nightmares."

Angelina smiled.

"You don't seem like someone who has nightmares."

Gurtha walked towards the window overlooking the street. An old woman mopped the cobbled paving outside her front door. She looked up at him and waved. He waved back.

"Nightmares. Doesn't everyone have nightmares? They're only what we fear most, expressing itself through our unconscious. We are all afraid of something."

Angelina sat in the rocking chair where Gurtha had sat before. She rocked backwards and forwards, slowly.

"Can I tell you what scares me?"

Gurtha spun around from the window. He walked towards her.

"Does this need a glass of wine?"

Angelina slowed the rocking chair.

"Wine sounds good. Although only one glass."

Gurtha made his way downstairs, opened the fridge and took out the bottle of Moet. He lifted two glasses from the wooden shelf and returned, taking the stairs two at a time.

He walked towards Angelina, setting the wine and glasses on a small table beside the rocking chair. He pulled out a bean bag which had been tucked in a corner, patted it into the shape of a doughnut, paused, filled two glasses and settled onto the cushion.

"I'm all ears."

Angelina's mascara had run down her face. She wiped the tears away and there were two horizontal black stripes under both eyes. She picked up the glass and began to sip it.

Gurtha sat his glass on the wooden table.

"I'm pregnant. That scares me."

She shivered in the chair.

Gurtha asked, "Why would that scare you? Most people would say congratulations and be thrilled."

Angelina hesitated, "Because the father is Barry and I have Cornelia to deal with."

"Do Cornelia and Barry know?"

Angelina shook her head and placed the glass beside Gurtha's.

"No."

She pushed the glass away from her.

I shouldn't have any more to drink."

Gurtha nodded.

"So neither Barry or Cornelia knows. That's complicated. What do you want to happen?"

Angelina threw her hands into the air.

"I told Barry that it was a mistake us being together. But I am beginning to see another side to him."

"Do you want to be with Barry?"

"I don't know."

She chuckled.

"I told Barry that maybe I wanted to marry you."

"That's crazy."

"Thank you very much. That's not a great compliment." She held out her glass. "Maybe a spot more."

Gurtha held up the bottle of Moet to see what was left. He helped them both to a small glass.

"Barry seems to like you."

Angelina nodded.

"That's true. I also understand why he could be intimidated by Cornelia."

Gurtha asked, "Why?"

The door downstairs opened and noisily closed. Footsteps moved quickly along the wooden floorboards. Angelina and Gurtha jumped to their feet.

"Anyone at home?"

Cornelia had reached the stairs. She climbed rapidly.

"Oh my God." Angelina caught Gurtha's hand. "What will we say?"

Gurtha handed Angelina a paper handkerchief from his pocket.

"Wipe your face."

Angelina had only managed to clean the mascara from her left cheek when Cornelia reached the top step.

Cornelia looked at the bottle of Moet, the two glasses side by side, the tear stained face of Angelina.

"What's going on here?" She snapped.

Gurtha moved towards her, giving her a kiss on the cheek.

"I suggested to Angelina that we should celebrate the success of the exhibition. Fantastic news – only five paintings unsold. Join us in a glass of Moet."

Cornelia's voice remained harsh, "I was keeping that Moet for your return. It doesn't look like a celebration that the two of you are having. I thought that we weren't getting together until tomorrow at Toni's party?"

Gurtha lifted the bottle into the air.

"You were keeping it for my return? Perfect – I have returned. And what a good choice – the Moet. There's still some left. Let me get you a glass. Now don't get fretful. I did say that I might call into the Gallery."

As Gurtha ran downstairs to get an extra glass, Cornelia turned to Angelina.

"You look as if you've been crying. What kind of celebration is this? What's up?"

"I just had a little bit of a health scare which frightened me. I'm going to be OK – but it shook me a little bit."

"What kind of health scare – cancer?" Cornelia's voice softened slightly.

"No – women's problems – but nothing serious."

"Sounds like you've told Gurtha what your health scare is all about but you don't want to tell me. Do you not think that's odd?"

Angelina stared unflinchingly into Cornelia's eyes.

"I've only told him what I've told you. What makes you think I would do anything different?"

Gurtha arrived with a clean glass. He poured a full glass for Cornelia and topped up the remainder into Angelina's glass.

"To friendship."

Cornelia drank the champagne quickly and handed the glass back to Gurtha.

"I will leave you two, then, to complete your business and see you tomorrow at Toni's."

Without looking at either of them, she walked briskly towards the stairs. They heard her feet stomp across the tiled floor and the front door slam shut.

DAY 28

SATURDAY 7TH SEPTEMBER 2013

"WHY DID you ask to see me?" Gurtha asked Angelina, munching on a croissant at Bar Stop on the road to Palma. They sat inside. It was a café which Cornelia would never visit - more a place for cyclists and a place where the local Mallorquins would have an early morning 'merienda' of bread, cheese, tomato, jalapeno pickles and wine. The ex-pat community preferred the cafes around the Plaza in Soller for a leisurely orange juice, coffee and croissant.

Angelina sipped her coffee.

"I wanted to thank you for listening yesterday. I can't believe what a relief that was - to feel listened to and understood. I have been going crazy over the last week. I invited Barry around last night and we talked."

Gurtha brushed the crumbs of the croissant from his lips and cut a slice of Mahon cheese which he placed on top of bread covered in oil and tomato.

"How did he react?"

"I told him about the baby and he seemed really happy. He said that more than anything else in the world, he wants to marry me."

"How do you feel about that as a possibility?"

Angelina sipped her water.

"The idea is growing on me. Nobody's perfect. It would have been better if he had separated from Cornelia before we got involved with one another – but that's life. We both have to accept responsibility for that. I can't say that it is all Barry's fault."

Gurtha helped himself to a spicy jalapeno pepper and olives which he heaped on top of a piece of white bread.

"What will be more complicated will be to work out when and how to tell Cornelia – especially when I tell you what else happened."

Gurtha placed his knife and fork on the plate and pushed his coffee to one side.

"OK. Let me hear it."

Angelina sat up straight in her chair.

"Before I texted him last night, Barry said that Cornelia was behaving in a frightening manner. He was really terrified about how she was acting and how her behaviour was escalating out of control. He is used to her major tantrums over minor problems, but last night she seemed to have completely lost her mind. She screamed that you and I had plotted to meet in the Gallery and that we had deliberately not told her. She said that was because we were having an affair. She blamed me and called me a …" She hesitated.

Gurtha nodded. "I can imagine."

"She insisted that I had laid a trap for you by quoting poetry to impress you. That enraged her as she said that she had never heard me express any interest in poetry before. It was my fault. You were not to blame. You couldn't help yourself falling into the trap because I was devious, manipulative and a nymphomaniac manhunter."

Gurtha laughed.

"Well there are more painful traps to fall into than a poetry trap. But how did she know about the poetry? I don't remember her being a part of that conversation."

Angelina, shook her head.

"Unfortunately Barry mentioned to her that we were talking about T S Eliot. He didn't expect her reaction. Gurtha, it isn't funny. Barry was really worried. She then threw two plates at him and then told him that he was no better than me."

Gurtha looked serious for a moment and then laughed again,

"It doesn't sound as though we're going to have a fun fiesta this evening. I hope Toni has paper plates."

Angelina placed her hand on his, and whispered, "The worst has still to come." She looked around the café. There didn't seem to be anyone listening – only the clatter of knives and forks and loud chatter from the locals at a few tables nearer the window. She continued, "She shrieked that she was going to put an end to it. Barry asked what she meant. She yelled at him, saying that she would put an end to our affair. Isn't that awful? How is she planning to do that when we're not having an affair?"

Angelina waited for Gurtha to say something.

Gurtha looked at her intently. Her face pale white, her lips trembling, anxiously waiting for him to speak. He felt bad now about being so flippant. It really wasn't funny at all. This could be more evidence to support the fact that Cornelia may have murdered Nuala. What could be more serious? Hadn't Andy Finn said that Cornelia had to be kept in a stable emotional state? He needed to ring Andy Finn, tell him about this latest outburst and get a perspective on how to handle this.

Gurtha urged Angelina, "Go on."

Angelina sipped again on her water, before answering.

"She doesn't know about the baby. Can you imagine what way she will react to that?"

Gurtha asked, "What did Barry do?"

"After throwing the plates at him, she began thumping him with her fists. He caught her by the wrists and tried to calm her down – saying that he was convinced that you were not having an affair with me. You know the way her face is always white. Barry said it turned a deep red, her eyes were wide open and bulging. She spat at him and told him to get out. He did."

"Did he go back after talking with you?"

"Yes, because he said if he didn't she would be compulsively churning mad thoughts in her head. That's what she always does, he said. He was worried that she might try to hurt me."

Gurtha leant forward in his chair.

"And how did he find her?"

"When he opened the door, he found her sitting cross legged on a rug in the sitting room. He asked if she was OK. She seemed extremely calm. She smiled at him and said that he wasn't to worry. That everything would sort itself out."

Gurtha shook his head in disbelief.

"Oh dear. I wonder what that means."

Angelina pleaded, "You must talk to her. I think you are the only one who can get through to her."

"The most important thing which we have to do is to keep her calm. We have the 'fiesta' this evening, which is good because Stephanie and Todd will be there, with other people. It sounds like she doesn't lose control when there are other people around – only when it's a one-to-one situation. I can talk to her but I don't think it will make the situation easier if she knows that we know how she has behaved and what she said and did to Barry last night."

♥

Gurtha phoned Andy Finn to update him about Cornelia's outburst.

"Thank you, Mr Maloney. This is exactly what you need to be doing – keeping us informed. She certainly sounds unstable. It also sounds as if she may be obsessed by you – so you could be at risk if she feels that there are any signs of rejection from you. However, as she currently appears to be protecting you, I would say that the person most at risk at the moment is Angelina. Her anger outburst appears to be driven by her jealousy of Angelina and the fear that she will lose you. This does not shed any light on why she would have wanted to kill Nuala but we are proceeding with our investigations at this end. The forensic team have been back in Nuala and Paddy's house. Unfortunately, as you did a good job cleaning the house when Paddy was in hospital, we may have lost some circumstantial evidence, but we are not giving up hope.

The important question is – how confident are you that she has returned to a state of emotional stability?"

Gurtha was unsure how to reply.

"I haven't seen her since the visit to the Gallery. However, we are planning to be together with a group of friends this evening. I will be able to gauge the situation then. I can ring you tomorrow, if that helps?"

"Sounds like a good idea. I also agree with you that she is unlikely to do anything to discredit herself whilst with others – so if you can do your best to ensure that Angelina, in particular, is not left alone with her – that will be not only important, but essential. Again I would recommend that you do everything within your power to defuse the situation. I have been promised the forensic update on Monday and am planning to be with you on Tuesday 10th September. That's only three days away. I will update the Soller Police of the situation and provide you the contact details of the Officer there who is our key contact. What questions do you have. Mr Maloney?"

Gurtha tried to think of a question but there was nothing. He merely repeated.

"So your advice is to keep everything low key until next Tuesday. Don't let Angelina be alone with Cornelia and try to keep as much as possible within a group?"

"Yes, Mr Maloney. That would be my recommendation. We are not saying at this moment that Cornelia has murdered Nuala. She is innocent until proven guilty but we do need to minimise any risks. It is quite common for people to display volatile behaviour in these romantic twists in relationships. We also have to be aware that one moment of madness can have severe consequences which destroy many lives. I think you are handling the situation well. Until tomorrow then."

Gurtha decided to ring Cornelia and check out how she sounded ahead of the 'fiesta'. She answered the phone within three rings. He ensured that his tone of voice was gentle. His strategy was to make no reference to anything which could inflame her.

"Hi Cornelia – I wanted to make sure that you are OK for this evening. Do you and Barry need a lift? I would be happy to drive down and collect you"

Cornelia replied, "That's more than kind of you Gurtha – thank you – but Todd and Stephanie have already offered to give us a lift. Looking forward to it. See you around eight then?"

"Perfect. It will be beautiful. We're expecting a starry night." Gurtha sighed with relief.

♥

Gurtha had met Toni briefly in his first week in La Torretta. Toni had knocked on the door and, speaking a few words of English, invited him to visit his house. He guided Gurtha through a gap in the fencing between the two houses, and showed him the barbeque area outside, including a large fridge, which he opened. It was filled with Cava. There were at least twenty bottles, laid neatly side by side. Toni turned to him.

"This is your house. You help yourself any time to the champagne. Here I put the key to the house." He placed a copper key under the mat in front of the door.

"If you need to go into my house – you take the key." He smiled at him, collected the key, opened the front door and showed him around. As Gurtha left to return to La Torretta, Toni slapped him on the back.

"Dinner. We have dinner together soon. Fiesta. Party time. Come to my birthday party on Saturday 7th September – bring your friends – all welcome."

♥

Gurtha walked down the path to Toni's house carrying one of the unsold paintings from the art exhibition and a Magnum of champagne as a present.

As he approached the candlelit table, a man and woman were standing around a microphone on a paved patio singing a Julio Iglesias song 'Por el amor de una mujer' – 'For the love of a woman'. There were three couples dancing a waltz around the patio.

Toni shook Gurtha's hand, accepting his presents.

"No need to bring a present. You are my present – 1,000 euros for your presence – thank you." He smiled and gestured to the table where people were buzzing with conversation and laughter.

"Where are your friends?"

He invited Gurtha to sit beside an elderly man who sat with his leg resting horizontally on a stool with a bag of ice on his knee.

"They're on their way. Thank you so much for the generosity of your invitation to include them. They are delighted."

Toni shook him again by the hand, "It's my pleasure. This is Paco. He had his knee replaced two weeks ago. Recovering. He's eighty years old."

Toni's outdoor table was made of stone, the upper half swivelled around so that people could choose what they wanted to eat.

Toni, the owner of the oldest bakery in Soller, poured Gurtha a glass of champagne.

"There are three things important in life. In order of priority they are … a good horse … a good bottle of wine … a good woman. We have two out of three here tonight."

Everyone laughed as the ceramic table top swung around offering a selection of jamon iberica, pimientos de padron, queso de Mahon and gambas de Sóller.

Paco talked to Gurtha about his work as a mechanic repairing the boats owned by the wealthy who docked them in the Port of Soller. He explained how he would crawl into small corners

THE SECRET WOUND

to reach the faulty parts of the engine and how, in the heat of the day, the spanners he needed were so hot that they burnt his hands. He kept a bucket of cold water to one side into which he would drop the spanners before using them. He said that his knees were worn out by kneeling and crawling through the small crevices of the boat. Gurtha joked,

"Do you mean that you didn't wear them out by praying?"

Paco laughed, leaned forward and poured Gurtha a glass of red wine.

"There was no time for praying. Catalina ..." He pointed to his wife across the table, "At the age of seven had to go collecting carob pods on a farm. She worked from seven in the morning until eight in the evening. She had a bowl of 'sopas mallorquinas' for breakfast and a glass of milk and that was all she ate until the evening when, at eight, she had another bowl of sopas. Do you know what sopas are?"

Gurtha shook his head.

"It's a poor man's soup, made from cabbage. If you were lucky there might be a few more vegetables like cauliflower but in those days it was usually cabbage and bread soaked in a broth. That was what people ate for breakfast, for lunch, for 'cena' – the evening meal. Look at this table – what have we got now? Are we any happier?"

With that question, Cornelia, Barry, Stephanie, Todd and Angelina arrived.

After kissing Toni and handing their present to him, Cornelia walked quickly to where Gurtha was sitting, kissed him and pointed to a free seat on Gurtha's left.

"Can I sit there?"

"Of course you can." Gurtha straightened a cushion on the circular stone bench.

She was wearing a long white silk dress beaded with pearls and pink flowers. Her hair was threaded with cerise bows and roses.

Gurtha poured Cornelia a glass of champagne and tried to work out what looked different about her. Then it was obvious. The plait had gone. He held his hands in the air,

"What have you done, Cornelia?"

She laughed at him.

"Glad that you noticed. I asked Barry to cut it off."

"Why?"

"I felt it was time for a change. A change is good for you."

She swung the table to reach the 'pimientos de padron'.

"Careful with those," Paco laughed.

"There are some so picante that they will blow your head off."

Cornelia tried one,

"So far ... so good. I like picante."

Toni tapped a spoon on a bottle of wine and the table fell silent.

"When we have the good times like now – we know it's good because we lived through the times of hardship. You appreciate it. You see that it doesn't matter having all of this." He swept his hands around the table.

"It doesn't mean anything."

Cornelia asked across the table, "What means anything?"

Toni raised his glass in the air holding Cornelia's gaze,

"Friendship. That's the only thing that means anything. Finding real friends."

He twisted open another bottle of red wine and popped open a bottle of cava as the suckling pig twisted on a spit above the charcoal barbeque.

As the table swirled, laden with food and wine, barbeque smoke drifted into the darkening sky, corks popped and Toni's son, Rafael, played the Chimbomba. Holding a small drum between his legs, he pushed a small stick through a hole in the skin where it repetitively droned creating the sense of a medieval banquet. Drifting back in time and sinking into something changeless.

On the other side of the table Barry sat beside Todd while Angelina laughed with Stephanie. There was more laughter from the shadowy figures sitting around the table. Gurtha looked up into the inky blackness of the sky. The stars were flickering in and out of existence. Mars was a steady orange like an unexpected dot on a Paul Smith shirt. A warm breeze ruffled Gurtha's hair like a friendly hand.

Then he felt Cornelia move beside him. All eyes turned to watch her as she glided towards the microphone and had a word with the man and woman who had just finished a song. They nodded, handing the microphone to Cornelia, who cradled it with both hands and then began to sing 'The Whisper of Love'. Everyone fell silent. Cornelia sang powerfully and emotionally, reminiscent of Amy Winehouse or Billy Holiday. She moved and flowed, embodying the sound, stretching her arms towards the table, bending forward like a swan as she circled before reaching both arms to the stars, pausing and singing the last phrase of the song with the purity of a violin.

Gurtha was the first person who applauded. Furiously. He pushed his chair back, stumbled to his feet and everyone else followed. Cornelia bowed, blew a kiss towards the table and handed the microphone to the man and woman who immediately began another song. Cornelia waved at the group smiling, then walked towards Gurtha, holding her hand out to him.

"Let's dance."

♥

Before the party ended, Cornelia had danced with Barry, Todd and Gurtha and had chatted to Angelina and Stephanie. She pulled them all into a circle where they held hands.

"Let's do the walk we said that we would do – to the cave of Ramon Llull near Valdemossa. It's stunning at sunset. There's a little path which weaves its way towards the cave with a sea view all the way."

Barry asked, "When?"

Cornelia answered, "Why not Monday – the day after tomorrow? We can close the Gallery for one day – after all there are only four unsold paintings. Let's take a long weekend and celebrate the Exhibition's success."

Everyone nodded in agreement. The mood was elevated. Angelina gave Gurtha a thumbs up and smiled. This was the Cornelia Gurtha remembered. The Cornelia who had been lost for a year and a half. It was wonderful to see her so happy, so full of spontaneity and fun. They broke their circle and went in search of Toni to give their thanks and then finally said goodbye to one another.

Later that night, Gurtha listened to thunder rumbling in the distance. Sheet lightning lit up the bedroom – the white mosquito net over the bed shivered as winds from the unexpected storm pushed their way through the persianas.

Gurtha was soaked in sweat. He turned onto his side and curled into the recovery position. He found it difficult to breathe. He tried seven-eleven breathing, the technique that he had taught Miriam a few weeks earlier. But his mind wouldn't stop racing. He rolled onto his back, then onto his stomach, pulled the pillow down to place his head on it and then pushed it away to lie on the sheet. There was no relief.

THE SECRET WOUND

How could he let Cornelia's perfect performance for one evening at a party, take away the reality that she was under suspicion of killing Nuala?

DAY 29

SUNDAY 8TH SEPTEMBER 2013

> "EXPLANATION BY THE TONGUE
> MAKES MOST THINGS CLEAR, BUT LOVE
> UNEXPLAINED IS CLEARER."
> **J RUMI**

GURTHA WAKENED early. It had been a troubled night's sleep. The storm had continued for several hours. It wasn't the storm that had kept him awake – in fact he was glad of the noise of the growling thunder as the lighting cracked around La Torretta. What had kept him awake was wondering how this was all going to work out. Since Nuala had died, the world had become chaotic. By coming to Mallorca, he had taken away the comfort and security of everything he knew. It felt as if he had thrown himself into the middle of a fast moving tornado which was cutting a path through his past and present and obliterating any sense of controlling the future.

After a quick breakfast, he rang Andy Finn.

"She seemed to be 'normal' last night – well more than that – happy – the life and soul of the party. She reminded me of the way she was when I first knew her. For a few hours, to be perfectly honest, I forgot that there was an unresolved murder. I can't believe that happened because since Nuala died, I have been thinking about her virtually all of the time."

THE SECRET WOUND

Andy listened. His tone of voice in reply wasn't stern, but cautious.

"It is good news that there is no obvious emotional instability, but we must not be fooled. We know that her erratic behaviour is only witnessed when with one other person. She may be a good actress. She knows you well. If she is intelligent, which you say that she is, she will have the potential to be a Mistress of Dissimulation. She may also be able to manipulate your unconscious energies – tapping into your personal weaknesses. She may know them more than you do. How did she react to Angelina?"

Gurtha tried to visualise what happened with Angelina at the party.

"Angelina acted like a frightened cat that had been poisoned and shot at. She tried to distance herself from Cornelia, mostly by spending the evening talking with Stephanie. I noticed that on several occasions Cornelia attempted to talk with her – in fact I heard her ask Angelina if she would like to dance. Angelina shook her head and said that she was tired. She scurried away to the toilets inside."

Andy sounded concerned.

"That is worrying. It is what I mean by dissimulation. There is no consistency between this behaviour and with what was reported by Barry to Angelina. We need to stay with our plan. You have the contact details of Ramon Gonzalez in the Police in Soller. He knows to expect a call from you at any time. What are the plans before Tuesday when I arrive?"

Gurtha replied confidently, "Today, Angelina has been invited to lunch with Stephanie and Todd. Barry and Cornelia will be alone. Tomorrow we have all been invited on a walk near Valdemossa."

Gurtha heard papers shuffling.

"Let's speak tomorrow evening, then, and we can confirm

where I can meet with Cornelia. If anything happens before that which is of concern, give me a call. I'm glad to hear that everything is holding reasonably steady."

♥

Cornelia made Barry pancakes for breakfast with maple syrup and brought him a mug of steaming milky coffee.

"It was a good party last night. Did you enjoy it?"

"Yes. Toni was very generous, the food and wine were superb. It was good to meet a few new friends. Did you enjoy it?"

"Of course."

"I've never heard you sing before. You have a beautiful voice."

"That was our song. I sang it for you. We listened to it together when we first met."

"I remember the song."

"I wanted to apologise for my behaviour the other night. I've been a little stressed, as you have experienced."

Barry wasn't sure what to say. He wanted to say that perhaps they should reconsider their relationship together and take a break from each other, but was worried that would send Cornelia into another 'episode'. He also wanted to be more honest and explain that it wasn't a break from Cornelia that he really wanted but a total seismic shift away from her – to have a total gap open up between them which would allow him to be with Angelina for the rest of his life. He did not know how to make this happen in a way which would be safe way for Angelina and so he nodded.

Cornelia continued, "Tomorrow will be fun – the walk with everyone. Why don't you prepare the picnic now so that we are not rushing tomorrow? I will do the paperwork for the Gallery. Then we can watch a film together later. How does that sound?"

Barry looked at his watch.

"How long will you need for the paperwork?"

"No more than a couple of hours."

Barry scratched his head.

"Don't you normally like to have a swim on a Sunday?"

Cornelia smiled at him,

"That's thoughtful of you to remember. Do you want to have a quick dip in the sea before lunch?"

Barry shifted from one foot to another.

"You know that I don't really like the beach but why don't I take my normal exercise and go for a walk to the Torre Picada, come back, organise the picnic for tomorrow and we can find somewhere to have lunch."

Cornelia frowned but only slightly and fleetingly,

"So we meet back here at 2.00?"

Barry smiled, "That sounds great."

♥

When Barry left the house, Cornelia didn't bother to follow him. She knew that Angelina had been invited to lunch at 2.00 with Todd and Stephanie. That meant that Barry had three hours to walk to Angelina's, meet with her, do whatever they did together and get back in time to have lunch with her.

She climbed the stairs to her bedroom, opened the drawer in the bedside table and removed Amelia's plait. She brought it downstairs, lit a candle, placed the plait and candle on the rug, took a cushion from the sofa and positioned it behind the candle, searched for granuals of frankincense and the charcoal burner, lit the charcoal with the frankincense and placed it beside the candle.

She recognised this feeling inside. She touched Amelia's plait. It didn't help to cut it off yesterday. She thought that it might allow the beast within to fall asleep again but she was powerless over it. It would sleep when it wanted to sleep. Now it was stirring, pacing around within her. It had its plans for tomorrow. She would have to obey.

After the beast killed Amelia, it had slept for many years. During those years Cornelia knew what it was like to feel safe, secure and in control of her life. When the economic crisis hit in 2008, Henry started talking about there not being enough money to retire. She felt the beast growl within her. Henry explained the need for austerity measures – cutting back – even about putting their Mallorcan home on the market.

When the beast was fully awake, she saw with its eyes. Henry became repulsive to her. As his health deteriorated, she reasoned that he couldn't be enjoying this gloomy situation he had created for them. The beast had a solution. She could find a younger version of Henry. He would have to have money, of course. He didn't need to be handsome. Then the beast came up with an idea of how to relieve Henry of his suffering. She only had to administer a slightly increased dose of warfarin each day and Henry would bleed slowly away – a gentle haemorrhage which would help him be released from the pain of his mind and body. It worked. Once admitted to hospital, the tests confirmed that Henry was in the last stages of heart failure. His vital medication had destabalised and his death was imminent. It only took a few days for him to die.

The beast then warned Cornelia that Nuala was a problem. Nuala was intuitive. Gurtha had said that Nuala was psychic. The beast told her that Nuala knew that she had murdered Henry. The beast said that Nuala would never allow Cornelia to marry Gurtha. That had always been the plan. Cornelia was born to marry Gurtha. She only had to wait for Henry to die. Of course, she needed an interim contingency plan, Barry, but that was never meant to be a permanent arrangement. The beast explained to her how simple it would be to murder Nuala. It worked.

When Nuala opened the door, she looked suspiciously at Cornelia. Then she wrote a note for Paddy. He was sent out. That made it all the easier.

There was resistance from Nuala to climb the stairs and leave the box of chocolates in Gurtha's room. On the landing she seemed to know that something dangerous was going to be played out. She refused to go into Gurtha's room and walked quickly back towards the stairs. Cornelia had to act quickly. The beast told her that Nuala could survive a fall down the stairs but there was another way which was certain death. Cornelia forced Nuala towards the bannister. Nuala fought back. She grabbed Nuala's hair with one hand and the plait with the other. Then she placed her hands around Nuala's neck and wrestled her, choking, to the bannister and tipped her over. After that the beast suggested that she pull up a piece of the carpet on the landing, walk downstairs and rearrange Nuala's body at the bottom of the staircase. The beast also suggested removing Nuala's shoe, a nice finishing touch.

DAY 30

MONDAY 9TH SEPTEMBER 2013

CORNELIA WAKENED with a sense of energy buzzing through her whole body. Today would be a good day. After today she was sure that the beast would want to slumber again. It's work would be complete. Maybe it would never awaken again. Cornelia would have everything she ever wanted. There would be no reason for the beast to have to help her.

Barry snored beside her. She rolled over and threw her arms around him. He jumped in the bed as if startled. Cornelia laughed,

"Did I waken you? Sorry. You sleep on. I'll make breakfast."

Barry pulled the sheets up over his head.

"Thanks. I'll be down in thirty minutes. I haven't properly wakened up yet."

She slipped on a dressing gown, opened the drawer beside the bed and removed Amelia's plait. She glanced at Barry. He hadn't seen. She put it in her pocket.

Downstairs she slipped the plait into her rucksack – in a zipped pocket. She prepared breakfast. As she sat at the kitchen table, she was filled with a sense of happiness – like a bride preparing for her wedding – anticipating a whole future ahead. A future filled with love, sharing, deep conversations, growing old with the comfort of someone you love and who loves you.

There was only a last effort which had to be made. There's always an effort to be made for anything worthwhile.

They packed the car with walking boots and rucksacks and Barry drove them towards Valldemosa. It was a beautiful drive – turning off the road from the Port of Soller and heading towards Deia – following the twisting road, a turquoise sea sparkling on the right. Small yachts left a white wake of rippling water behind them as they headed south. They passed the Residencia Hotel where Princess Diana used to stay, drove further along the road where Michael Douglas had his house and then could see where Bob Geldof lived. The mountains stretched up to the left ending in craggy cliffs reaching into a cloudless sky. On top was a path created by the Archduke Luis Salvador with magnificent views of the island.

Cornelia looked at the steep mountainside leading up to the Archduke's Way.

"That's another walk worth doing. The mountain is full of history. I love the way you have the mix of all the wealthy people from the past and present with the ordinary country folk. You come across 'sifjas' which are small charcoal ovens where men would spend night after night on the mountain ensuring that the smouldering charcoal didn't go out. There are also 'casas de neu' or snowpits where they used to store the winter snow and cover it with layers of ash. You can also see 'cacas a coll' which are thrush nets which the local hunters used to string between the trees. There were always two worlds living here, side by side. There still are."

Barry concentrated on guiding the car around the hairpin bends. He observed, "I'm surprised that you haven't been invited into the 'high society' circle."

Cornelia laughed.

"There's still time. I never give up."

They reached the car park near Valldemossa to find everyone had already arrived.

Cornelia took charge.

"Let's walk to Ramon Llull's cave first. There we can have our picnic."

Stephanie lifted her rucksack from the ground.

"Sounds great. Thinking of great – that was a fantastic party at Toni's, wasn't it?

Todd agreed and commented,

"Cornelia you were the life and soul of the party – you were fantastic. What a voice. You've kept that talent well hidden. What do you think folks – couldn't she be on stage?"

Angelina spoke, "Yes there was a wonderful energy at the party and Toni was so generous. Imagine letting strangers share such an intimate family evening. Wonderful."

Todd chipped in, "I think, Cornelia, you could come back with me to Los Angeles and we'll get you a singing contract no problem."

Cornelia smiled, walking at the front of the group who now filed down a narrow path,

"Stop it now. You're making me blush. Angelina, come up here beside me. You go first. I see you're wearing proper hiking boots – perfect."

Angelina carefully manoeuvred herself past Barry and led the walk.

Gurtha glanced to the right. The sky was a flowing emerald with streaks of ruby. Golden light reflected onto the waves, twisting in turquoise and yellow hues into waves which looked like molten olive branches. He pushed his hands into the pockets of his Barbour jacket and quickened his steps to match those of Barry. Todd tried to keep up, breathing deeply and breaking into a gentle run.

The olive trees on the narrow terrace to their left were covered in light green lichen. The dead branches of old dismembered olive trees lay scattered on the tilled rich red soil. Life and death living side by side. Todd stopped, rested a hand on the grey and orange stones still hot from the unbroken attention of the sun. He felt old, his body seizing up, unable to move in the way that it once used to move. He was more like a wrinkled olive limb than green lichen – more like the stone wall with some heat in it, but unable to move, than the sparkling waves below him. He sighed with the sadness that only one who knows what old age feels like is capable of sighing - a resigned sigh - similar to despair but not quite despair. It was the sigh of one who knows the closeness of body, mind, heart and soul to stone and dead wood.

They walked mostly in silence and reached Ramon Llull's cave an hour later. Gurtha enthusiastically climbed inside as Cornelia and Barry laid out the picnic on a large rug just outside the cave.

The view from the cave was magnificent – opening to a wide expanse of sea and a view of the golden disc of a sun sliding across the sky, gently dipping eventually into the horizon.

They sat in a circle together and began to help themselves to tapas – croquetas, Russian salad, olives, patatas bravas and baby squid.

Cornelia opened a bottle of white wine and placed a few chilled beers on the rug with sparkling water.

Stephanie asked, "Well – who knows about Ramon Llull? That would be interesting as we've made a valiant effort to find his cave."

Gurtha raised his hand,

"I can start. He was a fascinating character born in 1232 and died

1315. He was incredibly ahead of his time – a great philosopher and many give him credit for being the pioneer of computation theory – which is remarkable considering the century in which he lived. What I love most about his story is that he was born into a wealthy family. He was a troubadour and lived a licentious and wasteful life according to his own accounts. He had two children by Bianca Picary whom he married. Then his life changed. He had a couple of visions and decided to dedicate his life to God and became a Franciscan Tertiary. He spent the later part of his life converting Muslims to Christianity, not by violence or intellectual trickery, but through dialogue and by understanding their culture. An amazing man."

Cornelia asked, "I wonder what triggered his visions? If he was living what he called a 'wasteful life' why would he experience visions and other people don't?"

Everyone waited for Gurtha to answer.

"It's a good question. I'm not sure that I have the answer to that, to be honest. Perhaps we're saying that all human beings are born imperfect. Many will choose to lead what Llull would call 'wasteful' lives all their lives. Some individuals, like Ramon Llull, St Francis of Assisi or Rumi, who all lived around the thirteenth century, seemed to have a 'conscience' awaken in them. This became a rudder which then guided their lives to experience deeper and deeper love."

Stephanie raised her hand as if she was at school, "But what is this conscience? It sounds as if it's connected to the 'visions' that these individuals experienced. Cornelia's question is still unanswered as you would need to know what it is that makes some people have an awakening of 'conscience' and have 'visions' when others don't."

Gurtha laughed.

THE SECRET WOUND

"I didn't expect these questions today. I feel I'm back in my lecture hall. Modern psychology would probably say that we are mostly driven by our unconscious motivations – unmet emotional needs – for power, control, security, respect, approval of others etc. but as they are unconscious we don't accept responsibility for what we do. We look for comfort in the outer world, as Llull initially did. However, when these unconscious motivations become clear to us – you might call it having a 'vision' – or the experience of 'grace'– or seeing our 'woundedness' - we see ourselves as we really are, we take responsibility for what we do – and our actions change. St Francis of Assisi was another example of this. Born into a wealthy family and then giving all of this up for a life which respected not power but poverty, a love of nature and creation."

Stephanie looked at Todd and shook her finger at him.

"I hope you're listening to this Todd. I don't see you taking any notes."

Everyone laughed. Todd quipped, "Don't be looking at me for a 'vision'. I think they take all the fun out of life."

Cornelia silently ate a spinach croquette and stared towards a thick layer of purple on the horizon, layered on top with orange and pink. The more Cornelia looked at it, the more it took on the appearance of a rainbow shimmering on top of a flowing silky blue sea. Then the silky blue sea flowed into the sky above and Cornelia dissolved into the rainbow. She closed her eyes. Her body was undulating with rainbow colours circling within her. The colours were painting her, wiping away the darkness within. As the colours now were her body and the darkness had completely disappeared, for the first time in her life, Cornelia felt peace and knew that she was totally loved into being. Her own existence at this moment in time was perfect. Her being was love. The experience lasted a few minutes before she opened her eyes and saw Stephanie placing oranges on the rug for desert.

The remains of the picnic were gathered together and the rucksacks repacked. It was time to continue the walk.

Todd asked, "Do we turn back the way we came?"

Cornelia shook her head.

"Not yet. We walk a little further along this path and then we will double back on a different path. It's more interesting – you'll see. Angelina, let's have you at the front again. That seemed to work well. If that is easier for you?"

Angelina smiled and nodded in agreement.

Stephanie, Todd, Barry and Gurtha had fallen behind, engaging in conversation with Todd who was struggling to keep up.

She watched Angelina walk cautiously ahead of her. She wore a long white Grecian dress with a corded tie and hiking boots. Angelina looked good. Not many people could pull off that combination of hiking boots with an exotic, elegant draping dress. Then, unexpectedly Angelina twisted on her right ankle, her arms shooting into the air as she tried to balance. There was a small gash in the path – caused by a rock earlier breaking loose from the surrounding dry earth. She tried to recover her balance, but instead tilted further to the right, losing her footing and, as a golden sun dipped into a turquoise sea, she slipped over the edge of the path with a loud shriek.

Cornelia's eyes opened wide as did her mouth. She gulped at the air like a sand shark and raised her hands to cover her face.

Cornelia had planned to push Angelina to her death at the spot where the path twisted left. However, following the discussion over lunch and her experience of merging with the sky and sea, she had changed her mind. It had become obvious to her that killing Angelina would not give her a relationship with Gurtha which

THE SECRET WOUND

would be meaningful. She would be forcing herself into a life of continued lies which would not only 'waste' her life but would destroy that of Gurtha. She couldn't and wouldn't kill Angelina.

Cornelia screamed, "Gurtha!"

With Gurtha and the others out of sight, she instinctively threw herself onto the path, sticking only her head over the edge and then, instinctively, reached her right arm below.

Although Gurtha, Barry, Todd and Stephanie were not far away, the wind carried Cornelia and Angelina's cries in the opposite direction and they were only faintly heard like the distressed bleating of a young lamb's call to it's mother. Hearing the sounds of distress, Barry and Gurtha began to run. Todd, holding Stephanie's hand shouted from behind, "Slow down. Show mercy on an old man."

They reached Cornelia lying on the path, right arm stretched towards Angelina who, over the cliff edge, found herself hooked by the corded belt on her linen dress, grabbing with both hands at the wild strawberry bush which grew horizontally from the rock face. The branches of the strawberry bush visibly twisted and bent under her weight.

Cornelia looked for a moment at flickers from the sun´s corona disappearing into indigo blue. Moving her eyes to the distant streaks of tangerine clouds, she wriggled closer to the edge and reached a hand towards the strawberry bush. She touched the soft orange, fluid-filled wild strawberry first and quivered with fear, before forcing herself to look into Angelina's eyes. Angelina, panting, reached a left hand upwards to grab Cornelia's wrist.

It was a sudden, abrupt, unexpected movement. Cornelia closed her eyes, her cotton dress dragged over stones, being ripped apart, as she catapulted over the edge. She heard herself scream, yowling into the Universe.

When she opened her eyes seconds later, she found herself dangling, holding onto Angelina's left wrist. Her forehead pressed against Angelina's legs. She felt the cold rush of air into her nostrils and a sinking feeling in her gut as her feet searched the rocky cliff for a foothold. She dug her nails deeply into Angelina's wrist.

Barry and Gurtha threw themselves on the ground beside Cornelia while Stephanie and Todd stood dazed. Gurtha snapped opened his rucksack, pulled out the rope and made a noose.

"Get help," he screamed.

Barry shouted, "What's the number for the emergency services?"

As Barry dialled 112, Gurtha lowered the rope over the cliff edge. His body trembled with vertigo and nausea.

"Cornelia, put the noose around your wrist."

Cornelia reached a hand towards the rope, "I can't."

"Of course you can." Gurtha swung the rope closer.

Angelina sobbed, "I can't hold on much longer. The tree is …"

Angelina looked at the strawberry bush which was inching out from the cliff face, it roots increasingly visible as the soil holding it in place tumbled on top of them.

Cornelia screamed, "You have to hold on … Angelina … You have to … Angelina tell them … I did it … I murdered Amelia, Henry and Nuala … Ask them to forgive me."

Cornelia watched the strawberry tree shifting away from the cliff face. She had to act fast or both she and Angelina would die. Gurtha could not hold them both on this rope. Pebbles from the cliff face showered around them. If she held on any longer, Angelina would die. Cornelia grasped the rope with her left hand, placed the noose around Angelina's wrist and shouted to Gurtha, "Pull!"

As Gurtha tightened the rope, Cornelia let go of Angelina's wrist and plummeted below.

Stephanie screamed as the roots of the strawberry bush finally came away and the bush rolled down the cliff face after Cornelia, like tumbleweed.

Angelina swung on the end of the rope. Gurtha, Todd and Barry pulled on the rope, winching Angelina slowly to the surface.

Once at the top, Angelina lay stretched out on the path, gasping. She sobbed, "What about Cornelia?"

"She's fallen. Gurtha has gone down on the rope to see if there is anything he can do."

Angelina wept deeply.

"But she let go to save me. She could have saved herself."

Angelina held her hands over her face as Barry sat beside her. Cornelia, falling towards the sea below, triggering the memory of her father falling alone and helpless to his death in the Atlantic Ocean.

♥

Gurtha abseiled down the cliff face, passing the strawberry bush which had fallen onto a ledge – his breathing shallow and fast. He swung out three times, looking below, his body shaking as he saw waves crash against a small fern-covered outcrop. There was no sign of Cornelia.

DAY 31

TUESDAY 10TH SEPTEMBER 2013

"A THOUSAND HALF-LOVES MUST BE FORSAKEN
TO TAKE ONE WHOLE HEART HOME."
J RUMI

ANDY FINN arrived in a taxi at La Torretta at four in the afternoon. Gurtha had phoned him late Monday evening and explained what had happened. After that he had a two hour debrief with Officer Ramon Gonzalez in the Soller police station. In the early hours of the morning he talked with Laura who allowed him to ramble, telling and retelling what had happened over the last week.

He felt numb and confused. At a deep level he didn't want to believe that Cornelia had murdered Nuala. It would mean that he never knew who she was. Before letting go of Angelina's wrist, why had she confessed to Angelina and not to him. Why, if she held such anger against Angelia did she give up her life to save her? None of it made any sense.

Search parties worked through the night, without success looking for her body. Police Officer Ramon Gonzalez said that it was unlikely she had fallen into the sea as there were quite a few outcrops which could have possibly broken her fall. If she had fallen all the way to bottom of the cliff, her body should be visible and retrievable. The search was continuing by sea, air and land.

Andy shook Gurtha's hand warmly.

"I'm so sorry. This must be another tremendous shock for you."

Andy looked as Gurtha had imagined. He was a tall, well built man, with dark black straight hair falling over his eyes. Muscular, with a face wearing the lines of character. He had a steady penetrating stare. Today he wore jeans and a white shirt with dark trainers.

Gurtha blinked several times and was afraid that he might burst into tears. He bit the inside of his cheek.

"Thank you for coming. Let me get you a coffee."

They sat in the gazebo, listening as the train clicked its way towards Palma in the distance. There wasn't a breeze. The crickets were singing loudly. The town of Soller glittered in the valley below. With everything that had happened, it appeared both idyllic and horrific.

"Mr Maloney, first of all you mustn't blame yourself for what has happened. You have acted responsibly under extreme conditions. What I would like to do is to summarise the situation to confirm my understanding and then I will share with you what we have discovered from the additional data gathering and re-examination of existing evidence. Is that OK? Do you feel able to talk at this time? I know you must have had little sleep last night."

Gurtha whispered, "Yes. I am OK to talk."

Andy opened his notebook.

"Yesterday while walking along a cliff edge path, Angelina slipped and fell. Angelina has confirmed that this was an accident and that she wasn't pushed off the path by Cornelia, although both Angelina and Cornelia were out of sight of the remainder of the group when the accident took place."

Gurtha nodded, "That's correct."

"In the rescue attempt you lowered a rope towards Cornelia.

It appeared that the bush which was holding them both was dislodging from the cliff face. As Cornelia caught the rope she confessed to Angelina that she had murdered not only Nuala but Henry. She then managed to fasten the rope around Angelina's wrist and let go of her grip on Angelina. Angelina believes that Cornelia sacrificed her life to save her."

"That's correct."

"Cornelia's body has not yet been recovered and a search is still underway."

"That's correct."

"What other information do you feel we need to know, which you haven't previously shared?"

Gurtha nodded his head.

"Angelina said that Cornelia also claimed to have murdered her sister, Amelia. That was always thought to have been a childhood accident. Yesterday she placed the plait of her sister Amelia's hair in her rucksack. I don't suppose there is any way we will be able to confirm if it is true that she killed Amelia"

Andy took notes.

"It's unlikely. However, she was at a young impressionable age. It is not impossible that Amelia died accidentally and Cornelia thought that she was responsible. If she did not receive the appropriate counselling – this could have impacted on her later adult psychological needs. If she believed that she was a murderer, she could have turned herself into one."

Gurtha sighed.

"That's hard to process. What did your further investigations reveal? Although it hardly matters now that she is dead."

Andy turned back a few pages.

"We did find black hairs at the top of the stairs which may have been Cornelia's but we haven't been able to do a DNA match. I was hoping that would be possible after interviewing Cornelia. We decided to investigate Henry's medical records. It is true that he died from heart failure. It was considered at the time that there were no suspicious circumstances. However, an independent review of his records concluded that his warfarin count was higher than normal for the dosage he had been prescribed. Again – inconclusive evidence. I thought an interview with Cornelia may have shed light upon the facts. What else do you need from me?"

Gurtha shook his head, "Nothing, thank you."

"Mr Maloney I would like to talk with each member of the excursion yesterday to see if they have any additional information to share. I will stay a couple of days to collaborate with the Police and to see if Cornelia's body is recovered. Would you be able to provide me with the contact details of your friends?"

"Of course. Angelina is in hospital for observation. She should be getting out tomorrow. If you like, I can arrange for them all to visit you in the Gallery tomorrow."

"That would be excellent as I would like to see the Gallery and also Cornelia's house."

Day 32

Wednesday 11th September 2013

LAURA RANG early on Wednesday morning. After checking how Gurtha was, she shared some news, "Gurtha, I don't want to worry you when you have so much on your plate at the moment, but I need to tell you about a little incident with Paddy."

Gurtha sat down on the sofa.

"What Laura? Surely things can't get any worse?"

Laura took a deep breath, "It's nothing critical at the moment but Maggie thought that you should know. Paddy slipped in the shower. The Care Worker was with him but maybe he took a little dizzy turn and she couldn't hold him. He hit his head against the shower wall and was concussed for a few minutes. A Doctor was called and said that he was fine. They sent him to the Royal Hospital for a few routine checks and everything has come back clear."

"Do you think I should fly back?"

Laura hesitated.

"It's up to you – but you still have Police Inspector Andy Finn with you and Cornelia's body hasn't been found. I think that we can take the word of the Doctor that he is fine and that you should stay until this dreadful business is sorted out."

It was three days since the cliff walk and Cornelia's body had still not been recovered.

DAY 33

THURSDAY 12TH SEPTEMBER 2013

"I KNOW YOU ARE TIRED BUT COME,
THIS IS THE WAY."
J RUMI

CORNELIA USED a stone to scratch a tally mark on the wall.

It was the fourth day since the cliff walk. She looked around the cave. High above her was a long chard of light sporadically covered with ferns. That was the window to the crevasse into which she had fallen. The memory of the drop was vague. She had no idea of how long the fall had been. She remembered hearing Stephanie scream. She kept her eyes closed. There was a swishing sound as she fell first through thick ferns and then a lighter layer.

She hit a soft, watery muddy floor. She opened her eyes. Everything was in darkness. She wasn't sure if she had blinded herself. Maybe she had hit her head heavily against a rock. She lay in the shallow water, afraid to move. She must have broken something. If she had broken something it was certain to hurt.

She wasn't sure how much time had passed when she heard a helicopter fly overhead and decided to risk moving. She moved her legs first. There was no pain. Then her arms. They pulsated with a dull ache but she could move them. She rolled onto her side and struggled to her knees. Now that her eyes had become accustomed to the dark, she could see that she had fallen into a shallow fresh water lake. The water was an iridescent emerald colour, as if lit up inside by the fading sunlight held in the clouds.

The blades of the helicopter circled again noisily overhead. At one point she saw the helicopter's tail hover above the crevasse. She tried to cry for help but the words only came out as a whisper. She tried again, her body shuddering with the effort to scream, but again she could only make it whisper, 'Help'. She wondered if it was fear that kept her voice inside. The same fear that she had faced in nightmares.

She fell back into the water and gently sobbed. No-one would find her if she couldn't let them know that she was here.

She scrambled onto a small dry shelf of rock.

Each day she drank the fresh water from the lake. She watched the lake change colour from emerald green to obsidian black by nightfall. Sometimes the light from one star would shoot through the crevasse into the water below. She would crawl to the water's edge to touch the water and make it ripple.

That night, as she touched the star in her own private lake, the sea, land and sky rescue effort was called off.

DAY 34

FRIDAY 13TH SEPTEMBER 2013

CORNELIA SCRATCHED the fifth day on the wall and dangled her legs over the dry ledge which had become her bed. There had been no sounds from a helicopter for many hours. The cave no longer seemed threatening. It was a safe womb. She had reconciled herself to the fact that she would not be found and thought that she would enjoy whatever time she had left in this black and emerald watery womb. After all, when she let go of Angelina's wrist – she had thought that it would bring immediate and sudden death. She had been prepared for that. Now that she had a few more days, why not be thankful for them?

She remembered back to the rainbow-sky-sea merging experience outside Ramon Llull's cave. The intensity of the experience had faded but she felt penetrated by the knowledge she had experienced then. That she was loved. She had never been judged. She had judged herself. Instead, she found herself merged within the rainbow sitting on the 'mercy' seat – not the judgment seat.

The fear from the first four days of cave living had dissolved. It may come back, but for now it had gone. She found herself singing when the first light of dawn fell on the emerald water below. Her voice was strong. If anyone came by now, she would be heard. She would sing her way loudly and passionately to freedom.

DAY 35

SATURDAY 14TH SEPTEMBER 2013

"THERE IS A VOICE THAT DOESN'T USE WORDS.
LISTEN."
J RUMI

CORNELIA WAKENED early with the birds. She splashed her face in the emerald pool and then waved at the sunlight dropping through the crevasse.

Some time later, she wasn't sure when, she heard voices outside. She listened carefully. There were definitely male voices. There were sounds of ropes unfurling. They were abseiling down the cliff.

She got to her feet, stood on the ledge which was her bed and began to sing in her loudest voice, Leonard Cohen's 'Love Itself.'

It took five minutes of singing before she saw a dark curly head of hair peer over the edge of the crevasse and a voice call down to her.

THE SECRET WOUND

DAY 36

SATURDAY 15TH SEPTEMBER 2013

BARRY INVITED Gurtha, Todd, Stephanie and Angelina to dinner in Cornelia's house in the Port. Police Inspector Andy had returned to Belfast. Cornelia's body had not been found. It was hard to believe that so much had happened since the Saturday before when they were at Toni's 'fiesta', when Cornelia had been in such good spirits.

They arrived around eight o'clock. At first the atmosphere was tense. Nobody knew what to say. Barry opened a bottle of white wine and served some crisps.

"I'm sorry. I've ordered a seafood paella. I hadn't the heart to make anything. I hope that will be OK for you all. I know that Cornelia would have taken better care of everyone."

Todd got out of the sofa and hugged Barry.

"Don't be silly. We're all in a state of shock. There's nobody fit to do anything. You're more than kind to ask us round. There were so many things that we didn't know. Who would have thought that Cornelia was capable of murder?"

Barry looked at Gurtha without wanting to offend.

"I suppose we don't know what we're capable of until we face certain situations. We all have different coping mechanisms and maybe sometimes we can't cope – life gets too much for us."

Stephanie nodded and passed around crisps and nuts.

"I think that's the best way to look at it. Nobody knows what they are capable of, good or evil. Who would have thought that Cornelia would have given her life to save Angelina? You would never dream that she would have done that. It was almost like she was confessing to you, Angelina. She then accepted her fate."

Angelina sat at the table.

"Yes. That was amazing, unbelievable. I sometimes think that if you have a dark side, it is always balanced by a light side – you only have to find a way to let it be expressed. What I don't understand is why they have not been able to find her body. Did you hear anything from Police Inspector Finn or Ramon Gonzalez?"

Gurtha shook his head.

"They say it is inexplicable. The nearest that they have come to an explanation is that maybe she fell onto the grassy outcrop and, because of the force of the fall, she then rolled down the slope into the sea. The waves and currents are strong in that area. Certainly no-one would survive falling into the water. During the Spanish Civil War, Ramon said that the warring factions would bring their prisoners down to the water's edge and throw them in. Certain death. So that is the only scenario that has any credibility."

Angelina asked Gurtha, "How are you feeling now? I suppose you have been the most impacted by it all."

Gurtha sighed, "Cornelia invited me here. I thought of it as a sabbatical – something which would change my life. I had no idea what would happen. It has certainly changed my life. It's too early to say what I think. I know what I would like – a simple life."

Gurtha's mobile rang. It was Laura.

Everyone fell silent as he listened. His face looked shocked. He licked anxiously at his lips, the way a cat does when frightened.

"I understand Laura. Keep me informed. I'll get the first flight back tomorrow and go straight to the Milthorne."

Stephanie took hold of Gurtha's hand.

"What's happened?"

"It's Paddy. He's deteriorated. Laura has asked me to go back. It must be serious." He looked at his watch. "There are no flights tonight. I'll catch the first flight to Belfast tomorrow."

He folded his arms on the table and sank his head onto them.

"Give me a few minutes. I'll be alright."

The doorbell rang – the seafood paella had arrived.

DAY 37

MONDAY 16TH SEPTEMBER 2013

"THE QUIETER YOU BECOME,
THE MORE YOU ARE ABLE TO HEAR."
J RUMI

LAURA COLLECTED Gurtha at the airport. He carried two large suitcases.

"Thank you, Laura. I could have hired a car like I always do. This is too much of an imposition."

Laura shook her head.

"Don't be silly. By the way you're not staying in that Holiday Inn – you're staying at my place. I have a room ready for you."

"Are you sure?"

"I would be insulted if you said 'no'. Do you want to go and see Paddy straight away?"

"Yes – of course."

They drove to the Milthorne, Laura asking Gurtha lots of questions along the way, in particular wanting to know about developments in finding Cornelia's body.

"No. The Police have given up any hope of finding the body." Gurtha looked at Laura as she drove. He hadn't appreciated before how beautiful she looked. Her black hair lay sleek on her shoulders. Her features were fine. Her nose straight, but what was most beautiful was the shape of her lips which pulled into a moving smile – opening and closing – at times pulling into a smile to the left and then to the right. Her eyes were a hazel green – almond shaped rather than round, with thick black lashes.

She looked at him and smiled.

"I'm glad you're back. Paddy will be pleased. However, don't be surprised if he doesn't say much. He spends most of his time sleeping."

Gurtha nodded.

"You were right about Cornelia. I should have listened."

Laura tapped him on the hand.

"At times it's easier to see things when you're not emotionally involved – from a distance."

She pulled into the Milthorne carpark.

Maggie opened the door for them and kissed Gurtha and Laura.

"She's been brilliant. I would love her to work here with me. She's a ten out of ten." She stopped outside room 11. "You know Paddy had his fall. We don't think that is the reason for his deterioration. Sometimes dementia unfolds like that – you have a plateau when everything is fairly stable and then there can be a sudden worsening. We thought it best that you came home early as you can't predict how quickly it can … degenerate. I'll leave you together."

Gurtha and Laura pulled up a chair beside the bed. Paddy turned his head to look at them. He smiled.

"Gurtha. You've come home."

His face didn't look so red, more white, as if the colour had been drained out of him. He had lost weight and the skin sat on top of his face like a sheet that was too loose for the bed – it needed to be tucked in here and there. Because of the whiteness – Gurtha noticed the small spidery veins as they crawled over his cheeks and onto his nose. Gurtha felt a tightening around his heart.

Paddy's hand moved slowly across the sheet towards him – like a snail heading home.

Laura sat silently beside Gurtha and watched.

Paddy smiled again. His eyes were the same cornflower blue. They were bright, but they had more depth to them – two pools of blue which had deepened their way to new connections in Paddy's heart. It felt to Gurtha that the whole of Paddy's life was being drawn together from every cell in his body into his eyes. Gurtha didn't need to do anything more to know Paddy than to allow himself to sink into Paddy's eyes.

Paddy held tightly onto Gurtha's hand. He whispered. "You won't leave me now will you? I don't want you to go. It's frightening when you're not here."

Gurtha moved closer to Paddy's face. He wanted to kiss him on the cheek but he didn't want to frighten him. So he pretended that he wanted to whisper into his ear. Paddy move his head slightly on the pillow to make it easier for Gurtha to do that. Gurtha moved even closer until it was a kiss that he gave Paddy as he whispered.

"I'm not going away. I'm staying here for you. The holiday in Mallorca is over. I'm back." His lips touched Paddy's cheek.

He moved slowly back yet kept his face close to Paddy's so that he could see his eyes. Paddy began to cry but they were tears of happiness or even joy. He squeezed Gurtha's hand.

"Now we're all together again, like before. Nuala came to see me this morning and she said she would be back. When she comes back will you make us all a cup of tea and I'll have a digestive biscuit?"

Paddy's mouth began to move as if he was talking to someone but there were no words coming out. He kept talking, with his eyes fixed on Gurtha. His lips were moving the way Laura's lips move – to the right and left – up and down as if they were doing a dance.

THE SECRET WOUND

Gurtha leaned closer to Paddy's mouth to see if he could hear what he was saying. There was nothing, only movement and silence.

He pulled back until he could see Paddy's eyes again. Paddy swam into Gurtha's eyes. They were swimming together. Gurtha remembered the story Paddy had told about Alaya and Athaneus – when Athaneus recovered his speech but decided not to talk because he knew the power of silence and that you said more words or different words in silence than you did with words. Paddy was talking to him in silence. His mouth creating those silent words.

Gurtha wanted to say 'I love you' but he remembered that Athaneus didn't want to say that to Alaya. So he kept looking into Paddy's eyes until they slowly closed. Paddy shuddered a little in the bed as if the life within him had shaken its wings to leave him. He took his last breath.

DAY 38

TUESDAY 17TH SEPTEMBER 2013

TODD CALLED Barry and Angelina.

"Did you hear the news?"

Barry answered, "Yes. It was good that he got back in time. Only just, by the sounds of it."

Todd sounded different – not speaking in his normal brusque voice.

"Stephanie and I were wondering if you would like to have a coffee. It has been one Hell of a week. We felt we would like to have a quick chat."

Barry took a deep breath, "It's not more bad news is it?"

Todd laughed.

"No. No. Quite the opposite. How about 'The Albatross' in the Port in an hour? They do a good breakfast."

Angelina and Barry arrived at the same time as Stephanie and Todd and they picked a table in the shade. Beside the boats, a man sang doleful songs, strumming his guitar.

Todd said in a hushed voice, "Pity we didn't think of asking him to play for us the last few days – he captures the mood perfectly."

They ordered scrambled eggs and salmon as the seagulls circled

THE SECRET WOUND

overhead and the local wild cats sat patiently by the tables waiting for morsels.

Todd spoke first.

"Stephanie and I were talking last night after we got the news about Paddy and we were saying that, although it's been a difficult month or so, we feel we've learnt a lot. I've realised that I am a nasty, selfish piece of work. I don't know how Stephanie has put up with me. With all that has happened – Nuala – Henry – Amelia – Cornelia and now Paddy – we have decided that life is too short for more nastiness. We are going to get married in Santa Monica at Christmas and you are both invited to the wedding. We will invite Gurtha as well but let's allow him time to bury his father first."

Barry and Angelina looked at one another and then held one another's hands.

"Well, we were talking about darkness needing light. We weren't going to say to everyone so soon after the events of the past week but now that you are being so honest, why not? Angelina has agreed to marry me. We haven't set a date yet but it will be before the baby is born."

Stephanie got to her feet and hugged Angelina and then there were kisses all around and squeals of delight.

"Now we asked you first – so we have to be invited to the wedding.

DAY 39

WEDNESDAY 18TH SEPTEMBER 2013

> "WHEN SOMEONE BEATS A RUG,
> THE BLOWS ARE NOT AGAINST THE RUG
> BUT AGAINST THE DUST IN IT."
> **J RUMI**

POLICE INSPECTOR Andy Finn updated the file on Nuala's death. He read through his notes again to ensure that he had the correct dates for his interviews in Mallorca. There was a photo of Nuala on file. He fingered it for the last time. She had blonde hair pulled back into a scrunchie and a fringe which fell across her forehead. Her skin looked remarkably young for a woman of her age. She was smiling. However, it was her eyes that caught his attention. They seemed to be looking at him directly, as if she was with him in the room.

He was a man of facts and evidence – yet Nuala seemed to be demanding something more from him. Had he not done as much as anyone could? He read the comments which people had made about her:

A fearlessly honest woman

You won't pull the wool over Nuala's eyes

She would make a cat laugh

She was never one to get caught up in other people's business

She knew when to say something and when to be quiet

She didn't judge people but she knew what doing the right thing was

She was a mystic – she knew things beyond what normal people did

She gave you the sense that she had a personal relationship with God

Money meant nothing to her

Have never met anyone who had so little and enjoyed life so much

She was always grateful for what she had rather than moaning about what she didn't have

He had a stamp which he was going to put on the file cover – 'Case Closed'.

Instead he opened the drawer to his left and selected a different stamp – 'Case Open and Unresolved'.

Day 40

Thursday 19th September 2013

"Lovers don't finally meet somewhere.
They're in each other all along."
J Rumi

It was a cold September day with a strong northerly breeze blowing the remaining leaves from the oak trees in the Grove of Holy Cross Church. Gurtha climbed the steps holding Laura's hand. As he entered the Church , he could see that the pews were already full. At the front, near the altar was a pew reserved for Gurtha, Laura, Lily and Tom.

The evening that Paddy died, Gurtha returned to Laura's house. They were alone. They sat by an open fire and talked about life. Laura asked him, "Well, have you worked it out?"

Gurtha stoked the fire.

"Worked what out?"

"What you wanted to work out by going on your sabbatical to Mallorca."

Gurtha laughed.

"I think so. I know what I like now. I didn't before."

THE SECRET WOUND

Laura poured a cup of tea and handed it to him. "You said that you would tell me before anyone else. What is it?"

"Well I started to tell Barry, Angelina, Todd and Stephanie the night you rang, but I didn't finish."

"Well?"

"I learnt that I like simplicity, being in nature, being grateful for creation in all its forms, including animals. Needless to say I believe in non-violence but, most importantly, I discovered that human beings do have a conscience and it will triumph in the end."

Laura topped up his tea.

"Why do you think that? There are many people looking at the world and thinking that we are 'doomed' – and that it will not work out well in the end."

Gurtha sipped his tea.

"Yes – that's true. Maybe I felt the same after Nuala died. How could anything work out well. But, I now feel, how can it not? I think that we all have a radar, a conscience that will guide us to what we need to do. Simplicity will help."

"So how are you going to build this simple life?"

Gurtha took Laura's hand.

"If you would be so kind to help me, I would like to build it with you."

Laura blushed, held onto her cup of tea and nodded.

Back in the Church Father Jerome spoke.

"Many of us were here a year ago when we buried Nuala. We knew then that there was a risk that further murders could take place if Nuala's murderer was not brought to justice. Although the murderer was indeed amongst us and, in fact, I shook her hand, we know that in the end this person gave her life to save another. We should be grateful for her 'metanoia' or change of heart and pray for Cornelia. Today we celebrate Paddy's life and death. We recognise the value both Nuala and Paddy have added to our community. We must continue to look out for one another and to strengthen our community. There should be no strangers in our midst."

As the Mass ended and Gurtha lined up once more beside Tom to carry the coffin from the Church, he glanced down the aisle towards the front door. A woman wearing a long black coat, black gloves, black hat and a glossy black bob was watching him intently. Their eyes met for a moment, then she turned slowly and left the Church, silhouetted against the grey light outside. She vanished from sight. Feeling the weight of Paddy on his shoulders, Gurtha walked at a slow, measured pace and, as the coffin reached the door of the Church, he scanned to see where the woman, who looked like Cornelia, had gone. Inside, the church choir sang:

The rain tapped on the window
Calling from above
A quiet insistent yearning
That seemed to talk of love

Then there was a moment
When no one was alone
A fleeting, empty presence
Filled with all and none

What can you say
When words have gone?
What can you say when all alone?

What can you say
When all you hear
For sure
Is a whisper within the silence of love?

THE SECRET WOUND

THE SECRET WOUND

THE SECRET WOUND

ACKNOWLEDGEMENTS

This book would never exist without the continued support of my husband Martin and that of Matthew Smith the Founder and Director of Urbane Publications. They both open wonderful worlds of possibility, positivity and creativity.

Thanks to Laurence Freeman, Director of the World Community of Christian Meditation for his insights into the 'woundedness' of the human condition.

Thanks to Rachel Connor for her wonderful mentoring of 'The Secret Wound'. She is a true writing companion.

I have appreciated the friendship of other Urbane authors who have shared their writing experiences and are great fun to be around.

Thanks to my cousin Kathleen, husband Johnny McGreevy and my sister in law Heather Quiery for all their support.

Thanks to Alan and Agnes McLaughlin and to Kieran McNicholl.

In a world that increasingly seems fearful, angry and directionless and in a society which struggles to find effective responses, Deirdre Quiery brings a perspective in her work and in her writing that challenges many of the assumptions and standards that have evolved in the Western world during the four centuries since Newton and the dawn of science. What human beings need more than anything, she argues, is to think more expansively and inclusively and to go beyond traditional, rational thinking and embrace a wisdom which lies beyond thinking.

This perspective plays out in her studies (an MSc in Consciousness Studies and Transpersonal Psychology), in her life (living in a secluded olive grove in Mallorca which allows for space, peace and daily meditation), in her writing and blog on deirdrequiery.com, in her art (she has successfully sold paintings at two exhibitions in Mallorca and has one planned in London in June 2017) and in her other work (supporting corporate leaders and managers to be more creative and spontaneous, opening the door to true intuition and to the wisdom mind).

Her first book, Eden Burning, set in Belfast in the early seventies, the peak years of "the troubles", explores the destructive impact of fear and violence on the human psyche and the depths to which we all, as humans, are capable of falling given the right mix of genetic and personal history. It also explores the extraordinary heights which we, as humans, are capable of reaching when supported by the redeeming power of love and forgiveness.

Her second book, The Secret Wound, due to be published by Urbane Publications in June 2017 is set largely in Mallorca in 2014, explores in more depth the nature of love and relationship and how unconscious, deep-seated patterns of behaviour – what she would call wounds – fill our lives with unwanted and often unrecognised consequences which impede us from fulfilling our full potential. Until we learn to deeply undo the shackles of ego (because all of these unconscious wounds are ego-driven in one way or another), a painful process which requires tenacity and courage, we can never be free to flow effortlessly and joyfully with the universe in the dance of life. To do this successfully, we need to know that we are unconditionally loved.

ALSO BY
DEIRDRE QUIERY

EDEN BURNING

ISBN : 978-1909273900

£8.99

320pp, PAPERBACK

Northern Ireland, 1972. On the Crumlin Road, Belfast, the violent sectarian Troubles have forced Tom Martin to take drastic measures to protect his family. Across the divide William McManus pursues his own particular bloody code, murdering for a cause.

Yet both men have underestimated the power of love and an individual's belief in right and wrong, a belief that will shake the lives of both families with a greater impact than any bomb blast.

This is a compelling, challenging story of conflict between and within families driven by religion, belief, loyalty and love. In a world deeply riven by division, a world of murders, bomb blasts and assassinations, how can any individual transcend the seemingly inevitable violence of their very existence?

Urbane Publications is dedicated to developing new author voices, and publishing fiction and non-fiction that challenges, thrills and fascinates.

From page-turning novels to innovative reference books, our goal is to publish what YOU want to read.

Find out more at
urbanepublications.com